PARNO'S GAMBIT

The Black Sheep of Soulan: Book 3

Creative Texts Publishers products are available at special discounts for bulk purchase for sale promotions, premiums, fund-raising, and educational needs. For details, write Creative Texts Publishers, PO Box 50, Barto, PA 19504, or visit www.creativetexts.com

PARNO'S GAMBIT
The Black Sheep of Soulan: Book 3
by N.C. REED
Published by Creative Texts Publishers
PO Box 50
Barto, PA 19504
www.creativetexts.com

ISBN: 978-0692861301

PARNO'S GAMBIT

N.C. Reed

TABLE OF CONTENTS

PROLOGUE

-

The horses were laboring, sweat flecking off their necks and shoulders. Sherron McLeod grimaced as her hand came away from her mount's shoulder covered in horse sweat.

"Stop!" she ordered, looking at the Colonel next to her. "I want to stop!"

Callens sighed inwardly as he held up a hand, signaling the column of excellently trained soldiers behind him to slow and then to halt. He sat his horse expectantly, waiting for Sherron to address him.

"This is disgusting!" she seethed, reaching over to wipe her hand on his trousers, cleaning them on his uniform heedless of the insult. "I'm tired of riding this beast, Callens. Get me a carriage!"

"We haven't been able to secure a carriage as yet, your Ladyship," Callens reminded her evenly. "I have men out looking even now. So far, however, all we've managed to find are wagons. None of which have met with your approval."

"Well, you find me a carriage and a place to sleep because I'm not going any further on this filthy beast!" she screeched at him, uncaring of how that looked to the soldiers behind her. She had never cared for what men such as they thought. They were tools, nothing more. Tools of executive privilege for people like her to use and then throw away when they were no longer useful.

"We should keep moving at least until dark, Your Ladyship," Callens reminded her. "We have a long way to go and our lead will not be much. We have to keep moving."

"Not today, we don't," Sherron shook her head stubbornly. "I want a bath, a bed, and then tomorrow I want a carriage! You see to that and stop telling me what we have to do, Callens. I'm the one who decides what we have to do!"

"As you wish," he agreed. He turned to the officers behind him.

"Locate suitable quarters for the night," he ordered. "And someone find a carriage. Send parties in all directions as far as needed until one is found." The officers nodded, assigning men to the orders as Callens turned back to Sherron.

"Let us move forward at a walk, then," he suggested. "We'll have men before us, seeking a good place for Her Ladyship to spend the evening."

"Fine," Sherron waved her hand in dismissal. Callens fought off another sigh and wondered if it was too late for him to abandon the spoiled princess. Then he remembered that she had sank a dagger into both the King and the Crown Prince of Soulan and shook his head minutely.

Oh, yes, it was far too late for him to go back now. He had committed himself and his men to overthrowing the rightful rule of Soulan in favor of their former liege, Prince Therron McLeod, the twin of their current charge. And in time of war, no less. He would be fortunate not to be killed on sight.

He wondered what lapse in judgment had led him to agree to this madness. He was certainly doomed. His only consolation was that it was entirely likely that he would carry Sherron McLeod with him to hell when he went.

CHAPTER ONE

-

"No."

"But why not!"

Parno McLeod looked at the young woman before him and fought the urge to shake his head. Winnie Hubel was trying to be her normal, intimidating self and the effect of standing there, glowering, hands on her hips, really lost a little something with her wearing a dress of fine green and black trimmed silk instead of buckskins.

Of course, she still looked meaner than a wet hen, as the saying went.

"Winnie, you are not going into combat and that is final," he told her flatly. "There will be no women serving in the front ranks of this army so long as I command it."

"Women can fight just as well as men, Milord!"

She remembered, barely, not to call him by his given name. "There's no reason not to allow it!"

"There's every reason, particularly with you!" Parno shot back, tired of this argument.

"Why with me?" she demanded.

"You know exactly why," Parno fought the urge to roll his eyes. "You are courting the King of Soulan! Or rather, he's courting you," he corrected, frowning. "Imagine what a fine prisoner you'd make, Winnie, if anything went wrong."

"That's not fair," she said quietly, looking at the floor.

"Life isn't usually fair, Winnie," Parno nodded. "If it was, I…well, never mind," he cut himself off. "Look, not only is combat no place for you, but. . .truth is I've come to appreciate your being with Stephanie all the time" he admitted quietly after a look around. "I'd prefer if you would remain with her, at least when you aren't dallying with Memmnon," he couldn't resist adding.

"Dallying?" her eyes narrowed dangerously. "Does that mean what I think it means, Parno McLeod?" she demanded in a far too gentle tone.

"That would depend entirely on what you think it means," Parno replied innocently. "I merely specified that I did not want to impose upon your courtship to ask that you protect Lady Freeman on my behalf whilst I am forced to be away from her. Nothing more."

"You don't really expect me to believe that, do you?" she demanded, arms crossing beneath her breasts, a move that again wasn't nearly as imposing in a cleavage-baring gown as it might have been in a leather shirt. He admitted it was attractive, though.

"Are you insinuating that the Crown Prince of Soulan would lie, Miss Hubel?" Parno asked with mock severity. Winnie's reaction was priceless as she apparently finally remembered who she was talking to.

"Er, no Milord," she managed not to stammer. "Of course not."

"Good," he nodded firmly, fighting to keep from laughing. "Now. There will be no more discussion of your going to the front in order to participate in the fighting. The Nor do not take prisoners as a rule, Winifred," he told her more seriously. "I'm sure they would make an exception in the case of an attractive young woman, of course. More to the point, they might be just as likely to trade you to the Wildmen who are working in concert with them." He paused to let that sink in.

"I can't allow that, Winnie," he finished softly, yet firmly. "And if you have any respect for me at all, you will not only stop asking, you will stop trying to subvert others into this plan as well. Leave it be, and do not attempt to get yourself there by other means."

Winnie blinked at that direct appeal, her face showing a bit of shock. No one had so directly spoken to her about this up to now.

"You think you know what you'd be in for, but you don't, Winnie," Parno continued. "Don't ever imagine that seeing the wounded in the hospital at Cove, or here, can compare to the screams you would hear at the front, or in battle. There is blood everywhere you look and no matter how hard you try, you can't wash it away. Limbs cut off, hacked off, innards of men lying all over the ground… or on the floor if you are in the hospital, that is, if you're fortunate enough to have a floor. Sleeping on the ground when you sleep at all, a hot bowl of oatmeal the best meal you'll have for days at a time. Watching someone you've trained with and marched with, eaten besides, slept besides, stood guard with, die right in front of you as they beg you to save them." He stopped suddenly, aware that he'd been speaking too much.

"So, I ask you, please. No more." He looked at her solidly. "No. More. Allow Memmnon to court you. Be with Stephanie when she needs you. Stop dreaming of this notion. The only way you will do it is to defy me, and that would break Memmnon's heart, even if nothing happened to you."

"I…" Winnie tried to speak but couldn't manage it.

"Now," he took a breath, trying to clear the images from his own head. "I believe you have a luncheon to attend, and I have reports to look at. Since we both have our duties, we should be about them wouldn't you say?"

"Y...yes, milord," Winnie nodded shakily and left Parno's office without another word.

"Please, let this be the end of it," Parno whispered, his eyes closed as he looked to the heavens. "Please."

-

Parno did have reports to look at, that was true. Most were compilations of other reports, given to other people, but a few were to him alone... like the one he was looking at now.

Mister Parsons had returned from his adventure behind enemy lines to report that at least thirty thousand new troops were headed into the front along the Tinsee River. Were probably already there, Parno told himself, thinking of the time it had taken the message to get to him. He looked at the map on his wall, lips pursed.

While his estimate was that this new army would not make good on all Imperial losses, it would help. More to the point, the advantage that Parno had hoped to gain by pulling 4th and 5th Corps to the front would be blunted by this new Imperial force's arrival along with the necessity of pulling 2nd Corps out of the line for refit. Enri Willard had been right in his observation that 2nd Corps was fought out. They had borne the brunt of the Imperial assault from day one and their losses had left them a shell of the Corps' former strength. Until their losses could be replaced and their wounded returned to duty, it was better for them to be out of line.

Those new soldiers might put 2nd Corps back up to strength, but raw recruits wouldn't replace the fighting strength of the well trained and experienced soldiers lost in battle. He sighed, rubbing his temple.

He would still have sufficient forces to hold against a renewed Imperial assault, but would not have the ability to launch his own offensive as he had planned, which meant that the Imperial presence on Soulan soil would continue for the time being.

And all of this was almost secondary this afternoon despite the disaster it represented.

A week ago, he had dispatched a unit he badly needed at the front to hunt down his brother Therron's regiment. The regiment that had freed his insane sister from her confinement, allowed her to kill the King of Soulan and nearly kill the Crown Prince. Even now, Memmnon was working half-days and needed a cane to walk. Parno snorted to himself. One of the reasons that Memmnon was working half-days had probably just left his office in a tiff. He shook his head again. As if he didn't have enough troubles.

In any event, Parno had sent Brigadier Generals Beaumont and Whipple to chase down Therron's traitorous regiment, commanded by a Colonel named Frank Callens, and destroy it. It was almost certain that they were on the way to the Key Horn to free Parno's exiled brother, Therron. His twin, Sherron, had managed to get the location of the disgraced Prince from King Tammon McLeod before she had murdered him in his own bed and there was no doubt she would try to free him. Her plan all along had been to seat Therron on the throne rather than Memmnon. She would not stop until Therron was King, or she and he were both dead.

Parno meant for it to be the latter and the men he had sent after them had orders to make it so.

Warrants had been issued for both of them and Memmnon had allowed the news of the King's assassination to be distributed throughout the kingdom so that all would know the depths of Sherron's depravity and Therron's treason. Hopefully that would force any others who would lend them aid to abandon the twins, leaving them alone in their quest.

Investigators were still plumbing the depths of Therron's plot to assume the throne. Sherron's plot as well, Parno decided. There was no separating the two at this point, it seemed, and he didn't bother. Sherron might have planted the bug in Therron's ear, but he had pursued it knowing it was treason. He had managed to enroll at least one provincial governor in his scheme and where there was one there could be others. Atop that, Parno was almost certain that General Graham, commander of 1st Corps, had been enlisted. He couldn't prove it, and he wasn't positive about his suspicions, but the fact that he had them at all was troublesome.

Graham had tried to challenge Parno as soon as he had taken command of the army in Therron's place. Parno had crushed him in minutes, putting the man firmly in his place, but the doubt lingered, even now. The army had been Therron's for a long time. Long enough for him to have made many friends among the nobles in the officer corps and perhaps gain their support in his bid.

Parno had taken steps to root out the rot in the army but that took time. Time he wasn't sure he had. He hoped, again, that the news of the twin's treachery would dampen the desires of any of the army to support them. Assuming the throne ahead of his brother was one thing, but murder of the king, that was something else altogether. Parno had to hope that most of the men in the army, whether officer or enlisted, would draw a line there and refuse to back Therron.

If they didn't, then his promise to his father might not be...

"Parno?" a feminine voice broke quietly into his thoughts. He looked up to find Stephanie Freeman standing at his door. She was, as usual these days, wearing a dress of green and black colors, signifying her place in the McLeod family, as yet undefined but no less real. On her left breast, she wore a broach that displayed the McLeod crest, something he'd had made for her in the days after Tammon's funeral. As the, at least temporarily, Royal Physician following the death of her uncle at Sherron's hand, she was more than just Parno's 'affianced', as Winnie had put it. And, of course, she was also the friend and more or less patron of the young woman now being seriously courted by the new King of Soulan.

"Come in," Parno waved her inside, standing to greet her with a kiss on the cheek, which she returned.

"You look tired, Parno," she said, looking at his drawn face.

"I suppose I am," he nodded. "But I'm never too tired for you," he smiled and she blushed prettily.

"It's past noon hour, Parno," she reminded him. "You must be hungry by now."

"Is it?" Parno didn't have to feign surprise. Had he been drifting that long? "I honestly hadn't noticed. Have you eaten?" he asked and she shook her head.

"Well, we can't have that," Parno told her. "Let's go and see what we can dig up in the kitchen, shall we?" he offered his arm, and she took it, smiling.

And so, Parno escorted his Lady to lunch, leaving his troubles behind him if only for a short while.

-

General Henry Herrick was not in a good mood. Saddle sore, dirty, and tired beyond reason, he followed his escort into the camp of the Soulan 1st Army. His men were strung out for miles behind him, still marching after being on the road for just under three weeks. His orders had been to make the best possible time north, leaving behind only one militia division of cavalry and a smattering of guard units while bringing the rest of his 4th Corps to the western front as quickly as human and horse flesh would allow.

Well, here we are, he thought to himself as he took in the sprawling camp before him. He was surprised to see so many able-bodied men in the rear if his men were so 'urgently needed' on this front. He saw a small city of what could only be hospital tents in the distance, reminding himself that the war had been raging here for some time.

"Direct me to General Davies' headquarters, soldier," he ordered a passing sergeant, who stiffened and saluted.

"Straight ahead down this path, Sir," the man pointed. "You're about a mile distant, as yet, but it's right along this here roadway. Can't miss it, mind you, sir."

"Thank you," Herrick nodded and continued on his way. A mile distant? How far was this camp spread out, anyway?

Fifteen minutes later his men drew reign before a large tent that showed signs of hurried movement all around. Herrick dismounted along with his aide and tossed his reins to an enlisted man who served as a runner.

Casting a disparaging eye around him at what appeared to be disorganized chaos, Herrick entered what he assumed was the command tent, followed by his aide. He expected the men inside to snap to attention at his arrival, but other than a few glances to confirm who he was, no one made any note of it. Frowning, he walked to the large table in the center of the tent where he could see Davies pouring over reports.

"And you're certain of the numbers?" he was asking a rather disheveled looking man who was wearing more dust than Herrick himself was at the moment.

"No sir," the man shook his head. "We're reasonably certain about the minimum number," he stressed. "We can't account for what might lie beyond them, if anything at all. We tried for two days to get around them but their scouts seem to be learning as they go along. They're screening their movement very well, and Lord Parno ordered us not be seen doin' our looking."

"Very well," Davies nodded. "Thank you, Mister Parsons. You and your men should stand down and get some rest, but please make sure my aide knows where we can find you. I may have need of your services again."

"Aye, sir," the man nodded and walked tiredly away.

"Henry," Davies smiled, extending a hand. "It's good to see you."

"Bryce," Herrick nodded. "My boys are strung out for miles behind us but barring a problem should all be in here by day after tomorrow at the latest. Maybe even by tomorrow night, weather permitting."

"That is good news," Davies exhaled. "I'm sure you saw what's left of 2nd Corps on your way in," he added.

"Is that who it was?" Herrick was stunned. "I…I thought they were just…"

"Militia, maybe?" Davies raised an eye brow. "Shirkers even?"

"Not shirkers, no," Herrick shook his head. "Knew you wouldn't go in for that. They just looked. . .rough."

"They've borne the brunt of the assault since the war began," Davies said quietly, refusing to allow his men to be denigrated even by another Corps commander. "They have sustained losses on average approaching fifty percent or greater. After our last engagement, Marshall McLeod ordered them pulled from the line for refit. Now that you've arrived, I'm half expecting him to order them back to Nasil or even to Shelby while they incorporate replacements and repair and refit."

"Why Shelby?" Herrick looked surprised.

"As a back stop to Raines if needed," Davies replied, turning back to his map.

"What about this last engagement?" Herrick asked, turning his own eyes to the map table. "Last I'd heard was about a cavalry raid."

"Imperial troops attacked out position in strength three weeks ago," Davies informed him. "Came at us with all hands and the cooks. We managed to turn them back, but. . .it hurt." He handed a single sheet of parchment to Herrick who looked at it for a moment then whistled softly.

"Looks like you hurt them, too," he noted, returning the report.

"We did, but we can't stand those kinds of losses. They may can," Davies looked grim. "Marshal McLeod thought we had gained an advantage, perhaps even a decisive one, but. . .the man who just left here leads the Marshal's personal scout unit and they returned not long ago from a trek behind the Imperial lines. They've spotted at least three new Imperial divisions with numbers estimated at a minimum of thirty thousand strong heading this way. Their arrival will negate every advantage we thought we had gained… or would have gained with your arrival and the arrival of 5th Corps."

"Now, wait a minute," Herrick looked taken aback. "Between Freeman and I, we can muster probably. . .well, even allowing for the units we were ordered to detach, we should at least be able to bring another sixty thousand regulars plus the militia units we still have!"

"And we're already facing over one hundred thousand Imperial troops, not including this new army that's on its way down the valley," Davies nodded. "Even with both your Corps here, we would have been hard pressed to launch the Marshal's planned offensive. Now. . ." Davies trailed off with a shrug.

"Offensive?" Herrick looked even more surprised. "I assumed he wanted us to take over the defense so your troops could rest."

"Hardly," Davies snorted. "Marshal McLeod intended to launch an attack as soon as both you and Freeman were up and rested. Now, I don't know how this will affect his plans," he waved at the new notations being made on the map. "I think the news of their scouts worries me more than anything other than not knowing if they're going to change Generals."

"Why?" Herrick asked.

"Why the scouts bother me, or the changing of command?" Davies looked at him, then proceeded to answer both.

"The efficiency of their scouts leads me towards suspecting that these new divisions may be more experienced or at least better trained than what we're currently facing. As for Generals, well, we've bloodied this one twice now, assuming that their Emperor didn't kill whoever was in command of the first defeat. We're beginning to get a glimmer of how this commander thinks, at least somewhat. If they change, then their attacks may change. Funny, isn't it? What should be a weakness for them turns out to actually work to their advantage, at least a little."

"Except that it drives them to make stupid decisions because they only get the one chance to succeed," Herrick nodded.

"True," Davies allowed. "At any rate, I will issue orders for Graham to shift to the right starting day after tomorrow at noon," he got down to business. "That will allow your men to start moving into line on the left without risking our anchor along the river. Your men will end up with a bit over half the line, probably."

"All right," Herrick nodded. "I'd hoped for a day of rest for them, but after seeing 2nd Corps, my men can rest once they're in place. They haven't had to face any action and there's nothing hard about a long march that a day's inactivity won't cure, assuming the enemy allows it."

"Assuming," Davies nodded grimly. "Let us hope they do."

-

Lieutenant General Gerald Wilson surveyed the reports from his various commanders with about half of his mind. The other half was kept open for a member of the Imperial Secret Police, a shadowy if well-known organization that the Emperor used to execute his will among the elite of the Empire.

Since his second defeat at the hands of the Soulan army opposing him, Wilson had been expecting to see one of those assassins enter his office to eliminate him. He wondered if his family had already been killed. He had no way to know other than send someone to check, and that would let whoever was watching his family know that Wilson was thinking about it, which meant that he had done something worrisome that the Emperor would need to know, which would lead to a member of the Secret Imperial Police visiting him here in his headquarters, which made him wonder if his family had already…

Wilson shook his head, hoping to clear that rambling thought that cycled through his head about every two minutes. It was a constant wheel of circular thinking that presumed something would happen because something else had happened when he didn't know if the first something had even happened yet because he was...

He stood abruptly, realizing that he was doing it again.

"This is ridiculous," he told himself finally. "I'm the commander of this army until I'm not. So long as I am, then I have work to do." He grabbed his sword belt and swung it around his narrow hips, calling for his aide and orderly as he went. Both were waiting just outside the door.

"Sir?"

"Get my horse and my escort," he ordered his aide.

"Yes sir," the young Captain nodded eagerly. "Right away!"

Snorting at the younger man's exuberance, Wilson continued outside, looking at the organized chaos around him. It had been three weeks since the heinous losses of the battle that he himself had instigated and had intended to be the final push to destroy the Soulan army he faced. An army that was proving to be far more resilient than he would have believed before meeting them in battle.

At the height of the battle, with the enemy in sight and after taking so many casualties to their demonic weapons that had tore gaping holes in his lines and had taken scores of men at a time, a simple mistake by two idiot buglers had led to a mass retreat of his army. On the cusp of what might have been a great, if costly, victory, he had lost completely as his men had returned to their line of departure.

He shook his head once more as he thought back to that day and that most stupid of incidents. He still found it hard to believe, but there it was. It had happened and there was nothing to do about it but continue from here.

His men had refit as best they could after the battle, but in some cases whole regiments had all but disappeared from the battlefield in the face of the destruction the southerners had laid down before his men. Strange objects that burst like ripe melons, spewing fire and destruction with them in every direction. Men ceasing to exist in the face of those bursts and gaps many yards wide torn into an otherwise disciplined and well-dressed line. It had to be witchcraft. That was the word floating through the army and in some cases spread by the very officers that commanded it.

"Witchcraft," Wilson snorted, shaking his head yet again. His education in military arts had included history. Carefully guarded history of how things had been before The Burning. The Great Dying. The Plague.

Whatever name you gave it, it amounted to the same thing; the weapons his army was facing weren't from the future, they were from the past. The only wizardry at work here was science. Weapons such as this had existed in the Time Before as it was called, and Soulan had somehow resurrected them for their use in this war. Doing so gave them a tactical edge in the fighting that Wilson had no answer for save for heavy losses in the face of those weapons in a wild charge that he had to hope broke the Soulanie lines and allowed his men to overrun the weapons that were spewing that death and destruction into his troops.

Only just when that seemed to have succeeded, a stupid mistake had ruined the entire thing. Now an army that had once feared nothing other than their commander was literally shaking in their camps at the thought of facing those hellish weapons ever again.

Perfect.

Reinforcements arriving from home had been intended to strengthen his flank as he began to turn his army, cross the river and head for Nasil, the southern capitol. Now, their number wouldn't even make good his losses from the last two battles. They would help, but it wouldn't return his army to full strength and he dared not ask for more men. Even if by some miracle the Emperor hadn't decided to kill Wilson and his entire family, asking for more than what the Emperor gave him would indicate that Wilson lacked faith in the Emperor, and that was a one-way ticket to being beheaded.

No, he had to make do with what he had, which meant he had to fix the problems that his army was facing. Starting with their fear of the southern army and their 'witchcraft'.

As his horse arrived, led by the commander of his escort, Wilson began to formulate a plan to accomplish that, and get his stalled offense back on the move.

Before he lost his head.

-

Sherron McLeod looked at her surroundings, disdain written clearly on her face. Callens looked at her face and wondered, not for the first time, how he had ever thought that face was beautiful.

True, the Princess was beautiful in a physical sense, but inside she was rotten to the core. Too late he had realized that she was nothing but a hollow shell of the woman he'd once taken her for. A woman that he had hitched his wagon to good and proper, along with that of his men. Even if they managed to convince the authorities that they had no knowledge of their commander's treason, none of them would be allowed to remain in the army save as fodder for northern pikes. None would be trusted ever again.

I am a fool, he thought darkly even as his 'Princess' turned her scornful gaze upon him.

"This is the best you can do?" she demanded. "This. . .this farmhouse?"

"It is the nearest structure for many miles, milady," Callens told her for the second time. "You expressed a desire to be off the road as soon as possible and inside rather than outside. As such, yes. This is the best we can do."

"Ridiculous," Sherron huffed, looking away. "To think that I have to pass the night in this squalor."

It was the same every night. Each and every night there was something the matter. No accommodations were satisfactory to her, no speed sufficient (it was either too slow or too fast, one or the other), and no amount of placating her worked. Every night for three weeks, it was the same.

Callens now knew why Sherron McLeod had been referred to as the Royal Bitch.

"I suppose it will have to do, then," Sherron told him flatly, as if conferring a boon upon a lesser mortal. "Have my things brought inside at once!" she ordered.

"As you wish," Callens fought off a sigh and nodded to his aide. With a nod of his own in reply the aide stepped away to secure the Princess' luggage, another sore spot for the beleaguered Colonel. Having left the palace with nothing but the clothing on her back, Sherron had insisted that stops be made to ensure she was properly provisioned for the trip south. More than once he had been reduced to taking by force the things she had desired, knowing all the time that doing so was leaving a trail anyone could follow straight to them.

And still he obeyed her because the only way out of the mess he had placed himself and his men into was through it. With her.

Once we get Prince Therron it will be different, he promised himself as he stepped outside the farmhouse. The family that made their home here were now sequestered in their own barn, essentially made prisoners. Something no other member of this Dynasty had ever done to their citizens in all of their storied history.

All I have to do is get her to the Key Horn, he told himself firmly. Once there, Prince Therron will take her in hand, and I can put all this behind me.

He almost made himself believe it.

-

"Buford!"

Beaumont pretended not to hear his friend and second, Horace Whipple.

"Dammit, Buford we have to stop!" Whipple's voice urged. "We're losing men and horses left and right!"

"We have to be close," Beaumont shook his head stubbornly.

"Buford, they had a week's start on us. One day of rest isn't going to keep us from catching them and we know exactly where they're going. We don't have to trail them, just keep them bottled up when they get there!"

"Every day we don't manage to stop them, more people die at their hand," Beaumont replied.

"I know," Whipple nodded grimly. "But we won't stop them by killing our own men and horses! We've been in the saddle for five days with little more than a nap, and we'd ridden hard for three days when we arrived in Nasil. We'd been off the line less than five days when the Prince summoned us. We have got to let our men rest and our horses catch their breath or we'll be walking!"

For a moment, Whipple thought Beaumont would continue on regardless, but finally, reluctance showing in every move he made, Beaumont began to slow, reining in his charger and holding up his hand to signal a slow march.

"Very well," he sighed as he patted his horse's flank, soothing the tired animal. "We'll make camp now, rest one day, then start again. Agreed?"

"A full day?" Whipple stressed. "We rest tomorrow and start at sunup the day after?"

"Very well," Beaumont said again, nodding absently. "One day."

Whipple turned and began issuing orders to the men behind, runners who moved ahead to seek suitable areas for encampments and aides who hurried to spread the word through the command. That done, Whipple turned his attention back to his friend and commander.

The two of them had only recently led a highly successful raid behind enemy lines, returning just days before the Prince had summoned them to Nasil and ordered them to pursue and destroy Callens' regiment, returning the Royal Twins to Nasil for trial if possible and killing them if not. Beaumont seemed more driven than usual and it was wearing on Whipple more than he wanted to allow it to show. The man he had come to know was generally more professional than this.

"Buford, are you going to be like this the whole time?" he asked carefully.

"Like what?" Beaumont looked at him, puzzlement on his features.

"You're driving the men into the ground for one thing, and killing horses doing it," Whipple replied. "You don't speak unless you've no choice. You ignore your officers when they approach you. You aren't aware of your surroundings; the list could go on."

"I'm aware of my surroundings!" Beaumont scoffed.

"What was the last town we passed through?" Whipple asked him calmly.

". . . ."

"That's what I thought," Whipple nodded, a look of satisfaction passing across his face. "Buford, we can't keep this up. I want the bastards as much as you do, but we can't destroy our unit getting them. Once this is done, we have to return to the Prince still able to fight. We can't win this one battle at the expense of the war."

Beaumont had slowed his horse to a walk now, his face pensive as he considered Whipple's words.

"You're right or course," he agreed finally. "I just... I can't imagine what Callens was thinking," he said suddenly.

"From what I hear, he wasn't thinking," Whipple shrugged. "Not with his head, anyway."

"What do you mean?" Beaumont asked.

"The Princess beguiled him," Whipple shrugged again. "She's a looker, if you've never seen her," he added. "Met her at a ball once," he explained. "Cold hearted wench if ever I met one, and that's no lie nor exaggeration. Word has it that Callens fancies her, and she's prone to using that to encourage him, if you know what I mean."

"Are you serious?" Beaumont looked shocked. "He killed the King and nearly the Crown Prince for a woman?"

"Well, to be fair he didn't actually do any of that," Whipple reminded his friend. "Her Wenchship did that all on her own. Her own hand took the King's life and nearly that of Prince Memmnon. For my money," he lowered his voice a bit, "Callens was as shocked as anyone else in the kingdom when she killed her father. But having helped her that far, he's committed now. He's no choice but to continue."

"You think so?" Beaumont asked. "I admit I'd prefer to think that than think the son of the man who trained me had turned traitor. His father has to be rolling in his grave," the cavalry man shook his head.

"His father?" Whipple frowned. "You knew his father?"

"I did," Beaumont nodded firmly. "Was my first regimental commander when I made officer. He was doing a stint in the Militia as part of a training regimen. His tutoring enabled me to rise to company command and later to Second officer. He was promoted to Brigadier after that and moved to staff. I left soon afterward myself and went to teach horsemanship at Donson."

"So, do you know his son?" Whipple asked.

"Never met him, and now I'm glad," Beaumont's voice was flinty. "Makes it easier to kill the little bastard when I finally do."

CHAPTER TWO

-

"So, what are you planning, Parno?"

Memmnon was sitting uncomfortably in his chair, his movements obviously pained. Parno was convinced that his brother was up and moving only because he had sworn he'd not try to court Winnie until and unless he could do so more or less under his own power.

"I can see only one alternative at the moment," Parno admitted, studying the map he had himself lain before the new King of Soulan. "It's a gamble, Memmnon, to be sure," he added. He picked up a pointer.

"I had already taken 2nd Corps off line due to their losses," he indicated the position of the 1st Army. "We're incorporating replacements into their ranks already, but. . .untrained men are no true replacement for the professional soldiers we've lost to this point."

"True," Memmnon nodded.

"I'm going to move 2nd Corps to Shelby," Parno moved his pointer to the river port along the Great River. "There's room a plenty to train and to camp, and that will place them in a position to backstop General Raines if the enemy tries to cross the Great River. I don't think they can force a crossing over the bridge, but if they somehow manage to get a large force across in boats, especially if they can do it by catching us by surprise, then they could establish a bridgehead there and then…well, we're finished," he said bluntly. "There is no way we can contain two such offensive thrusts at one time. We don't have the manpower or the horsepower."

"I know," Memmnon nodded. "Something else to thank Therron for," he muttered darkly.

"With 2nd Corp there as a reserve, I plan to pull back the men I just sent to Raines, and I'll be keeping his cavalry division as well. With those units, plus the additions of Freeman and Herrick, we'll be approaching something like a reasonable force against the Imperials in the Valley, even with this new force Parsons found, assuming that's all there is."

"You'll still be outnumbered," Memmnon warned.

"We'll always be outnumbered," Parno nodded. "We'll always be outnumbered and there's nothing we can do about it, so there's no reason to dwell on it. And we can't just sit here while the Imperial Army camps out on millions of acres of farmland and grassland. We need that land to be producing food and we have untold thousands of people displaced by the invasion who need to be able to go home again."

"What's being done about the refugees that are coming from the north?" Memmnon asked. "I should be keeping up with this," he muttered to himself.

"No, you should be assigning someone to keep up with it for you," Parno corrected. "Trust me, I've had to learn the same thing. You can't do it all, Memmnon. Even if you weren't still recovering you couldn't do it all alone. It's too much. Get someone to take charge of them and find them a place to live, even if it's in tents outside the city."

"I have to start thinking about how to feed them," Memmnon looked peaked.

"Let them work to do that," Parno shook his head. "Provide land, tools and seed and let the able bodied among them till and plant and maintain every inch of space you can with gardens and row crops. Have teams of refugees gathering fruit and nuts as they come ripe, wherever they are. How many bushels of berries do we leave on the vine every year? How many apples, pears, peaches do we leave on the ground for the deer? This year, the deer will have to make do with greens, that's all."

"You've put thought into this," Memmnon complimented/noted.

"No more than a passing interest," Parno shook his head. "I've had to learn to think quickly, that's all."

"Who would you suggest I give such a job to?" Memmnon asked, sitting up straighter and wincing only slightly as he did so.

"Well, now that you mention it..."

Winifred Hubel scowled at the scene before her, clearly unhappy.

"Why hasn't something been done about this already?" she demanded of her escort. 'This' was a field outside the city that was overflowing with refugees fleeing from the Norland invasion. A few scattered tents, the occasional wagon, but mostly people with little more than the clothing on their backs and a few meager possessions. Hungry children crying for relief that weary mothers had no way to provide. Sick and injured untended in the dirt, or if they were fortunate, lying on a blanket.

"This is a disgrace," the young redhead scolded.

"My Lady, I'm sorry, but I had no way of. . ." the young Captain tried to defend himself. Having just been appointed by his battalion commander as Winifred's personal escort along with his company of the King's Own, Andrew Case had no idea that there were refugees anywhere, let alone just outside the city. He had been consumed for the last three days with nothing more than ensuring that Lady 'don't call me Lady' Winifred's movements were screened and her safety assured. Before that, he had been equally consumed with his duties securing the palace after the death of the King and near death of his own Prince.

"Listen to me," she looked at the young man, her eyes blazing. "I'm not interested in blame, understand? We have to do something about this. Now." She paused, weighing what her most important duties should be first.

"I need runners sent to the nearest warehouse," she ordered. "I need enough food for. . .five thousand people for. . .one week," she estimated. "I will also need sufficient camp ware for that food to be cooked in, and if possible, bowls and utensils."

"You," Case pointed to the nearest man. "You heard the Lady. Get moving!" The younger man nodded nervously and kicked his mount into action, spurring his way toward Nasil as fast as the startled mount could carry him.

"Send someone to Lady Freeman-Corsin," was her next order. "I need medical attention for these poor people. She needn't come herself, I think a regular surgeon and physician should be sufficient for their needs, but we need bandages, litters and above all clean water. There should be medical students at university," she added suddenly. "Advise her that this would be excellent training for them, I should imagine."

"Corporal," Case snapped and a man with the inverted chevrons of a junior NCO came to near attention in the saddle. "Lady Corsin with Lady Hubel's orders. Now!" Again, a horse was spurred into frantic movement as a startled NCO jumped to obey.

"Water," Winnie repeated. "We have to get them clean water before cholera or dysentery kills the lot of them," she went on. "I know there are tankage wagons the army uses to move water to camp. Do we have any of them in the city?" she asked.

"I'll have someone check at once, milady," Case assured her, snapping his fingers to get the attention of a junior sergeant and waving him off to check for water tanks.

"We need tents or perhaps existing buildings to give them shelter," she mused. "Are there any abandoned factory buildings in the city? Or perhaps outside it?"

"There are a number of older buildings that are not in use at the. . ." Case trailed off as a sudden thought came to him.

"What is it?" Winnie demanded.

"Milady, 1st Corps barracks are empty," he said softly. "Have been since they headed for the front. Thousands of bunks, latrines, mess, everything you need."

"Catch the runners then and have their orders changed," she told him at once. "Everything asked for is to go there and then I need every wagon that can be had. We'll pull them with oxen if we need to. Mules are even better but I'm sure they are in short supply. Those here who can walk will have to do so. Have the wagons bring some water and jerky for them to eat along the way, and have the doctors meet us at the barracks. Meantime, secure the services of a few people to cook for them for tonight and tomorrow."

"Just tonight and tomorrow?" Case asked.

"We can't take care of them forever," Winnie told him. "We'll give them a day of rest, then a day or two of acclimation and training. After that, they will have to care for themselves. Which reminds me," she added. "We will need seed, garden tools, things of that nature. Are there open grounds around the barracks?"

"Yes, milady," Case nodded eagerly. "Many acres of parade and training ground for infantry and cavalry alike."

"Excellent," Winnie nodded firmly. "This is what I want…"

-

"It would appear that placing Winifred in command of the refugee issue was indeed a wise suggestion, Parno," Memmnon commented dryly as he watched the hustle and bustle about the palace.

"She's a hard charger," Parno nodded. "Stephanie is using the refugee care as a training ground for medical students, too. At Winnie's suggestion, no less," he smiled. "She'll make a fine Queen, brother," he added softly, delighting in Memmnon's deep blush.

"Damn you," Memmnon muttered. "Why is it that I cannot successfully tease you about Lady Stephanie as you do me about Winifred?" he demanded.

"I've had more practice," Parno shrugged, unrepentant. "At any rate, I know I'm right. You've chosen well. In fact, you couldn't possibly have chosen better, in my opinion."

"And giving her this duty keeps her from trying to get to the fighting," Memmnon added, and was pleased to see a bit of red rush to Parno's face.

Finally.

"That is a plus," Parno admitted. "But I also knew that once she saw the problem, she'd seize it and move forward. And she has."

"So, she has," Memmnon agreed. "Parno, I'm sorry, but I have to rest," the King said gently. "I've been on my feet a good bit today and I'm played out, I'm afraid."

"Of course," Parno nodded. "I'll be departing tomorrow," he added, looking back to where Stephanie was overseeing still more preparations. "I have to get back and get things moving. We lose by doing nothing."

"Very well," Memmnon nodded, a gasp of pain and fatigue escaping his lips as his attendants assisted him. "Please see me at least once more before you go. Perhaps supper this evening? Or after?"

"Afterward," Parno nodded. "I'll be there."

"Until then." Memmnon moved away, out of sight of most of the people in the area, but not his doctor. She approached Parno with concern on her face.

"Does he need attention?" she asked.

"No, just rest," Parno assured her. "Do you have some time?" he asked her suddenly and she looked at him.

"You're leaving, aren't you?" she said in way of answer, and he simply nodded.

"I knew it was coming," she sighed. "I just didn't want it to be so soon."

"I've been here for weeks," Parno protested. "And I have to get back. I have too much to do."

"I know," she nodded, her hands folded carefully before her.

"Walk with me," he urged suddenly, and offered his arm. She took it at once and her weight on his limb was a comfort all out of proportion to what it should have been.

"To the gardens?" she smiled up at him.

"As you desire, my Lady," he smiled back. They left the hustle and bustle behind them for a while to enjoy what might be their last afternoon together.

-

"Sir, I'm going to need more men."

Captain Andrew Case had reached that decision only a few hours into his charge's handling of the refugee crisis. She was using his men as runners, litter bearers, teamsters, whatever her need was.

"You have a reinforced company under your command, Captain," Major Carl Vaughan, 2nd Battalion, King's Own, Commanding replied, a slight frown on his face. "Are you telling me that one hundred and fifty men can't take care of one teen-age woman?"

"Take care of her? We can't even keep up with her! Sir," he hastened to add, face red. "Sir, since taking the refugee situation over, she is using the men to care for the refugees rather than herself. None of the men mind that, sir, and neither do I. I admire her for it, to be honest. But my men are spread too thin. If a raid hit, we'd never be able to get her to safety, let alone protect her. And sir, begging your pardon, but there's always the chance of Nor spies and saboteurs amongst the refugees, too. Was a Nor heathen to get word that her Ladyship was the King's intended..."

"I see your point," Vaughan nodded sagely. "Let me confer with Colonel Raymond and I'll get back with you. Today."

"Thank you, sir," a greatly relieved Case saluted. Chuckling to himself, Vaughan rose to walk over to the regimental commander's office.

-

"So, he stuck it out nearly a whole day?" Raymond smiled.

"Nearly," Vaughan chuckled again. "And he wasn't complaining. He was concerned about the girl's safety. And he made some excellent points as well I'd have to say," he added. "We might want to think about seeding some people into the refugees ourselves. Just to keep a pulse on what's happening."

"Good idea," Raymond nodded. "I'll speak to Grey about it later on. Meanwhile, what to do about young Case?"

"Other than not having combat experience, he's as qualified as can be," Vaughan shrugged. "He's got the training, the talent, and the raw material. And he's shown today he's not afraid to ask for help when he thinks he needs it, but only after seeing if he can handle it himself. He's nearer the girl's age than anyone else we have and will come closer to identifying with her. That being said," he held up a single finger, "we need to have a female Constable assigned to her. Maybe more than one. And she needs a secretary as well. The men can continue to serve as runners, to a point, but Case will have to put his foot down somewhere on how many of his men he's willing to allow to be out running and waiting tables."

"Agreed," Raymond made a note to himself about the female constables. "Good idea. All right," he nodded. "Pull the additional men from other companies, but no more than one platoon each. I don't want the other battalions too short handed to protect His Highness."

"I'll see to it," Vaughan promised as he rose. "You know, this leaves me short a company, not to mention one of my most promising young commanders," he grinned.

"You'll manage, I'm sure," Raymond snorted. "And it was your idea."

-

"What? I mean Sir?" Case straightened.

"You're being promoted to Senior Captain, Mister Case," Vaughan repeated, working to hide his mirth at the younger man's antics. "You aren't senior enough to be given leaves, but you'll be commanding a short battalion so we've dusted off an old rank used for such occasions. Your duty to Lady Hubel will now have a command of three companies of roughly one hundred men each. The new men are being drawn from around the rest of the regiment so all of them are King's Own. Some may not be happy about their new assignment, though," he warned.

"Sir." Case nodded.

"As to your manpower issues, it's your responsibility to ensure that you have enough men to meet your obligations, Captain," Vaughan turned more serious. "That means telling Lady Hubel 'no' when she draws your manpower too low. Suggest that she begin drawing her helpers from the refugees themselves and reserve your men for acting as runners. They aren't security risks and they know the city. Better to use them than the refugees for something like that."

"Yes sir," Case agreed. "But sir. . .refusing her can be. . .difficult," he managed not stammer.

"Get over it, Senior Captain," Vaughan ordered him sternly. "You aren't there to babysit her or make her wishes reality. You're there to protect her and that includes from threats within as well as without as you said. Watch for Nor spies and saboteurs among the refugees like you've been doing. If present and they get wind of who she is, or of what she means to the King, then you could have an attack coming at you from out of nowhere."

"Yes sir," Case nodded. "I'd thought of that, actually, but. . .it would help if I had some women in the service, sir," he admitted. "There are times and places that a man just shouldn't be accompanying a woman, Major."

"So, there are," Vaughan agreed. "Colonel Raymond will be asking for female Constables to be assigned to her this afternoon. They'll be with her around the clock while your men form her outer shell. You've done well, Case. I have no reservation about you having this assignment, as I know you'll continue to do well."

"Thank you, Major," Case stiffened again out of habit.

"Now get back to your command, Senior Captain."

-

"You're leaving in the morning?" Stephanie asked softly, distressed.

"Yes," Parno kept his voice just as soft, but also firm. If he didn't, it wouldn't take much for her to talk him out of going.

"When will you be back?" she asked, deliberately ignoring the fact that he might not return at all.

"I have no idea," he replied honestly. "I have to try and get things moving again. We need to try and move them back, at least back into the Kenty Plains and free up some of our bread basket. If we don't, we'll face a starving time before winter is over."

"The flowers are still trying to bloom and we're already talking about winter," she snorted delicately, her small hand caressing a rosebud.

"We have to plan months ahead in times like these," Parno reminded her. "If we don't, we suffer. Our people suffer."

"I know," she sighed. "I'm just tired. I want things to return to the way they were."

"That isn't going to happen, Stephanie," Parno told her gently. "Far too much has changed, and not just with the Imperials, either. Things won't ever be like they were, ever again."

"I know that too," she nodded, still looking at the bloom as if it were the most amazing thing she'd ever seen. "I don't like it, but I know it. I accept it," she added, finally looking at him.

"I wish we were closer," she said softly, laying her head on the chest. "I wish we were much closer."

"If we were much closer, we'd be a spectacle spoken of for years to come," Parno chuckled and she slapped his chest lightly with an open hand that closed on a fistful of his jacket.

"Stop trying to cheer me up," she told him. "And stop making fun of me," she semi-protested.

"I'm not making fun," he promised. "I wish were back at Cove Canton and the biggest problem we had was where we were going to build our home and whether to raise cows, horses, or both!" he said, softly kissing the top of her head.

"But we're not," she sighed again.

"No, we aren't," Parno echoed her sigh with one of his own.

"This war won't end soon no matter what," she said suddenly, lifting her head to look at him.

"No, it won't," he told her firmly. "There will never be peace between us again, in all likelihood," he added. "Times of non-war may be the best we can look forward to."

"I don't know if I want to raise children into that kind of world," she admitted, then her face colored at what she had said implied.

"You won't have to," Parno promised her and she looked at him, startled.

"I intend to destroy the Empire once and for all," he told her flatly. "When I'm finished, there won't be an Empire for us to be at war with. Our generation may know only war, but the next will know peace. Our children," he stressed to her, hands gripping her shoulders firmly, "will know peace. I swear that to you. If God grants me mercy to live long enough, our children will know peace on all sides."

"Marry me," she said suddenly. Impulsively. "Today. Right now. When you leave tomorrow, leave here as my husband, Parno."

"No," he shook his head, hiding his shock as best he could. "Tempting, but no," he tempered his refusal with a smile. "What you ask is very tempting, Lady Stephanie, but I cannot."

"Why?" she all but demanded.

"Edema would kill us if we married without her present, let alone without letting her plan the event," he managed to get it out without laughing, but then broke into a broad smile as he lost his battle with laughter. Stephanie looked at him in near anger for a few seconds before she too descended into laughter.

"I suppose you're right," she nodded. "But I meant it," she insisted. "If something were to happen to you, at least I'd have. . .I mean I might have…" her voice died out as she looked away, face reddening once more.

"A child?" Parno asked her, and she nodded jerkily, fighting tears.

"No," his voice was even more firm this time. "I would not leave you like that," he told her. "I can't imagine anything less responsible than abandoning you when you were with child. I will not."

"Even if it's what I want?" she asked him, not looking at him.

"Even if it's what you think you want," he replied. "There is too much to do, Stephanie, and I know you well enough to know that you will be in the thick of it, no matter what. I can't and won't try to stop you, because that would be like telling you not to be the woman I fell in love with. But I will not add to that difficulty with something like that. But if the Lord wills it, there will be a time, I promise."

"Before you go north," she looked at him sharply. "Before you leave Soulan."

"Yes," he replied just as firmly as he'd refused minutes ago. "Before I go north. And that is something I must ask you not to repeat. Few know of my plans, and I need it to stay that way. They are for far into the future. Years, in all likelihood. So yes. Before I leave Soulan."

"I will hold you to that, Parno McLeod," she straightened herself, pulling at her clothing to straighten it as well. "You will do as you've promised."

"I always have," he smiled one more time. "I always have."

-

"What do you mean 'no'?"

Senior Captain Andrew Case drew himself up, steeling himself against the onslaught he was sure to come.

"I mean no, My Lady," he repeated, trying to hold eye contact with the smoldering green orbs that Winnie Hubel had turned upon him. "I have almost half my command at your disposal now, running errands and waiting tables. No more. I have to have enough men remaining to ensure your protection. As it is I am granting you more leeway with my command than I should, and that will end in a day or two."

"Not all of them," he indicated the refugees that were even now receiving their first good meal in many days, served in many cases by men wearing the green and black livery of the King's Own, "are ailing, My Lady. Some of them are able, and most likely willing to work. You must begin pressing them into service to help themselves as you yourself said before. My men have responsibilities that extend beyond this work. In fact this work is not what they are here for at all."

"Too good to serve the common folks?" Winnie asked, eyes narrowing even further.

"I am a commoner myself, My Lady," Case's voice was chilly now; insulted. "I have no noble lineage to call upon or defend. I am where I am because I'm good at what I do and I work hard. And if I did think I was too good to serve, I wouldn't be in uniform," he added tersely. "There is no higher service."

Taken aback, Winnie was actually the first to break eye contact as she looked back to the refugees.

"It doesn't make sense not to use your men to help," she told him.

"We are using my men to help, but we won't be using all of them," Case said calmly, getting hold of his own temper. "Enough is enough, My Lady. Many of my men are working now and will have to stand guard tonight. Those lucky enough to be resting now and pulling guard tonight will have to work tomorrow. If I continue to allow all of them to be used in such a way, then soon I'll have troopers who aren't watching what they're doing. Not paying attention from lack of sleep. And all it takes is one mistake, My Lady."

"You act like there's someone lurking about even now to kill me," Winnie snorted.

"For all I know, there is," Case surprised her. "There could be Norland spies mixed in with the refugees, or teams intending to use the ruse of posing as refugees to commit acts of mayhem and sabotage around them as they go. Once word gets out who you are then yes, My Lady, you become a target."

"And you should also consider this," he lowered his voice, looking around to ensure that no one else was near. "You are now the intended of the King of Soulan. Prince Memmnon is now King Memmnon and you are all but betrothed in the eyes of the palace. Word of that will spread, My Lady, and there are many fine young noblewomen whose families will not take kindly to missing the chance to marry into the McLeod dynasty. Families to whom intrigue and assassinations come easily and naturally."

"You have to be joking," Winnie snorted derisively. One look at his pensive face was all it took for her to realize he wasn't joking. He was as serious as he knew how to be.

"Perhaps you should discuss this with Lady Corsin, My Lady," Andrew told her. "You are in a different world now, My Lady. Things are not always what they seem at this level."

-

"We leave tomorrow?" Karls asked, standing before Parno's desk in the office that had once been Memmnon's.

"With the sun," Parno nodded. "I want you to choose a small guard for Stephanie from among the Black Sheep," he told Karls. "I know she has an escort already, but I want it strengthened. At least to Company level. In the meanwhile, I'm searching for suitable female escorts. I had hoped Winnie would be that for Stephanie, but Memmnon ruined that for me," he snorted.

"I'm sure he's broken up about it," Karls grinned.

"I'm sure," Parno nodded. "I'm expecting Sebastian Grey any minute," he continued. "I'm going to request a brace of female Constables to be her close escorts. While I'm thinking about it, I want good swordsmen among the men of her escort. By which I mean men who can serve as instructors. And men skilled in hand-to-hand as well. I want everyone around her well trained and that will include training the women."

"Very well," Karls nodded. "Does that mean you want the man currently in charge of her escort replaced?"

"Who is it?" Parno asked.

"Winters," Karls replied. "Jeffrey Winters, Senior Lieutenant."

"One of yours?" Parno asked, by which he meant one of the original regulars that Karls had brought with him to form the Black Sheep.

"Yes," Karls confirmed. "He was with us at the Gap and served with distinction, promoted from Third Lieutenant for bravery and then from Second for merit. He was brevetted Captain to command her escort after he recovered from injury."

"He was wounded, wasn't he?" Parno asked, thinking back.

"Yes, but continued fighting," Karls nodded.

"Are you happy with him where he is?" Parno asked.

"He's a good man," Karls nodded.

"Then officially promote him to Captain and leave him," Parno ordered. "Stephanie hasn't complained about him so I assume they get along. No sense in upsetting that balance."

-

"What do I need with Constables?"

"They aren't here as Constables but as security," Parno replied as both Stephanie and Winnie complained. "You need women to accompany you places a man really can't go. These ladies are well trained and have been part of the Royal Constabulary for some time. They will work in shifts and accompany you at all times. They are not runners," he looked at Winnie, "nor are they orderlies," this to Stephanie who had the grace to color a bit. "They are here to protect you and you will let them do it."

"Or what?" Winnie demanded.

"There is no 'or what'," Parno said simply. "It's going to happen. Anything else?" Both women blinked at that but nodded agreement.

"Wonderful," Parno tried to sound exuberant. "I'm sure you'll all get along. Now, Lady Stephanie, may I escort you to dinner? I'm afraid I have to make it an early evening," he semi-apologized.

"Certainly," she smiled, taking the offered arm.

"Can we speak later?" Winnie asked, a hand on Stephanie's arm.

"Of course."

-

Dinner was more subdued than Parno had hoped and still went better than he'd expected. The discussion earlier in the day in the garden hadn't necessarily ended on a great note after all, and Stephanie wasn't the most docile of people. Her quiet acceptance had therefore set Parno on edge.

They were having a private dinner, just the two of them, in the small dining room that Tammon had used for family only gatherings. The meal was excellent, the cooks going all out because of Parno's impending departure. Parno couldn't enjoy it for fear of the impending explosion he was expecting at literally any second. He was starting to wonder what she was waiting fo-

"So, you will leave at first light?" Her voice was deceptively mild.

"As soon as we can see well enough to travel," he nodded carefully. "One of the reasons for such an early supper. I need my beauty sleep," he tried a small joke, which promptly fell flat.

"And there is no way of knowing when I will see you again, is there?" she continued on as if he hadn't spoken.

"No, I'm afraid not," he admitted. "Things have changed so much in the last three weeks that I don't know what I'll find when I get back. I have a lot of movements to make and I need to see what's going on before I can make them."

"I see."

Uh-oh.

"I think I shall retire early," Stephanie said suddenly, standing abruptly. "I can't do this," she admitted softly. "I can't sit here and pretend nothing is wrong. That you won't be gone when I wake up."

"I'm sorry," Parno stood. "I really am. May I walk you to your rooms?" Technically his rooms, at least before. He'd never likely get them back, now.

"No," she shook her head, clearly fighting to maintain her decorum. "No, I don't think that. . .that would be wise," she said. "Please be careful," she all but whispered as she hugged him tightly. "Please. And come back to me."

"I will," he stopped short of promising but tried to reassure her. "I will miss you," he added.

"And I you," she kissed him gently and then pulled herself away.

"Go with God, Parno McLeod." Gathering her skirts in hand she then swept out of the room with a haste that belied her grief.

Parno returned to his chair though his appetite was now gone. He toyed with his food for a few minutes before shoving the plate away and standing.

Eating alone was no fun.

-

"Are your plans finalized?" Memmnon asked. Parno had gone to see his brother one last time before turning in.

"Yes," Parno nodded. "At least for the most part. There will almost certainly be some changes I must make at some point, but no plan survives contact with the enemy."

"True enough," his brother tried to settle into a more comfortable position and failed. "Is there any hope?" he asked.

"There is always hope," Parno shrugged. "We are not beaten. We aren't even close to beaten as things stand now, in fact. But for us, leaving so much of our growing land in their hands is the same as losing, really. Without that acreage, we will be in trouble. We've lost too much in the way of cattle and horses already, not to mention other stock that play lesser roles in feeding our population. I have at best a month to force them back or we will have to make do with what we have left. We will face a hungry time before next spring, which will leave our army weaker right when it should be stronger."

"They are already planting, and they have more people than we do," he continued with a sigh. "And they are determined. I don't know," he shrugged finally. "We will do all we can."

"I know that," Memmnon smiled faintly. "Is there any word from your men about Therron and Sherron?"

"No, but I expect none unless they succeed or they run into trouble," Parno replied with a head shake. "The two men I sent are excellent with independent command. They don't need constant guidance, just instructions and limitations, which they have."

"I am hearing vague rumors coming from the south about an army unit taking by force from people as they go," Memmnon mentioned. "Grey is convinced it's Callens trying to appease Sherron, based on the items generally taken. Dresses, vanity items, comfort items, that sort of thing."

"She's learning that being in the saddle isn't quite as romantic as she thought," Parno smiled grimly. "Maybe that will slow them down. We'll see. But I've done all I can on that score," he admitted. "This plot of hers has taken nearly a full division of fighting men away from the front when I needed them most. Well trained men at that."

"I know," Memmnon nodded. "It should all have been handled differently," he admitted.

"Too late now," Parno shrugged. "At any rate, I will leave at first light. I'm leaving a small detachment of my regiment as a guard for Stephanie. Please ensure that they aren't 'misappropriated' for anything else," he requested.

"I shall," Memmnon promised. "Be careful, Parno, and please take care of yourself. We cannot spare you. I don't say that lightly, either. We literally have no one who could replace you. So please, have a care."

"I will," Parno promised. "Take care of yourself and follow the doctor's orders," Parno grinned.

"I will," Memmnon smiled in reply.

With that Parno took his brother's hand and then left his quarters, heading for his own.

"A pensive look, my prince," Cho Feng's voice came from the dark of the room as Parno closed the door.

"How can you tell in the dark?" Parno asked, turning up the lamp along the wall.

"You have just left your lady and your liege," Cho shrugged in the growing light of the lamp. "It was not a difficult guess. Darkness has come earlier than I had guessed."

"Not yet summer," Parno nodded. "Days will get longer soon enough and we'll be wishing they were shorter, to deny the light to the enemy."

"Possibly," Feng agreed, returning his gaze to the city below. Despite the war there was light everywhere showing from street lamps and windows.

"Bright place at night," Parno observed. "Lights always drew me when I lived here," he admitted. "Well, lights, lager and ladies," he chuckled. "Life's necessities you know."

"You have left those habits behind, I have noted," Feng's voice sounded humored, though his face was still turned from Parno.

"Had to," Parno nodded, removing his sword and then his tunic. "Especially now."

"Yes," Feng nodded. "What do you know of your enemy, Parno McLeod?" Feng changed the subject suddenly.

"He is more numerous than we are, and well trained," Parno replied after a few seconds. "Moderately well led, at least on the nearest front to us, and fairly well determined. I believe that determination was shattered, or at least broken somewhat with our repulsing of their last attack, but that will not prevent them from attacking again. Having begun, they have no choice but to continue."

"And your other enemies?" Feng asked.

"They are ruthless, bloodthirsty and highly intelligent, yet that intelligence is tainted with arrogance, disdain and not a little madness," Parno's voice darkened a bit. "Sherron is mad. Therron is an ego stroked moron with delusions of grandeur."

"Which of them is the more dangerous?" Feng asked.

"Sherron almost certainly, at least for now," Parno replied at once. "It is her machinations and scheming that has made all this possible. We ignored her in favor of watching Therron, a mistake that cost us our King and nearly our Crown Prince. It also cost us several other good men."

"What do you know of yourself, young prince?" Feng shifted gears quickly, testing his young charge.

"I am outnumbered and pushed against a wall," Parno admitted. "My troops are better led, and moderately better trained, but far too many of them lay dead on the field and their replacements will not, cannot, do as good as they did."

"Too much of my grain and pasture lands lay in enemy hands," he continued. "My army is too small and spread too thin. The enemy has the initiative and I cannot find a way to seize it back. I have made two attempts to do so but been stymied each time."

"I need time, but I cannot trade space for time because I cannot spare any more farm land in enemy hands. I need men, but I can't grow them like grain. I need horses but trained war horses take time. Years. I need supplies, which at the moment are plentiful but not unlimited." He paused and looked at Feng.

"My enemy occupies a position that he knows I must attack sooner rather than later," he sighed. "If he has patience, he need only wait for me to come to him. In the end I will have no choice."

"Very good," Feng complimented. "What are you doing about this?" he asked.

"I'm moving 2nd Corps to Shelby and taking Raines' Mounted Infantry as well as the Mounted Infantry I sent him just a few weeks ago back. 2nd Corps will be able to rest and refit while serving as a reserve for 3rd Corps and I will have additional usable manpower where I need it."

"Once all my forces are up and concentrated, I plan to take the combined cavalry strength of the army and sweep around the enemy right, coordinating that strike with a determined infantry attack against his right flank. I will have to maintain my line and the anchor on the river while threatening their right at the same time. If successful we maybe can roll them up from the flank as we did the first time, but with greater success and better results."

"A risk, but an acceptable one," Feng noted. "What are your other options?" he demanded.

"I see none," Parno admitted, hands raised in a helpless gesture.

"Then you are not looking," Feng replied, arms crossing over his chest. "There are always options, Parno. They may not be tenable, but they are there. What else can you do here?" he demanded.

Parno looked at his teacher. Feng was trying to Make A Point, he knew. This was what he always did when trying to Make A Point.

"Cho, I cannot see another alternative," he said finally. "I must have that land to feed my people, let alone my army. I can't let them stay there."

"How many of your men die because of this attack?" Feng asked, pressing his charge. "How many horses? How much treasure expended to return how much land to your use? Land that you might ultimately lose again if the enemy mounts a strong counter-offensive?"

"I…" Parno began a reply but halted it as he considered. He would lose men there was no doubt. Horses too and expend a great deal of resources. But try as he might he couldn't see an alternative.

"What am I not seeing?" he asked, sitting down and looking for all the world like a kid in school.

"What is the objective of this offensive?" Feng asked.

"Retaking crop land," Parno replied.

"So actually, the objective is to secure more land to plant crops, no?" Feng prompted.

"Yes," Parno nodded, still not seeing it.

"So then, is there no other way to secure land for planting than to hurl your army recklessly against a prepared enemy in a place of their choosing?" the oriental sword master's words were almost scornful.

"I…" Parno tried to reply but brought himself up short. Was there another way?

"Is there no land in this kingdom not currently in use that can be pressed into service to maintain stock or grow food?" Feng's eyebrows rose.

"Well yes, of course, but you're talking about places strung out all across the kingdom!" Parno protested, finally seeing Feng's point. "Some of them barely accessible, even!"

"Could they sustain a group of people sent there with the tools to care for themselves for the duration?" Feng asked.

"I suppose so," Parno nodded, though reluctant. "But wouldn't it be better to retake all this prime farmland?"

"Can you be assured of holding it?" Feng asked. "What happens if you expend so much in resources to take this land back, then to plant it, only to lose it before the grain can be harvested? You have fed your enemy's army in your own front yard and lost how much in doing so? How much labor, time and resources expended for no return of any kind save loss?"

Parno sat back in his seat, his entire plan crumbling before his eyes, cut to ribbons with just a few short swaths from Cho Feng.

Had he become so accustomed to casualties that he had begun to ignore them? Had he been so focused on kicking the Nor out of his Kingdom that he lost sight of the real objective, which was to never have to do anything like this again?

He had known that any plan he had devised would include losses and so he had ignored that as a consideration? Since he couldn't prevent it, he wouldn't factor it into his thinking?

"Now," Feng continued. "If you can feed your army and your people without sacrificing so much to the enemy to do so, on a gamble that may not pay off for you, why not do so and allow them to keep that land for now?"

"Because it's ours!" was Parno's immediate reply.

"How long to grow grain?" Feng demanded.

"Four to six months depending on the grain, the soil, things like that," Parno shrugged.

"How long to grow soldier?" was the next question and it caught Parno flat footed. Cho's accent tended to come out much more when he was exercised. Which he was now.

"I-you can't just grow soldiers!" he complained.

"Of course, you grow soldiers, just as you grow craftsmen and artisans," Feng snorted. "Soldier growth starts at birth! Foolish boy," Feng was pacing now. "Soldier must attain adulthood before training can begin. How long?" he demanded.

"Sixteen to eighteen years," Parno nodded, the light beginning to dawn.

"How long to train soldier?" Feng was relentless.

"The way we're doing it now, nearly another year, total."

"So…nineteen, perhaps twenty years to replace soldier who falls in combat," Feng stopped pacing and faced Parno suddenly, having made his point. "Six months to grow grain. Starve a little now, or allow your enemy to overwhelm you later. Make sacrifices at the table, or on field of battle. From which can you recover more quickly?"

"From the table," Parno wasn't even paying attention to what he was saying anymore. Instead his mind was far away, turning over what lands were available to him, to everyone, for producing the food they would lose from this year's harvest.

"Your position is a strong one," Feng pushed on. "Your army is resting and they need it. Many new soldiers. Need time to train, to learn from those who know what war is now. Your enemy is afraid of your new weapons and may hesitate to push you further, at least for now. Attack in haste. . .?" he prompted Parno to recall one of his earlier lessons.

". . .retreat in defeat," Parno murmured, standing. "I have to go," he said suddenly, reaching for his sword. "I have much to do. Please find Karls for me and tell him we will not be leaving as I had planned. Our departure is delayed at least one day and perhaps as long as three. And have a courier ready at dawn to carry a message to Davies for me, and another to carry one to Raines."

"Very well," Feng fought off the urge to smile. "It will be done," he bowed slightly.

"Thank you," Parno said softly before stepping out into the hallway, on his way back to see his brother.

"You are most welcome, my Prince," Feng smiled at the closed door. "Most welcome indeed."

CHAPTER THREE

-

"You want to make all these people move when I've only just gotten them situated?" Winnie's voice was as hard as her gaze. Memmnon has chosen well it seems, he thought with a dry mental chuckle.

"We don't have a choice, Winnie," he told her flatly. "We can't feed them indefinitely from stores and there isn't enough tillable land here to feed them either. They are going to have to work to feed themselves and anything extra will go to feed the army that's defending them."

"They are sick and exhausted!" Winnie objected, forgetting that it had been her own idea just a day ago to do the same thing.

"They aren't all sick and they've had two days rest already," Parno was shaking his head. "It will take a week at least to get things organized to the point that they can head for areas that are open enough to allow them to grow food. Once they've planted, they'll have the summer to prepare shelter and firewood for the winter. Yes, I'm aware of how hard that will be, but aren't you forgetting that a great many of the refugees themselves are farmers and ranchers? They have the knowledge to take care of themselves and to teach others to do the same. Let them use that knowledge and share it with townsfolk driven out of the towns and cities north of the lines."

"A lot of them are children," Winnie's protests were growing fainter.

"Children who are accustomed to working," Parno nodded. "And moving them south gets them further away from the war," he added. "The climate improves during the winter months for every one hundred miles you travel south, too. Here in Nasil the winter can be horrific at times and it's no better in Shelby. Don't even get me started on the Plateau and I shouldn't have to tell you about winter in the Apple

Mountains."

"No," Winnie agreed. She knew firsthand how hard winter could be in the mountains she had grown up in. "When will we have to do this?" she asked, resigned.

"As I said, it will take a week or so to gather the needed supplies and sufficient wagons to carry them. Let them rest during that time, but begin organizing them now. Find leaders among them who can get things done and others that know how to grow. Those who can handle stock as well," he added. "We don't have a great surplus at the moment but we do have enough to allow some swine, sheep and even a few cattle. They will need to allow them to breed and slaughter the new stock for meat, but over the next two years they should grow herds large enough to feed themselves and help feed the army."

"Years?" the word was echoed up and down the table, including Stephanie who was there to advise on health issues.

"Yes, years," Parno nodded. "We have to be smart about this," he told them. "We only have so many soldiers. We can only replace so many soldiers each year, and we have to have some able-bodied men to do other work as well, including assist with farm and stock operations and harvest trees. To build ships and forge weapons. No matter how many people you give me, I can find uses for them and still need more. You'll soon find the same to be true for your own work if you haven't already," he warned.

"That is true," Stephanie nodded, thinking about work in a military hospital in time of war. "No matter how many orderlies you have, it's never enough. There is always work waiting for those just coming on duty."

"But years?" Winnie asked again and Parno noted several heads nodding at her comment.

"If I launch an offensive and fail, then the Nor remain in the Tinsee Valley for the foreseeable future," he said flatly. "If I succeed, but lose so many men I can't hold our ground, then we still fail in the end and the enemy remains at our door." He leaned forward.

"The only way to ensure that we throw the enemy off our doorstep is to build up to the point that once we get them in retreat, we can press them all the way to the Ohi and hopefully destroy them as they try to cross back over." He stood abruptly, the need to move making him pace a bit behind his chair.

"I will only have one shot to make all that happen," he told them. "If I fail, or even if we succeed and the victory is Pyrrhic, then we're finished. The Nor have one huge army in the Valley, another army at least half that size across the bridge in Shelby, and now a new army, at least thirty thousand strong, has joined the army we currently face on the Valley plains." He stopped pacing and looked at the people before him in turn.

"If we try and fail, one of those armies will make it into the heartland and we have nothing left to stop them or even slow them down."

Heads rocked back as if physically pushed at hearing this.

"I had planned to risk everything in one big push to force the enemy back, at least as far as the Kenty plains, freeing up as much crop land as possible. But the point was made to me that every soldier I lost, every ounce of treasury that I expended, every seed we managed to plant and horse that was lost would be for naught if the enemy managed to push back and take that land from us a second time."

"Worse, we would have fed the enemy for the winter while our own people starved," he finished. "Which leaves us with the problem we originally faced; we have to feed our people and we have to keep the army supplied. We either do those things or we fall. It really is that simple, people. I should have seen it sooner," he admitted, sitting heavily once more, somewhat dejected himself after having said all of that aloud.

"You have already done more than anyone else to ensure that we remain free," Memmnon spoke for the first time from the head of the table, his voice calm and reassuring. Every inch the King. "Do not take blame upon yourself for something we all should have thought of, Parno."

"I agree," Gideon Philo, Minister of Agriculture nodded firmly. "This is my area of expertise, my Lord, and I too failed to appreciate the importance of what you have shown us. There are vast acres of unused lands that we can tap into for production of grains and maintaining herds. For that matter, there are thousands upon thousands of acres held in Royal Reserves around the Kingdom that can be planted and where trees can be harvested for dwellings, ship building, and to clear more land for planting."

"I dislike the idea of so many women being pressed into the labor force," Sebastian Grey shook his head. "It isn't right. And younger women who are of child bearing age? When they are with child, how are they to harvest crops and work fields?"

"Women are already working in all of those areas," Roda Finn scoffed, two seats down from Parno. "There are women working in the Foundry right now in work at least as dangerous as being on the front lines of combat, and equally important to the war effort."

"What?" Winnie's head came up at that.

"Talk to him about that later," Parno cut off that discussion before it started. "The point is that women are already working in dangerous occupations throughout the Kingdom. And when we mustered the Militia for service in the Army, who remained to tend the flocks and the fields, Chief Constable? Women." Parno's voice was flat and final. "Lady Stephanie is perhaps the finest surgeon in the Kingdom, and Lady Winifred one of the best archers in the history of our people. She has spent the last year teaching thousands of men the art of the bow at Cove Canton. Men who are even now the scourge of the Wild Tribes in battle, I remind you."

"Indeed?" Grey looked at the blushing Winnie with new respect.

"Indeed," Parno nodded firmly. "So, we will table any more discussion of how suitable women are for working anywhere. There are observation posts along the Great River and our seashores that are manned and in some cases commanded by women. All of them doing an excellent job. Let us move forward."

"Very well," Grey withdrew his objections.

"I will see to gathering the resources needed for new settlements to be self-reliant," Philo said, standing. "Tools, seed, implements and stock, at least to the degree we can in one week," he amended. "We may have to send the stock by way of herdsmen later on as we gather it, but that can be done. We must ensure in each group that there are those strong enough and able enough to handle a team of oxen behind a plow. We have few horses or mules available for such work at this point."

"I will find them," Winnie promised the Minister. "We must also be careful not to separate families," she added. "These people are traumatized enough as it is."

"I see no reason to separate family groups at all," Memmnon agreed. "In fact, I submit that such groupings will make everyone want to work harder to ensure that their families are cared for."

"True enough," Philo nodded. "Very well, I must get to work at once. With your permission, My Lord?" this to Memmnon.

"Of course, Minister," Memmnon nodded and the older man hustled from the room followed by two aides that had been making notes during the meeting.

"This will work," Memmnon said to those who remained. "Remarkable how this changes things, is it not?"

"It removes part of the strain from the army," Parno nodded cautiously. "So long as the enemy cooperates, this should help buy us time. We need time."

"What will you do with that time?" Memmnon asked.

"Train our replacements for one thing," Parno admitted. "Work them into the units that have suffered such heavy casualties so far, especially 2nd Corps. They are at half strength in most cases. It will also allow for those wounded who can return to duty to do so. Getting back experienced soldiers to fill the holes in the ranks is far better than taking a raw farm boy and placing him in the ranks with a bow or a sword."

"True," Memmnon nodded in agreement.

"We'll also use raids and feints to keep the enemy off balance," he mused. "We have to watch the river now, too," he added, eyes unfocused as he saw the position of the army in his mind's eye. "After we hurt them so badly last time they attacked, they may well try to bring those boats down river to make a landing behind us. Not to mention. . ." he trailed off as a new thought occurred to him.

"What?" Memmnon leaned forward, wincing as he did so.

"The Cumberland," Parno almost breathed. "They can use those boats and float down the Cumberland," he voiced it aloud. "I have to go," he stood abruptly again. "I have messages to send. If you need me I'll be in your old office," he told Memmnon, who grinned despite the situation. Parno still resisted calling the room his office.

"I should go and talk to the refugees I guess," Winnie said, once Parno was gone. "Start trying to organize them into groups."

"Let Philo handle that," Memmnon shook his head. "That will allow you to be the one they come to when they have complaints. You can solve their problems, which will make you ever more favorable to them. That way when you must ask hard tasks of them, they will respond better."

Winnie looked mulish for a moment, but Stephanie intervened just then.

"I needed to speak to you, anyway," she said quietly and the redhead nodded reluctantly.

"We all have work to do it seems," Memmnon said, looking toward Grey, Finn and any others in the room. All of them took the hint and departed, leaving the two women alone with the King.

"You may use this room for as long as it is needed," the King said, rising without aid, though an attendant stood close by. "I would appreciate the pleasure of your company this evening at meal time, if it pleases you," he told Winnie formally.

"Of course, My Lord," Winnie nodded gracefully, as Stephanie had taught her.

"Then I take my leave, ladies." Memmnon departed with his attendant hounding his steps, leaving the two alone.

"What is it?" Winnie asked, turning to Stephanie.

"You wanted to speak to me and we haven't had the opportunity," Stephanie said, reminding her friend. "I had intended to try and do it today anyway, so why not now?"

"Oh, yes," Winnie looked momentarily surprised but regained her composure quickly. "Captain Case suggested that I talk to you about how things work at this 'level'," she said, clearly looking for the words she needed. She was trying very hard not to embarrass Memmnon with her glaring rural manners and rudimentary education.

"What things, exactly?" Stephanie asked kindly.

"He suggested that there were families who might take great comfort in something happening to me," Winnie tried again.

"Ah," Stephanie nodded in understanding. "Court intrigue and machinations, yes," she sat back. "And yes, dear, I'm afraid that is true. I am surprised that he would mention it to you, however. It's his job to prevent such things from happening, after all. That's what he and his men are for. To keep those events distant from you. What?" she asked as Winnie's face grew more and more red while listening.

"I…I didn't believe him," Winnie began. "I've been pressing his men into service to help the refugees these last three days or so and he resisted me the last time, claiming that he needed at least some of his men to be working at their real jobs. I might have insulted him a bit about that," she admitted, more red faced still.

"Insulted how?" Stephanie asked.

"I might have said or implied that he was too good to help commoners in their time of need, or something like that," Winnie tried to blow it off.

"And he isn't of noble birth, I take it," Stephanie mused.

"No, he isn't," Winnie confirmed.

"Then yes, you gravely insulted him, Winnie dear," Stephanie sighed, leaning back. "You are going to have to learn to get that tongue under control young lady," her sponsor told her flatly. "These aren't the mountains, and these aren't backwoods people or former prisoners who speak that kind of language. And men like Case are rare indeed to make it into the King's Own on nothing but merit."

"He did seem proud of that," Winnie nodded, still stung from her dressing down.

"He has every right to be," Stephanie told her flatly. "Until recently the King's Own was more ceremonial at times, but these days it's nothing of the sort. Now as to your problems," Stephanie leaned forward again. "Yes, there are a number of families in Nasil alone who will not be glad nor happy to see you in the King's company, let alone to hear that he considers you marriage material. Families that are not above the use of assassination to remove someone they perceive as being in their way," Stephanie emphasized. "You would think in a Kingdom such as ours that things like that couldn't happen, and they are rare, or were," she frowned. "I'm afraid that Therron and Sherron McLeod's influence on the nobility has not been a good one, by and large. Where their father tended to keep them in check, and their mother I'm told kept them at bay, the twins have instead allowed them not only to run amok but have encouraged that separation between noble and commoner to a place far in excess of anything in at least recent history."

"So, Case wasn't just trying to get me to do what he wants," Winnie murmured.

"No, he wasn't, and his job is hard enough as it is without you making it worse," Stephanie chided. Winnie's face flushed even further at that but she nodded in understanding.

"Now I suggest you start with an apology to him, and then by heeding his recommendations when he has any. Men aren't chosen for such a position without cause or reason, so he's undoubtedly able. When he tells you something should be or not be done, heed his advice. And in the future, it would be good not to lean too heavily on that 'commoner' tag as well," she warned. "It might surprise you to learn that a great many people around Parno and Memmnon both are not 'noble' in birth. Neither has time for mere cosmetics."

"It will be as you say," Winnie promised.

"And speaking of behavior, you have missed your etiquette classes the last three days," Stephanie's tone grew even more firm if possible.

"I don't have time to-" Winnie began but Stephanie's voice cracked across the table cutting her off.

"You will make time, Winifred," she told her ward firmly. "If things continue to develop between you and Memmnon then you will one day be Queen of Soulan and your children will be the heirs of the Crown, young lady. You will make time for those classes and you will apply yourself to them. Don't give your enemies any more ammunition than they have already to use against you." Stephanie leaned back again and relaxed ever so slightly.

"Your work with the refugees has already gained you a great deal of respect and notoriety among the commoners of the city, who incidentally are far more numerous than the nobles in this kingdom. The refugees also respect and adore you for helping them in their time of need, and using Minister Philo to separate them into new groups to head off to work was a good idea that insulates you from any hard feelings over that. It will allow you at some point to visit them again and ensure that all is as well as it can be, and we can always have Philo make a few odd mistakes on purpose for you to correct. He knows how these games are played and will not object to being a heavy, provided it does not impugn his honor."

"That's dishonest," Winnie muttered.

"It's politics," Stephanie corrected. "Do you like Memmnon, Winnie?" she asked suddenly. The renewed blush on the younger woman's face was answer enough but Stephanie wanted to hear her say it.

"Yes," she said softly. "He is very kind and warm hearted when we are alone," she admitted. "He doesn't. . .he's not the King when it's just the two of us. He's just himself."

"Do you want to be his wife, Winnie?" Stephanie asked.

"He hasn't actually asked me," Winnie replied.

"That isn't what I asked you," Stephanie refused to be put off.

"I. . .I think so," Winnie nodded. "I'd never thought much about marriage at all but. . .Memmnon is different from anybody else I've ever met. And I don't me cause he's the King, either. I can see myself being his wife. I just don't know if I can see myself being his Queen."

"There's no separating the two," Stephanie said flatly. "I don't necessarily want to be 'Princess Stephanie', either. But if I want to be Parno's wife, and I do, then I have to be Princess Stephanie as well. And I hold no title of nobility either, dear," she added as almost an afterthought.

"What?" Winnie's head shot up. "But your parents-"

"Have more than one child and I am not the oldest, nor am I a son," Stephanie finished for her. "I hold no title other than 'Doctor' and I earned that title, so I wear it with some pride."

"Of course," Winnie nodded. "I just thought, I mean. . .you know so much and everyone calls you 'Lady' or 'milady'. . ."

"Because of Parno," Stephanie nodded, her own face reddening just a little. "I'm afraid that where Memmnon is well thought of and liked if not loved, Parno is a somewhat different story. Many respect him, yes. Many also fear him. And I honestly don't think he cares for the difference either way," she admitted. "As his 'Lady', that fear or respect transfers to me, just as the respect for Memmnon does to you in your present circumstances. Which makes your classes that much more important, by the way," she used this point to hammer home another.

"I see," Winnie nodded, and she did, finally.

"Good," Stephanie stood. "Now, I have been given at least one more day to convince Parno to marry me before he leaves, so I'm afraid I have work of my own to do," she smiled.

"Marry you now?" Winnie's eyes widened.

"If I can make him, yes," Stephanie nodded. "One of the good things about not be a 'noble' dear," she smiled broadly. "I can pretty much do as I please and no one cares."

-

"I don't care how hard it is."

Parno's face was a slowly erupting volcano as he spoke in terse terms to the man in charge of the River Guard. Unlike the Navy, the River Guard worked only the navigable waterways of the Kingdom, protecting commercial and civilian traffic alike from river piracy and raids. As the idea of the Nor using their boats to creep around his army had struck him, he had become obsessed with finding a way to prevent it.

"Milord," Commodore Steven Williamson licked suddenly dry lips, "it's not that it's difficult in and of itself. Our small boats are not equipped to battle against soldiers, that's all."

"I'm not asking you to fight them," Parno said, his calm tone of voice making Williamson even more nervous. "I'm ordering you to send boats and men to guard against them sneaking by me. All you need do is raise the alarm. That alone may be enough to stop an incursion."

"Our boats are spread over much of the kingdom, milord," Williamson tried again. "And many of our able-bodied men are now serving in the ranks, either in the Army or the Navy. Our manpower is limited."

"Commodore," Parno spoke with exaggerated patience. "I don't care where you have to pull men from, understand? I want boats patrolling that stretch of the Tinsee, as well as the Cumberland, and I want it done as soon as possible. By which I mean as soon as a boat can make it to where I want it, even if it has to be hauled by mules!" Parno took a deep breath to calm himself before continuing.

"Lay lines across the river, drive piles in rapids, do whatever you think it might take to slow an advance along the river by the enemy, do you understand? Why haven't you already thought of this anyway? Must I do all the thinking in this kingdom!"

"I will get right on it milord," Williamson promised, seeing Parno's hand creeping toward his sword. "We should have men on the way by first light."

"See that you do," was the terse reply and then Parno was gone, out the door and into the street.

"You must calm yourself," Cho Feng said quietly from his side.

"I'm calm," Parno told him.

"People in the streets could hear you 'talking' calmly," Cho's voice was dry with near sarcasm.

"I'm tired of being told how difficult something is," Parno shrugged. "Nothing is impossible with enough work. You taught me that. You and Darvo," he amended.

"I understand," Cho Feng nodded. "Many do not yet fully understand the gravity of the situation," he observed. "Until they do, they do not see the urgency of things as you do."

"Well they better start if they want to stay in their cushy jobs where it's safe," Parno said darkly. "My men are bleeding and dying all the time while they complain about how 'hard' something is. I'm sick and tired of hearing it."

"I understand," Cho repeated.

"Stop trying to make me calm down," Parno almost growled. "I need people to start thinking."

"So, you do," Cho's voice was still smooth and gentle. "And threatening them is certainly the way to do that," he added just a moment later.

"I didn't threaten him!" Parno objected.

"You didn't put your hand near your sword while speaking to him?" Cho asked, eyebrow raised.

"Did I?" Parno was suddenly less sure of himself.

"I am afraid so," Cho sighed. "You have become far too comfortable with that sort of thing my Prince."

"Well," Parno's reply was lame and he knew it but he didn't know what else to say. "Now I have to scratch up some kind of force to send up river from here and keep an eye out," he changed the subject. "Don't you love it when things just fall into place so well?" he asked rhetorically.

"Had you stayed with your original plan, none of this would have occurred to you at all," Cho reminded him. "As it stands now, you have the chance to repair this oversight. You are beginning to see the value of defense beyond merely winning one battle."

Parno considered that. He had no problem with defensive thinking when preparing for battle, but when merely looking for contingencies, he stuck with his background in horse soldiering. Movement, power, speed and agility were the way to win a battle.

"I have to start thinking like I want to win a war," he said aloud and missed the pleased expression that flitted across Cho's face before being schooled away.

"Indeed," he settled for saying. "Your battles to this point have been all or nothing, make or break affairs. Your enemy has been bloodied and are now reevaluating. You must look to do the same. You made a good start this morning, taking the long view of things. You must continue."

"Yeah," Parno nodded. "I need to see Roda Finn," he said suddenly.

-

"The river?" Finn frowned in thought. "I don't know, milord. What did you have in mind?"

"I had it in mind to lay the problem at your capable feet and you solve it for me," Parno smiled winningly. "It's called delegating I'm told."

"I've heard of it but rarely been able to put it into practice," Finn nodded, suddenly jumping to his feet and throwing open the door to his office.

"Who told you to move that!" he screamed at the top of his lungs, causing several people to jump nervously. "Put that back where it was and get back to work!" he slammed the door without waiting for answer or explanation and sat back down.

"What kind of problem do you expect to encounter along the river, my Prince?" he asked amiably, his ire from seconds earlier nowhere in sight.

"Ah, small boats mostly, ferrying troops down the river to land behind my army or perhaps all the way to Nasil, assuming they could make it this far." Parno couldn't help but glance out the window at the factory workers, wondering how Roda's outbursts were affecting them.

"Those rivers are closed to our own traffic are they not?" Finn mused, hand stroking his chin.

"Yes," Parno nodded. "Only supply ships are allowed to go up the Tinsee, and the Cumberland is closed as well. For the duration of the war or at least until we clear the Nor from our lands and force them back across the Ohi."

"Well, the easiest thing to do would be to erect some sort of coffer dams I suppose to limit navigation, but that's a hard job that would require some time and it would ruin the river for our own use as well," Roda said absently, scratching idly on a sheet of papyrus. "There is an idea I had for the Navy that might work," he said, looking up suddenly.

"What?" Parno asked.

"A double shot ballista," Finn told him as he rummaged through the papers on his desk. "Instead of two ballistae needing to be fired at the same time to propel say a length of chain between two bolts, we string both bolts on the same system and they fire in tandem-ah, here we are!" he unrolled a sketch and laid it open for Parno to see.

"What would this do to a small boat?" Parno asked. There was no point in pretending he could understand what he was seeing in all the chicken scratch that decorated the paper before him.

"Shoot tandem bolts that could carry chain, or tar-soaked rope, things like that, and hurl it into those small boats as they tried to navigate the river," Roda explained. "Also," he hesitated, "I've developed a way to fire the ballistae from a safe enough distance that we can return to using the exploding rounds I developed for them at Cove. We can't risk them at the front, but using them against a river target would be completely acceptable and safe, I should think."

"Wouldn't the water prevent that from working?" Parno frowned.

"Not with small amounts of material such as magnesium added to the bolts warheads, no," Roda smirked. "Magnesium will burn ever hotter if you try to extinguish it with water."

"I never heard of it," Parno admitted.

"We don't have much of it," Roda admitted. "But uses for it are very limited. It can be mined in some places but we usually get it from a complicated process using static from a hand cranked turbine-"

"Short version, Roda," Parno held up a hand before the fussy inventor could launch into lecture mode.

"We can get more," Roda said simply. "It will take a while and will require some manpower and skilled labor, but I know where to get most of it. Shipping from the coast will require a wagon, and possibly a small escort, I don't know," he admitted.

"And you can use this. . .magnesium, was it? to make the fire in the. . .warhead, did you say? burn hotter? Right?"

"Yes, and as a bonus it will provide a good deal of illumination in the event it must be used at night," Roda promised. "I was initially using it to experiment with a way to provide you with what the old world called 'flares' but. . .I have yet to devise a safe method of launching such a device into the sky," he admitted.

"We used them in my homeland," Cho Feng spoke for the first time. "The mechanics are not known to me, but their uses are many and not limited to warfare, either. Navigation aids for one thing," he added.

"Yes," Roda nodded to the oriental in thanks. "Just so. An imminently usable material for many things, milord."

"Anything else you can think of right off hand?" Parno asked.

"If I could figure a way to use the mines along the river that would be ideal," Roda mused. "That will take some thought, however," he shook his head. "I will need to make them float, and then figure a way to insure that the boat striking the mine would make it explode. I'm sorry, milord, but I will need to study on that one," he admitted.

"That's all right," Parno assured him. "I need it as soon as possible, but if it doesn't work then it's useless anyway. Do what you can."

"I will," Roda promised. "And I'll finalize the work on the double-shot ballistae as well. They will help right away if I can get them into service."

"Whatever you need, use it," Parno ordered. "Sooner the better."

-

'Milord!" Parno halted as he heard this call on his way out of the foundry. He turned to see Whip Hubel heading toward him, face set.

"Oh, boy," Parno murmured softly. "Hello, Whip!" he called with a smile. "How are you?"

"I'll be needin' a minute of your time, milord," Whip told him. "A matter of serious concern, Prince."

"Let me guess," Parno tried to keep his voice light. "What are my brother's intentions?"

"Exactly so," the old man nodded firmly. "I didn't raise my daughter to be no noble man's play toy, no matter who the man might be," the old man was clearly working himself into a fit. "I like you, milord, and it would grieve me for us to have words of hardship between us, but-"

"Wait, wait!" Parno held up his hands to stop the older man. "Wait," he repeated, frowning. "What are you talking about? Play toy?"

"Word is that your brother, the King, is trying to play house with my Winnie," Whip was smoldering. "I won't be having that, milord, from no man I care not who he might be."

"Have you spoken to your daughter, Whip?" Parno asked, looking at the older man.

"I can't get to her," Whip replied. "And that's another thing-"

"Come with me," Parno cut him off once more, motioning for the older man to follow. "We'll go now and see her. And along the way I'll try and explain what's really happening. And I'd be most interested to know where you got your other information, as well," he said amiably.

Cho Feng was not fooled.

-

"Let me get this straight," Whip said as the palace came into view. "You mean to tell me that the King of Soulan is sparkin' my little girl and wants to actually marry her? Make her the Queen?"

"Courting is the word we use, and yes," Parno assured him. "That's exactly what's happening. As it happens, your daughter isn't keeping house or anything else. She's living with my own fiancé in my old apartments in the palace and she has her own escort now as well as some very capable women constables to escort her where a man shouldn't be, including her rooms."

"Huh," Whip looked taken aback by that. "That ain't how I got it," he admitted.

"I'd be most interested to know where you 'got it' from," Parno said calmly.

"Just rumors floatin' around," the old man shrugged, now embarrassed. "One man in particular been talking a good bit about it during making delivery from here in town out to the foundry," he added. "Took great relish in describing the King's 'toy' in fact, to the others at the Foundry. Word made its way to me a few days ago but I ain't been able to see my little girl since she's been staying here."

"I'll fix that today," Parno promised him. "As for this man in particular, I'm going to need his name, Whip. I'll need to talk to him."

"Name's Denton," Whip replied. "Havrel Denton. Makes delivery to the canteen two, three times a week, he does."

"Does he now?"

"Aye."

"Well, we'll have to talk to Mister Denton then," Parno was entirely too calm. "Meantime," they pulled up at the gate.

"You again," the officer at the gate said, seeing Whip. Then he spotted Parno and came to attention. "Milord!"

"You've been refusing this man permission to see his daughter?" Parno didn't bother with niceties.

"He doesn't have permission to be here, and there's no way his daughter is-"

"His daughter is Winifred Hubel," Parno forced his anger down, saving it for Mister Denton. "You know her as Lady Winifred? King's intended?" he allowed the words to sink in and was pleased to see the man's face pale.

"While I'm on the subject, this man is my personal friend," he added, not noticing how Whip straightened proudly at that. "Not to mention perhaps the finest bowman in all of Soulan," he continued conversationally. "Now, I'm not castigating you for doing your job," he told the man. "But did you at least check with someone in the palace to see if his story was true?"

"N-no, milord, I did not," the man admitted. "I assumed-"

"Never a wise thing to do," Parno told the man, shaking his head in mild reproof. "Now, you're doing an excellent job here soldier, but I do want it fixed so that Whip can see his daughter whenever the notion takes him. Is that clear?"

"I'll see to it, milord!" the young officer promised, saluting stiffly.

"Outstanding!" Parno slapped the man's shoulder affectionately. "Now, carry on. I'll escort Mister Hubel inside to see his daughter. Right?"

"Right! I mean yes sir!" the young Lieutenant stammered.

"Carry on then," Parno nodded. "This way, Whip," he said. "Have Mister Hubel's horse place in the palace stables. He'll be staying the night," Parno ordered the enlisted man holding their reins.

"Aye milord," the young lancer grinned, having been highly entertained as seeing his wet behind the ears lieutenant taken down a peg.

"Milord, I'm not rightly the kind of man that ought be stayin' in a palace," Whip said softly. "I just wanted to see to Winifred's wellbeing."

"Nonsense," Parno scoffed at the statement. "You're as fit as at least half the nobles who have stayed here, I promise you. You'll likely have dinner with Memmnon and Winifred tonight, but if not, you can dine in the canteen. We'll have you a room assigned and you can stay here anytime you want to visit your daughter. Though I warn you that her days are pretty busy," he added.

"What do you mean?"

"Well, she's been overseeing the refugee care for the last few days, and attending classes for Stephanie, Lady Corsin," Parno clarified, "and she's also been attending civic and formal functions with Memmnon when he's able to attend."

"I'd heard he was injured," Whip nodded. "That's one thing that made me question what I was hearin', to be honest," he admitted.

"You were wise to question, but I don't think you'll have any more problems getting in," Parno assured him. "Understand that after my father's murder, security here is a great deal more stringent that it had been."

"I've no doubt, though it could be a mite better," Whip nodded and Parno stopped short, looking at him.

"What do you mean?" he asked.

"Begging pardon, milord, but there's at least seven ways inside this place that I've already found in the last week, and that's sneaking in without violence. I'm sure there's more."

"Do tell," Parno encouraged. "In fact, after you've seen Winifred and satisfied yourself that she's not being mistreated, I want you to come see me. I want you to meet the commander of the Palace Guard."

"Aye, milord."

"Now, I need to see someone."

-

"Denton?" Karls made sure he had the right name.

"Havrel Denton," Parno nodded, handing over a slip of paper. "He makes deliveries to the foundry from here. I want him taken. Quietly if possible but taken no matter what. Once you have him, take him some place quiet and let me know you have him."

"Aye, milord," Karls nodded. "I'll have someone on him today, and try to take him this evening."

"That will be fine."

-

"Papa!" Winnie smiled broadly as seeing her father for the first time in weeks. She hugged him tightly and he returned it, relieved to see his daughter in such high spirits and good health.

"Hello, girl," he said softly. "You look a right fetchin' picture, lass," he grinned and she blushed from head to toe.

"A lot has happened, Papa," she admitted.

"So the Prince informs me," Whip nodded. "How about we find a place to talk and you tell me all about it?"

-

"Colonel Stang, this is Whip Hubel," Parno introduced. Strong eyed the archer with a raised eyebrow. "Whip, this is Colonel Mason Stang, commander of the Palace Guard. Colonel, if you recognize the name Hubel, Whip is Lady Winifred's father. He's also my archery instructor at Cove Canton. He's had some issues getting in to see his daughter lately. Now," Parno leaned back, "I've fixed that problem for him, but during the time that he was trying to see his daughter he discovered a number of ways into the palace that bypass the security we have in place."

"Sir?" that got Stang's attention. Tammon McLeod's personal regiment had been incorporated into the Palace Guard upon the King's death, and Stang given command. He had served for years working to keep Tammon safe and the murder of the King had stung him to the core. Not just as a failure to protect his Sovereign, but his failure to protect a man that he had great respect for. A man he had served for over ten years of his career.

"That's it, Colonel," Whip nodded, his voice calm. "I've found seven ways so far that a determined man could get in here without being seen, was he a mind to. Probably others as well, though I'd have to look to see."

"Seven ways," Stang looked skeptical. "Without being seen or detected?"

"Aye, Colonel," Whip replied.

"You'll both forgive me I hope if I find that hard to believe," Stang fought to keep his composure. "We've worked since. . .the incident, to find and close any and all holes in our security, milord," this to Parno. "I do not doubt that Mister Hubel believes he can get inside without detection, but I do doubt that he can actually do so. We've identified and closed a number of places that someone might be able to infiltrate the palace or the grounds, and secured them or posted guards."

"What about a test, then?" Parno asked, a slight smile on his face. "No warning to the troops, mind you," he held up a finger. "Your normal security measures in place and nothing else. We'll see if Mister Hubel can put his money where his mouth is, so to speak."

"Sir, that would be extremely dangerous for Mister Hubel," Stang objected. "My men might injure or kill him in the performance of their duties, sir. I would not like for that to happen."

"What do you say, Whip?" Parno asked, looking at the older man.

"I doubt they can do it," he said simply. "They have to catch me to hurt me, and they won't."

"Colonel?" Parno turned back to Stang.

"Sir, with the assurance that my men and I will not be penalized when he ends up hurt or killed, I will allow it," Stang agreed, stung by Whip's easy confidence. Plus, if this was something Prince Parno really wanted to do, there wasn't anything Stang could do to stop him.

"Very well, but remember; no warnings, no extra security measures. This is between the three of us. Whip, when do you want to do this?"

"Next night or so, I guess," Whip shrugged. "No sense putting it off, milord."

"All right then," Parno agreed. "I'd like to be here when it happens and I need to leave in the next day or so. I'll agree to that. Remember Colonel," he looked back at Stang. "No heads up to your troopers. If you warn them it's not a real test, right?"

"As you say, milord," Stang nodded jerkily, on the border line of anger over this questioning of his men and their work.

"Then what say you and I escort Mister Hubel off the grounds so you know he's not here anymore?"

-

"I thought we were expecting your father to join us for dinner," Memmnon looked at the empty place setting at the table in his private dining area. It was a small room adjacent to his apartment in the palace and he rarely entertained anyone other than Winnie there.

"He will be here soon," she promised, smiling. "He said he had to do something for the Prince and then he would be along. He did say we did not have to wait for him," she added, trying very hard to speak and enunciate as she had been taught recently. Winnie had admitted to herself that she had come to care very much for Memmnon in the last few weeks and she wanted to be someone he could be proud of.

"I would prefer not to start until he arrives if that is alright with you?" Memmnon replied. "We can enjoy the appetizer while we wait. And I would welcome hearing about your day," he smiled gently.

"My day?" Winnie laughed softly. "How can my day compare to yours?" she asked.

"My day was much the same as yesterday," he sighed. "And tomorrow I am sure will be more of the same."

"I spent a good part of the day in class, and working on the refugee resettlement issue," Winnie admitted. "I have made some progress working with Minister Philo."

"I'm glad to hear that," Memmnon said as he poured tea into her cup. "I admit that I worry about them. I wish we had been able to prevent the invasion and they didn't have to flee their homes."

"I do too," Winnie sighed. "But we're doing the best we can for them, I promise," she squeezed his hand as she took her tea from him with the other. "Their lives may not be as good as they were before, but they will be able to feed themselves and have shelter. And it won't be forever," she reminded him.

"It may well be a long time," he told her sadly. "If not for Parno we would have already fallen you know," he told her flatly. "I doubt many know it, but his work before the war is all that kept us from being caught unaware and bowled over."

"You mean his work with the Black Sheep?" Winnie asked.

"No," Memmnon shook his head. "That work was important and is still bearing fruit even now, but no. I'm referring to his work in sniffing out the Norland plot to attack us. Without his warning we would have been caught completely unaware."

"I didn't know that," she admitted.

"Not many do," Memmnon confided. "I still remember the fit my brother threw over it," he shook his head sadly. "He was more concerned that Parno had done something he wasn't supposed to than the fact that the Empire was about to invade."

"Why wasn't he supposed to do something?" Winnie asked. "I don't understand. He did something that needed doing, and the Kingdom got the benefit, right? So where is the problem?"

"In Therron's head," Memmnon admitted. "And my father wasn't a great deal better. He did at least listen and commend Parno in the end, but he started out by telling Parno that he had acted outside his authority."

"That's silly Memmnon," Winnie frowned. "What authority does he need to protect his people?"

"I didn't say it was right," Memmnon nodded. "And this is why I'd much rather hear about your day," he smiled, trying to change the subject.

"I can see where my day would be more encouraging to you," she smiled back.

-

"What are you looking for?" Stephanie asked as Parno looked out the door of their own small dining area. Parno would get up and move to the door every five minutes, look down the hallway, then return to the table.

"Nothing," he smiled distractedly. "How is your meal?" he asked solicitously.

"My meal is excellent as it always is," she raised an eyebrow. "What is going on, Parno?"

"What makes you think anything is going on?" he asked, smiling again.

"Parno, I am an educated and highly intelligent woman," Stephanie smirked slightly and her voice took on an amused tone. "And I know you quite well, too. You're obviously up to something and I want to know what it is!" Her tone was light despite her demand for information. It was clear that whatever was happening wasn't dangerous, at least judging by his attitude.

"I'm not personally up to anything," Parno told her truthfully. "I'm just enjoying the show."

"What show?"

"Wait for it."

-

Colonel Stang made the rounds again, checking every post of the Palace Guard and every gate, entrance way and door to the palace itself. He was not going to allow some backwoods archer to embarrass his unit or his job. It wasn't personal, and he would never disrespect the father of Lady Winifred, but there was simply no way that man was going to be able to penetrate the grounds of the palace.

Having completed his rounds for the third time, he approached the King's apartment to check on security there. The two men at the door stiffened to attention from standing rest as he approached.

"How are things?" he asked tersely. "All secure?"

"Aye Colonel," the senior man at the door reported. "His Highness, Her Ladyship, and her Ladyship's father are dining at the moment."

"Excellent," Stang nodded absently. "I want to know at once if-what did you say?"

-

"It is a pleasure to finally meet you, Mister Hubel," Memmnon said politely, standing as Whip entered the room.

"Ah, the pleasure be mine, Your Highness," Whip was clearly nonplussed at Memmnon's behavior. "I'm right sorry for being here late."

"Quite all right I assure you," Memmnon waved the apology away. "Winnie informed me that you were doing a project for my brother. I must also thank you for all the work you have done for us to this point, as well. Parno says that your assistance with his training program was invaluable to him and he speaks most highly of you. Something I assure you he isn't known for doing," he added with a wry smile.

"I'm glad he has such a good opinion of me, Your Highness," Whip managed not to stammer.

"Please, call me Memmnon," the King smiled.

"I, ah, don't think I could do that, sire," Whip looked uncomfortable at the suggestion. "That's a mite informal for someone like me to be addressing the King."

Before Memmnon could answer there was a knock at the door. Frowning he rose and went to answer it. He was surprised to find a red-faced Colonel Stang standing there.

"Colonel," Memmnon said. "To what do I owe the pleasure?" It was clear that he wasn't pleased, however.

"Sire, I was informed that her Ladyship's father has joined you for dinner?" Stang managed to get out without strangling.

"Yes," Memmnon looked a bit puzzled. "How does that concern you?"

"I would be most interested in knowing how he entered the Palace, sire," Stang's face reddened further.

"Oh?" Memmnon raised an eyebrow.

"Yes, sire," Stang actually tried to see past Memmnon into the room.

"Colonel," Memmnon's voice took on a warning timbre. "I am in the midst of dining with my prospective bride and her father. Your interruption for any reason that does not directly involve our safety or that of the Kingdom is unwelcome. I trust I've made myself clear?"

"Sire," Stang straightened to attention. "I apologize for the interruption, begging your pardon," he bowed stiffly.

"Then I'm sure you can converse with Mister Hubel tomorrow. Now unless there is a circumstance of security as I detailed earlier, I will bid you a pleasant evening." With that Memmnon closed the door soundly in the Colonel's face and returned to his dinner.

"I apologize for that," he smiled. "Shouldn't happen again. While I am thinking of it Mister Hubel, I would welcome the opportunity to visit with you tomorrow, if you have the time?"

-

"I want to know how that man got into this palace," a seething Stang informed his second and third in command and his assembled battalion commanders. "I want to know who let him on the grounds and I want to know right now!"

"We've checked with every post, sir," his second informed him. "There is no record of his entering the grounds and none of the sentries report seeing him entering the grounds. The only men on duty who report having actually seen Mister Hubel are the sentries at the King's door. We don't know how he got in."

Resisting the urge to throw something, Stang looked at his assembled officers. Somehow, someway, Hubel had managed to get inside the palace, not just on the grounds. His men had no idea how the man got onto the grounds or even how he got into the building or to the King's own door without being spotted. This was a waking nightmare for a man responsible for the security and safety of the King of Soulan. The only thing that could make it worse at the moment would be-

"So, Colonel," Parno's voice floated to him from behind. "I understand that Mister Hubel managed to penetrate the grounds and make it to the King's door?"

"I'm in hell," Stang muttered as he plastered a smile on his face and turned to face the Crown Prince.

"Yes, milord, he did," he acknowledged. "We're working even now to discover how he managed it."

"I see," Parno didn't look overly smug. "I assume that you'll be taking him seriously after this?"

"Yes milord," Stang sighed.

"We'll talk tomorrow then," Parno nodded, already on his way out. "Good evening, gentlemen." Stang waited until Parno was gone before wheeling on his officers once more.

"I want to know how that man got in here," he growled.

-

"So, Winnie's father managed to elude security?" Stephanie asked.

"Completely," Parno nodded. "The only men who saw him were the sentries."

"You put him up to this, didn't you," Stephanie accused.

"Possibly," Parno admitted. "Whip said he had found ways into the palace to try and see Winnie. He hadn't tried to enter yet, but he would have soon if he hadn't come across me."

"And you think this was a good idea?" she asked.

"We'll see."

CHAPTER FOUR

-

"Colonel, I trust that you are ready now to listen to Whip and let him lend you a hand?" Parno's voice made it clear that Stang had better be.

"Milord I've yet to discover how he got on the grounds or into the palace itself," a red-eyed from lack of sleep Stang nodded. "I would be most appreciative to know how he managed it."

"I can show you," Whip nodded easily. "There's a bunch o' ways a man can get in here, was he determined enough, Colonel."

"I have to assume that our enemies are determined," Stang said evenly. "Some of them more so than others," he added darkly, thinking of a certain pair of twins.

"And they have an intimate knowledge of the palace and grounds," Parno agreed. "Let's not settle just for Whip's counsel in this matter, Colonel. Talk to the staff, especially those who have been here a long time. If there are secret ways in and out of here, some of them will undoubtedly know them. Find them, and seal them. I want nothing happening to my brother."

"It will be done, milord," Stang promised, then turned to Whip. "Are you free to show me where and how you managed to get inside?" he asked.

"Sure thing," the older man said easily. "Have to hurry though. Got to meet with the King this afternoon about something."

"Meet with the King," Stang repeated softly. "Of course."

-

"You're enjoying that a little too much," Cho Feng said once Stang and Whip had departed.

"Am I?" Parno smiled slightly. "Surely not."

"What profit is there in aggravating Colonel Stang?" Cho asked.

"I need him to be on his toes, that's all," Parno replied. "He's responsible for Memmnon's safety, and to a lesser extent for Stephanie's. He's got to be on the ball and Whip proved that he's not. It also proved that Stang wasn't even willing to consider that he hadn't thought of every possible way into this place. I can't have anything happening to Memmnon."

"Because that would make you King," Cho fought off a smile.

"Exactly. I can't have that. The last thing I need right now, or ever comes to that, is to be King. Or even Regent, now that I think on it."

"For you to be a Regent, there must be an Heir," Cho mentioned.

"Memmnon's working on that."

-

"I appreciate your time today, Mister Hubel," Memmnon said as he limped along through the garden, an attendant far enough back not to overhear but close enough to lend assistance if needed.

"Reckon a man of my station gets asked to speak to the King, he speaks to the King, sire," Whip said carefully.

"Do not think of me as the King right now," Memmnon told him seriously. "I realize that might be difficult, but I would appreciate it if you tried. I am talking to you as a man right now and nothing more."

"Alright," Whip's eyebrow rose at that but he nodded.

"I know that it came to your attention only recently that I was courting your daughter," Memmnon stopped to look at Whip, leaning heavily on the staff in his hands. "I am sorry for that, Mister Hubel. I had no idea that her father was anywhere near us at the moment and assumed that Lady Stephanie was acting as her ward."

"Might as well have been," Whip nodded. "Girl was supposed to be teaching the bow to a bunch o' new folk at the Canton. I came down here with Finn to work on his gadgets as he calls 'em. Reckon Miss Stephanie took it on herself to invite Winnie along with her when she came down. Didn't know she was here myself until someone got to runnin' off at the mouth about. . .well, that's no never mind," he waved his hand away. "Anyhow, ain't no need of an apology, Sire. I seen you're treatin' my girl right and proper and that's all that matters to me."

"Indeed," Memmnon nodded. He began walking again. "I am pleased to hear that, and I thank you for your forbearance. Now then," he paused as they came to a bench and looked at Whip.

"Would it trouble you if we sat?" he asked, clearly struggling.

"Course not," Whip told him. "You hadn't ought to be on your feet much as yet, way I hear it."

"Yes, so Lady Stephanie takes great pleasure in telling me," Memmnon chuckled as he sat heavily on the bench. "Thank you. Now then," he repeated. "I wanted to speak to you concerning your daughter, Mister Hubel."

"Reckon you should call me Whip, Sire," the older man shook his head with a wry smile. "Having the King call me Mister. Ain't that something."

"Well, for this I feel it needful Mister Hubel," Memmnon demurred. "Though I look forward to a time when you and I are better acquainted and such formalities are behind us. Speaking of which, the reason I wished to speak to you was concerning my intention to ask for your daughter's hand in marriage."

"I see," Whip tried to keep a straight face. "You reckon my little girl, raised in the mountains like she was, 'thout a Ma and all, she'd be a suitable Queen for you?" The question caught Memmnon off guard. Of all the things he'd thought he might hear from Winifred's father, this hadn't been on the list.

"I'm not looking for a Queen, Mister Hubel," he replied honestly. "True, any woman who weds me will be the Queen, and her children Heirs to the throne. But I am looking for a wife," he stressed. "I wasn't looking for one, I freely admit, until I met your daughter. I have to tell you that I'm sure I made less than a sterling impression upon her at first meeting. In fact I was likely unconscious at our very first 'meeting' considering I was being kept under sedation. She was escorting Lady Stephanie at the time and came with her to my quarters where I was being kept while they tried to keep me alive."

"She wasn't raised to look down on folks on account of such," Whip shook his head. "Doubt she thought anything of it, especially considering the circumstance."

"Fortunately, that seems to be the case," Memmnon ventured a small smile. "At any rate, when I saw her, I admit that was the moment I began to think about a wife. No, that isn't accurate," he shook his head and looked off into the distance for a moment.

"At that moment," he continued finally, "I began to think about her being my wife."

"And why would that be?" Whip asked, again catching Memmnon by surprise. Anyone else would be fawning over him by now, thrilled with his wanting to marry their daughter. His respect for Winnie's father climbed a notch.

"Her beauty of course," he acknowledged freely. "But more than that, her strength. There she was, bow in hand, short sword on her hip, protecting Doctor Corsin from any threat, including me apparently," he laughed at the memory. At Whip's questioning look Memmnon began to relate the tail of those dark days.

The two spent an agreeable time together, talking as just two men. It was the best hours Memmnon had spent outside Winnie's company in a long while.

-

"That him?" Sergeant Carl Anders asked. The owner of the sundries store nodded jerkily as Anders pointed to his delivery driver, Havrel Denton.

"That's him, but he-" the man dried up as cold-eyed troopers looked back at him. "That's him," he managed to squeak out again.

"Thanks," Anders nodded. Motioning for the other three troopers to follow him, Anders waited until Denton was out of sight behind the building before sending two men around one direction and taking the other with him a different way. A minute later they approached Denton from both sides.

"Havrel Denton?" Anders called out. The man looked up sharply.

"Who's asking?" he called, then froze as he recognized the livery of the Sergeant and his companion. Two seconds later he was running, only to plow straight into two more troopers coming from the other direction, one of who felled him with a blow to the forehead.

"Havrel Denton, we need to talk to you a bit about that mouth of yours," Anders looked down at him. "Take him boys."

-

"No."

"I'm not asking for that much, am I?"

"Stephanie, we already had this discussion," Parno sighed. "And if not for my realizing what terrible mistakes I was making, I'd already be gone. I gave you my reasons, and I feel they're good ones. I've heard nothing from you that outweighs those reasons, either."

"Then you aren't listening," Stephanie almost pouted. She was seated on a sofa in the receiving room of what was now Parno's office, stocking feet drawn up beneath her in a most unladylike but comfortable pose.

"I am listening or I wouldn't be replying to you, now would I," Parno stated more than asked. "As bad as I hate to admit it, there are protocols I need to follow here. I'm the stupid Crown Prince now," he sighed, shaking his head. "I can't just elope for God's sake!"

"I'm not asking you to 'elope' Parno McLeod," Stephanie huffed. "I'm asking you to marry me now, before you go and get yourself killed. At least give me the chance to give you an heir first!" she almost stormed.

"I'm not going to get killed," Parno tried to calm her. "I'm not allowed to get close enough to anything dangerous to get killed."

"You're at war and entirely too disposed to be close to the fighting," she shot back. "There's every possibility that when you leave here you won't return."

"I admit that I have done that in the past," Parno tried being more reasonable. "But as I've said, it's been pointed out to me rather firmly that I am no longer a mere regimental commander. As such I can't run off on foolish flights of fancy and engaging in combat. I have to command. And so, I am. I am delegating my duties to others and commanding."

"That is still not a good reason not to-" she broke off at a knock on the door.

"Come!" Parno called as Stephanie put her feet back down, straightening her clothing from where she had been reclining on the soda.

A trooper wearing Parno's colors entered and offered a message to the Prince without speaking. Parno read it, nodding as he did so, then looked at the trooper.

"Tell him excellent and I'll get back to him. Meanwhile, let him stew."

"Sir," the man nodded, nodded respectfully again to Stephanie, and then exited, closing the door behind him.

"What was that about?" she asked.

"Oh, just a man I need to have a word with about something."

-

Lieutenant General Gerald Wilson stood studying his wall map, trying to formulate a plan that would get his army out of the rut they were in at the moment. He had to find a way either to attack and carry the Soulan Army's positions, or to go around them.

Engaging their cavalry was a non-starter he admitted. Stone and his men were excellent soldiers and fair horsemen, but the initial meeting of the two forces had proven rather successfully that Stone's men were better utilized protecting his flank and rear areas than in actual combat against the southerners. Added to that little bit of wake up was the fact that Stone had lost several thousand of his troopers in that engagement, leaving his units a hollow shell of their former strength. For now, Stone and his men would protect the trains and guard rear areas. It wasn't the way it was supposed to be but it was all he could do. Committing his cavalry against Soulanie cavalry in open combat was an invitation to wholesale slaughter.

The Tribal warriors were also reluctant to engage the southerners after getting their asses handed to them in the cavalry battle that had seen Stone's men hurt so badly. On the one hand, it was difficult for Wilson not to smirk at their reluctance after all the arrogance that Blue Dog and his fellow 'chiefs' had shown the Imperial troopers. But on the other hand, it deprived Wilson of a good raiding force that he could have encouraged to go behind enemy lines and rampage through the Soulan rear. It disgusted him to think of the havoc the savages would wreak on civilians, but the thought of himself and his family dying disgusted him more.

He was sure that he outnumbered the Soulan Army on this front and equally certain that his counterpart across the Great River, Jackson Andrews, outnumbered the forces he faced as well. The problem was that the Soulanies had developed those weapons from the old times and used them to wreak havoc on his army.

He paused for a moment to curse his own complacency in rejecting the claims of the survivors of Brasher's force as they ran back to 1st Army with tales of dragons and wizards and witchcraft. Had he not blown these off as the wild statements of an army that had been crushed by inept leadership and a determined enemy then he might have realized then that the southerners had developed something so destructive. He had no excuse other than the fact that Brasher had been an idiot and he had assumed that the idiot had gotten his command tore to pieces with his idiocy.

Then his own command had been torn to shreds by the same 'witchcraft'. He shook his head at his own foolishness. Dwelling on that would not help him. It was gone and done with, time to move on.

Only he couldn't seem to figure a way to do that. His men were still jumpy weeks after the disaster that had befallen them in the previous battle. The losses of 1st Army had been horrendous. Far higher than the rest of the war combined to that point. His staff was still working to reorganize the army, combining regiments that had all but ceased to exist into new regiments, and them into new divisions. They could do that work without his supervision. It fell to him to decide how to put those reorganized regiments to best use.

And best use did not include another head long attack into the face of those devastating artillery weapons that had broken the back of his first attack. But what else was there? What he had told Daly still held true; they were hurting the south simply by sitting on so much valuable crop land. Their people would be hard pressed to feed themselves and their army without the millions of acres his men now occupied or controlled. Had the Emperor been more patient then he could simply stay where he was, fortify his position, and wait for the enemy to come to him. Which they would eventually be forced to do.

The Emperor was not possessed of such patience however, so that plan was also a non-starter. Asking for more time was akin to asking for more resources; a sure way to end up dead. That meant he had to find some way to get his offensive moving again, whatever it took.

It seemed incredible that after such a rousing success at the start of the war, his powerful forces had been brought to a standstill. Who would have thought when those boats had carried the first waves of the initial attack across the Ohi River that he would find himself standing here, stymied as to-

Boats. The boats! He looked at the map before him with renewed interest. Rivers. Always rivers. These rivers were a natural resource of course, but because they flowed south-north no one considered them acceptable invasion routes. But. . .maybe that was a mistake. There was no need to limit the use of the waterways to invasion routes. While using them to actually invade would not work, maybe they could serve to get his troops moving again. If he could use the boats to get troops behind the Soulanie lines then perhaps he could spring a surprise attack.

But to what end? He continued to look at the map. He needed more than that. He couldn't stand another defeat. The army couldn't stand another defeat. He needed to do something that weakened the southern position to a point where his army could attack them and have a chance of success even with the hellish new weapons.

Moving down the Tinsee far enough to attack the Soulan rear would not help him. True, the distraction would pull some troops away from the front, but not to the point that the army was actually weakened. A spread and disjointed enemy was not necessarily a weakened enemy. He needed to separate troops from the Southern army and force them away from this front.

An attack by Andrews from the west, across the bridge into Shelby would be the ideal thing, but it would take weeks for a courier to arrive there and then Andrews would want confirmation. Then he would send word to the Emperor and on it would go, meanwhile nothing would be done. No, that would not do.

But what about the other river? For some reason no one ever seemed to look at the Cumberland River, despite the fact that it flowed right to the southern capitol. Or perhaps because it did, he wasn't sure. Nasil was known to house the Soulanie's 1st Corp, traditionally their best units and officers. And again, the river flowed north, not south as the Great River did. As an invasion route it wouldn't work well. But as a raiding route? Could he use the boats to send a raiding party down, well up, the Cumberland River?

First, were the boats even still available? Were the sailors still there? Could he get them overland to the army or would he have to send them back to where the Cumberland emptied into the Ohi? Would the sailors respond to his authority if they were still there? Would they come south and help ferry his troops still further south for a raid in force?

There was only one way to find out; "Captain!"

"Are you satisfied that this new plan is better than the old one?" Memmnon asked. He and Parno were in the King's office, speaking privately.

"I think so," Parno nodded. "The thing is, what I had planned to do could have crippled the army even if we were successful. Cho Feng made me realize that I was overlooking too much, Memmnon. I was reaching too far because I was looking too far ahead. I wanted so badly to push the Nor back and then take the war to them that I. . .I forgot that I first had to win here. That I had to make sure that we could survive."

"I don't understand," Memmnon admitted. "Well, I understand that you want to preserve the army, but at some point, we'll have to use it, Parno. It seems the longer we wait, the stronger they'll be."

"So, will we," Parno replied. "I'm going to amend my original orders and send 2nd Corps to Cove to start through the same training regimen that the Black Sheep went through. Once they're finished and back up the strength, we'll pull them back and send 1st Corps. Then send them to Shelby and pull 3rd Corps and so on. We'll retrain our army and train our new recruits and militia at the same time. Train them the same way I did the Black Sheep. Our army will be stronger than it has ever been in our history, Memmnon. And we can do it in a year. Two at most."

"And you have the strength to keep the Nor at bay until that's done?" Memmnon looked doubtful, though he clearly wanted to believe.

"No," Parno admitted. "Not on paper, as the saying goes. I don't. But I have the strength and the trickery to keep them off balance and stall their push south. It will mean reinforcing Raines further than my original plans in case the force they have across the Great River is strong enough to make a serious push and they decide to do so. That's always a risk," he sighed. "But overall, this plan is still much better than the one I had before."

"Sending the refugees south and having them plant there instead of on the plains relieves us of the need to free up the crop land the Nor are sitting on," Memmnon nodded thoughtfully. "They might settle for staying static thinking that so long as they keep us from having all that land during growing season then we'll face a starving time before next year."

"And we still may," Parno sighed. "Those on the coast will have to depend more on the fishing trade than ever before, especially on the Gulf. The damage Semmes did to the Imperial Fleet will help our fishing fleet stay moderately safe, and the Gulf Squadron is still on station to help keep pirating down. We'll have to marshal as much grain as we can for the army without literally starving our own people, but we'll also need beef and pork, not to mention leather, wood, iron and so on. We can't simply take every able-bodied man into service with the army, as I said before. Some trades are going to have to maintain healthy young men to keep them going. Or at least healthy older men," he shrugged at the difference.

"How strong do you think you will need to be to push the Nor out of the valley?" Memmnon asked after a minute's thought.

"If our men are all trained up to the same standards as mine, then our static strength should be more than sufficient," Parno surprised him. "Their men are trained about to the standard our militia were at the start of the war or a bit better. It was only superior training and leadership that let our army withstand the assault as they did. With all five Corps plus their militia attachments trained up to that standard, then we'll have more than sufficient strength, assuming we're at or near full strength. Say. . .seventy five percent of optimal, roughly. That would give us about one hundred ten thousand men, give or take."

"We certainly don't have that many horses," Memmnon noted.

"And won't by that time either," Parno agreed. "Actually, we do have that many horses, but not that many trained war mounts. And we still can't have that many in that time, either. What we can have is enough horses to have our mounted infantry all on horseback. They can and will supplement our cavalry as we advance. Bottom line will be to have six to eight highly trained and well-equipped cavalry units on the line and ready when we launch our counter-offensive. Call it seventy-five thousand total."

"Half or better of your projected needs," Memmnon mused.

"Yes," Parno nodded. "That's another advantage though. We'll have a year-and-a-half to two years to raise and train new horses. Not enough time to have horses raised and trained from start to finish, but enough time to begin raising horses to replace those we lose in combat. It's a never-ending cycle," he sighed.

"All this is dependent on your being able to keep the Imperial Army in check this entire time, however," Memmnon pointed out. "How are you going to do that while pulling so many men off line?"

"We'll have to keep the Nor off balance with feints and raids," Parno shrugged. "We'll also have to watch for incursions and raids of theirs. I'm especially concerned with their alliance with the Tribes. If they turn them loose behind our lines, it could be a massacre before we managed to run them to ground."

"Yes," Memmnon grimaced. No Soulan King had ever had anything approaching rapport with the Tribes. They were singularly uninterested in anything approaching peace. He wondered what the Emperor had promised them to get their cooperation.

"Anyway, compared to what I had originally planned, this plan not only stand a better chance of overall eventual success, but may be far less costly, especially in the short run. It's still a gamble, but the risks are less."

"There will be risks no matter what we do," Memmnon sighed. "Lessening them is always desirable where possible. If you must gamble, go with the better odds."

"I think this is the best I can do," Parno held his hands out in a gesture of helplessness. "I have too many fires and not enough water buckets."

"Well, as you try to fight the fire, I will look for more buckets," Memmnon promised.

Neither brother mentioned the biggest fire of all.

-

"Milady, we should keep moving until at least dusk."

Callens was getting very tired of Sherron McLeod. Every day it was constant picking and bickering and insulting his men, himself and everyone they passed. What in the hell had he been thinking? He shook himself mentally at that; he knew what he'd been thinking.

"I'm tired and I need a bath," Sherron replied absently. "I want to stop. Find me a place to rest."

"Milady, you do realize that they will be sending someone after us, don't you?" he asked.

"Nonsense," Sherron waved the protest away. "They don't know where we're going to start with, and they will all be in a turmoil with both my father and brother dead. Parno, that idiot, will be there by now and be trying to keep things together. He will have made a fine mess by the time we get back with Therron. By then everyone will be so glad to see us no one will worry about anything else. Trust me, Callens. Now find me a place to pass the night. And no more farmhouses, do you hear?"

"Of course, milady," Callens fought off a sigh. There was no reasoning or arguing with her. Again, he had the thought that once they did reach Prince Memmnon she would be his problem.

But at the rate they were being forced to travel, that was going to be a long trip.

-

Therron McLeod stood once more on the white sands of the ocean front, watching a distant storm. Lightning crackled across the sky but the storm was still too distant to hear any thunder. He wondered idly how far out the storm was and which direction it was moving. It was difficult to tell with dusk approaching.

He idly picked up a stone and tossed it into the waves that crashed onto the shore, the ripples it made instantly lost in the surf. Much like himself, he snorted. His power, prestige, everything gone in an instant. Even the servants here, pleasant though they might be, were in no way cowed by his presence or his name. He couldn't say his position, for he no longer had a position. He had thought more than once that his father's 'mercy' was more like punishment than actual death would have been. To be regulated to this...

He shook his head, clearing the thoughts away. It did him no good to look backward. Instead, he had to find a way to free himself from this hell he was in. What many might consider to be paradise and yet for him it really was a form of torment. Away from the seat of power that he felt was rightfully his, away from the army, which was his backbone, led by officers loyal to him and grateful for his patronage, in the thick of the machinations at court.

There had to be a way out of here, and back to where he belonged. He just had to find it.

-

"I want you present, but you are not to interfere."

Parno was looking at Sebastian Grey as he spoke, preparing to enter the building on the edge of the city that Havrel Denton was now being held in.

"Milord, this should, rightly, be a matter for the-"

"That sounds like interfering," Parno cut him off, his voice as flat as his eyes.

"This man may or may not be a spy, or agent provocateur. He is most certainly in dire need of an attitude adjustment for running his mouth about Winifred, assuming he is just a stupid man who delivers goods. Either way, we will handle it. I wanted you here in case he does turn out to be a spy, so that you can hear what he has to say and perhaps think of questions to ask him that we've overlooked. Understand?" Parno's tone made it plain that he expected a 'yes' and nothing else.

"I do, milord," Grey nodded, reluctance in every syllable.

"Then let us go and see about this man," Parno opened the door and led the way inside, Berry and two others following while the rest of the escort took up station outside.

"Milord," Anders stood to as Parno entered.

"Any problems, Sergeant?"

"None, milord," Anders shook his head. "He's mouthy, but not much on the physical. He's been alternating between threats and pleas since we got here. We ain't spoke to him over just instructions, as you ordered, milord."

"Good job," Parno nodded. "Take your detail and go get some rest, Sergeant. I appreciate this."

"No problem, milord," Anders nodded, then waved for his detail to fall in and led them out. Parno stood looking at where Denton was surrounded by the glow of lanterns in the darkened building, even though the sun had yet to set. The man looked off, somehow. He wasn't sure what it was, but there was just something about Denton that set off bells in Parno's head. It was time to find out why that was, and why Mister Denton had felt the need to engage in idle gossip about the King and his prospective bride. He stepped into Denton's view, followed by Cho Feng, Grey holding back as ordered.

"Mister Denton, I'm Parno McLeod," he said simply.

"Thank God!" Denton exclaimed. "Milord, I've been set upon by ruffian soldiers who were-"

"Acting on my orders," Parno interrupted him softly, watching for Denton's reaction. The man's face stilled and all pretense seemed to leave him.

"What is it that I've done, then, to deserve this?" Denton asked.

"Why don't you tell me, Mister Denton?" Parno asked, taking a chair and sitting down to the front of where Denton was tied to a chair of his own. Cho Feng remained standing.

"How would I know?"

"Well, truth is, you've been running your mouth a good bit, Mister Denton," Parno smiled. It wasn't a pleasant smile. "You've been saying some very bad things about a fine young woman that happens to be a friend of mine. He father also happens to be a friend of mine. You have many friends Mister Denton?"

"A few," came the cautious reply.

"I don't," was the flat rebuttal, Parno's voice going cold. "So, I'm understandably upset whenever one of the few I do have is maligned. I'm sure you can understand that." Denton nodded but didn't speak.

"So, tell me, Mister Denton," Parno leaned forward. "Where did you get the information you've been spreading about the King and his. . .what was the term he used?" Parno turned to look at Cho Feng.

"Play toy, my Prince," Feng's reply was even. "I believe the term was play toy."

"Play toy," Parno nodded, returning his gaze to Denton. "I'd be very interested in knowing how you came to that conclusion, Mister Denton, and why you chose to run your mouth about it in public."

"That's what this is about?" Denton laughed harshly. "Because I saw some skirt that the new King is playing house with and told a few people abou-" was as far as he got with his reply before the back of Parno's hand crashed into his jaw, rocking Denton's head and sending stars in front of his vision. By the time he looked back around, Parno was already seated again, calm as ever.

"Let's try this again," the Crown Prince said amiably. "Where did you come by this information, and why did you choose to spread such malicious gossip about someone you know absolutely nothing about?"

"You can't do this," Denton said harshly, blood dripping from the corner of his mouth. "The Articles of Constitution-"

"Are suspended for the war," Parno smiled again. "Bet you didn't know that, did you. I suspect they don't teach that sort of thing in Norland."

"What do you mean suspended!" Denton demanded, then pulled up short. "Norland?"

It was clear to every man watching that he was a poor actor. He realized he was caught out and was trying to brazen his way through.

"Our public education system is much better than yours," Parno told him. "All children in Soulan know these things by the time they finish mid-forms. Common knowledge throughout the Kingdom, actually. So," Parno leaned forward again, his voice was more cold, "You don't have any rights to stand on at the moment, Mister Denton. Even if you were a Soulan subject and not a Norland pawn sent here to stir up trouble. Now let me ask you again, where did you get your information and why spread it around that way?"

"I don't know what you-" Denton's head rocked the other way this time as Parno used his off hand to smack Denton's other jaw.

"I really can do this all evening," Parno told him, once more already back in his chair before Denton looked around. "I won't though, because I have more important matters to see to. I'll leave you in the capable care of my assistant, here," he indicated Cho Feng. Cho did not smile.

"He's not from around here, as you may can tell," Parno continued conversationally. "He has had some training and experience in talking with people like you over in the East. Prisoners and what have you, kind of like you are right now. He assures me that he can have you talking in short order and tell me everything I want to know."

As Parno spoke, Cho removed a leather roll from behind his belt and pulled a low table to him. Setting the roll down where Denton could see it clearly, he slowly and methodically unrolled it, revealing a number of wicked looking blades, hooks, needles and other instruments that severely damaged Mister Denton's ability to remain calm. Cho's face never showed an iota of emotion as he worked, setting a small brazier before him and lighting a single piece of charcoal inside before standing back a step, hands behind him, feet shoulder width apart.

"What the hell is this?" Denton began to struggle a bit. "You can't do this!"

"Why?" Parno asked. "Because the Imperial spy master told you that our laws prohibit such things, and would protect you if you were caught?" he chuckled harshly. "That was before your armies came screaming across our borders in alliance with the western Tribes, killing and maiming as you came. I assure you everything of that nature went right out with the wash when that happened. The days of using our laws against us have ended, Mister Denton. It's interesting," Parno leaned back once more, making himself comfortable. "You appeared about eighteen months ago and took work at a sundries store, making deliveries. Before that there's no record of you anywhere. Your boss says that whenever he would ask about where you were from you'd be very vague, 'back west', 'a little south of there', and so on. No real answers and a lot more questions. It's as if you just popped up out of the ground, full grown. Isn't that something Cho?"

"Indeed, it is, my Prince," Cho replied stoically.

"Now look here," Denton began to stammer. "I don't know what the hell you're talking about. And it was never nobody's never mind where I-"

"Where were you born, Mister Denton?" Parno cut him off. "Quickly now!"

"W-w-what?"

"Where were you born!" Parno yelled, on his feet suddenly.

"I-I-I was b-b-born a little ways west of here," Denton stammered.

"Town!" Parno demanded.

"Town?" Denton paled.

"Enough," Parno was suddenly still again. "I'm convinced he's the right man. Now we extract what we want to know from him."

"Extract?" Denton looked even more scared if that was possible.

"I will pull it from you like teeth," Cho said gently, picking up a set of pliers commonly used by farriers to pull shoe nails from horse hooves. "I do so enjoy that kind of thing," he said flatly.

"Well Cho, looks like he's all yours," Parno shrugged. "He's not going to tell me anything and I'm not going to stay out here all day just so he can let some of his friends have a few extra hours to sow their discord. How long, you think?"

"Wait a minute!" Denton yelled, but was ignored.

"Perhaps two hours," Cho intoned. "He has all his teeth it appears, as well as all his digits. I will alternate between them, cauterizing the wounds as I go to prevent much blood loss. He will still be able to speak."

"Wait a minute! There's no need for that I tell ya!" Denton yelled, but was again ignored.

"Two hours?" Parno looked doubtful. "Not that I don't think you know your business, but do you really think he'll last two hours?"

"Ask me something!" Denton cried out. "Anything!"

"He is healthy and young enough to withstand the rigors, my Prince," Cho nodded. "He also has his ears, I noticed," Cho said, picking up a long, wicked looking needle. "There and the nose are ideal places to inflict pain that will not kill."

"Ask me anything!" Denton was crying now, struggling against his bonds without success. "Just ask me dammit and I'll tell ya!"

"Still, two hours is a bit much, I think," Parno mused, hand to his chin. "I'll make a wager with you," he said suddenly with a snap of his fingers. "He lasts two hours and I'll give you a month's extra pay. Sound fair?"

"Dammit you ain't asked me nothin' yet!" Denton blubbered. "All you gotta do is ask! I came down here almost two years ago when the peace treaty and trade agreements was signed! I was s'posed to get work and lay low till things kicked off and then work to create strife and difficulty here in your capitol!"

"Hear that Sebastian?" Parno asked suddenly, looking into the shadows. The form of Sebastian Grey emerged, his eyes flinty and hard.

"I did, milord," he nodded.

"Mister Denton, this is Chief Constable Grey," Parno turned to the now broken Imperial spy. "He's going to be questioning you since he knows more what to ask than I really would. Remember that if you don't cooperate with him, then Cho will be back. I won't of course," he brushed imaginary lint from his uniform. "Far too important for this rubbish, but Cho, he needs a hobby. You look like a pretty good hobby to him I bet. Ain't that right, Cho?"

"Indeed, my Prince," Cho nodded gravely, as if terribly disappointed at the loss of opportunity.

"You ain't got to worry about that!" Denton cried. "I'll tell 'im anything he wants to know just keep that lunatic away from me! Talking about ears and teeth and 'digits'. You ain't right in the head!"

"I have been told that," Cho assured him as he returned his 'tools' to their roll and extinguished the coal.

"You got this?" Parno asked Grey, who now was struggling not to laugh.

"I do, milord," he nodded. "Have my men come in when you go out, please," he added.

"Sure thing," Parno patted the man on the shoulder before he and Cho exited the building. Parno sent the waiting Constables and scribe inside to Grey before he burst out laughing.

"I didn't know for sure that would work," he admitted.

"Fear is a powerful motivator," Cho told him. "Often fear itself is the greatest enemy."

"Don't forget to return those sewing needles to the women at the palace," Parno said as they mounted their horses. "And make sure Doctor Spurgeon's kit gets back to him. He may need it."

"Of course."

-

"Gal, what are you aiming to do?" Whip asked as he and his daughter walked together in the palace garden.

"He hasn't asked me to marry him, papa," Winifred shrugged. "Nothing I can do until he does."

"You know he aims to," Whip fought the urge to roll his eyes. "If you ain't figured it out then I can tell you; he flat out asked me about it not long ago. He wants you to be his wife."

"I'm no Queen," Winifred shook her head.

"Says he ain't looking for a 'Queen'," Whip shrugged this time. "He's looking for a wife who will happen to be his Queen once they're married."

"I don't know nothing about being royalty," Winifred fought the urge to snort, something she was trying to stop as part of her 'etiquette' training.

"Made that point myself," Whip agreed. "Didn't seem to faze him none."

"I know," her voice was quiet. "I'm scared, papa," she almost whispered.

"Of him?" Whip asked. His daughter wasn't scared of much.

"No," she shook her head. "He would never do anything to harm me. You know that as well as I do."

"Was my impression," Whip agreed. "So, what is it scares you, Ginny?" Ginny was short for 'Ginger', a nickname from her childhood.

"I'm scared of being Queen," she admitted. "I'm scared of making him look bad. Of making a mistake and being laughed at. My life would change a whole lot in ways I can't even imagine."

"That is absolutely true," Whip couldn't argue. "I can't even imagine how much you're gonna go through, baby gal. I can't. You know you ain't got to do it, neither," he reminded her.

"I know," her voice was soft again. "Thing is though. . ."

"You think you want to," Whip fought a grin as his baby girl's face took on a deep shade of red.

"Yes," she nodded, her gaze fixed on the ground in front of her as she walked. Whip looked at the finery she was decked out in and shook his head slightly. Seeing her in the lap of such luxury was something that would take some getting used to.

Something else that would take getting used to was having a simple conversation with the King of Soulan. As Winnie's father he was impressed that Memmnon made the effort to approach him as 'just a man', regardless of how unlikely it was that anyone could do so. He hadn't pressured Whip in any way nor had he offered him any incentive to convince his daughter to wed him.

He had flat out asked for permission to ask Winnie to marry him. He had done so as properly as Whip could have expected any young man to approach him for such a matter.

Whip had been inclined to give him permission to ask, and should she say yes, his blessing for the marriage.

"What did you talk about?" she asked, breaking Whip out of his thought process.

"Just told you," he replied. "He was fairly formal and what not, right well-mannered young man to be honest. He told me he was taken with you, and had been pretty much since he set eye to you. Told me a funny story about how you thought he was making eyes at that little lady doctor only to find out it was you all along," he chuckled.

"Yes," her face was red again. "I really did think he was set on sparking Stephanie. He was just wanting to talk to her about me."

"And now he's talking to you direct," Whip drew the word 'direct' out.

"Has been a while," she agreed. "I have dinner with him most every night, and lunch some times when he ain't-, when he's not busy," she corrected herself.

"Uh huh." Whip said nothing else.

"I've gotten to know him pretty good," Winnie went on. "He's a good man, daddy," she looked up at him. "He's kind. He's not loud or brash and he don't talk harsh. When he's with me, or when I'm with him I should say, he acts like I'm the only other person around, no matter who else is there."

"And you like that, don't you?" Whip smiled at her. He reached out and wrapped his arm around her shoulder.

"Yes," she nodded, once more looking at the ground a few feet in front of her. "I do. I like him a great deal. And I think I can see myself being married to him. What I can't see is me being no Queen."

"I can," Whip told her gently. "You can do anything you set your mind to, baby girl. I can see a difference in you already just since we been apart. You talk better, you walk better, you got mannerisms you sure never learned from me," he laughed quietly. "That lady doctor has helped you a bunch, ain't she?"

"Yes," Winnie nodded. "But I don't know if it's enough."

"You ain't done yet, are ya?" Whip pointed out. "She's still helping ya, and you're still taking them classes you told me about, right? And he ain't looking to marry ya tomorrow."

"You want me to do it?" Winnie smiled at him and he was instantly serious.

"Oh no," he held his hands up, waving them side-to-side. "I'm not making this decision for you gal. This is all on you. I'm telling you that you can do anything you want to. Anything you set yourself to. I got faith in you girl."

"I know," she smiled at him, laying her head on his shoulder as he wrapped an arm around her again. "Thank you."

"I told him," Whip continued, "that he had my permission to ask you. I then told him that so long as you said yes, then the two of you would have my blessing. You been doing an adult's work for a long time and been doing serious work for the last year right alongside everyone else that was training them men that follow the Prince. After all that, I reckon you can sure enough make the decision whether you want to marry somebody or not."

"So, you do what you want to do," he finished. "What you feel like is the thing to do. What's best for you, girl. You do what makes you feel right, and what feels like it's best for you."

"Okay."

CHAPTER FIVE

-

"Why are you still on about this?" Parno fought the urge to sigh. Stephanie had just finished another round of arguments over why they should get married, tonight, so that she could try and conceive a child before he left in the morning. Something he thought had been settled already.

"Is that all you have to say to me after that?" Stephanie demanded. "An impassioned plea to do right by me and give me the one thing that I have ever asked of you?"

"One thing?" Parno looked at her. "You've asked only one thing of me?"

"Only one thing like this," she clarified, a bit uncomfortable.

"Stephanie, please," Parno did sigh this time. "Be reasonable. I'm leaving in the morning and headed back to the army. I've already explained why we can't do something like that. Let me get things started on the road we've chosen and make sure that I've got things headed in the right direction. Once I can do that, I'll be back and we'll talk about it. We can make our plans and-"

"I don't need any plans!" Stephanie cut him off.

"Have you even talked to your family about this? Your parents at least?" Parno demanded suddenly, catching her off guard. She blinked.

"You haven't, have you?" he demanded, though not unkindly.

"Well, I've been rather busy since I got here," she managed not to stammer. "Caring for your brother and trying to assist Winnie with her education and training. I'm also looking to establish another school to train surgeons here in Nasil, and that takes effort and time as well, so-"

"So, you haven't," Parno finished for her. "Okay," he turned away from his plate reluctantly. "Let's look at this. You haven't even told your mother and father that you and I are even talking about marriage, let alone that we've decided we're going to marry. I'm guessing that your family on the whole has a very high opinion of me to start with, so finding out that we just up and got married without a proper courtship let alone without telling them would go over great, wouldn't it?" Stephanie began to fidget but before she could respond he continued.

"We're at war. A war that may last for years and right this minute sees a foreign army on our soil that I can't find a way to force back, at least not for some months to come. I have to spend the next two years playing cat and mouse with an army twice the size of mine that is attacking us from two different directions while at the same time trying to train up my army to the same level we managed with the Black Sheep, because only with superior soldiers are we going to be able to win."

"My brother and sister have colluded and conspired to seize power from my father, put Memmnon off the throne, my sister killed my father and almost killed my brother who is now King, and is even now on her way south to release my brother from exile on the Key Horn. She will then almost certainly attempt to bring him back here determined to see him on the throne! Doing so will of necessity include killing me."

"And now, on top of all that, you want us to basically marry in secret and try to conceive a child the one night we'll have together before I return to the front of said war?" he concluded.

"Yes," came the firm reply. "It so happens that this is the time that I'm most ferti-"

"Stephanie!" Parno cut her off dramatically. "I have no interest whatsoever in hearing that! It-it's not proper!"

"Why not?" she seized on his discomfort. "If we were already married, I'd be talking about it all the time! It's a part of the process of having chi-"

"We aren't married!" Parno complained. "And we aren't going to get married without your family there, and knowing in advance so they can be prepared. We will be inviting the people that are important to us to be with us when we take our vows and I will not be running off to the front as soon as it's over. I will not get married and leave the next morning going to war and I will not try to father a child only to possibly leave him or her without a father!"

"Fine," she almost spat out. "Be that way."

"You told me not so very long ago that you were a very intelligent and highly educated woman," Parno raised an eyebrow. "More than once in fact, now that I think about it. How intelligent and educated are you being right now? I am now the Crown Prince as well as the Lord Marshal of the Army of Soulan. I can't keep acting like Parno, the Prince Who's Not. I have to consider what I look like to others whether I like it or not. And the Crown Prince taking a wife is going to be a big deal, regardless of the fact that it's me and not Memmnon."

"There are a whole slew of protocols involved in the marriage of a Crown Prince, not least of which is an official announcement from the Crown and a suitable courtship period. We will have to host a formal dinner, to which most nobles will bring gifts and well wishes to the happy couple and pretend that they like me and hope that our union is blessed with peace, prosperity and children. There will also be a formal ladies gathering, called a 'shower' for some reason that I have never understood, where they will bring you gifts and presumably tell you all about how it is to be married. A few of them will no doubt try to talk you out of marrying me because I simply am not good husband material."

"There are other less important functions that the Protocol Office will see to, such as formal invitations to the head of the Coastal Provincial Coalition, all the Provincial Governors, and of course assorted socially important though undoubtedly inept bureaucrats who would be offended if not included."

"And once we are married, we will be going somewhere pleasant and private for a wonderful honeymoon of peace and quiet. Where no one will bother us for at least a little while of blessed silence. Time that we will have just to ourselves and share with no one else. So for all these reasons, we can't simply get married tonight and try desperately to make a baby before I am up and riding with the sun headed for the front. We can't do it, Stephanie." His voice was calm, reasonable and patient. He felt sure he had managed to make her see reason.

"I can see there's no point in talking to you," she stood up, wiping her mouth and hands on a silk napkin which she tossed on her plate. "You've made the decision for both of us it seems without even bothering to take into consideration how I feel about it, or how I want things done." Parno looked at her, incredulous.

"You know that's not true," he objected. "You're practically the only person whose feeling I do take into consideration! And the decision was made for me the day I was made Crown Prince by default. Like it or not, and I don't, there are protocols that have to be observed here. Not doing so will just make it that much harder on Memmnon and cause problems right when we need all the smooth sailing we can get."

"Oh, stop blaming it on protocols!" she snapped back. "I'm sick of hearing about them! You didn't want to get married to start with and this gives you a way out. You could have just said no!"

"Stephanie, I am not trying to say no," Parno spoke with great care and precision. He didn't like being called a liar. "I just told you, did I not, that as soon as I could manage it I would be back and we would make plans for our wedding. Invitations, shower rituals and everything else that goes with it. Because I'm now Crown-"

"Stop blaming that!" she almost shrieked.

"There is a difference between blaming, and explaining," he said evenly. What the hell was going on here? Where had this come from all of a sudden? "I'm not blaming anything on the Crown, and I'm not trying to get out of anything either. Please, sit down and lets finish our meal and talk about this more cal-"

"I've had enough," she snapped at him, moving around the table. Whether she meant the food or the conversation or him in general he didn't know. "I'm going to my rooms."

"You mean my rooms," Parno shot back playfully, still trying to lighten things a bit. He was right, he knew it and he wasn't going to change his mind. That didn't mean he wasn't going to try to be peaceful.

"Fine, I'm going to your rooms!" she huffed. "You aren't going to listen and I'm tired of talking to someone who won't see reason or look past their own selfish needs and desires. Good night."

"Selfish?" Parno's face betrayed his shock. "Selfish?" He looked up only to see her headed for the door.

"Are you really leaving like this? I'll be gone at sunup," he said to her back as she pretty much stalked toward the door.

"And the sun can't rise too soon!" she almost snarled. "Have a safe trip," she hissed, not bothering to look back, seconds later slamming the door behind her. Things had happened so quickly, escalated so rapidly that Parno was still sitting in his seat. For a moment, he was simply stunned, not knowing how to react to what had just happened. Gradually however he felt his temper rising and soon was eating again, stabbing at his food with real anger.

"I knew better," he told himself. "I knew better and did it anyway." There was a reason he didn't trust people or let them get too close to him. He couldn't trust them.

The one person he actually trusted more than any others had just slammed the door in his face after calling him selfish. He had known that becoming involved with her was a bad idea, yet for just a while he had allowed himself to believe that it was going to be okay. That despite everything that was happening, he had found someone that would treat him decently. Even love him.

Now, because he wasn't in a position to immediately do what she wanted he was selfish? All his life he'd been looked down on for doing the 'wrong' things, and now it seemed he'd get the same treatment for desperately trying to do the right things as well. Parno took a few seconds to review what he'd said. How was anything he'd said in any way selfish? Just because he didn't agree with some desperate, last minute effort to marry and create a child? Bring a child into a world that he wasn't even sure he could protect and preserve smacked of irresponsibility. How in anyone's estimation was that selfish? Wasn't refusing to give in to your own base desires the exact opposite of selfish? He closed his eyes for a moment to try and fight off the stress induced headache he felt coming.

This night had started so well. He had been completely blindsided by Stephanie's anger and her lashing out at him, but it was her comments that actually hurt him. He had trusted her. Believed her when she said she loved him. Wanted to marry him. To make a life with him.

Once more in his short life someone he had placed his faith in had turned their back on him at a time when he most needed them. Needed their presence, their understanding, needed their support.

"I will never learn," he said aloud to himself as he flung his utensils down on the table in disgust. He stood, cleaning his face and hands with his own napkin which was then slung on to the table top. His appetite was gone and his head was hurting, and though he would never admit it his heart was aching as well. But he had a cure for that.

"Never again," he swore to himself as he left the small dining room to return to the apartment he'd been using, needing only to see his brother first.

"Never again."

-

"You look unhappy brother."

"Do I?" Parno asked as he settled into a chair across from Memmnon. "Can't imagine why."

"Sarcasm," Memmnon nodded. "Classic defensive mechanism against-"

"Spare me," Parno cut him off with an upheld hand. "I'm leaving at sunup. Any last orders or advice?"

"You are in a snit, aren't you?" Memmnon's face wore a slight grin.

"I'll take that as a no," Parno sighed, preparing to stand again. "I'm too tired for verbal fencing, Memmnon. Tired and have a headache."

"I understand you caught an Imperial spy today," Memmnon changed the subject.

"Had him caught, yes," Parno nodded. "I gave him to Grey. He was talking when I left."

"So, I understand," Memmnon snorted. "Something about torture and foreign devils?"

"No accounting for what the Nor teach their young," Parno shrugged.

"I suppose not," Memmnon nodded. "I assume you will be going ahead with your plans as soon as you reach the army?" he changed the subject again.

"Yes," Parno nodded. "I have almost decided to move the training site, but otherwise nothing has changed. And I'm not certain I'll change the site, either," he admitted."

"What are the advantage to either?" Memmnon asked.

"Sending them to Cove gets them away from the front so they can train in relative peace, and puts them at a higher elevation which will be cooler with the coming summer," Parno noted. "On the other hand, leaving them in the west puts them closer to where I might need them in times of urgency. It's a tossup," he admitted.

"Can you not do both, assuming that sending 2nd Corps to Cove would leave you enough instructors to train 1st Corps behind the lines once Freeman's troops are on the line?"

"Take both off the line at the same time?" Parno raised an eyebrow.

"As you said, it's a gamble either way," Memmnon shrugged. "And I'm not offering suggestions or orders, Parno. Just asking."

"It's worth considering," Parno admitted. "2nd Corps would almost certainly benefit from being sent to Cove. They're worn out and their losses have rendered them nearly ineffective on the Corps level. Giving them time to incorporate new troops into their ranks before they have to fight again would be ideal."

"So it would," Memmnon nodded in agreement. "Whatever you decide to do I trust your judgment," he added.

"Amazing what a year and an invasion can accomplish," Parno snorted at that and Memmnon nodded.

"So, it is," he settled for saying. He would not be drawn into an unproductive argument. The past was behind and Memmnon could not change it no matter how he might wish he could.

"Well, I'm going to retire, I think," Parno stood. "I'm tired and I have a long way to go over the next several days and a great deal to get done."

"Sleep well and travel safely, brother," Memmnon stood, offering his hand. "Good luck."

"Thanks."

"Well, you're in a funk."

Winnie's voice was almost amused as she watched Stephanie slam items around in their shared sitting room, her face marred with anger and eyes red with unshed tears.

"I take it you didn't have any success with your campaign?" Winnie tried again.

"Oh no!" Stephanie's voice was full of sarcasm. "I had great success in discovering what a pig-headed, obstinate, disagreeable ass my 'affianced' really is."

"My, you are in a snit tonight, aren't you?" Winnie mused, keeping her distance from the irate physician. It might have disturbed her to know just how much like Memmnon she sounded at the moment.

"I am not in a snit!" Stephanie snapped. "I'm mad!"

"Yeah, I got that," Winnie nodded. "I take it you're still single."

"Shut up!" Stephanie growled. She sat heavily on the sofa across from Winnie and hugged a pillow to her torso tightly, clinging to it as if she would die if she let go. Suddenly she burst into tears. Winnie frowned, rising to her feet and going to sit beside her friend and mentor, wrapping an arm around her shoulder.

"I made a terrible mess of things," Stephanie admitted between sobs. "I was so mean to him!"

"Why would you be mean to him?" Winnie asked.

"I didn't like what he was saying," Stephanie admitted. "It was true, but I didn't want to hear it so I walked out on him. After I had said some terrible things to him," she added.

"I see," Winnie hugged her tighter, fighting a grin over her friend's head. Leave it to Stephanie to get mad over being told the truth.

"He's leaving in the morning and all I could do was be angry with him," Stephanie continued.

"Well, you can't let him leave with things like that between you two," Winnie declared flatly. "It's not right. Not for either of you. You can't let that fester while he's gone. You need to make it right."

"How can I make something like that right?" Stephanie asked, sitting up and wiping her eyes.

"You need to be waiting for him when he gets ready to go in the morning and admit you were wrong, then apologize," Winnie shrugged, stating it as if it were the simplest thing in the world. Which to her it was. "That's a good place to start."

"What an interesting look," Karls observed when Parno stormed into the sitting room of the visiting dignitary's quarters that he and his entourage were sharing.

"Shut up," Parno growled, though without the heat he might have used with Memmnon or someone else he wasn't so close to.

"And an attitude to go with it," Karls nodded, unperturbed by the response. "Bad meeting with your brother? Or bad news from somewhere?"

"Neither," Parno sighed, plopping down on a stuffed chair near the window. He rubbed his temples but his headache was there to stay a while it seemed.

"Dare I ask then what it is that has caused this?"

"I had dinner with Doctor Corsin," Parno told him.

"I can see how that would leave you in such a state," Karls nodded, carefully not reacting to Parno calling her 'Doctor Corsin' rather than Stephanie like usual.

"We had an argument," Parno clarified absently.

"Well that's not really a new development," Karls smirked. "I mean the two of you used to have some really epic arguments at Cove Canton."

"Not like this," Parno shook his head. "Doesn't matter," he suddenly stood again. "Not long ago I was looking for a way to make her see sense and realize that I wasn't a good match for her. This should probably do it," he said with a careless shrug. Karls had to work to hide his concern at that statement.

"Parno, I know you don't mean that," he chose to say.

"Sure, I do," Parno said absently. "She's better off with someone who can give her what she wants isn't she?" his tone was suddenly very reasonable. Too reasonable. "I think she made it clear tonight that someone isn't me. Suits me if that's what she wants," he shrugged.

"Now Parno, don't be making hasty decisions," Karls was becoming more concerned by the minute. Parno wasn't usually so. . .accepting about something like this. So fatalistic.

"We're leaving before sunup," Parno ignored Karls' statement. "There will be enough light for us to make it out of the city and be on the road north by dawn. That's what we'll do. Have the word passed to everyone if you will. Be ready to ride an hour before dawn. I want to be on the road as soon as we can. I need to get back where I belong. We've been away too long as it is. "

"Of course," Karls knew when to let go of a subject. He would try again tomorrow. He rose from his seat.

"Do you want everyone else notified?" Left unsaid was that 'everyone else' meant Stephanie Corsin.

"No need," Parno said over his shoulder, moving toward his bedroom. "We don't need a sendoff. I'm going to bed. I've got a terrible headache that won't go away and I no longer seem to have a doctor to help with that so I'm going to lie down. And I don't want to be disturbed by anyone other than the King. Pass the word to the guard. Anyone," he stressed just before he shut his door.

"Alright," Karls said to a closing door. He stood there for another minute, concern for his friend etched on his face. He knew that friend well enough to know, however, that pursuing it would not bear fruit. That in mind, he pulled on his boots and headed for the door to pass messages to everyone who needed to know they would now be leaving some two hours earlier than previously planned.

He would skip the fatalistic attitude that his friend and commander now seemed to have.

-

The group of horsemen was challenged by a sentry standing in the middle of the road. The lead rider drew reign, calling for a halt.

"Advance and state your business," the sentry stated tersely. A single rider left the group and rode into the torchlight.

"I'm General Freeman, soldier," the rider said tiredly. "On my way to Army headquarters by orders of the Lord Marshal."

"We're expecting you, sir," the sentry snapped a salute. "You are still about two miles distant from General Davies' headquarters. Stay on this road and it will take you straight there with no troubles, the road is lit the whole way. Expect to be challenged at least twice more on the way. Security is especially tight because of the presence of Tribal horsemen among the Nor."

"Tribals?" Freeman scowled. "What are those devils doing among. . .well, no matter," he waved the question away as irrelevant. "We'll be watchful. My troops are still on the road even in the growing dark. Some of them will no doubt attempt to push on in an attempt to make it here tonight. And there's a cavalry division not more than five miles behind I'd imagine."

"Very good, sir," the sentry nodded, standing aside. Soon Freeman and his men were on their way again.

"Tribal warriors among the heathen, eh?" his aide mentioned casually. "Sounds like the war is a bit more serious than we've been hearing, sir."

"Does, doesn't it?" Freeman admitted. The last they had heard was that a major cavalry battle had been fought and won by the King's youngest son of all people. Freeman had also heard about the Pyrrhic naval victory fought by Rafe Semmes. He had tried to get to Savannah to see Semmes but orders to move north were already waiting, pending the news from the Navy engagement thus Freeman had put his men on the move the very next morning. Now, almost five weeks later, he was within walking distance of his destination.

The next challenge was from a Captain rather than a sergeant and Freeman informed the officer that if an area had not been set aside for his men to make camp, please see that one was. The Captain promised to see to it at once and waved the General of 5th Corps onward.

The last challenge was by a Major, who saluted and gave more detailed directions to General Davies' tent.

"Davies?" Freeman frowned.

"General Davies is Commander of 1st Army now, sir," the officer informed him. "Also in command of this front in absence of the Prince."

"The Marshal isn't present?" Freeman's frown deepened. Where in the hell was the Playboy Prince while the Soulan Army was engaged in a fight for the Kingdom's survival?

"Expecting him back soon," the man informed him. "He had to ride to Nasil on summons of the Royal Couriers, sir."

"Ah," Freeman nodded. That explained it. Not even Parno McLeod ignored a summons of the King. Whelp probably would be disrespectful once he got there, but he would go, nevertheless.

"Thank you, Major."

"Service, sir," the man bowed slightly, then saluted. "You may pass," he said with a tired smile. Freeman laughed and led his company sized escort on. Ten minutes later they were dismounting before a large but otherwise nondescript tent that was marked as important only by the four-man guard at the entrance.

"General," the Sergeant at the flap snapped to. "We've informed General Davies of your arrival, sir. He's waiting for you now."

"Very good," Freeman nodded. He turned to his aide.

"With me," he said simply, then to his escort commander, "Care for the horses and find us a place to billet tonight. We'll establish our own quarters when the train arrives."

"Sir," the Captain nodded and led the General's horse away, followed by his men.

"Well, let's see what the story is," Freeman sighed and stepped inside.

The cavernous tent was glowing with the light from several lanterns and lamps. Boards were set on easels throughout with maps displayed. Some notated friendly positions, others suspected enemy positions. Still others showed geographical features that might be beneficial or problematic to the army in defending their ground. Freeman nodded in appreciation at that.

"Hello Willis," Bryce Davies said warmly. "Good to see you," he offered a hand.

"I should be saluting you, apparently," Freeman grinned at his old friend and classmate. "I hear you command an army now and not just a corps."

"That is true," Davies nodded. "Though half of my 'army' is camped behind the line now, recovering from their efforts to stall the Imperial advance."

"Losses?"

"Fifty percent overall," Davies said grimly. "We'll get some of them back but. . .a lot of them are gone."

"I'm sorry, Bryce," Willis Freeman said sincerely. A good general never took losing men lightly.

"Me too," Davies nodded. "You have to be tired," he changed the subject, noting Freeman's dusty appearance.

"We've seen some miles," Freeman agreed. "My men are still two or three days out in some cases, but some of my cavalry should arrive later tonight, nothing happens. Them and their horses are worn out, but they'll be here."

"We'll give your men time to rest before placing them into line," Davies promised. "Say five days, starting tomorrow. I know that means not every unit will get five days, but it should let them get some rest at least. After that, we'll feed you into the line, replacing 1st Corps for the time being and allowing them the time to rest and refit. They've fought two major engagements, the last one being a real brawl that saw the enemy knocking on the door. Their losses aren't as bad as 2nd Corps, but they're bad enough."

"I see," Freeman nodded. "Last I'd heard was about the Playboy Prince leading a cavalry charge against the Nor."

"Watch how you say things like Playboy Prince, Willis," Bryce warned casually. "The Army loves him and would take offense to anything that sounded like a slur. And yes, he led that one himself. Gave the Imps a thorough lashing, too."

"So, what was the second engagement?" Freeman, nodding his acknowledgment of Davies' warning.

"The Imperials came at us with everything in the inventory," Davies said, moving to a rough copy of a map that had the known history of that battle on it. "They were right on us when they finally broke. We still don't know why they fled other than thinking they'd bitten a dragon by the ass," he chuckled harshly.

At Freeman's frown, Davies explained the impact of the new weapons on the Imperials. By the time he'd finished the look on Freeman's face was warring between outright disbelief and joy.

"To think we actually have something like that to use against them," he shook his head. "If we have all that, why hasn't he driven them out already? And why would the King summon him to Nasil when we have such a huge army on our own soil? For that matter, why replace Prince Therron with. . .with him?" he caught himself before saying anything disparaging about Parno McLeod.

"I see there's a great deal to catch you up on," Davies sighed. "Hungry?"

"Very," Freeman nodded.

"Then let's get a bite to eat and some coffee while I tell you what's happened."

-

"My God."

Freeman's meal sat before him, less than five bites taken. The look on his face had begun in horror and grown steadily worse as Davies informed him what had happened.

"The King dead?" he repeated. "By his daughter's hand? And Therron a traitor? What the hell is going on around here?"

"Apparently, Prince Therron believed the officers of the Army would back his claim to the throne over Crown Prince Memmnon," Davies said neutrally.

"Then he's a fool," Freeman snapped at once. "Like him? Yes. Follow him in revolt? Treason against the Crown? Not if Hell froze over," the man shook his head, long hair waving behind him. "What could he possibly have been thinking?"

"Don't be so quick to assume that no one would follow him," Davies warned. "At least one Provincial Governor was in on the plot, and I have my suspicions about a certain corps commander as well."

"Graham?" Freeman guessed it at once. "Figures. He's an ass-kissing idiot. Probably how he got that command."

"Could be," Davies' shrug was non-committal. "Prince Parno put him in his place rather firmly, however," Davies managed not to smirk as he explained the first meeting between the two men.

"I admit I seem to have severely underestimated that boy," Freeman shook his head. It was clear there was no disrespect intended in the word 'boy', but a mere reference to age. "I'm glad the King lived long enough to see it."

"Me too," Davies admitted. "And that we got to see it at all. Had Therron still been in command, you would have much less further to travel, I'd say. We would never have held here this long."

"Well, if Henry and I are both up now, maybe we'll be strong enough to hold out and begin to push back," Freeman said, turning once more to his cooling meal. "I hope the men the new Marshal sent for that murdering wench are successful."

"So do we all."

-

"I don't want to hear any more complaints," Buford told his assembled officers. "We're on the road at sunup and we ride until dusk each day. We will eat in the saddle and we will walk the horses to rest them. We will catch this bunch of traitors and we will do it as soon as possible. Now does anyone have anything to say?"

Heads shook around the fire as the regimental commanders and their seconds decided not to try and point out potential problems. That's leave that to General Whipple.

"Then get back to your commands and get your orders issued," Buford ordered tersely. "We ride with the light. Dismissed." The men broke apart and returned to their own camps. Soon it was just Buford and Whipple.

"Think I was too hard?" Buford asked his silent friend.

"No, it has to be done," Whipple shook his head. "Just remember these men are yours and mine, not Callens' and not Therron McLeod's. We don't have to threaten or bully them, Buford. They followed us behind enemy lines for three weeks or more and they'll follow us here. It isn't necessary to ride them into submission when they are already obedient to orders."

"So, you do think I was too hard," Buford snorted.

"No," Whipple's answer was slightly harsher this time. "I think you're on the edge of alienating a good command over something that you couldn't have stopped and that wasn't their fault. They know what's at stake and will follow without question. No need to relieve your own tension by passing it on to them. If it were too hard for them, I would tell you. What I'm telling you is that it's unnecessary," he stressed. "It doesn't accomplish anything."

"Callens can't be making that good a time," he went on after a moment of silence. "The witch loves her comfort and is a 'noble' in the truest sense of the word. I guarantee you that she's making his life miserable at being on the trail without her usual amenities. I doubt they're making as good a time as we are, even allowing for today to rest and refit."

"From the reports I'd have to agree," Buford agreed. "The things they're taking. . ." he shook his head in disbelief. "No soldier would take those things at sword point when he's on a mission like that. They're useless. And he has to know that. Why let her slow them down that way?"

"He has to hang on to her and deliver her to Therron," Whipple shrugged. "Once he does, then he can wash his hands of her and she'll be Therron's problem. But he's committed now so he has to follow through. You can bet he's had the same thoughts you have, there's just nothing he can do about it."

"Likely," Buford nodded. "He was raised and trained better than that I'm sure."

"Well, make sure you don't make the same mistakes he's making, then," Whipple rose from the log he'd been sitting on. "I'm for bed. I figure things will be rough tomorrow."

"Undoubtedly," Buford agreed. "But we have to catch them."

"We will."

-

The Black Sheep were accustomed to hardship. There were no complaints other than good natured grumbling as they stumbled out of barracks to prepare for the trip north. A hot meal, probably the last really good food they would see for a while, eaten even as company commanders briefed their troops.

Next was preparing horses, something the hard-bitten troopers would not leave to the wranglers of the Royal Stables, good though they may be. In half-an-hour, good time considering, the Black Sheep were mounted and ready to ride despite the lack of light. If moving in the dark gave any of them pause, they neither showed it nor spoke of it.

"Are you sure you aren't making a mistake?" Karls asked a still brooding Parno quietly, ensuring no one else could hear.

"There's no mistake," Parno said simply, mounting his charger. "I already made the mistake. Maybe this will correct it," he added wryly. "Are we ready to ride?"

"Parno-"

"Are. We. Ready." The way Parno bit the words out left no room for discussion, even for someone as close to him as Karls Willard.

"We are, Milord," Karls replied formally. "All men mounted and ready."

"Then let's ride," came the terse order. Parno spurred his horse to moving and rode out of the parade ground without looking back. Karls looked at Cho Feng, who returned the glance impassively, and then nodded to Major Simmons, his second in command and the highest-ranking former prisoner in the ranks aside from the ambiguous rank of Cho Feng as Parno's 'adviser'.

"Let's be under way, Major."

"Aye, sir," Simmons nodded and raised an arm. The signal was repeated down the line with no sound, and soon the arms began to fall again, moving this time from back to front. The signal that all were ready to move.

"Move out," Simmons told the front ranks simply. The column began to move as the highly-disciplined troopers began to follow the column in front of them out of the palace grounds and onto the road.

While this was going on, Harrel Sprigs and Cho Feng had ridden to catch up to Parno, who was riding along as if he didn't have a care in the world, a sure sign that he was deep in thought or mad.

Or both.

"You are in an ill mood this morning," Cho said calmly as he drew abreast of his Prince.

"Don't you start," Parno sighed. "Did Karls put you up to this?"

"He did not. I have eyes, do I not? You do not hide your aggravation well, my Prince," he pointed out.

"Suppose I don't," Parno agreed with a nod. "Don't worry. I'll ride it out between here and the front."

"Are you certain you are not making a foolish mistake?" his most trusted adviser asked him softly.

"Positive," was the firm yet simple reply. There was no more talk as the column caught up and they increased speed. It was a long way to the front.

Winnie had left instructions that she was to be awakened an hour before dawn. She had woken Stephanie and then the two had bathed and dressed quickly, intending to be downstairs before Parno and his retinue. Stephanie would have only a few minutes to speak before he would be gone, but she vowed to make the best of those minutes trying to repair the damage from the night before.

The two went down the back stairs and into the kitchen, where the staff was already moving about preparing for the day.

"Has the Prince ordered breakfast yet this morning?" Stephanie asked, smiling. The cook looked at her for a moment, clearly nonplussed.

"Well?" Winnie asked.

"Beg pardon, milady, but the Prince left word he'd be eating with his troops this morning as they set out," the cook managed to croak.

"Of course," Stephanie nodded. "Thank you. I'll catch him there." When the cook looked ever more nervous, Winnie frowned.

"You got something to say, say it," she ordered, her newly found 'proper' speech left behind.

"Milady, again begging your pardon but. . .ma'am, the Prince and his men have been gone for an hour or more," the man finally answered. "I'm sorry you weren't informed," he offered hesitantly to a stunned Royal Doctor.

"No reason I should have been," she said into the odd silence. "None at all." She turned and departed, walking slowly and with no apparent direction. Winnie followed her, not exactly sure what to say.

"He said he was leaving at sunup," Stephanie said numbly. "I know that's what he said."

"Plans change in time of war," Winnie offered, having nothing else to offer at the moment.

"He left without saying goodbye," Stephanie murmured, sitting heavily in on one of the heavily cushioned bench seats that lined the palace halls.

"You did say he was still trying to talk to you when you walked out," Winnie reminded her. "Maybe he assumed you wouldn't be interested in hearing from him," she sat down next to her friend.

"He couldn't possibly think that, could he?" she asked, looking at the floor. "Surely I wasn't that bad." She sounded as if she were trying to convince herself, not Winnie.

"I don't know," the younger girl had to admit. "I wasn't there. Look, send a message to him," she said. "You can tell him you're sorry and that you hate you missed him. That you miss him and wait eagerly for his return. Stuff like that."

"No," Stephanie stood suddenly, smoothing her dress even though there were no wrinkles. "No, I don't think that would be appropriate," she shook her head. "If you don't mind dear I think I'll return to the room and rest a bit more. I'm sure to have a busy day today."

"Stephanie don't just let this lie," Winnie warned. "Don't make one mistake worse by making another."

"Mistake?" Stephanie looked at her. "I didn't make a mistake, Winnie. I made a royal mess. Literally. I worked and worked to convince him he could trust me, that I cared for him and supported him regardless of his reputation or how his family regarded him, enlisted Edema of all people and Dhalia even to assist me. All that I have done, all that I had managed to accomplish, destroyed with a temper tantrum of selfish desire." With that she walked away, slowly and stiffly.

Winnie watched her go but there was nothing else she could do at the moment. She thought for a moment about riding after Parno herself but a glance at her 'escort' killed that desire before it could take flight. They would have an apoplexy, and despite what freedoms she enjoyed, simply leaving wasn't among them at the moment.

Funny how having a little power suddenly took away all that freedom.

-

Stephanie made her way to her rooms, flanked by two members of Parno's regiment who kept a respectful distance. They had worked out an arrangement with Major Case where the King's Own was responsible for guarding the residence, while the Prince's Own would guard Lady Stephanie. It kept the ridiculous sight of seeing more soldiers protecting one apartment than were guarding many of the gates into the palace proper and ensure that fresh men were always prepared to go wherever either woman wanted to go.

Within reason of course.

Stephanie had no care for any of this as she stumbled her way back to her room. Parno's rooms she corrected herself. Maybe she should move out of them now? She didn't know what to do anymore. For the first time in many weeks she was at a loss for what to do. She had made a terrible mess and she had no way to fix it. She didn't even know if it could be fixed for that matter.

She entered her room without a word to her guards, something she almost never did. They noted it and exchanged glances. None spoke but it was clear that their charge was unsettled by something.

Inside, unaware of their worry, Stephanie went to the bedroom she had been using, Parno's as it happened, and collapsed on the bed. Safely out of sight of everyone else, she finally began to cry. She continued until she drifted into a shallow, dreamless sleep that would provide her with little rest and no relief of any kind.

CHAPTER SIX

-

Hard riding saw Parno and his men arrive back in camp late afternoon of the third day. Approaching dusk actually, there was still enough light to see that the size of the encampment had swelled considerably.

"Freeman must have made it up," Enri Willard said carefully. Parno's mood had not improved on the ride up and his staff was now wary of speaking unless it was needful.

"Looks like it," was the Marshal's only reply. He had been terse like that for the entire journey, speaking only when he had to, or when explaining his plans, which wasn't often at the moment. It didn't look as if that would change now that they had arrived, either.

"They seem to be in camp," Enri ventured another remark. "I would estimate that they haven't been here long and General Davies is allowing them a limited rest and refit before taking their place in line."

"That's good, actually," Parno shocked him with a reply that wasn't a few one syllable words. "It will save me some time."

"Time?"

"I'm going to move 1st Corps off the line and replace them with Freeman's men. 1st Corps will go into extended retraining back this way somewhere," he waved around him absently.

"What about 2nd Corps?" Enri asked.

"They'll be heading to Cove Canton, where they will make camp, work up with their replacements to fill out their ranks, and then go through the same training regimen. When they return, they'll be much better soldiers."

"I see," Enri nodded, thinking about how long that would take.

"It will take about six months," Parno told him, almost as if he could read his Chief of Staff's mind. "Not nearly as long as it did the original regiment. They won't need basic training or horsemanship, and the training regimen is set now. In fact, it might not take a full six months if we're lucky. The hardest part is the conditioning."

"As you say, milord," Enri nodded.

"Who's going to train 1st Corps if we're sending 2nd Corps to Cove?" Karls asked, silent up until now.

"You are," was the simple reply.

"That's a good idea," Karls nodded absently. "That way you ca-what!?" he cut himself off as Parno's words sank in.

"You and the Sheep will do it," Parno told him again. "I don't expect you to do it personally, but there's no reason the regiment, some of them anyway, can't serve as instructors. A few of them already have while recovering from injuries, remember? And Cho will be around to give you pointers when you need them."

"Parno, why would you send us to do that instead of keeping us with you?" Karls asked.

"I'm not going to be doing anything but planning," Parno shrugged. "We're on the defensive for the foreseeable future, Karls. I'm not going anywhere that I'll need you, and if I do, I'll pull some of you away, but training them is more important than anything else we can do for now. Other than holding the Nor at bay," he amended after a second.

"How about when you travel back to Nasil?" Karls asked.

"I won't be going back, save for Memmnon actually summoning me," Parno told him flatly. "There's no reason for me to be there while the army is in the field. This is where I belong, so this is where I will be."

Behind him the two brothers exchanged a glance, but neither spoke. There wasn't much to be said to that, and in truth neither knew what to say anyway.

Or wanted to risk the wrath of the Lord Marshal if he took offense to it.

As they drew near the headquarters tent they could see General Davies waiting at the entrance to the enclosure, having received word through sentries that the Marshal was returning. Parno dismounted and handed his reins to a waiting trooper, nodding his thanks.

"Welcome back, Marshal," Davies smiled slightly.

"General," Parno nodded. "I take it all is well for the moment?"

"Yes sir, for the moment," Davies agreed. "General Freeman and his Corps arrived three days ago and are in camp. I had planned to allow two more days of refit and then move then into line, bringing 1st Corps out to refit."

"Excellent idea, and falls into line with my own plans," Parno nodded approvingly. "We'll move 1st Corps back about three miles and place them into camp where their new training will begin. Meanwhile, 2nd Corps will head for Cove Canton to begin the same training. The training my own regiment went through to be precise. They'll have a better time integrating their replacements into their ranks there, I think. The instructors there are almost finished training the rest of my men who joined us after the Gap." He looked at the map.

"We are going to have to detail at least one division into the central highlands north of the Cumberland, however," he mused. "To guard against an incursion by Imperials by boat."

"I had thought of that," Davies surprised him. "There is a separate brigade of Mounted Infantry in General Freeman's Corps, the 31st, made up about evenly of regulars and militia. I was going to send them across the river and into that territory."

"That's a good start," Parno nodded, "but I'm afraid a group that size would be overrun without support."

"We can send other unattached units with them, of course," Davies nodded. "We have a number of individual battalions that are part of either General Herrick or General Freeman's commands. Attaching them to the 31st would both give them added strength and allow units that have no parent division to serve as patrols in strength in the highlands."

"Good idea," Parno nodded thoughtfully. "Since it's your idea, I'll leave it to you. Which reminds me, have you selected someone to replace you at 2nd Corps?"

"My second in command, General Gavin, is a good man, milord," Davies nodded. "He's been with the Corps long enough to know all the commanders and many of the men quite well. He is an excellent tactician, at least on a tactical scale, and has managed the command well since my movement to command 1st Army. He lacks true experience in leading so large a command, but I will be leaving him my Chief of Staff to assist him. And at that level you can really only learn by doing."

"True," Parno agreed. "Well, if you're sure of him, give the job to him," Parno told him. "I have faith in you, General. Just make sure he's the right choice and will do a good job. As to the 31st and their attachments," Parno mused, looking again at the map which showed the Central Highlands, "that's going to have to be someone who can exercise independent command and use good judgment in absence of orders. He'll be supervising patrols of the area as well as some other units that will be similar to the artillery units we're using here. Unusual in other words," he smiled thinly. "He'll need to be able to work with the River Guard, and with the unusual application of the new weapons against a possible river incursion. That will include reacting to any incursion by either boat or land." Parno faced Davies.

"His prime marching order will be to slow any large incursion while notifying us and Nasil of the enemy's approach, and crushing anything small enough to handle himself. So he'll need to know his own limitations, but not be hamstrung by indecision."

"I'll need a bit to ponder that, milord," Davies admitted. "I would suggest that we send the independent units combined under that one person's command. That will prevent any possible competition or friction between the unit commanders."

"I am singularly uninterested in dick beating, General," Parno surprised everyone with his coarse description. "I'll kill any man, regardless of rank, who endangers this Kingdom because his feelings were hurt or he was trying to make someone look bad. Or good, for that matter." He paused and looked at the collection of me around him. "Be a good idea to make sure that message spreads I suppose," he told them after a moment's pause. "No sense in me killing someone for being ignorant and stupid instead of just stupid. See to it," he ordered Davies abruptly.

"I will, milord," the General promised.

"I'll be in my tent if you need me," Parno wheeled abruptly and departed, having issued all the orders he felt were necessary for the time being. Davies shot a glance at Enri Willard, who shrugged, shook his head, and then followed his commander out of the tent.

"Well, you heard the man," Davies told the assembled staff. "As you talk, make sure everyone knows the penalty for 'dick beating'."

Muted murmuring accompanied by affirmative head nods met with the statement as the staff returned to work. The new Lord Marshal was interested in results. Nothing else.

Good to know.

-

Imperial General Gerald Wilson read the response to his query to the boat commander, his face tightly controlled. In no uncertain terms the man informed the General that while yes, he and his men were still on station, not having been recalled as yet, he had no orders from the Admiral to assist further downriver, and in the absence of said orders could not in good faith abandon his assigned post to assist him in getting his stalled offensive moving again.

In other words: No.

Crumpling the paper in his hands, Wilson allowed himself a few seconds of unbridled fury before forcing himself to be calm and calculating. Fury would not help, at least not unless he could direct it at the right man. Which he couldn't. He needed someone to go and make the man see reason, that was all. Someone who could, if necessary, force the naval force to bring their boats here, or to a point across the small strip of land between the Tinsee and Cumberland Rivers, and prepare to take a force down river. Or up river, as it were.

"Captain!" he called out, looking around. His aide was right beside him and flinched at the volume.

"Sorry," Wilson apologized, very uncharacteristically. "Has General Stone and his command returned yet?"

"This morning, sir," the man nodded.

"Get him," Wilson ordered. "I want to see him as soon as possible."

-

"So, you want us to go and make this Commodore, or whatever, bring his men and boats down this way?" Stone was looking at the map.

"I want you to send enough men to make sure that they bring the boats and come here," Wilson nodded. "I want you to take the rest of your command and whatever I can scrape up to go with you into the central areas, here," he pointed to the region above the southern capitol and the river that flowed through it. "Threaten the capitol if you can, but be sure to be seen in the area so they'll report it. I want them stripping men and resources from elsewhere to face a new threat."

"Like Brasher was supposed to be," Stone mused, nodding slowly. "We'll have to carry supplies with us," he noted. "There won't be any kind of supplies we can seize in there. Be lucky to find enough grazing to feed our horses."

"I'll give you until light tomorrow," Wilson said flatly. "I want you on the road as soon as its sunup. You'll cross the rivers back there and proceed down once the boats are on their way to me. Make sure whoever you leave in charge there will get the job done."

"There's no way I can be sufficiently prepared for a campaign like this by daybreak," Stone said simply. "My men and I have been in the saddle for the best of three weeks chasing ghosts. Our horses are exhausted and so are we. Our few wagons are empty other than empty barrels. It will take a day just to re-shod our mounts and refit our gear."

"Daybreak tomorrow," Wilson repeated. "Or I find someone who can."

"You're sending us to fail," Stone sighed but nodded. "We will not be able to fight effectively and in a major engagement We'll be overwhelmed for lack of support. You're throwing us away for no gain." He set his hat on his head and started for the door.

"Had you been more efficient against the southern cavalry I might not need you to go," Wilson shot at his back.

"Had you given me the support I needed, we would have destroyed them in our first meeting," was Stone's simple rebuttal. "We'll be gone with the sun." And with that he was gone.

Wilson knew he'd just turned a loyal subordinate against him in all likelihood, but his options were extremely limited. He needed to make a move and he needed to do it soon. Stone had to be a part of that. His troops were consuming an enormous amount of stores and so far hadn't produced a single major accomplishment in return for them. Maybe a lean trip into the wilderness would get results from them that living well had not.

Meanwhile, he needed those boats and Stone was available. Simple as that.

He put the thought from his mind and returned to his maps.

-

"I admit, milord, I don't see the importance of this new training cycle," Herrick said. It was well after dark now and the assembled Corps commanders were back in the headquarters area, talking to their Marshal over a simple supper.

"The training regimen that I put my men through was strenuous, General," Parno told him. "Strenuous and in some cases fatal," he admitted. "But the results speak for themselves. My men are the equal of troops three and four times their number easily. With terrain on their side they can hold a position against even greater numbers, as they proved at the Gap. It's a matter of conditioning more than anything else. My men can march twenty-five miles in less than a day and arrive where they're going still able to fight. They can do that day after day for over a week, too. Their swordsmanship is second to none in most cases, and every man is cross trained on at least two other weapons in addition to whatever his primary weapon may be. My swordsmen can serve as archers, my archers can serve as pike-men, my pike-men can serve as swordsmen. My archers can hit targets at one hundred yards distant.

My swordsmen can engage and defeat the enemy two-on-one. My lancers can pick up a tent peg with their lances from the back of a galloping horse. I could go on but I assume you're getting the idea?"

"Yes sir," Herrick nodded. "I am."

"I'm not bragging, and I'm not putting anyone else down," Parno explained to the four men, plus Davies. General Darrel Gavin had replaced Davies as 2nd Corps commander and had joined them for this meeting in his new position. Graham was still in command of 1st Corps for now, but was silent in the presence of the Marshal.

"My men aren't superior to any of yours in strength other than what they've learned," Parno continued. "They aren't supermen and they die just like yours. Too many of them already have," he added grimly. "It's just a matter of conditioning, as I said. Training. We developed an entirely new training regimen at Cove Canton, and I think the results speak for themselves. That regimen was developed by experts in every field, including Colonel Nidiad before his untimely death at the Gap. All I did was gather the right people and tell them what we needed."

"Your artillerymen will be trained in using and handling the special ordnance by Major Lars, my Artillery Chief. He helped develop the protocols we use for them and was there from the beginning of their development. Short of having the inventor or one of his chief assistants with us, which we can't at the moment, there's no one better to train them, I promise."

"The best archers from the Black Sheep will serve to train your archers to a higher standard of conditioning using the techniques taught to them by Whip Hubel. If you've not heard of him, he's known as the Archer of the Apples. He is without a doubt the finest bowman in Kingdom and that is not hyperbole. I've seen that man do things with a bow that will keep you awake at night."

"For the swordsmen, again some of the finest blade handlers in my regiment will serve as instructors and they've earned their positions in battle. They know their business. Know what works and what doesn't. In many cases taught by my adviser Cho Feng himself. If you haven't seen him handle two swords at once, it's a sight to see I assure you."

"In addition to everything else, your men will learn a series of hand-to-hand combat techniques that Cho taught to the entire regiment. Even disarmed my men are capable of taking on an armed combatant and prevailing. It's not ideal of course, but far better than seeing a man run through because he lost his grip on his sword or bow."

"This sounds like a very involved process, milord," Gavin noted.

"It is that," Parno agreed. "I'll be pleasantly surprised if your men can finish it in less than six months. It took my men a year, but much of that was spent in basic training and even in basic horsemanship. You can't tell it now, but many of them had only the most basic horseman skills at the start and some had no skill at all, having never owned a horse. That's how effective what we've done can be, gentlemen. I took criminals and poachers and thieves and turned them into a regiment of soldiers that could fight a division of Imperial troops and hold. I trained them to the point that just over four hundred of my men attacked and defeated a force of some eight hundred Tribal warriors on horseback, inflicting roughly three hundred casualties on them at the cost of four men wounded and four horses lost."

That got a stir from all of the assembled generals.

"Tribals?" Herrick voiced their amazement, or disbelief, for all of them.

"Attacked the rear units during our cavalry engagement as they tried to canvas for wounded," Parno nodded, leaving out that the rear units were defying orders to do so. "My men were watching the flank, and hit the Tribals before they could get in range, tearing their number to shreds. Believe it, gentlemen; this new regimen will put your men on par with anyone, on foot or horseback."

"Assuming they survive," Freeman noted wryly.

"Assuming that," Parno didn't disagree. "General Gavin, you'll be heading to Cove Canton with your Corps. You'll have an easier time integrating your new troops into your units without the distraction of what's happening here. In the event of an incursion into the Highlands, you'll serve as a strategic reserve while there, so always be prepared for that."

"Yes, milord," Gavin nodded.

"General Graham, when your men come off the line, they'll pull back to an area that my regimental commander has selected and make camp. Their training will be here. Your losses, while in no way light, are not nearly so grievous as 2nd Corps. You should be able to work replacements into existing units without much difficulty during the training and your presence so close to the front will let you serve as the reserve for this area. As it grows hotter you will need to warn your officers to guard against heat stroke since it will be warmer here than in the higher elevations of Cove Canton. And while in normal camp we don't train in inclement weather, there are no such rules here. We don't train in lightning, but otherwise we're in the field. Regardless."

"Yes sir," Graham said simply. He knew that the Marshal was looking for a reason or excuse to kill him and wasn't entirely sure the Prince would actually need one. As a result, he was most careful how he spoke and acted.

"Your men aren't expendable," Parno told them. "We will suffer losses I know, but we will not lose a single man to carelessness or neglect. Warn your officers about that as well. They will be held personally responsible for the wellbeing of their men. Losses to dehydration, heat stroke and other needless and avoidable problems will see them facing a court martial. Make sure that is understood. And you are not exempt," he warned them all. "We're on the verge of annihilation. We need every man, and we need to be smarter than the enemy because every other advantage is theirs for the moment. Am I clear?"

"Clear sir," the men answered in unison.

"Outstanding," Parno nodded. "Please don't consider this a threat, or think I'm being needlessly harsh. Our soldiers are our greatest resource right now and they have to be well cared for. Not coddled, just taken care of. If we do that, then when we need extraordinary feats from them ordinary men will answer that call." He stood.

"1st Corps will prepare to hand off their place in line day after tomorrow. The two of you," he looked between Graham and Freeman, "work out the details so that the hand-off goes smoothly and with the enemy none the wiser if possible. General Gavin, your men should be sufficiently rested by now?" he made it a question.

"We can march on your orders sir," Gavin nodded. "I would ask for a day's advance if possible, but we could be underway with less if absolutely necessary. Moving camp takes time however and the extra warning will enable us to do that with less difficulty."

"Then two days from now, once the line exchange is complete and we know things are going to stay static, I want you on the road to Cove Canton. Your replacements are in place?" he asked.

"Yes sir," Gavin sighed. "They're a far cry from the veterans we lost, but they have had their basics at least. We'll get it done, milord," he promised.

"I'm sure you will," Parno nodded firmly. "We've never faced a threat like this, gentlemen," he said flatly. "We have to be better. We have to be smarter. I depend upon you for that as does the King and every man, woman and child in this Kingdom. Remember that, and when your men are tired and complaining about how hard the training is, remind them of it as well."

"Are there any questions?" There weren't, and all five men stood.

"All right," Parno sighed. "Godspeed and good luck to us all. General, I'll leave it with you," he told Davies.

"Aye, milord," Davies nodded. Freeman waited until Parno was gone to look at Davies.

"Now that, by God, is what a Marshal is supposed to look and sound like!"

Not even Graham disagreed.

-

"Are you in any better mood now that you've rode us all into the ground on the way here?"

Parno looked up from the report he'd been reading to see Karls Willard standing in the entrance to his small 'office' tent. He frowned slightly as he tossed the report on his desk and leaned back.

"Why is my mood of so much concern to all of you?" he asked rather than answer.

"Well, for one thing you're our commander," Karls entered the tent and sat down unbidden. "Moody commanders tend to make mistakes and those mistakes end up costing the soldiers. Secondly, the rest of the army will catch it sooner or later, and that's bad for morale. They're going to wonder what you know that they don't that's causing you to be moody and miserable and may just assume that it's something horrible and may lead to our defeat. And lastly, for many of us, you're a friend. We don't like to see you like this. It isn't good for you. You've got enough on you as it is."

"So, it's self-preservation, first and foremost," Parno chuckled, though there was no humor in it. "Makes sense," he nodded. "Well, first of all," he replied in kind, "I don't command the regiment anymore, you do. Second of all, I'm not around the army that much anymore so it's unlikely they see my 'mood'. And if they're worried, they have every right to be. They aren't stupid, especially those who have survived the last two or three battles. We're facing an onslaught of massive proportions and turning it will be as much a matter of divine will as martial skill. And lastly," Parno's voice might have softened the slightest bit, "I appreciate your concern, and I mean that whether it sounds that way or not. But my problems, one, are mine, not yours, and two, my problems aren't anything you can help me with."

"You can help me by training 1st Corps into as fine a fighting unit as you can over the next few months while I try to keep the Nor off balance. That will be difficult, especially without Beaumont and Whipple here raising hell behind enemy lines but I have to do it, nevertheless. I can't afford to let the Imps get settled enough to come at us with all hands and the cook again. Whatever made them withdraw last time wasn't anything we did. We can't count on that happening again."

He stopped there, seemingly having ran out of steam. He closed his eyes and rubbed his temples.

"Headache?" Karls asked.

"Just eye strain I'm sure," Parno shrugged. "Doesn't matter. Pain is part of the job. I do think I'll rest a bit, though," he stood and stretched. "I've gotten everyone their marching orders and I'm sure Davies can do all that without me looking over his shoulder. Nothing left for me to do but read reports and wait. I can do both tomorrow just as easily as I can tonight. Good night, Karls."

And just like that, Parno had put an end to any discussion of his problems. He hadn't been so abrupt this time, but the message was just as clear;

Butt. Out.

-

"Your quarters are ready for you, sir," Harrel Sprigs said quietly and Parno had to work not to jump.

"I need to get you a bell," he groused. "How did you know that's where I was going?" he demanded.

"Well, it's my job to know," Sprigs shrugged. "And I heard you tell Colonel Willard good night, as well," he grinned. "I knew you would eventually want to retire so I made sure your quarters were ready."

"Thanks," Parno laughed just a small bit, shaking his head slightly. "Are you still disappointed that you didn't get into a line unit, Harrel?" he asked suddenly.

"No, milord. I am not," the young officer shook his head. "I've served the Kingdom much better here than anywhere else I could have gone. I'm satisfied of that."

"Good," Parno nodded. "And good night, Captain," he added at the mouth opening of his tent.

"And to you, sir."

-

"I don't know what we're going to do about this."

Karls was sitting at a fire with Cho Feng, his brother Enri seated across from him as well grasping a bottle of the home-made beer that Karls had once more procured.

"What is it you think you can do?" Enri asked, taking a long pull from the bottle. "That is really good," he looked at the bottle.

"There is no action we can take that will solve this problem," Cho offered into the dark. "This is a problem that he must deal with himself. Whatever the good physician did or said, she struck an extremely sensitive place. I suspect that he has compared it to betrayals past, such as his brothers before the start of the war. If this is the case, then he will right himself before long. It will take longer simply because the betrayal will be worse here, in his mind. But he is strong and he knows the path he must walk. He will be fine."

"I'm not so sure," Karls resisted the temptation to just take Cho's words for it. "I'd like to think so, but this. . .this is different. I don't know what happened between the two of them but it hit him hard. Hard," he stressed, looking at the other two men.

"I'm not comfortable delving into the Marshal's personal affairs," Enri said finally, shaking his head as he rose. "Not at all."

"He's not just the Marshal to me," Karls replied evenly. "Or to Cho."

"I know that," his brother smiled gently. "Nor would I try to stop you. But I do not enjoy the same relationship with the Marshal you two do. I cannot place myself into his personal business as easily as you can. I will have to concentrate on making sure things run smoothly while the two of you work on restoring the Marshal's equilibrium."

"You only use big words like that when you're drunk," Karls laughed. "How many of those have you had?"

"At least one more than I should have apparently," Enri admitted before draining the current 'one' in his hand. "Now, I am off to bed where I hope that this fine beer allows me to fall into a deep sleep."

"Good night, brother," Karls told him. Enri waved over his shoulder as he made his way toward his tent.

"Your relationship has improved," Cho noted.

"Yeah," Karls admitted. "Kinda glad for it. Hard to work with your older brother looking over your shoulder though," he chuckled.

"I am sure."

"You really think he will be okay?" Karls asked.

"He will have to be," came the steady reply. "He has no choice. And he is aware of that."

"I wonder what she said to him?" Karls shook his head. "I mean, I would have sworn she was all about him and nothing else."

"That is not always a good thing," Cho said evenly.

-

"Doctor, are you alright?"

Memmnon was easing himself back into his chair after an examination by his physician. He was sore, but not so sore that he hadn't noticed Stephanie's distraction of late. Or Winifred's for that matter.

"I'm quite alright, Highness, thank you for asking," she smiled at him. The smile was not as bright as it might once have been, however. Nor were her eyes.

"Look here, Doctor," Memmnon's voice sharpened slightly, though not in a commanding way. "I may not be terribly bright in some ways, but I can see that you are at least somewhat distressed. Over what I do not, indeed cannot know, but the distress itself is apparent. You have done a great deal for me over the last several weeks. Surely there is some way I can help you, even if it's just to lend you an ear."

"You're very kind, Your Highness," Stephanie said after a few moments to gather herself. "And I deeply and sincerely appreciate your concern. I'm afraid however that there is no real help in the situation I find myself in. To put it simply, I did something foolish and now I must live with it."

"I can sense the hand of my brother here somewhere," Memmnon sighed. "Tell me doctor, and be truthful now; has he in some way violated your trust or disrespected you in any-"

"No!" Stephanie looked so shocked at the question that Memmnon was momentarily nonplussed by it. "In no way," she continued more calmly after a few seconds to compose herself. "I assure you that Prince Parno has done no wrong, Your Highness," she said very correctly. "If anyone has acted poorly between us, it was I. He has always been every inch the gentleman in my presence."

"I-really?" Memmnon didn't know quite what to say and found himself stammering a bit.

"Really," Stephanie affirmed. "Your lack of faith in him does you a disservice in this case," she decided to go ahead and cement the idea that Parno had indeed done no wrong. It was the least she could do she decided, considering.

"That is possible," a red-faced Memmnon nodded in agreement. "However, it has been his pattern for many years to act in just such a way."

"Perhaps because no better was expected of him," she said simply as she put away the last of her instruments. "Forgive me, for it is not my place to lecture," she said, standing. "I believe that I can pronounce you fit again, Your Majesty," she declared to him. "You will continue to experience twinges of pain for a while yet, as well as stiffness and soreness, both of which should lessen over time. Your physical activities will still need to be limited, but that will change as you regain your strength with more activity than you have been allowed to this point."

"You speak as if you are leaving, Doctor," Memmnon said quietly.

"I am indeed, Your Highness," she nodded. "The need for my presence has thankfully passed and there is no need for me any longer. I am of course at your service should any medical need arise in the future," she promised him. "But I feel confident that you are on the road to recovery."

"I was not thinking of me, Doctor," Memmnon observed carefully. "Then again, perhaps I was," he decided after a few seconds to ponder. "What will become of Winifred in your absence, Doctor? I cannot think it would be acceptable for her to remain here in the palace without you as her chaperon and ward, so to speak. I know she would miss you, as would I. And I do not know that she would remain here without you, nor could I blame her."

"Nonsense," Stephanie scoffed. "For all her headstrong ways at times, Winnie is a grown woman who is more than capable of making her own decisions. She is intelligent and strong. And I am certain she is in good hands here."

"That is not what I meant," Memmnon shook his head. "At the moment no one questions her honor staying here because of your presence. And she is not uncomfortable here again because of your presence. Should you depart, I am not certain either of those things would remain true."

"I understand your concerns, Your Highness-"

"Please, can you not at least when we are in private just call me Memmnon?" he cut her off gently. "You have been my doctor all through this most trying of times and it's safe to say I have few secrets left from you. And we will one day be in-laws as well," he added with a soft smile. As soon as he said those words, Stephanie looked away slightly, her face falling.

"Ah," she heard him say ever so softly. "I see."

"No, I doubt that you do," she shook her head slowly. "You will blame him, as you always have, but. . .this is not his burden to bear. There is no blame for what has beset me now but me. And merely calling you by your name rather than addressing you properly would be wrong," she added.

"I must have someone to talk to," Memmnon shrugged. "I always knew things would be like this, but. . .my father had advisers and friends that he had accumulated through the years. What friends I have made are few, and they are far away from here, mostly serving in the army. A few scattered nobles that don't give me a headache just looking at them but they are likewise busy trying to make sure we can survive the war. And burden? Doctor, that sounds very much as if you are-"

"No, I'm not," Stephanie sighed, having known as soon as she said the words that she had chosen them poorly.

"I see then," Memmnon nodded, though he clearly didn't. "So what has happened that you and Parno are no longer. . .close, shall we say? I must admit that he seemed very taken with you on the rare occasion when he spoke of anything personal to me. I believe you had made him the happiest I have ever seen him."

It was too much, that last, and Stephanie burst into tears. Gathering her things, she nearly ran from the room, ignoring Memmnon's calls.

-

"What did you do to her?"

Approximately fifteen minutes after the doctor had fled his apartment, Memmnon now faced the wrath of a redheaded Fury.

"I did nothing, I assure you," Memmnon held up a placating hand to try and calm the raging tiger. "I tried to engage the doctor in simple conversation. She spoke of leaving the palace and I tried to get her to stay. I wanted her to remain and be my, our, physician, and be here for you. I did not want you to feel alone or uncomfortable here in anyway. I also asked her to use my given name, at least in private, as we would one day be in-laws."

"That may not happen," Winnie almost growled.

"I know that now," Memmnon was sweating by this time. "I didn't know it then. The last I had heard, she and Parno were to be married at some point after the war.

Or at least at the point where our defeat was no longer so possible. I did not know there had been any change. And even if there has, I still want her to remain here and be the Royal Physician, as well as be here for you to lean upon."

"You think I need her to lean on?" Winnie asked, a dangerous light in her eyes.

"I think you want her here, and that you consider her your friend," Memmnon nodded. "And I know that she has been assisting you with issues of court and other things that you may think you need in order to please me."

"So, I'm just trying to please you," Winnie actually smiled, which by now Memmnon had learned was not always a good thing.

"I think you have been trying very hard to please me, though your efforts are not necessary because your very presence pleases me and you need do nothing else in that regard that you do not wish to," a very wary Memmnon replied. The change in Winnie was abrupt.

"What?"

"I said it isn't necessary for you to bend to the pressure of court to please me," he repeated. "If you want to learn those things, then I support that, fully. If you do not, then it isn't necessary. I do not want you to change, to try and become what you think I want you to be, because you are already what I want you to be; you. It was not a socially conscious woman of court who stood in my bed chamber and challenged me when I thought Parno was in danger or when I wanted you to leave so I could discuss sensitive information. Nor that stood ready with bow and sword to protect her friend from possible attack while she labored to save my life, either." He took a deep breath, then plunged ahead.

"That was the woman I fell in love with on near first sight, Winifred. I love you because of your strength, your loyalty, your beauty and your determination. I don't care if you wear silks or buckskin, I don't care if you know which plate goes where or what colors are in season or any of that other rubbish that so many 'noble' women seem to be fascinated by." He leaned forward slightly and a furiously blushing Winnie took a step back in spite of herself.

"I want you just the way you are, or any other way you chose to be," he said simply. "Do not change one hair on your beautiful head because you think I want you to. I want you to be happy, Winifred. I want you to be happy, here with me, for as long as we live. I want you to be my wife, and yes I'm afraid that means be my Queen thanks to my sister, and I want you to bear and raise my children. Raise them to be strong like their mother and not weak like so many of our blood have turned out to be. As my brother and sister turned out to be."

"I want you to marry me and stay with me and never leave me," he finished, reaching into a small pouch on his belt he removed a box and opened it. Inside was a ring with a single large emerald.

"This was my mother's," he said simply. "I wish you to wear it, if you will consent to be my wife. I have already spoken to your father and he has given me his blessing to ask you for your hand, and I am doing so now. I had not planned. . .that is, I had planned for this to be different," he stammered slightly. "However, regardless of how it happens, I want you to marry me."

For the second time in less than an hour, a woman fled Memmnon McLeod's rooms, crying.

-

"I don't understand," Memmnon said an hour later.

"There's little enough a man can do to be understanding a woman's ways, milord," Whip shrugged, his voice sympathetic. He had answered an urgent summons from the King thinking something was wrong with his daughter, only to find that the King needed someone to talk to.

"But I...everything I did was for her!" Memmnon continued as if Whip hadn't spoken. "I didn't mean to make the doctor cry! Or make Winifred cry, for that matter! I thought she would want the doctor to stay here with her as well! That it would make her more comfortable than staying here alone!"

"She like as not would have wanted her to stay even had you not said anything," Whip nodded. "Yon lady doctor has been a good influence on the girl, there's no denying." He was at a loss to explain anything to the young King. His only foray into courtship had ended with Winifred's birth and he'd never had the nerve to try again.

"I don't understand," Memmnon was shaking his head again. "I just don't. . ."

-

". . .understand," Winnie was shaking her head. "Why is it you feel you have to leave? Just because things may not be the same between you and the Prince doesn't mean you can't stay here!"

"Winnie, I need to get away from all this," Stephanie shook her head. "It's too much. Every time I look around. . .everything here reminds me of him," she settled for saying.

"I need you to be here," Winnie pleaded, eyes wet. "Memmnon just asked me to marry him!"

"You knew that was coming," Stephanie told her. "What did you say?"

"Nothing," Winnie admitted. "I went there mad because I thought he made you cry, and he told me that all he'd done was ask you to stay on here for my benefit, and then he pulls out this honking great ring and asks me right there to marry him!" she almost cried. "I ran out crying after that," she admitted.

"Oh, Winnie," Stephanie hugged the younger woman. "You can't leave him like that, it isn't right!"

"Well, if I knew what to do, I wouldn't have!" the redhead shot back. "Yes, I knew he was thinking about it, but he admitted he had planned to do all that another way. Said my being upset about you had kinda changed his plans a mite."

"Winnie, my battles are my own to fight," Stephanie told her firmly. "While I appreciate your being so loyal and caring for me, you need to concentrate on your own life and the changes that are coming. Starting with what will you answer?"

"I can't stay here alone," Winnie shook her head. "And we can't get married until he's King. I. . .I don't have anywhere to go but back to Cove Canton," she sighed. "I only came here because you offered me the chance to come see the Royal City, remember? My pa ain't got a house here, he's just sleeping in a room at the

Foundry, he said. Which is okay for him, but there ain't no room there for me. At least back at the Canton I got a house to live in." She stood suddenly.

"Reckon I'll go back," she said finally. "I got a home and a job there waiting. I can't stay here without you. I don't know nobody else and I ain't gonna be here alone and by myself."

"You can't do that!" Stephanie protested at once.

"You can," Winnie shrugged. "Reckon I can do as I please, being as I'm grown and all. This was a fairy tale anyway, and fairy tales ain't real. I know that much if I don't know nothing else. I can't be here alone. I make too many mistakes as it is. This bunch would eat me alive if you weren't here. And I don't react well to that sort of thing."

"So, reckon I'll head back where I belong," she nodded. "What you aiming to do? Go back to the hospital or stay here?"

"Winnie you can't leave!" Stephanie ignored the question. "You're. . .the King. . .I mean you just can't!"

"I can too, and I am," Winnie told her. "Done made up my mind. I need to see my pa first though and let him know. And I guess I need to see 'bout getting a ride," she mused. "You don't reckon I could get that carriage to carry me back, do you?" she asked suddenly. "I mean, don't it belong there, anyhow? Or is that yours?" she asked suddenly.

"What? No! It isn't mine," Stephanie shook her head. "And it doesn't matter because you can't go!"

"I already said I can," Winnie told her flatly. "I'm not staying here alone. And no matter how many people may be around, without you I'm still alone. I came here not knowing nobody, just riding along with you. I didn't ask the King to be sweet on me, and didn't encourage or lead him on neither. Ain't none of that my fault."

"Winnie we're talking about the King!" Stephanie continued to protest. "You can't just. . .things like that just aren't done!"

"Reckon it was you told me that not being a noble meant I didn't have to care what people thought," Winnie shrugged. "And how they don't care no way, since I ain't nobody to start with."

"That wasn't what I meant!"

-

"This is Parno's fault," Memmnon almost murmured. "Somehow, someway, he's responsible for this, you mark my words," he said to Whip.

"Now I can't see how he would go and do something like this," Whip protested.

"He probably didn't mean to," Memmnon allowed. "But he's a lightning rod. He attracts, encourages bad luck and misfortune. Creates it almost, leaving destruction in his wake almost everywhere he goes. Comes as naturally to him as breathing."

"Milord, perhaps you ought to try and find out exactly what the problem is before you go assigning any blame for it?" Whip did his best to sound reasonable.

"What? Oh," Memmnon seemed to take note of what Whip was saying finally. "Yes, yes of course," he nodded. "Send for them both at once," he ordered. "Have the guard send for them both. Together. We'll find out what my brother has done this time to get all this going."

"Aye, milord," Whip sighed, shaking his head as he made his way to the door.

-

"What does he want?" Winnie demanded, arms crossed. "I'm busy at the moment."

"Winnie, dear," Stephanie managed to intervene. "This is an official summons of the Sovereign," she pointed out. "There is no ignoring this. Or putting it off, either," she sighed. "When?" she asked the arms man.

"It was immediate, milady," the man kept his face neutral.

"We'll need a minute," Stephanie said.

"I'll be here," the man promised/threatened. Stephanie closed the door and leaned against it.

"Well, now you've done it," she said quietly.

"I've done it?" Winnie looked at her crossly. "I'm not the one who ran out cr-" she stopped abruptly as she remembered she had done exactly that. "I'm not the one who started all this," she settled for saying, feeling somewhat justified.

"You certainly haven't helped any!" Stephanie shot back, moving to the mirror to check her appearance. "You had better prepare yourself unless you want Memmnon to see you like that!"

A look of dawning horror on her face, Winnie fled to her bedroom leaving Stephanie to shake her head.

"For someone who isn't interested in a fairy tale, you seem very determined that the King not see you look a fright, dear."

-

By the time the two women entered the King's audience chamber, Memmnon was working into a fine temper tantrum. He was the King, dammit. While he might wish he weren't, he was, and that meant that he got to know what was going on around him. And he meant to know what was going on today.

"Why here?" Winnie almost whispered as the two were shown into the seldom used room. Well, never used for them before. Neither had been here.

"I think Memmnon is reminding us he's the King," Stephanie said just as softly. "As in he wants to know what's going on and he's not going to take no for an answer."

"I don't have to-!" Winnie hissed but was cut off by Stephanie's glare.

"He is the King!" she hissed right back. "So yes, you do have to. Now be quiet and let's see what he wants."

Biting back a reply Winnie followed Stephanie into the main room where Memmnon sat upon his seat waiting, crown perched atop his head. He seldom wore it and Stephanie took this as another sign that Memmnon meant to have his questions answered this time.

"Ladies," he said curtly as the two curtsied before him. "I want to know what is going on around here, and I want to know right now without any further beating around the bush. And no crying and running away, either," he added. "I've had quite enough of that today, thank you. Start whenever you're ready."

"Now you wait one da-" Winnie started off angrily only to get an elbow in the ribs from the doctor.

"Milord, this has been, all of this has been a complete misunderstanding," Stephanie said politely. "The fault for this lies entirely with me and I sincerely apologize that my problems have caused you any irritation."

"I'm not interested in finding fault since I assume that Parno is somehow to blame," Memmnon told her flatly. "He always is. What I want to know is what is it that he has done that has led to all this . . . drama," he settled for saying.

"Milord, I assure you that Prince McLeod is in no way to blame for any of this," Stephanie told him, her voice tightly controlled. "He has done nothing untoward nor caused any problems of any kind. Even were he so inclined I doubt he could find the time."

"I didn't say he did it on purpose," Memmnon nodded. "Still, as I told Mister Hubel, Parno is a lightning rod for trouble. He doesn't have to make an effort, it comes to him naturally. And you still haven't answered my question," he added with a raised eyebrow.

"Now you look he-" Winnie tried again only to receive an elbow to her stomach this time, cutting her off nicely.

"Milord, the night before he left, Prince Parno and I had a disagreement that was completely my fault," Stephanie decided she had to just come out and admit it. "I tried. . .I attempted to force his hand on something that I knew he didn't want to do, and when he refused again I... I became angry. I said a great many things to him in that anger that I should not have. Things I didn't mean. I meant to try and make amends with him the morning after before he departed, but he left earlier than anticipated and I... I missed him. I am afraid that I have bungled our relationship very badly. To the point that I seriously doubt we still have a relationship," she admitted, looking at the floor.

"So, when I mentioned being in-laws. . ." Memmnon mused.

"I'm afraid I became somewhat emotional and fled your presence lest you see that and assume, as you did, that Parn-, Prince McLeod was somehow to blame," she nodded.

"And you?" he shifted his gaze to a smoldering Winifred. "I assume that your accusations toward me were because you just assumed that I had done something to the good doctor that caused her to cry?"

"She had been here and came back crying," Winnie crossed her arms under her breasts, refusing to be cowed. "So yes, I did assume that. And that was wrong," she barely managed to choke out. "So, for that I reckon I owe you an apology too." Memmnon nodded regally, accepting her apology.

"While I understand the doctor running out as she did, why did you do so?" he asked her a bit more gently this time. "Does the thought of being married to me really cause you such grief?"

"You caught me by surprise or that wouldn't have happened!" she shot back, red faced with embarrassment. "I didn't expect it, that's all."

"I see," Memmnon was fighting off a smile now. "And Doctor, why is it that you feel you need to leave the palace? Just because you and Parno are having difficulties does not mean you aren't welcome here. Surely you know that. I did not ask you to become the Royal Physician because of your relationship with him. Nor out of simple gratitude, though you have that and always will. I need a physician. It is that simple. Your family has provided physicians to the House Tyree since. . .since there has been a House Tyree, in fact," he shrugged. "It is entirely appropriate that you should take up that mantle yourself, should you so desire. If not then of course you don't have to, but I would be disappointed. And I believe that Winifred would be sad to see you leave."

"I'm le-" Winnie managed to dodge the elbow this time, but it still cut her off mid speech.

"Milord, while you needed me it was entirely appropriate for me to be here," Stephanie began after a warning glare at Winnie. "So long as Prince McLeod and I had a suitable arrangement it was also not entirely inappropriate that I use his residence here in the palace, since he wasn't using it and I needed to be close by. But none of those things apply, now. He and I... we will likely never. . .I made a terrible mess of things," she sighed in defeat, having no better way to describe it. "I like as not cannot repair the damage I've done, and thus there is little likelihood that he and I will reconcile. That being the case, I am extremely uncomfortable using his rooms anymore. It simply feels wrong, Highness. And it saddens me," she admitted. "It reminds me too much of him."

"I see," Memmnon mused. "You're aware I assume that there are other rooms available? That this palace is an extremely large place that can accommodate many people? That being the case, finding you suitable permanent quarters that will not remind you of my idiot brother will be no trial."

"He is not an idiot, Highness," Stephanie said at once.

"If he left here without trying to mend his relationship with you, regardless of who was at fault, then yes, he's an idiot," Memmnon said flatly. "I know there is nothing I would not do within my ability to reconcile any rift that occurred between myself and Winifred," he added, ignoring the furious blush on Winnie's face at his words.

"I left him with impression there was no reason to do so," Stephanie shrugged, her voice small. "As I said, the fault here is entirely my own."

"Be that as it may," Memmnon decided to cede the point, "I still need a physician, and Winifred desires your company here. I dare say that without you here she will not want to remain. I will do anything I can to prevent that short of actually forcing her to stay. If she desires to go, she may at any time and with my blessing. It will break my heart, but that is not reason enough for her not to do what she will. That being said, if she is leaving solely because you are then I implore you yet again to remain. I will order a new apartment prepared for you today. One the two of you can share if you like, and decorate as you see fit. So long as you are here to act as her chaperon then there can be no attempt at creating a scandal. I will not have her slandered." His voice was a bit dark as he said that.

"I. . ." Stephanie started and then stopped. Her arguments had been very handily repulsed so far.

"I'll stay if you will," Winnie said softly. She turned to see the younger woman looking at her imploringly, green eyes pleading with her to say yes.

"Winnie," she began but then halted once again.

"Please," Winnie added, on the verge of begging. Suddenly Stephanie realized that for all her bluster, Winnie wanted very badly to stay. Not because of the palace or the finery or anything like that, but simply because Memmnon had managed to win her heart. She hadn't yet admitted it to him, but it was evident to Stephanie as she looked at her young friend.

"You must answer the King," she said suddenly, her voice as soft as Winnie's. "Provide him an answer, and I will go wherever you want to go. If you say no, then we will both return to Cove Canton. As you said, we have homes and jobs waiting there. If you say yes, then. . .then we'll remain here and I will act as your chaperon."

"That's blackmail!" Winnie hissed angrily, her face flushed.

"Yes, it is," Stephanie nodded. "And it's my final word on the subject," she added primly, crossing her arms in a defiant posture. Two could play that game.

"Humph," Winnie tossed her hair and looked away. Looked away to hide the smile that she couldn't contain any longer. She had done it. It had cost her, but she had done it. Schooling her features, she looked back at Stephanie and then at the King.

"Ask me again," she ordered. "Ask me again and do it right this time," she clarified. Eyebrows raised, Memmnon rose to his feet, stepped down from his dais, and walked to where Winnie stood waiting. Without flourish or fanfare, he knelt before her wincing only slightly and held the ring before her once more.

"Winifred Hubel, this ring was my mother's," he said quietly. "My father placed it on her finger the day he asked her to be his wife. To be his Queen. I do not know how many generations this ring has been used for this very occasion and doubt anyone does. But I offer it now to you as so many of my predecessor have done, asking that you consent to become my wife. That you become my Queen at the proper time and rule beside me, bear my heirs and raise them to be strong and honorable, just as their mother is."

By the time he was finished Winnie was blushing furiously once more, her face so hot that she had to make a conscious effort not to fan herself, especially at the 'bear my heirs' part as that implied, well, you know. Her heart beating almost out of her chest, blood running hot, she looked down at the man who had won her heart not as King, but as a man.

"Will you, Winifred Hubel, marry me?"

"Yes," she nodded, only a single tear falling this time as she knelt in front of him and let him slide the ring on her finger. "Yes, Memmnon McLeod, I will marry you. And I will do my best to give you strong heirs to one day, long in the future, follow in your footsteps. I love you," she almost whispered as she hugged him tightly. They stayed that way for perhaps a minute before…

"All right, that's quite enough of that," Stephanie said firmly. "That kind of contact could be misread after all. The proprieties must be observed at all times from henceforth until the wedding."

"What!?" an enraged Winifred was on her feet in a second.

"You heard me," Stephanie smirked. "As your chaperon, I have sway over these kinds of things and this type of conduct is extremely unbecoming. A brief embrace upon meeting, another upon parting, and that will be quite enough. Anything more is excessive."

"Why you-" Winnie was about to explode when Memmnon, still on his knee, took her hand.

"A little help, here?"

Winnie was beside him in an instant, helping him to his feet. Stephanie watched, hiding a smile of satisfaction. Winnie thought she was so smart. Well, she would show her!

"I will prepare a schedule of arrangements for you today," she informed Memmnon haughtily, and winked at him when Winnie wasn't looking. The King had to fight to hide a smile as he nodded gravely.

"Very well," he managed not to choke with laughter.

"What!?" Winnie screeched. "Are you gonna let her get away with that?" she demanded.

"I have no choice," he shrugged. "I asked her to be your chaperon and ward and now I must accede to her authority in this matter. She will be in charge of our courtship until our nuptials. It is the custom, and even the King cannot ignore it."

"You planned this," Winnie hissed, turning on Stephanie like a she-wolf. "All this time you-"

"That surly behavior will simply not be tolerated, young lady," Stephanie had to really fight now not to laugh. Over in a corner, forgotten, Whip Hubel was having the same trouble, watching his fire tempered daughter be caught in a snare she had made herself.

"Now, we will repair to our rooms until the King has prepared our new accommodations, at which time we will be moving. You may attend the evening meal with His Highness, assuming he has no pressing court business, but at no time will you be unsupervised while in his presence. Now come," she whirled at once, less the outraged Winifred see her grin.

"You seriously can't do anything about this?" Winnie demanded of Memmnon, who shook his head gravely.

"It is all but law," he told her truthfully.

"What good is being King if you can't change things the way you want?" she demanded.

"I ask myself that daily," he sighed. "You had best go, lest she ground you."

"Ground me!?" Winnie almost howled in rage. "I'll be da-"

"Language young lady!" Stephanie's near shout cut her off. "Now come with me!"

"You have to go," Memmnon made himself look forlorn. "We will see each other at dinner," he promised.

Looking to make sure Stephanie wasn't looking, Winnie rose on her tiptoes and kissed Memmnon's cheek.

"I saw that!"

"Until dinner," Memmnon promised again as Winnie silently implored him to have Stephanie executed. Or banned. Something. Anything.

"Fine," she sighed. "Until dinner." With that she trudged after Stephanie, muttering the whole way under her breath. As soon as the door was firmly closed Memmnon was laughing, joined by Whip as the older man made his way across the room.

"You do realize, I reckon, that once she finds out this is all a bunch o' hogwash, she'll kill you both," he said easily.

"I suspect so," Memmnon wiped the tears from his eyes as he managed to get his laughter under control. "But I shall enjoy it until then!"

CHAPTER SEVEN

-

Tinker watched from a distance as the men of 2nd Corps set out on their march to Cove Canton. 1st Corps was settled into their new camps not more than a mile from his inn, a development that would allow his operation to delve into General Graham's command and see how deep the rot went. Tinker was sure that the only reason Graham wasn't dead was because the Prince didn't know who to replace him with yet. And so long as Graham remained, those loyal to him would make themselves known without fear of reprisal unless he had warned them not to, which Tinker doubted.

He had not spoken to Graham himself, but had observed from a short distance more than once. Having watched the man and listened to him speak, Tinker was convinced that Graham was merely waiting for his own opportunity. What exactly he intended to do was still a mystery, but Tinker intended to find out, one way or the other.

"Mornin' Mister Tinker," Aaron Bell said quietly as he came up behind his 'boss'.

"Good morning indeed, Mister Bell," Tinker replied, smiling. "We have new neighbors," he indicated the massive camps of 1st Corps.

"So, I hear," Bell nodded. "I don't know about this," he admitted. "I'd not have started with that bunch myself. Like as not be difficult to trust 'em too far."

"What difference does it make?" Tinker asked. It was clear he honestly wanted Bell's opinion.

"Once they go through what we did, that bunch will be a lot more soldier than they are right now," Bell told him. "That's not to say they ain't soldiers now, mind, but. . .it takes more than that to be a Black Sheep. Once done, assuming they can finish it, they'll be the equal of any Imperial force twice their size on open ground, all other things being equal."

"Things?" Tinker asked. He had learned early on that Aaron Bell had a very sharp mind and Tinker never wasted resources.

"Artillery and such," Bell clarified. "Supplies in the field, quality weapons and what not. So long as the other side ain't got a noticeable match, they can stand against 'em and win near ever time, assuming good leadership."

"I see," Thinker nodded thoughtfully. He had been absent for much of the now famed Black Sheep Regiment's training and was not familiar with their methods. He did know that the Prince's Regiment was the talk of the army and that many young men and officers had tried every way possible to wrangle assignment to the elite formation that rode with the Marshal.

"So long as ole Graham is a question mark, maybe we ought not trust his men this much is all I'm saying," Bell continued. "But I reckon the Marshal knows what he's doing."

"Indeed," Tinker nodded again. "And it up to us to try and make sure that the rot doesn't run too deep," he added. "Being so close should be a great benefit I should think."

"Don't count on it," Bell shook his head, surprising Tinker. "When you're doing this, all you want at the end of the day is a bed. And you don't want no one sharing it, neither. You want to sleep is all. And the officers is in for a rude shock too," he grinned maliciously. "They may think they ain't gotta do the same training, but the Prince, he did it right alongside ever body else. I can promise you that he'll see to it that bunch over there does the same thing," he nodded toward the camp.

"Really," Tinker was impressed.

"Really," Bell's nod was emphatic. "That bunch is in for a rude awakening."

-

"Move, move, move! Into formation now! On the double quick you slaggards!"

The men of 1st Corps stumbled around confused at the yelling and ordering about. They had assumed they'd have a few days rest before this new training and refit began and had taken the opportunity to unwind with a bit of raw spirits the last two nights.

They were paying for it now.

Men were racing to their new assembly grounds still pulling on boots, and in some cases pants, all the while wondering who these men in black and green livery were and why they were issuing orders in their camp.

"What the devil is going on here!" General Arnold Graham stormed out of his command tent, hair askew and shirt unbuttoned. "Who are you and by whose authority are you disrupting my camp!"

"General." The voice was quiet and firm, and Graham turned to see a man dressed in the Marshal's colors looking at him casually.

"Who are you?"

"I'm Colonel Karls Willard, General," the man replied calmly. "And today is the first day of your new training. Fall in," the Colonel ordered calmly. Graham looked at him with incredulity.

"Who the hell do you think you're talking to, solider!?" he demanded, thundering toward this upstart colonel with a death wish. "I'll have you-" which was as far as he got before he was forced to stop lest he be impaled on a sword that was only inches from his chest. Graham followed the blade to find a grim-eyed trooper looking at him as if all he wanted in life was an excuse to run Graham through and have done with it.

"I'll have you in irons and whipped!" he snarled.

"No, General, you won't," a new voice said and Graham whirled to see Marshal McLeod behind him. "You will fall in with everyone else and you will participate fully in the training your men are about to endure. You will complete that training or else you'll be out on your ass, guarding a horse camp somewhere. Understand?"

"I'm a General in the Soulan Army!" Graham shouted right in Parno's face, his fury making him forget who he was talking to.

"You are for the moment," Parno nodded. "I can break you with a word, Graham, and send you back to Nasil in disgrace. I should do just that in all likelihood considering your closeness to the last Marshal. You remember him. The Marshal that would be King? How involved were you in that little plot, Graham? What did Therron promise you if you supported him when the time came?"

"What?"

Parno fought to hide a frown. He didn't think Graham was that good an actor, and right now he looked poleaxed.

"What plot?" Graham asked, his bluster and fury gone. "Does this. . .is that what happened to the King?" he asked quietly.

"It is," Parno nodded. "My sister killed the King herself, and nearly the Crown Prince. She is even now on her way to free Therron from his exile on the Horn and bring him back to place him on the throne. She thinks she killed Memmnon as well I'm sure, leaving only me in her way. Therron's regiment, led by a Colonel named Callens, helped her escape detention, kill the King and nearly the Crown Prince and are now taking her to Therron with plans to escort him home to take the throne by force."

"My God," Graham breathed rather than spoke. "She killed her own father?" he looked aghast.

"She did indeed," Parno nodded. "Now knowing that, how far do you think I should trust Therron's right hand man. Hm? How much trust can I safely put in you, General Graham? Are you waiting to knife me in the back and help Therron take the throne from Memmnon, the rightful heir? Are you waiting for his call to lead your men to his side and use them to secure his place on the throne and then what? My job, perhaps? Is that what he promised you?"

"I. . .I didn't know," Graham looked lost. "He never spoke of such a thing to me, milord. Had he done so I would have reported it at once. I am many things, Marshal, but I am no traitor. Loud, braggart, arrogant even? Certainly. Traitor? No."

Parno actually believed the man. He hadn't expected this. He had thought to catch Graham by surprise, make him angry, and trick him into admitting his connection to Therron. Instead the man's bluster had fallen to pieces under that attack, and Parno was fairly sure that his shock and surprise were real.

Now, Parno wasn't sure what to do.

"Milord," Graham came to attention, looking faintly ridiculous with his hair uncombed and his shirt outside his pants, suspenders still down.

"Milord," he repeated. "I swear to you, for whatever it's worth, that I had no inkling of what your brother had planned when he was Marshal. As for your sister, I've met her only a few times and that never more than a hand before dinner, milord. I could not say that I know her even slightly, to be honest. Begging your pardon, but… I never cared to spend much time around her because she seemed. . .odd. I'm sorry to say that, but it is true."

"Oh, it's true," Parno assured him. "You have excellent judgment if you have nothing else. She's quite possibly insane, so odd is actually something of a compliment."

"It wasn't meant to be, again begging your pardon," Graham shook his head. "Your brother was always on about the nobility and what have you, but I wrote that off as arrogance of his birth more than anything else, milord. He was never shy about reminding someone who and what he was."

"No, that is true as well," Parno nodded. "So what do I do with you, General?" he got the discussion back on track. "What am I to do with Therron's favorite general, commanding his favorite and most pampered Corps?" Graham's face flushed at the barb but he didn't take the hook.

"That has to be up to you milord," he said simply. "My men may be, or have been 'pampered' as you call it, but we've stood against the Imperials and held our ground. We shed our blood doing it and we did our duty. We will continue doing our duty so long as we are able. To a man I give you my word on that."

"I really want to believe you right now, General," Parno said softly. "You have no idea how badly I want to believe you. I need to be able to believe you because I don't have time for this. Any of it."

"All I can do is try to prove it to you milord," Graham shrugged helplessly. "I doubt my word is any good at the moment, considering my association with your brother, but it's all I have to give you other than hard work. If I had anything else I'd offer it, but I don't."

Parno considered that for a moment, appraising Graham carefully.

"You look like you're in pretty good shape, General," he said finally.

"I'd like to think so, milord," Graham was clearly puzzled by the comment.

"Then if you can survive the training alongside your men, that will be a good start to proving to me that you're not a part of Therron's cabal. I warn you now that it's grueling, hot, dirty work. You'll want to kill the instructors, then you'll want to kill yourself if it means escaping. But if you survive, if you can finish it, you'll be more formidable that you can possibly imagine. Of course some would say that I'm being foolish to leave you in command at all, let alone leave you in command and train your men up to the same level as my own."

"You speak as if you've done this yourself, milord," Graham noted, eyeing Parno carefully.

"That's because I did," Parno said simply. "I marched, rode, slept, ate, trained with every weapon right alongside my men. Start to finish. In addition to my other duties."

Mentally, Graham's estimation of Parno McLeod climbed several notches. He hadn't imagined that the Playboy Prince had bothered to get dirty. He should have known better after everything that had happened since he'd taken command.

"I will do all that I can to do the same," Graham said simply. "If I fail then I'd expect the same treatment as any of my men who fail."

"Good, because that's exactly what will happen," Parno nodded firmly. "And remember this General; when you're training, you rank no higher than the man next to you. Every man you see wearing my colors has already done this. And all of them are survivors of more battles than anyone on this field. Don't forget that. Regardless of their backgrounds, their education or anything else, every one of them is a fighting man from head to heel. They will make it rough on you because they know that the harder it is here, the less you bleed on the battlefield. They know that because they've proven it."

"Then so will I." Graham's voice held nothing but grim determination.

"I hope you do, General, because I need you," Parno's voice fell to a near whisper. "I need you and every other man in this army to ensure that our people don't end up as Imperial slaves, assuming we live. So prove it to me, General. Prove to me that you have what it takes, that you can toe the line, and most of all that I can trust you."

"I will," Graham's voice was firm. "If you will excuse me, milord, my men are beginning their new drills."

"Go then, and good luck," Parno said.

"Thank you, milord." Parno watched the man hurry away, joining is staff officers who immediately began complaining to him. Graham bellowed them into submission in record time and then turned to the instructors himself, ignoring whatever muttering there was in the ranks. It wasn't his responsibility to quiet them. It was the instructor's.

"Perhaps not the enemy you feared?" Cho Feng's voice floated to him as if on a breeze.

"Perhaps," Parno nodded. "We shall see."

-

"What are you doing?"

Stephanie looked up from her book to see Winnie standing at the entrance to the small garden alcove. Stephanie had retreated here to read in silence, relishing the absence of constant chatter found in the palace.

"So, you're talking to me again?" Stephanie smiled, closing the book after placing a mark to keep her place.

"Humph," Winnie turned her head, looking out over the rest of the garden. "I shouldn't speak to nary a one of you ever again!"

Stephanie couldn't help but grin at that. For two days she and Memmnon had kept up the charade of enforced societal norms on the younger woman, Stephanie bearing down on her every move and whim, enforcing even the slightest protocols in her young friend's relationship and courtship with the King. Finally, it had been too much and both had broken at supper three nights ago, laughing so hard that tears had rolled. Winnie had been somewhat less amused and had not spoken to either of them since until now.

"Then why are you?" Stephanie laughed, getting to her feet. "You must need something," she teased and Winnie's face reddened.

"Winnie, you're going to have to learn the difference of friends picking at you and bullies picking on you," Stephanie told her firmly. "Yes, Memmnon and I had some fun at your expense, but you had that coming for you behavior. And for thinking you had trapped or tricked me into staying here with you as well," she added. She was rewarded with a slow creeping flush that began below Winnie's neckline and rose to color her entire face.

"Fine," she admitted. "I might have had it coming," she said it so reluctantly that Stephanie could imagine it causing actual pain.

"So, what have you been doing while you've been pouting?" Stephanie asked her.

"I wasn't-" Winnie began, then cut herself off, refusing to rise to the bait again. "I've been doing my classes and practicing my speech."

"Good," Stephanie nodded seriously. "That's good. Your studies?"

"I'm doing them," Winnie sounded a bit more unsure of herself there. "That's not as easy."

"You just have to concentrate," Stephanie told her encouragingly. "You really need to know the history of the kingdom and it's dynasty, considering you will be Queen soon."

"Yeah, no pressure," Winnie snorted.

"There isn't any," Stephanie nodded in agreement. "Memmnon already told you that. You need this for your children, when you have them. They will come to you as their source of trusted information. You want to be able to provide it and this will help you do that."

"What about you?" Winnie asked, getting to the reason she had looked her friend up to start with.

"What about me?" the doctor asked.

"What are you going to do about you and Parno?" Winnie asked more directly.

"There's nothing to do," Stephanie sighed. "I told you Winnie. I burned that bridge pretty thoroughly. My fault, but it's still done. Parno has been betrayed so many times in his life that it has become the regular state of things for him. There's no way he will see what happened with me as anything else but another betrayal. My carelessness ruined everything I'd worked for," she sighed again, taking her seat once more.

Winnie frowned. She hadn't meant to make Stephanie more despondent.

"You can't just leave it like that," she insisted, joining her friend on the bench.

"Even if you're right and there's no hope of fixing it, you can't really know that 'til you try. And if you don't try, then you'll regret it your whole rest of your life."

"It's either 'your whole life' or 'rest of your life', Winnie," Stephanie corrected. "Not both."

"Don't change the subject," Winnie shot back at her. "You know I'm right. You can't just give up."

"The problem is not knowing when to give up," Stephanie sighed. "Had I stopped pestering him when he asked me to then I'd not be in this mess. When he explained so very calmly and rationally why my way wouldn't work, I should have let it drop. Instead I kept pushing and then got angry with him when he just repeated the same arguments. And I let my anger lead me to say a great many things I shouldn't have. He needed, he deserved my support in all of this and all I did was make things worse for him. And then when he didn't do what I wanted, I spoke terribly to him. Now what kind of wife will I make?" she asked her friend with a sad smile. "My prospective husband saddled literally with the survival of the Kingdom and he rides to war with the last words I said to him being basically that he was selfish and I was glad to see him go."

"Ever' body makes mistakes," Winnie insisted. "You ain't no different than nobody else."

"It's not the mistake that makes it difficult dear," Stephanie replied softly. "It's who makes it and who it's made to. I probably couldn't have done anything worse than what I did."

"He'll forgive you, but you have to ask him first," Winnie was steadfast. "Only you're too stubborn to do it, seems like."

"You don't know him as I do, Winnie," Stephanie settled for saying. "He has had a very hard life and has learned to be distrustful as a defense mechanism. He let me inside that mechanism, only to have me do what I did. He will not make the same mistake again. He learns quickly."

"He'll forgive you if you ask him," Winnie said again. "And you know it, I think. You're just punishing yourself for what you did by doing this. Only problem is you're punishing him too."

"I really don't wish to discuss this anymore," Stephanie stood again, her face suddenly rigid. "I do appreciate your attempts to cheer me, but I do not want to continue dwelling on this."

"If that's what you want," Winnie nodded. "I came to see if you wanted to take a ride with me. I'm tired of sitting here and I'm getting out for a while. I'm going to go and visit the refugees and see how they are, and maybe have a look see around the city."

"I'd like that," Stephanie nodded at once. "Getting out of here would be a break, even for a little while."

-

Sarah Williams blew hair from her face as she washed her son's clothes for the first time since she had been forced to take her two small children and flee her home ahead of the Nor invasion. She took a minute to look around her and make sure that her son Micah, four, and daughter Lucinda, seven, were within her line of sight. She had allowed them to play with other children while she worked, knowing the two needed the distraction as much as she did. Things had been hard for that last several weeks, and only in the last few days had her children actually had enough to eat or clean water to drink, not to mention been able to bathe properly in far too long.

She had left with little more than the clothes on her back when she saw the beaten soldiers of 2nd Corps retreating through her small town. Her husband dead for two years, Sarah made a living for her and her two children doing laundry for most of the rest of her small town and by serving as a midwife for expectant women in her area. Being educated, she also assisted in teaching school three days each week which had helped her manage to keep her head above water and leave a little left over for the things her children wanted.

All that was gone now, left behind in the mad dash to get to safety ahead of the Nor heathen invading their land. At less than thirty years old, full of figure and not unpleasant to look upon according to more than one lecherous old man, she was all too aware of what fate awaited her at the hands of their invaders, and what that fate meant for her children. Taking what she could carry in a small backpack and preparing a small pack for each child to carry a random toy or doll as well as a change of clothes, Sarah had set out within an hour of the first ambulances rolling through town ferrying wounded south. While others had mocked her for doing so, she noted that she had seen none of them since.

Maybe they were safe and sound still in their own homes while she as stuck living in a soldier's barracks, but she doubted it. That wasn't the Nor way. And she had heard more than once that the horrible Tribal Horsemen were among the invaders as well. A shiver she couldn't suppress ran through her at the thought of the hellish horse soldiers running rampant through the south. Her children wouldn't be safe from them and neither would she.

Nor would anyone who remained behind and got caught by the paint wearing devils, that was certain.

She admitted that this was far from ideal, living in a barracks and dependent on others for feeding and caring for her children, but at the moment it was all she had, and she was grateful for it. Wishing you still had your own living and your own home wasn't the same as being ungrateful for what you did have.

And there were several able-bodied men among the refugees that had given her the eye more than once over the last week that were no longer allowed around the women and children. That lone was worth being at least somewhat dependent on others, just to be in relative safety.

She wasn't the only woman here with small children either. And there were men as well, though most were well past the age of serving in the military, unlike those who had given her the eye before. None of those scoundrels had apparently had wives or children either one to care for and spent their days being mouthy and threatening. She was certain that had Lady Winifred not come upon them and used her own guard to protect and care for them that her own safety would not have been certain more than another night or two. And with her went her children.

She hoped that the guard had drug the lay-about bastards away to be forced into the army. That way the Kingdom could get some good from their useless hides and protect their victims at the same time. It would serve them right for preying on the helpless in such times as these.

A stir among the crowd of refugees her attention and she stood up, washing still in hand, to see two women, heavily escorted, riding her way. The two were looking over the camp with a judging eye, and even in the distance Sarah could recognize the red mane of Lady Winifred. Smiling, she hurriedly finished her chore of washing, wringing the small suit for her son out and hanging it across a fence to dry as Lady Winifred drew reign before her barracks.

"Hello Miss Williams," Lady Winifred smiled. "How are you faring?" Sarah was flattered that the young woman remembered her name from among so many.

"I'm well, milady," Sarah promised, walking to where the two women still sat their horses. "How are you?"

"I told you it's just Winnie," Winifred semi-scolded. "I'm well, thank you. Are you getting along alright?"

"We are," Sarah assured her. "I must thank you again, milady, for all you've done. My two children are much better off than at any time in recent weeks thanks to you. I shall never be able to repay your kindness."

"There is no payment required," Winnie promised. "It is the Kingdom that owes you. The army is doing all it can to push the Nor back, but until your homes are freed we must look after our own as best we can. Speaking of which, has Minister Philo been through to see you all?"

"The Agriculture man?" Sarah clarified. "Yes, he was here two days past," she replied to Winnie's nod. "He spoke of our moving soon to areas where we could plant and grow food and establish new living areas until the current crisis has passed."

"Yes," Winnie nodded. "I had hoped to be able to keep everyone here, but there isn't enough room for so many to raise a garden to help feed yourselves. Also, Minister Philo believes that once the camps are established, we will be able to provide at least some stock to each area for milk and eventually meat, provided we have sufficient breeding stock in each camp."

"That is what I was told," Sarah affirmed.

"Is there anything you need right away?" Winnie asked her.

"Well," Sarah mused. "There are a number of pregnant women among the refugees right now. I've served as a midwife for some time myself, so if I could get access to the supplies I need I could continue to do that now. I don't need much, really. A scope and a few other instruments, along with a few tools to make supplements and extract vitamin nutrients."

"How much training do you have?" the second woman asked suddenly, a slight frown of concentration on her face.

"I apprenticed under an older woman in my town for two years, and assisted the doctor before he went north with the army," Sarah replied.

"Sarah, this is Doctor Stephanie Freeman-Corsin, the Royal Physician," Winnie introduced.

"Pleasure, miss," Sarah bowed slightly.

"Mine as well," Stephanie smiled slightly. "Do you have time to answer a few questions for me, Miss Williams?" she asked.

"Of course," Sarah nodded. The dark-haired woman dismounted then and passed her reins to a green and black clad cavalry man.

"Tell me what you know about…"

-

"How is. . .trying to kill. . .us. . .making us bet. . .better soldiers?"

This was a question asked by more than one 1st Corps soldier as the first day's training came to an end. Graham was gasping for air himself as he heard one of his officers asking the same question he and others were thinking.

"I'm. . .told that it. . .it's a matter of. . .conditioning," he offered. "The mo…more we do. . . this, th. . .the easier it be. . .becomes."

"I di. . .did note that. . .the instructors ran right alongs... alongside us," another said, nodding jerkily. "And they don. . .don't seem to be breathing. . .so hard."

"They been do. . .doing this a lo. . .lot longer," Graham told him. "Prince Parno did it too," he gasped out in one breath.

"Really?" that perked the nearby officers up. "The Mar. . .Marshal went through this?"

"Right along with his men," Graham nodded. "And if. . .if they can do it then s. . .so can we!" he forced out. "I don't want to see a single man falling out of line, do you. . .you hear me?" he stood before them despite his heaving lungs. "If a bunch of criminals and pansies can get through this, then 1st Corps can damn sure do. . .do it too," he was finally getting his breathing under control.

"Yes sir." The collected gasp of his officers would have been funny if he hadn't been gasping right along with them.

Several yards away, a group of green and black clad men stood comparing notes.

"Weak as water," one said flatly. "Ain't none of 'em could make a day in the Regiment."

"Neither could we when we started," a second noted and the others, including the first speaker, nodded.

"True that," a third agreed. "And none of 'em quit, I note," he added.

"That is true," the first speaker agreed. "They ain't nothing if not determined. And the General included," he chuckled. "Be lucky he don't kill his fool self trying to make sure he leads the way."

"Reckon that will make his men follow through," someone else said.

"I think they can make it, assuming they keep this up," was the general consensus when spoken by the leader of the group. "Reckon we can tell the Colonel they'll probably make it a day or two anyways."

"Be Cho's turn tomorrow," one chuckled. "Least they'll get to sit down some for that."

-

"Miss Williams," Stephanie said after quizzing Sarah for several minutes, "your knowledge seems to exceed that of the usual mid-wife. You're almost a nurse in terms of knowledge and ability."

"Thank you miss," Sarah nodded. "I learned a great deal from the doctor these two years before the war. He had a small library and I was able to borrow and read a good many of his books. I learned a great deal from them, and from him."

"Don't thank me, I'm just being honest," Stephanie shook her head. "As it happens, I run a school for military surgeons at Cove Canton and am establishing another school here for both surgeons and nurses. Is that something that would interest you? Serving the Kingdom as a nurse? Perhaps even as a physician, assuming you can handle the study load?"

"Ph...physician?" Sarah was stunned. "Miss, I...milady I don't know that I could-"

"You're obviously well educated," Stephanie cut her off gently. "And intelligent. There's no reason you couldn't do it if you were so inclined. The decision is yours of course, but I think you would be perfect for it."

"Miss, I have two small children," Sarah said softly. "I...I have to see to their care above all else."

"Rightly so," Stephanie approved of the woman's dedication. "But what if I can arrange suitable childcare for you? Someone to watch over and safeguard your children while you study? You would attend class and serve in the hospitals around Nasil as well, your time split about evenly between the two. You would be paid for your work of course, a small stipend, and I will ensure you have a place to stay and are provided with meals. I admit it may not always be varied much but it will be filling and plentiful. You and your children will be taken care of, assuming you wish to participate. And you would have time for your children in the evenings before bed time, at least when not working in the hospital once your training is finished."

"I...I don't know that I could do it, Miss," Sarah admitted. "What if I tried and failed?"

"You can't fail the nurse part," Stephanie shook her head. "As I said, you're almost there now, and a woman of your obvious education will have no trouble finishing the program. You will be able to test out on the beginning part of the course I feel certain. Even if you can't, you will still be well ahead of the norm. We aren't desperate for nurses yet, but that time is coming," she confided softly. "I'm trying to get ahead of the need by finding people that can serve now and having them ready to meet that need when it comes."

"I...I didn't think the military allowed women to serve," Sarah temporized. A physician? Her?

"They don't allow it on the lines," Stephanie nodded. "For good reason. It's no place for a woman and I speak from bitter experience," she added, thinking about the Gap. "But with so many men serving, women are having to fill the gaps left by their absence, and the medical field is one of those areas. A large one at that. It's not just military, either," she pointed out. "We all have need of medical help at some point, military or civilian. There will be a shortage of doctors for some time to come I fear, and nurses especially will be in short supply. As you pointed out yourself, if nothing else there are expectant women to be cared for."

"I will see to it that an adequate care facility for your children and any others is provided, Sarah," Winnie offered. "There are likely some women among you who wouldn't be able to work a farm but can and would care for children, including continuing their education where needful. You probably aren't the only woman among the refugees who might be qualified for Stephanie's programs."

"There are a right few women here who have at least as much education as I do," Sarah nodded in agreement. "And there are at least a handful of school teachers. They've already been working to make sure the children don't suffer too much disruption in their learning."

"Introduce us then, at least to the ones you know," Winnie ordered, stepping down from her own horse and passing the reins over. Four men and two female constables dismounted with her but remained unobtrusive.

"Please," Stephanie agreed. "We need all the help we can get."

-

"Well?" Parno asked as Karls walked into his small camp later that evening. "How'd it go?"

"None of them died," Karls chuckled. "Honestly, they did about as well as you could expect, not having done much of that sort. And Graham hung in to the last as well," he added.

"May have had him wrong," Parno nodded thoughtfully. "I don't think he's that good an actor, and he was stunned to learn what all Therron had done. Swore to try his best to complete the course and expected the same treatment as any of his men should he fail."

"That's a good start anyway," Karls nodded in agreement. "And he worked. Didn't complain, didn't try to pull rank, nothing. Didn't offer to entertain his officer's complaints either. He let the instructors do the talking when it was needful and just concentrated on getting through the day himself."

"Well, he was true to his word for one day, anyway," Parno sighed. "Have to see if that continues."

"What about your day?" Karls asked.

"Same as always," Parno shrugged. "Reports, meetings, issues to solve, that sort of thing. With 2nd Corps on their way, all I need do is finalize the plans for the units headed into the central highlands and I'll be done for the moment. After that it's hit, feint, repeat for the foreseeable future."

"Any word from Beaumont?" Karls asked.

"I don't expect any unless they have trouble," Parno replied. "And honestly that's Memmnon's headache now that he's awake and aware and doing well. I have enough on my plate as it is. Not to mention that I need to stay as far from Therron as I can so that I don't have to try and overpower the urge to kill him."

"I see," Karls nodded. He had thought he and Enri had difficulties.

"Anyway," Parno stood up, stretching. "I need to go meet with Davies. The man he's selected to lead the troop into the mid province above the capitol is coming and I want to meet him. Welcome to come along if you'd like," he added.

"Okay."

Brigadier Nelson Pierce was uneasy. He had been singled out from his own command in 2nd Corps and told to stay behind, reporting to General Davies this evening. He knew of no reason why he would be relieved of his command, having performed well, or so he thought, since the war began. He had led the retreat from the bridges in good order, having been promoted to full Brigadier following that action and had continued to lead his men well since.

Yet what remained of his men and the new men that had replaced his losses were even now on their way to the Marshal's home posting for retraining, rest and refit while he himself stood here waiting to see General Davies.

Perhaps it's a staff assignment, he told himself. He didn't want such a posting, but working for General Davies would be fine. He had served the General for many years and now that Davies commanded an entire army group, he would want experienced officers to staff it.

"Good evening Nelson," Davies' voice cut into his rumination and Pierce shot to attention.

"Evening sir."

"At ease," Davies told him, waving the man forward into a chair near his field desk. "I know you're wondering what this is about," Davies said at once. "First of all let me assure you that you've done nothing wrong. The fact is that I have a new assignment for you, and your past performance is one of the reasons I've chosen you for it."

"Sir," Pierce nodded.

"The Marshal has ordered a force prepared from organic units that answer to no higher command and sent into the central Tinsee highlands, north of the capitol and the Cumberland River as a screen against attack from that direction and down the river itself." He indicated the map before him. "The Cumberland itself, if they can navigate it down, is a natural invasion route to the capitol and with 1st Corps in the field, there's little left there in the way of defense."

"Yes sir."

"I've decided to give this command to you, pending the Marshal's approval, and send you into this area to prevent the Nor from being able to approach the capitol undetected."

"Sir," Pierce leaned forward, interested now. It wasn't a staff assignment after all.

"I'm sure you'd rather have your old command, but that won't be the case here," Davies was apologetic. "Your men need the rest and time to refit, and their retraining will take time. Normally I'd have sent you along with them but the truth is you're more than capable of exercising independent command and that's what this is for the most part. You'll have to decide what you can handle on your own and what you'll need to send for help over. In addition, you'll have to support the River Guard. They are currently pulling all available forces they can together and placing them here to guard against incursion by boat, supported by some experimental artillery units that should be able to deter any boat parties. They will require land support which you will have to provide from your command."

"What kind of artillery, sir?" Pierce asked.

"I'm told it will be very similar to the highly effective rounds we used in repulsing the last Imperial attack on this position," Davies assured him. "Their orders are to remain undetected unless and until a major incursion is spotted, at which point their orders will be to destroy it if at all possible. That's why they will need support from you. In the event that the boat force is able to land, your men will have to either protect the artillery forces as they withdraw, or help them reduce the enemy, whichever is more practicable. Meanwhile," Davies moved his hand back to the area north of the river and the capitol, "you will have to patrol this area on a regular and random basis, keeping an eye out for Imperial troops, especially cavalry raids and any possible force that might threaten a river crossing into Nasil. You will have to evaluate each one and determine if you can hold unaided, and if not then send for help." He looked at Pierce.

"And there's the rub. Every time you call for help, it will have to come from somewhere we need the troops already there. From here, for instance, or elsewhere. There is a small force of the Prince's Own finishing their training cycle at Cove, and a larger force that is a few weeks into it. I'm told once the Prince's Own contingent is finished, they will move into the area to support you in a likelihood, and that the cavalry division now training at Cove Canton will be available to backstop you as necessary. But if you can handle the threat on your own, that is preferable to pulling men from other areas."

"I see, sir," Pierce nodded. "What kind of force will I have to call upon?"

"Your strength will be centered on the 31st Mounted Infantry, Independent Brigade. Their strength is around thirty-five hundred effective at the time of their arrival here with Freeman's Corps. Here is a list of other units, all separate and independent units, that will be attached. Cavalry, a Pioneer company, additional mounted infantry and even one regiment of foot soldiers to garrison choke points or other areas you feel the need. They would be a good choice to backstop the River Guard for instance, but I leave that up to you. All totaled, you'll have about six thousand men, all well trained but for the most part unblooded."

"A good number, sir," Pierce nodded, looking over the organization of the unit he'd be commanding.

"It is until the scope of your operation hits home," Davies sighed. "That's a lot of ground to cover."

"But not all of it is passable, sir," Pierce said, rising from his seat and moving to the map. "A lot of this area is so rough that even unsupported cavalry would have a difficult time getting through it without loss. Some of these roads are little more than mountain trails and they aren't well kept simply because very few people use them. The people living here are hardy and often wild as well, sir. The Imperials will lose men to random archery attacks simply because the people of that area will see killing them as a challenge. They'll also see their presence as a challenge that has to be answered. If the Nor do send men into this area, those people will fade into the hills and then hit and run against them, stealing horses, killing sentries and so on."

"There are a few passes where a sizable force could come through, and I'll have scouts well ahead of them while using the Pioneers and any available local help to prepare blockages for those passes. Anything to slow their advance and make targets of them. And as you said, assigning the foot regiment to the River Guard is the most sensible thing to do in this case. Their lack of mobility would limit their usefulness in the highlands, but make them ideal for the static defense needed along the river itself. I can assign a company of cavalry to act as runners and scouts for them from wherever they decide to set up shop."

"That's an excellent idea," a new voice spoke and both men turned to see Parno McLeod standing just inside the tent, flanked by a colonel wearing the black and green of the McLeod Dynasty and a foreigner wearing similar colors though not in uniform.

"Marshal," Davies nodded while Pierce came to attention.

"Stand easy," Parno ordered, moving forward. "Sounds like you chose the right man for the job, General," he said to Davies.

"Then Colonel Pierce led the rear guard as we withdrew from Lovil," Davies nodded. "Held far longer than anyone had any right to expect as well. Were it not for him, I don't know how much worse things might have been."

"You speak as if you know the area well, Brigadier," Parno turned to Pierce.

"Somewhat, sir," the man nodded. "I was raised around this area in different places until I joined the army. I was singled out for officer school and then War College because I also had a decent education thanks to my mother. Her family have lived in these hills since before Tyree's time, milord."

"Outstanding," Parno was glad to hear it. "That makes you doubly able for this position then. Do you see any problems we've overlooked?"

"No sir, I don't," Pierce admitted, looking back to the map. "Supply shouldn't be a problem as We'll have Nasil to our back, and we'll have sufficient manpower to keep scouts out along any likely trails. The only thing I could ask for would be additional Pioneer units if they're available to hasten our ability to block roads and passes. It's hard, dirty work and one company would be hard pressed to do it all in a timely manner."

"Well, it so happens I can do that," Parno nodded. "I operate an Engineering school at Cove Canton and this would give them some much needed hands on training. I'll send a messenger to them tomorrow ordering them to send all those ready or nearly ready to graduate to assist you. Where will you try to make your headquarters, Brigadier? Since you know the area, I think it best to let you decide where to meet up."

"I think Springfield, sir, assuming we don't get there and find Imperial troops already in the area," Pierce said after a minute, pointing to a small dot on the map. "It's well north of the capitol and there are good roads to and from. We can scout the provincial line between there and Kenty, blocking the roads and passes I spoke of, enlisting the aid of the locals, as well as deploying scouts of our own."

"Sensible," Parno nodded. "Very well Brigadier," Parno said finally. "General Davies' confidence in you seems most well founded. Assemble your men and prepare them for immediate departure. The sooner the better in fact."

"Assuming that all commands are in good stead we should be able to leave tomorrow, though it will likely be approaching noon," Pierce mused. "I will speak to the assembled commanders as soon as I can this evening to ascertain readiness. If we can depart on time and have no issues, I estimate we can be on site and working in a week to ten days, depending on what we find."

"Excellent," Parno nodded again. "Godspeed, Brigadier."

"Thank you, Marshal."

CHAPTER EIGHT

-

"So, we'll be keeping some of the refugees here after all."

Memmnon was seated at the head of his conference table, with Winnie to his right and Stephanie to his left. Minister Philo was there along with Sebastian Grey and Howard Govan. Aides were in attendance as well as scribes to record what decisions were made.

"Yes," Philo nodded, glancing at Winnie. "Lady Winifred's notion to keep underage children and their parents here in the city bears some merit, Highness. Simply put, children too young to be of use in farming or other operations would be at risk and their education will probably suffer as well. If we are to maintain any sense of normalcy, we must include learning for the next generation."

"That is true," Memmnon nodded. "They are the ones we fight for the most, after all. I understand you have made arrangements to create care for the children while their mothers work in some capacity?" he looked at Winnie.

"Yes," she nodded. "There were a number of school teachers in the refugees and other educated women as well. While we debated on sending teachers with each group and the children with them, in the end we decided to send teachers with each group that has children, and try to group the children so that more than one teacher can be sent with that group or groups. Some groups will be made up of people who have no children and aren't likely to have any. Those work groups will be sent into areas that will let them provide for themselves as well as support the war effort with things like logging and mining where needful. Some will also participate in industry throughout the Basin. There are a number of men who can work in those arenas that are unable to serve in combat."

"Excellent idea," Memmnon approved. "And I believe you have recruited from among the refugees as well, Doctor?" he turned to Stephanie.

"I have, Highness," she nodded. "Several women of higher learning and some who already have medical experience will be incorporated into my new School of Nursing here in Nasil. Some of them will no doubt show aptitude enough to move into medicine themselves with a bit of experience and education. We will have need of many more nurses and surgeons before this is finished. Already we are shorthanded due to the high number of injured from the battles already fought. It will only get worse."

"Also true," Memmnon nodded.

"Women surgeons?" Sebastian Grey semi-objected. "Are we really contemplating women surgeons in the army?"

"And what might that problem be?" Stephanie's icy voice floated down the table.

"It's not done!" Grey thundered, forgetting who he was talking to for a second.

"I've heard that all my life," Stephanie said calmly. "And yet, here I sit. The Royal Physician, founder of the Cove Canton Military Surgeon School, and now the Nasil Military Medical Academy. And I remind you that I am the sole person at this table that was at the Battle of the Gap." Her voice was like iron for all it was soft.

"I believe she has you there, Sebastian," Memmnon smiled sardonically. "It's time we stopped limiting women in their roles, gentlemen. In Tyree's time women served in combat if you recall your history. I admit that was a different time and their weapons were much better than our own, allowing women parity in battle. My own betrothed is one of the most accomplished archers in the Kingdom and has trained more archers to expert level than anyone else I know personally. While I agree with my brother than serving in open combat is not acceptable for our women, restricting them in their roles elsewhere is stupid and wasteful. Parno told me of a woman he met in the west who commands a listening and observation post on her land along the Great River, and does so with skill." He leaned forward slightly, getting the attention of everyone at the table.

"There will be no more talk of restricting women in roles they can fulfill in support of the Kingdom's war effort. Nor will I entertain any more objections to it. Enough is enough. Women want to serve, and in areas where they can they will be allowed to do so. I trust I have made myself clear on this?"

"Aye, Highness," Grey muttered as the other men at the table nodded their assent. Winnie practically beamed at Memmnon's side but not where he could see it. Stephanie felt vindicated as well by the King's pronouncement but didn't push that. Her point was made, that was all that mattered.

"The first refugee resettlement groups will be moving out tomorrow," Philo returned to the business at hand. "Three groups headed for Royal Reserves in the Basin, south of the river. The area north of Bingham in fact."

"I want a strong presence in that area to keep down banditry," Memmnon ordered. "With so few able-bodied men they will make an inviting target."

"We've seen to it," Govan nodded. "These three groups are large and well equipped, and will be near each other as well. No more than ten miles between them at the furthest point. As soon as their crops are in they will be stockading their living areas as well. We have a Pioneer company and a platoon of Royal Engineers going with them. They aren't pleased about that, by the way," he added.

"I'll speak to the Chief Engineer today," Memmnon promised. "They'll be delighted by this afternoon."

"Now that I'm thinking about it," Memmnon mused, "I want all the women who are able to draw a bow to be armed with one and given proper instructions in using it. There's no reason for them to be victims of a crime simply because they have no means to defend themselves. Every woman who wants one should be issued a dagger as well, and a short sword if they wish. I know for a fact that women can wield them with proper training. I will make sure that Colonels Moore and Stang provide sufficient men to accompany the refugees and provide such instruction."

"Sir, weakening the capitol isn't a good idea," Grey objected.

"It's for a limited time and in limited numbers, Sebastian," Memmnon parried. "And it will be done. We have failed our people quite enough of late. There will be no more of it."

"We will likewise begin offering the same training to women here in the city," he decreed suddenly. "There are many healthy women here who would no doubt make fine archers if given the opportunity. We shall give them that opportunity if they desire it. That I will leave to you," he turned to Winnie. "You have served as an archery instructor before, and seeing you shoot should embolden even the most timid of women to try the bow should they desire."

"Of course," Winnie managed not to stammer. "Whatever pleases you, my Lord," she bowed her head regally and Stephanie had to fight to keep from beaming proudly. Winnie had come a long way in a short time.

"Anything else?" Memmnon asked the assembled group.

"The Generals from the War College want to meet with you about the strategy we are using in the war," Howard Govan spoke. "They believe that we should be pushing against the Nor now, regaining our crop land in time for planting."

"Parno has put forth an excellent reason for that not to be done now," Memmnon replied. "If they feel they must object, they may do so, but warn them now," he leaned forward again. "Their arguments had better be based on fact and figure rather than some dislike for my brother. He alone had produced victories in combat against the Imperial invasion. All they have done is posture and support my brother Therron in his ruinous command. If they want to keep their heads about them, suggest they keep their heads about them, if you take my meaning."

"I do," Govan nodded, fighting off a smile. "I'm sure none of them will have the fortitude to face you directly."

"That means they will try to do it surreptitiously, which I like even less," Memmnon frowned. "Sebastian, are we keeping an eye on Therron's friends?"

"We are, milord," Grey nodded firmly. "Including them. Not all of them were loyal to Therron, and some of those who were have abandoned that line in light of the death of your father."

"Good," Memmnon nodded. "Allow the three most ardent objectors to see me. Schedule it for tomorrow, I suppose, though you'll need to check with my secretary to ensure I have an opening."

"As soon as we adjourn, Your Highness," Govan nodded.

"Well then, I believe we can adjourn."

-

"You're not doing this just to pacify me, are you?" Winnie asked as the meeting broke apart. She and Memmnon were alone other than Stephanie.

"Doing what?" Memmnon frowned. "The archery instruction? In what way will that pacify you?"

"You know what I mean," Winnie developed a frown of her own.

"For once, I do not," Memmnon told her. "One of the things Parno is concerned about is a raid in force making way down the river to the capitol. As Grey pointed out, we are weak here at the moment. Should a sizable force indeed make it this far then having a force of women who can man the fortress walls and shoot accurately might make the difference in a bit of damage here and there as opposed to a high casualty count and a raid that could do real damage and hurt morale. It is simply a matter of making use of every resource we have."

"You aren't afraid they'll be injured in combat?" Winnie asked.

"Of course, I am," Memmnon replied, exasperated. "But will they be any less injured if they are wounded or killed or. . .what have you, by a raiding force? I think not. At least this way those who want the means of fighting back will have them."

"Okay," Winnie nodded, satisfied with the answer. "There are a number of young women from the refugee group that wanted to remain here. I could train them as sort of an auxiliary unit to supplement the City Guard and what have you."

"No," Memmnon shook his head. "Those who are going in the groups need the training as well, and they will get it, but we need them where they are just as bad. Growing food and producing war material is just as vital as anything else they could do here. We must limit our numbers in the capitol to what we can sustain here on our own. And every one of them you remove from the refugee resettlement is a bow lost to them should the need arise."

"True," Winnie frowned, not having thought that through. "Still, we could lead-"

"No," Memmnon's voice was firm this time. "I want them able to defend themselves, and help defend their homes or this city if it is their home, but there will be no field unit of women warriors, Winifred. The risks are too great and I will not take them. I would ask that you not foment such a plan to others, either. Do not try and go around me in this. I will bend so far but no farther and that is too far."

"As you wish," Winnie sighed. "I think it's a mistake," she had to add.

"It may well be but it is my mistake to make," Memmnon replied. "And you will have quite enough to do I should think teaching archery to so many."

"So, I will," she admitted. "So I will."

-

"We will stop at the next house," Sherron declared. "I'm tired."

"No."

Callens' voice was calm and firm. It took Sherron McLeod a second to realize what he had said.

"What?" her voice was sharp. "What did you say?"

"I've knuckled under to you enough," he said flatly. "We are being pursued whether you believe it or not, and every time we stop when we should be moving they gain on us. We will keep moving. We will keep moving until we cannot see the road. At that point we will stop, care for the horses, rest as we can and be back on the road with the sun. You will complain, but you will do as you are told. You are no longer in charge."

"How dare you! I am the Prince-"

"You are nothing without Therron and we can't get to him stopping after ten miles a day for you to 'rest'," Callens cut her off flatly. "We must get to Prince Therron. Thanks to you he is now the legitimate heir for a kingdom that is at war and essentially has no leader. Enough. Make yourself comfortable in your carriage and be silent."

"When we get to Therron I'll have you-"

"Have me what?" he asked her suddenly. "Killed? Don't you think I'm already a dead man? I was standing there when you killed the King and the Crown Prince. There is no escape for me, you vile witch. I allowed you to ensnare me with your promises and hints and teases, but there is nothing for me now. And to my shame I have dragged my men, loyal soldiers of Soulan all, along with me straight to hell following your whispers and teasing."

Sherron looked at him, blinking.

"So, keep your teeth together, be silent and enjoy the trip." With that he rode ahead, leaving a sputtering Sherron McLeod behind him, speechless for the first time since he had known her.

-

Therron McLeod was walking the beach once more, his feet bare, shirtless, he basked in the warm sun as he ambled down the beach.

He wondered why he had ever worked so hard. This wasn't a bad life at all, he decided. True, he lacked real freedom, but other than that, living here along the ocean in a nominally temperate climate with almost eternally good weather? He had a small staff in addition to his 'guard', and the food was first rate. He had books, he had everything he could wish for other than freedom.

Perhaps freedom was overrated? Perhaps ruling was overrated? Had he made a mistake in thinking that he really wanted to be King?

No. His thought process came full circle as he continued his walk. It had never been about him. It had been about what was best for the Kingdom. The Kingdom needed a leader. A strong leader. His brother was not a bad man but Memmnon would never make the strong leader that Soulan needed.

And now the army, the magnificent fighting machine he had spent years building and bending to his will was being commanded his inept younger brother. His army, his stepping stone to power in the hands of Parno of all people. He wondered how much damage his brother had done to the army already.

Kicking the sand that was no longer so comfortable, Therron McLeod continued on his way down the beach. His temporary moment of self-doubt gone as he reminded himself that it was always about what was best for the Kingdom. Not him.

Therron was selfless. He was willing to sacrifice for the Kingdom. He would return and take the throne from Memmnon and lead the Kingdom to victory because only he, Therron McLeod, could do that. That was what he told himself. What he had always told himself to justify what he did or planned to do.

He had to get away from here and back to Nasil before his brothers destroyed everything. Only he could save Soulan.

-

"Have you considered that we're going about this wrong?" Whipple asked.

"What?" Beaumont looked around in the saddle.

"We know where Prince Therron is, so why follow Callens? Let us go straight to the Horn and take custody of the Prince and be done with it. We can be there waiting for them when they arrive."

"We're gaining," Beaumont shook his head. "We should stay on the trail."

"There's no reason to chase after them, Buford," Whipple persisted. "We can force an engagement there and run them to ground. There won't be any way for them to take the Prince, and that's the main thing. He is the only legitimate threat to the throne."

"She killed the King!" Beaumont shot back. "And Callens helped! We are not going to let them go!"

"I'm not suggesting that we let them go," Whipple fought to prevent his exasperation showing. "We won't be letting anyone go. We'll simply be setting a trap for the people we want by using the person they want as bait!"

Beaumont had his mouth open to reply when Whipple's comment seemed to hit home.

"See what I mean?" Whipple seized on the moment. "We let them come to us. They don't know we're after them. They don't know that Prince Memmnon is now King. They think the Kingdom is in tatters because she killed the King and the Crown Prince. They intend to return to Nasil as conquering heroes and place Therron on the throne."

That was all true. Beaumont knew that. He also recognized that he was intent on catching the Princess and Callens because of the murder of his Sovereign.

"I see what you mean," he admitted, almost against his will. "What if they don't go to the Horn?" he asked.

"Where else can they go?" Whipple countered. "They have to have Therron to survive. They literally have no choice but to go to him and free him. They can't make it without him."

Also true.

"How much damage can Callens do if we let him continue running unchecked?" Beaumont asked.

"As news spreads?" Whipple asked. "There's only so much he can do. True, he has an elite unit that can cause a great deal of damage, but it's still one regiment. That's all. And once we secure Therron, then we can ride them down and kill them all."

At times like this Beaumont was reminded that Whipple, for all his noble suave, was underneath his calm exterior a violent man who lived for combat.

"All right," he made a decision based on Whipple's argument. "Let's head for the Horn now. No more delay and no more tracking. We'll get ahead of them if we can and be waiting for them. And kill them all," he repeated, much to Whipple's obvious delight.

"Now you're talking!"

-

It took three days instead of two to get the resettlement groups on the road but they were finally moving. Wagons drawn by horses that were not capable of combat and by oxen that would double as plow animals when the refugees began to plant were loaded to the gills with seed, tools, tarps, clothing and anything else that Winnie and the others could imagine them needing. There was some grumbling among them as they moved out, many feeling they should have been allowed to stay in the Royal City. The simple truth was that there wasn't enough room for them. Refugees were still pouring in though the number was slowing as the bulk of those displaced by the invasion found their way somewhere safer. Many had found places with family further south, others had found work with the booming war economy.

But many more had nowhere to go. Nowhere except into the mass of refugees that were headed for places like Nasil. Places where they assumed safety awaited.

In that same three days Winnie had secured numerous bows and a goodly supply of arrows suitable for practice. A total of one hundred and eighty-seven women from those remaining behind and from women living in the city had stepped forward to ask for training in archery.

Stephanie had found an even dozen women and five men unable to serve in the army that were interested in the nurse training, including Sarah Williams. All of them were higher than average educated and showed promise. Even now they were being inducted into the school. Winnie had hired eleven women from the refugees with small children that would be staying to open and maintain a childcare facility for those who were participating in any part of the war effort.

A part of this massive operation that was kept secret was the secretion of Royal Constables into each group as refugees. Their mission was simple; keep an eye on the groups and inform Sebastian Grey of any rabble-rousing activity among the refugees.

The Prince taking Havrel Denton into custody and making him talk had been a stroke of great fortune. He had readily given up over a dozen lower and mid-level spies and agents that had been secreted in Nasil alone before the war began. Each of those in turn were slowly being convinced to give up others that they knew not only in Nasil but in other cities as well. Grey's constables were even now following up on that new information and rolling up small cells of agents that were waiting for the right moment to strike. With hard work and vigilance, he felt they would be able to continue to make progress before the agents in place could cause the havoc they were in place to create.

Of course, that was in a perfect world. Grey didn't believe in perfect. For that matter he didn't really believe in good fortune. It stung that the Prince had uncovered the initial spy by simply realizing that this was a man who was set on causing problems wherever he could.

But Grey was a man who learned from his mistakes, hence the constables seeded into the refugee groups, and the others even now circulating through Nasil and the outlying areas. Looking for people who were trying create strife among the Kingdom's citizens or cause trouble for the Crown. He might be caught by surprise, but it wouldn't be because he wasn't looking.

-

"There are five dangerous faults that can and usually will have an effect upon a general," Cho spoke calmly. "What are they?"

"Recklessness-" Parno began.

"Why?" Cho cut him off.

"It can lead the army to destruction. Rushing headlong into a situation results in being susceptible to traps that can destroy the army. Even if the army survives, their confidence in their leader will be shot."

"Continue."

"Cowardice leads to capture," Parno continued. "The loss of the army, even surrendering intact because we lack the courage to fight. Because the leader lacks the courage to fight," he clarified.

"A quick temper. Reacting to an insult without thinking can lead to recklessness. If the leader can be provoked by mere insults into committing his forces without planning, then he invited defeat. A tendency I have in personal matters," he sighed.

"Good," Cho nodded. "Next?"

"A delicate honor that can be shamed into rash behavior," Parno sighed. "Such as the way I tend to jump into things without thinking. These last two are definite failings of mine."

"The fact that you recognize that means it can be overcome," Cho assured him. "Go on."

"Being overly solicitous of the army," Parno concluded. "Of the men that make up the army," he amended. "I can't. . .I can't be afraid to spend them. I shouldn't waste them, but I can't be afraid to use them for fear of losing them." He leaned forward, elbows on knees.

"I concocted this. . .this gambit, this gamble, because I was afraid of losing my army, or of doing so much damage to it that it would be ineffective. How is that different from being overly solicitous? How is it different from being cowardly? It's too late to change now, really, but did I, have I done the right thing?"

"Is it over solicitous of the army to worry that they would lose sufficient strength in the planned offensive to no longer be effective? Where was your concern?"

"It was in preserving the army until we could meet the enemy with some kind of parity," Parno nodded.

"As to cowardice, you have personally led more than one action despite calls from all involved that you not do so," Cho looked rather smug this time. "You have faults, my Prince, rest assured. However, cowardice has never been among them."

"Thanks. I think," Parno grimaced. "I hope that this works," he sighed. "If we can keep them off balance until we can get some better organization, and some better training, then I think we have a chance to really take it to them. The problem is that once we do, we can't let up. We have to keep the pressure on and make them break. I want them streaming back into Norland telling tales of superhuman soldiers who tore through their ranks and left them decimated."

"You wish to use their defeat to spread fear and panic among the northerners," Cho said rather than asked.

"Yes," Parno nodded. "I want them terrified," he said savagely. "I want them so afraid of Soulan troopers that when I take my army across those same bridges they run for their lives. That their army, what's left of it, is quaking in their boots from fear of facing the same soldiers who destroyed their greatest army in an age and sent them reeling." He looked up at Cho.

"That kind of fear can only help my cause. Fear will swell our ranks in their minds, give us numbers greater than we could ever really have. They will spread the rumors of our 'witchcraft,'" he snorted, "and of how we routed and destroyed their armies, and the Nor will think 'surely there must be more of them than we can see. How else could they have done all this.'"

"A good strategy that can be very effective if employed properly," Cho nodded, his face a mask. Parno didn't miss that.

"What is it?" he asked.

"I have said nothing," Cho told him, looking directly into his eyes.

"Cho, you are my most trusted adviser, and my teacher," Parno said softly into the fire lit night. "With Darvo gone, you are all that I have to depend on when it comes to preventing me from making a costly error. From doing something that I can't undo. You can't do that when you don't talk to me."

"What you propose is not an unknown method of warfare in my Kingdom," Cho said suddenly, his voice crisp. His hands clasped behind him, he began to pace slowly about the fire. Parno recognized this as his lecture mode, or at least one of them, but. . .there was something different about it.

"You seek to use terror to aid your cause," he said flatly. "It is an ages old tactic that has worked effectively in many realms, when used correctly. But there is a price, young prince, for using such tactics. A heavy price that is sometimes, most times, difficult to pay. In fact, you will never truly stop paying for it."

"How so?" Parno frowned.

"The use of terror as a military and political weapon is almost as old as warfare and politics itself. Used to spread fear of oneself into areas before an invasion, it can clear non-combatants away and even cause armies to retreat without offering a defense because they fear to engage such a fearsome and deadly foe."

"Good," Parno nodded. "That's what I want!"

"It can also lead disparate and otherwise unfriendly groups to band together against you," Cho told him. "Using the adage, 'the enemy of my enemy must be my friend'. This is not always true."

"I can't see how it would ever be," Parno shook his head. "An enemy is an enemy. Period."

"That alone makes you more intelligent that the majority of leaders in times past or present," Cho actually smiled serenely at hearing his protégé speak so. "But this is not the price I speak of, though it too can be problematic."

"Stories spread by your own mouth will soon become embellished by others, eager to be heard and to be believed. They will enhance your reputation to the point that some will see no hope of stopping you and many will even take their own lives and the lives of their offspring to 'spare' them from your wicked and depraved ways. To prevent their children from being sacrificed to your dark gods, and their flesh from being consumed by your demon soldiers."

"Hold on now!" Parno objected. "Who said anything about sacrifices and demons?"

"You want the enemy to fear you and your 'witchcraft', do you not?" Cho answered. "You wish the Nor to tremble at your name and bow at your feet, no? To be too afraid to stand against you and your men in combat? To think you. . .superhuman was the word used I believe. To think of you as unbeatable. Their people and land as indefensible. Their future as hopeless."

"Sounds so much worse when you say it," Parno muttered, poking the small fire with a stick.

"As I said, the tactic is not unsound, but it can get out of hand." He paused, his head down for a moment. When he looked up again, he face was once more like a mask.

"There was once rumored to be a regiment of great prowess in the highlands near the border of my kingdom. A land of great warriors, these were greater still. So powerful that their leader only made use of them in times of great need. He could not risk calling upon them for minor things it was said, as they might well turn their wrath upon him."

"Neighbors to the north grew bold one season and looked south to fair fields and fresh water, and women. They coveted what this smaller kingdom had, yet the presence of this great war tribe made them hesitate. What good would it do to launch a successful campaign only to have them unleashed upon you when it seemed victory was in your grasp?"

"Finally, a small group of men ventured south disguised as traders and craftsmen. They would spy out this good land and see what they could see. For many weeks, they traveled and visited many towns, plying their trades as if they were really what they seemed. And one day, they encountered a man in an odd uniform. He bore the mark of this feared and hated regiment, and many of the men began to panic."

"He was just one man, however, and the leader of the caravan managed to calm them. Even engaged the man in conversation. He discovered that the man was just as human as he was, much to his surprise. With a wife, children, a small farm of his own. He had a few hands work the farm for him as he rode to supervise the area assigned to him and ensure that all was well."

"The caravan leader managed to convince the soldier to dine with him in a local inn, where he plied him with liquor well into the night, and with strong drink the great soldier revealed the truth about his famed regiment. They were not demons at all, but merely a tribe of well-trained men who worked together, trained together and fought as a group rather than as individuals once the battle was joined. They were better trained and equipped, nothing more. Not bigger or stronger, not strengthened by dark powers or human sacrifice, just. . .hard fighters who were willing to do whatever it took to protect their land. A charge they had never failed in. Ever."

"The caravan leader found himself admiring the soldier and was somewhat saddened that he had to part with him. He was almost certain that in any other time they could certainly have been friends."

"What happened to him?" Parno asked as Cho fell silent. "To the soldier I mean?"

"I killed him and his family two years later after I had destroyed his famed regiment in battle and decimated his tribe, having learned their secrets and turned them against him. He recognized me as my sword fell and the look of betrayal on his face was one I will never forget."

"His family?" Parno looked ashen now. "Cho, why would you-"

"Their titles, their lands, their soldiery was hereditary, you see," Cho was looking into the flames now, obviously lost in his own past for once. "We could not spare his heirs, less they rise up one day and invoke the names of their fathers and lead a revolt against us. Naturally the mother fought to the death to protect her children. Most of them do," he added absently, still looking into the fire. Suddenly he became aware of his surroundings again and stood.

"So, you see, young prince," he said, his 'lecture' persona back in place, "such tactics are good to a point, but can be taken too far. Temper your need for revenge with wisdom, and where possible with mercy," his face softened for a fraction of a second. "Always with mercy, where possible. Now," he straightened his robe and then his back, "it is time I retired. There is still much to be done and the wise worker gets an early start."

"Cho, I-"

"Good night, my prince," Cho bowed slightly and disappeared into the night, apparently to his tent.

Parno sat still for a long time after that, searching for all the lessons he could find in what Cho had just told him. First was the awareness that Cho Feng was at one point a leader of men, of course, and a wise one at that. A daring one as well, to head into enemy territory that contained men rumored to be demons.

But he had scouted that area and gotten to the truth of the matter, finding out how those men maintained their illusions and then finding a way to cut through them. Literally.

And he had been bloodthirsty and remorseless while doing it, too. Parno punched at the fire harder and harder as he imagined himself being forced to kill a child or a mother, but suddenly he stopped short, looking up and then in the direction in which Cho had disappeared. An epiphany had hit him. A moment of clarity for this tale told by his teacher.

Parno wouldn't be the one killing the mother and child. In this story, Parno would play the soldier. The soldier who lost his wife and family to a rumor. To a tale of terror that led a smart soldier to believe there had to be an answer to the problem and who had looked until he had found it.

His men would be the soldiers forced to bear the mantle of being the fearsome warriors that couldn't be beaten. And what happened when one of his men was taken prisoner and the enemy discovered that they were just ordinary men like themselves? An enemy that had been fooled that badly would be emboldened to greater heights in order to regain their honor, would they not? And they would be motivated to commit horrendous acts against an enemy they now knew was not supernatural, or even super, but was merely well trained and disciplined.

"There has to be a middle ground," Parno mused as he resumed poking at the fire before him. "There has to be."

He would stare into the flames for a long time looking for an answer that couldn't be found there.

-

Tom Hildebrand sat down beside his commander, his very bones seeming to ache with even that simple effort.

"I wish we'd never asked to do this," he moaned.

"I've had the same thought at least a dozen times today," Colonel Bret Chad nodded his agreement. "Look on the bright side," he grinned tiredly.

"There's a bright side?" Hildebrand asked, a look of feigned astonishment on his face.

"We aren't dead yet," Chad chuckled.

"Yet," Hildebrand seized on that one word. "Not yet."

"I didn't say it was all that bright," Chad chuckled darkly. "But we're doing quite well according to our instructors. And our men haven't quit. They're still plugging away."

"Because they feel indebted to the Prince," Hildebrand nodded. "They don't want to disappoint him. Nor do I, if I'm honest," he admitted. "I really want us to be admitted to his Regiment."

"We will be," Chad assured him. "If we earn it," he added, getting wearily to his feet and taking his empty tray and cup with him. "That being said, I'm for a shower and then bed. My group leaves at light on The March."

"We go in a week," Hildebrand nodded. "About the time the group that's out now returns, I think. Good luck."

"Luck is for fools," Chad snorted. "Good training. That's what we say. Good training."

"Good training then," Hildebrand allowed. "At least we're doing better than that cavalry outfit," he snorted slightly.

"We're a cavalry outfit now, Tom," Chad reminded him. "And yes, we are," he smirked as much as he could in his exhausted state.

"Sleep well," Hildebrand told him. "I'm to the canteen and get a stiff drink and then I'm off myself."

-

"I have muscles aching I didn't know I had," one trooper commented. "Where in the hell did they get this training plan of theirs?"

"They developed it themselves," a young lieutenant told him, stripping off his boots as he did so. "They invented all this to make their men strong. Worked, too," he added, shaking rocks from his boots.

"How so, sir?" another trooper asked.

"No rank here, soldier," the young officer shook his head. "Until we finish, we're all the same rank. Nothing recruits," he chuckled. "And it worked because this bunch managed to crush an entire Imperial Field Army that outnumbered them ten-to-one, that's how so. These fellas that are training us, and them others that are already ahead of us, they fought with the Prince, the Marshal, at the Gap. Five thousand of them against fifty thousand Nor. Ripped their guts out, too."

"Really," the first trooper mused. "That had to take some tough men," he said thoughtfully.

"Well, you'll note that the instructors are doing all this right alongside us and not even breathing hard," the young lieutenant said as he fell into his blankets, exhausted. "One day, assuming we live through this, we'll be able to do that. Think how much that will mean on the battlefield when we have to face the Nor again."

"True that," the second trooper said, falling into his own bedroll. "I can already tell a difference."

"I guess if I could feel anything I could too," the first chuckled darkly. "Ah well, I didn't die today. I'll take it."

The other two didn't hear him, already snoring with exhaustion. He followed them seconds later.

CHAPTER NINE

-

General Brent Stone was in a foul mood when he and his men reached the area outside Lovil where a certain piss-ant Naval Commodore had made his very comfortable camp. He and his sailors had apparently been enjoying themselves immensely in their time there, terrorizing the populace that hadn't had the opportunity or the foresight to flee before the war started. Sailors were running through the small town even now chasing women who were clearly unwilling, carrying goods that clearly weren't theirs.

Seeing the damage to people and infrastructure almost made him snap and order the entire bunch put to the sword. Only the knowledge that Wilson needed them kept him from it.

"Get the first regiment in line up here and get this bunch under control," he snapped to his aide, who nodded and turned his horse to gallop back down the line. "Come with me," he ordered his escort company grimly. The men followed him, their own anger up at seeing how these naval buffoons had taken advantage of their hard work and bloodshed.

Stone drew rein before what had once been the town hall of a small Soulan town in Kenty province. A hand painted sign now declared it to be the '1st Imperial River Force Headquarters'. Two men stood guard at the door and eyed the troopers warily as half dismounted, holding reins for the rest. Stone took the steps two at a time. A look of mild incredulity crossed his face as the two stepped before him, blocking the door.

"Commodore said no visitors, horse soldier," one said, his tone just beneath where it would have gotten him whipped for insolence.

"Did he?" Stone asked gently. "How 'bout that?" he turned to his men. "Commodore said no visitors, boys. Guess we'll have to come back later, eh?"

He then grabbed the speaker by the throat and threw him down the stairs, two of his men taking the other and following suit.

"Let 'em go," Stone ordered as the two ran off into the growing dusk, his men set to pursue. He stormed into the 'office', looking around him. The place was a pig sty. Half eaten meals still sitting on desks, trash everywhere strewn on the floor and the smell...

"Open the windows," he ordered, then held his hand up for everyone to halt.

"Did anyone else hear that?" he asked suddenly. Again, he heard a muffled sound, almost like...

"Turn this place out, now!" he ordered the men behind him. As two of them moved to open windows, the rest started kicking in doors. The third door open elicited a startled yell.

"General!" the trooper called stepping back and grasping his sword. Moving to the door, Stone looked inside and froze for an instant.

Lying on a bed was a girl that might have been fifteen, tied spread eagle to the metal frame and naked as the day she was born. Beside the bed was a man struggling to get into a pair of naval uniform trousers, cursing and sputtering all the while.

"Take him," Stone ordered calmly, belying his fury. He grabbed a nearby trooper.

"Go and find a woman," he ordered. "One with some age on her, and preferably one with some medical expertise assuming this lot hasn't killed her. Bring her here at once. Kill anyone who tries to stop you."

"Sir," the trooper nodded and ran out the door. He had seen inside the room.

"You two," he pointed to the two nearest men as two others drug the struggling naval officer from the room. "Order Colonel Hill to start gathering this lot up and put them somewhere under guard. Kill anyone who resists. Regardless of rank."

"Yes sir," the men nodded and ran for the door, eager to be away from their General's icy calm. That was always a bad sign.

"I'll kill you for this!" the naval man was stammering. "I'll have you know I'm-"

"Dead," Stone turned to him, eyes flinty. "You're dead. The penalty for rape is death. I was going to ask your name but I don't really care. A unmarked grave on foreign soil is still too good for you."

"Now you see here!" the man yelled, still in the grasp of two beefy troopers. "Who do you think you are!"

"I'm Major General Brent Stone, Imperial Cavalry Corps," Stone replied evenly. "You may have heard me say I don't care who you are. I assume though that you're Commodore Hacking?"

"Haskings!" the man corrected.

"Who's your second in command?" Stone demanded. "He may be about to get a promotion."

-

Captain Lucas Silven was slowly drinking himself into a stupor when he heard a commotion at the

canteen door. He looked up to see a quartet of cavalry men walk into the place and start throwing sailors outside. Another foursome soon joined them and in record time the canteen was clear except for him. A large sergeant flanked by two privates walked to his table.

"Please tell me you're here to stop this," Silven said softly, corking the bottle he'd been drinking from.

"We are indeed," the sergeant nodded. "Are you Silven?"

"I am Captain Silven, yes," the man stood up slowly, straight despite his alcohol intake. "Who sent you?" he asked. "Someone with authority I hope?"

"General Stone, Imperial Cavalry Corps," the sergeant replied. "He wants to see you."

"Why?" Silven asked. "I couldn't stop this," he waved an arm around him. "I tried, mind you, as did some others, but. . .too many of the men sided with Commodore Haskings. We aren't all bad people, you know," the Captain said sadly. "Some of us are men of honor, despite what you see here. There simply weren't enough of us. When the army left, the Commodore and those like him. . .well," he shook his head. "Where is the General?" he asked, taking his cap and setting it on his head. "I must make my manners to him."

"We'll take you to him."

-

Stone looked up at Lucas Silven, his fury at Haskings taking a back seat as he looked at the beaten man before him.

"I must apologize for my disrepair, General," Silven said very correctly. "I'm afraid that I have taken to drink in order to get through the days here, surrounded by debauchery as I am. Or was. My compliments to your men for being able to do what I am my boat crews could not," he added.

"And just why was that, Captain?" Stone asked.

"I command the equivalent of three of your companies, General," Stone replied. "All good men. None of them would have been engaged in the embarrassing behavior you saw on display when you arrived. However, the Commodore's command was just under five thousand men in total. The few crew commanders who thought as I did were simply too few to stop the activity that the Commodore endorsed. We have a number of dead and injured men to prove that," he added. "Including two Captains. Perhaps we should have tried harder, but we total less than a quarter of the entire command between us. Not enough," he shrugged. "Not enough for men who are not nearly so well trained in hand-to-hand warfare as your men undoubtedly are. And we were defeated in detail, more or less," he added. "Commodore Haskings knew who would object and made sure they could not do so."

"You could have sent word to someone!" Stone half stood, his anger getting the best of him.

"Sent three men, General," Silven nodded. "One by horse and two by foot when horses weren't available. The horse returned without a rider." The implications of that were pretty clear, even through Stone's anger.

"I'm told you're next senior to Haskings," Stone said suddenly. There was no point pursuing this line. He would put an end to Haskings soon enough.

"I have that dubious honor, yes," Silven nodded. "Will you execute us, General?" he asked. "We deserve it. All of us."

"Even those not guilty of crimes, Captain?" Stone asked, eyebrows rising.

"No," Silven shook his head. "No, my men and many others are guilty of no crimes, General. Myself on the other hand, I have allowed Haskings to use his rank to defile and deface our honor as well as this small haven. I should have allowed him to kill me rather than doing nothing."

"Why didn't you?" Stone demanded.

"Because he would have killed my men as well," Silven shrugged, his liquor hitting him hard now. "My men are good men, General, despite the company they are forced to keep. They deserve better than being killed for no other reason than their Captain is a coward."

"Doing what's best for your men isn't cowardice, Captain," Stone said quietly. "Go to your quarters and sleep your drunk off. When you wake, you'll find things in better repair. At which point you will take command of this rabble and take them south to assist General Wilson with a new operation along the river. I'll give you the details in the morning."

"Sir," Silven snapped a painfully correct salute which Stone returned and then turned to stumble out of the office.

"See to it he gets safely where he's going and then post a guard on his door," Stone told the sergeant quietly. "That might be the only good man in this devil's den."

"Sir," the sergeant nodded his agreement and followed the naval officer from the room. Stone got to his feet and walked out into the foyer and across to the room where the old mid-wife was tending the girl.

"How is she?" he asked gently from the door.

"She'll never have children," the old woman spat harshly, looking up at Stone with hate filled eyes. "Why is it you devils come here, anyway?" she demanded. "Is this all your kind is good for?"

"I'm afraid some of us, yes," he nodded sadly. "I daresay there are such among your own kind," he added.

"Not like this," she shook her head. "Nothing like this. It's no wonder our men beat you like children in war. None of you deserve the title of 'man'. Heathen swine!"

"Please see to her as best you can," Stone didn't berate the woman. She was right, after all. "Whatever she needs that I can provide, I will. My surgeon should be along shortly if you need and will accept his assistance. And it won't help, but I intend to kill the man who did this to her within the hour. It isn't enough, but it's all I can do at this point. I can't undo it."

"You'll get yours soon enough," the old woman promised him.

"I imagine you're right," he agreed and left her before she could say anything else. He stepped outside, grateful for the fresh air after being in that foul office for so long. A work gang taken from the sailors was even now clearing it away under the watchful eye of his aide.

Why did we come here? he asked himself suddenly. Why do we come here and give men like this a chance to do such damage?

He knew the southerners thought of them as heathens and miscreants at best, and with examples like this why shouldn't they? He closed his eyes against the memory of that girl, that child, and the fear on her face. Even through his exhaustion his fury boiled up again and suddenly he was unwilling to waste the time for the formality of a trial. He turned back to the door behind him.

"Bring him," he ordered simply. The aide nodded and signaled for the three men guarding the 'commodore' to bring the bucked and gagged man outside.

Haskings had apparently realized the strait he was in at some point as his belligerence had ceased, replaced with fear as he tried to see around him. The troopers deposited him on the street outside, still manacled. Stone drew his own sword and stood before the pathetic troll.

"You were caught red handed committing an act of rape in time of war," Stone said flatly, his voice devoid of emotion. "As the senior commander of this area I have the authority to determine crime and punishment for offenses and pass sentence. Your sentence is death."

Haskings was still screaming protests into his gag when Stone's sword fell, cutting the man's head off cleanly.

"Better than you deserved," he muttered to himself. He wiped his blade on the dead man's jacket and then stood. He motioned to the body as he spoke to the senior trooper.

"Find a pike and have his head mounted on it," he ordered. "Burn the body along with the body of anyone else caught in the act. Collect the heads the same way. I'm going to bed."

"Yes sir."

Stone didn't look back as he made his way to the barn where he had made his quarters for the evening. He'd be damned is he slept anywhere this rotten lot might have laid their heads.

-

Lucas Silven stumbled out of his bunk at the crowing of the cock the next morning. Going outside he doused his head in the flow of water from a well, then decided he needed a shower and fresh clothes before meeting with-

He stopped short. There was a general here, wasn't there. Someone had cleaned up this madhouse, or at least started to, last night. And hadn't he mentioned a mission of some sort? Galvanized in a way he hadn't been in weeks, Silven picked up the pace despite his hammering head and hurried to bathe and change, his mind racing the whole time.

It had to be an offensive along the river. Nothing else made any sense. There would be no need of his crews unless they were going to using the boats to ferry men down, or up, river. Perhaps moving supplies, he allowed, but their boats weren't designed for long treks with such loads and would be far inferior to even the worst wagons. Not that he'd refuse of course. Anything to get out of here and get his men away from this dung heap.

In record time, he found himself standing before the town hall, where the impromptu sign was gone and Commodore Haskings head was on prominent display atop what looked like an infantry pike. Silven decided it was a good look for him and nodded.

"Like it?"

Silven turned to see Stone standing a few feet away, apparently sizing Silven up for size.

"I'm ashamed to say I do, sir," Silven admitted. "I suppose that's unbecoming of an officer of the Imperial Navy but. . .he deserved that and more."

"I agree," Stone grunted. "My men should be about done rounding up the refuse around here, Captain. I'm going to tell you straight. Anyone caught in the act of rape or theft is being executed. Probably already done in fact. I hope your crews were as sterling as you said because if not then some of them will be looking just as peaked at the good Commodore, there," he pointed at Haskings' head.

"If they were caught in the act they deserve it, sir," Silven shrugged. "You mentioned a mission last night? Or did I dream that?"

"No, there's work and plenty for you and your men, Captain. I've decided to let you replace Haskings for the time being. Three of your fellow Captains have sadly lost their heads over recent events," he deadpanned. "I'm afraid the number of commanders is dwindling rapidly."

"That's all right, sir," Silven replied. "It's the men who do the work, anyway. What is it you need us to do?"

-

"We can do it," Silven said at once after hearing Stone outline Wilson's plan. "It means transporting the boats overland though, and that's something we can't do easily. We only had three men per boat, General. We'd never be able to carry the boats far in a day's time. Five miles if we were lucky, and I mean very lucky." He frowned, looking at the map. "Is he wanting us to help land a force south of the Soulan Army, or use the Cumberland to threaten the capitol?"

"The last I heard he needed you to carry enough men by the Soulan Army position to create a distraction in their rear areas," Stone replied.

"Then we can just pole the boats down the river," he told the general. "Empty they aren't that hard to handle. We will need some wagons to ferry gear and supplies alongside, but the boats can make the trip okay in most areas. Where they can't we can carry them."

Stone was impressed. His first impression of Silven hadn't been favorable, but observing the man today, after he'd been given a shot of hope, he was seeing him in a different light.

"I will detail a battalion of cavalry to side track you back to the army's position," he told Silven. "Their orders will be to assist you in getting there anyway they can. They can guard your train during the day then help secure your camp at night, and when necessary help haul your boats. How long you estimate until you can reach the camp?"

"It depends on the river," Silven said after a moment to look over the map. "There are a few areas where poling will be difficult but not impossible it looks like, but. . .other areas we'll have to get out and carry. I don't know the river there well enough to give you a definite answer, general. Sorry."

"I'd rather have an honest answer," Stone shook his head. "Best guess will do. I just something to send General Wilson by courier. Three weeks? Four?"

"I'd say three weeks give or take three, maybe four days," Silven replied. "I admit that's a rough guess and doesn't take into consideration bad weather and what have you, but it should be close. Again, it all depends on how strong the current is."

"I'll tell him a minimum of four weeks then," Stone said after a minute. "If you get there early, just makes you look good, what?" he grinned, probably the first time he'd done so since arriving.

"I'm all for looking good," Silven snorted, then remembered himself. "Sir," he added.

"I'll give you today to get things organized and ready. I want you on your way tomorrow," Stone ordered.

"Yes sir."

-

Newly promoted Brigadier Nelson Pierce watched as the wagons assigned to his command labored over rough areas of the trail. He had known it would be difficult, especially ferrying men, horses, wagons and supplies across the river and yet the ferrying was beginning to look as if it was the easy part of this journey.

Roads he remembered being in fairly good shape had become scant trails that his pioneers had to cut trees from to allow the wagons to pass. That slowed his advance and tired his horses and draft teams more quickly. But there was little help for it. His men wouldn't be very effective without their gear and supplies. Still, he had other issues to deal with as well.

"Major Bradfield," he told the man next to him. "You will take your battalion and move ahead of us. Carry three days provisions and scout the area well ahead. If you can find a better route than the one we are on, secure it and send back runners to guide us forward. We'll continue on this road until we hear from you. I'll expect you back in three days if you've found no better going than we have here."

"Yes sir," the man sketched a salute and spurred his horse down the line. Soon his men were moving back up the road past the wagons and then moving off into the distance. Pierce nodded at their efficiency. Next order of business was the infantry.

"Colonel, you know your assignment and the rendezvous point. You will take your gear from here and move your regiment into position, awaiting the River Guard and River Artillery force if they are not already in place. They will be along, so establish your camp and set watch. I've assigned a company of cavalry to use as scouts so you should be able to keep good watch along the river and still man your posts. Remember to keep enough of the cavalry back to send warning to me and to

Nasil should a large boat force attempt to pass you. They'll be working against the current so they should be slower. We can't let the capitol be taken by surprise."

"Sir," the infantry man nodded. "Understood."

"Godspeed then, Colonel, and good hunting," Pierce said, returning the man's salute. Less than an hour later the infantry regiment broke away from the column, heading for the river post assigned them earlier, flanked and led by the reinforced cavalry company he'd sent along with them.

His two immediate needs seen to, he turned to the pair of scouts he'd employed who were familiar with the area they were headed into.

"You know what I want," he told them. "Stay out of sight for the most part, other than when you speak to people. If they've seen or heard of enemy troops raiding, I want to know it. I expect you to meet up with us somewhere along the line in a week's time with whatever news you have. Understood?"

"Sir," the older man, all of nineteen, nodded.

"Off you go then," he ordered with a wave, and the two civilian dressed men took off, galloping ahead toward the column's ultimate destination; Springfield.

Pierce, satisfied he'd done all he could do for the moment, rode forward with a small escort to see what the Pioneer captain thought about their expected progress. Once he had a better idea of how long this might take, he'd need to send a courier back to the Marshal and General Davies.

Right now, though, it was a hell of a mess that he hadn't expected.

-

Major Billy Bilbrey was sweating. And with good reason he felt.

Pushing and pulling on wagon after wagon of the questionably stable compounds needed to make Roda Finn's 'gadgets' work was enough to make anyone sweat a little however, and Bilbrey was very new to those gadgets. Four weeks ago, he had been Captain Bilbrey, commanding a three-catapult battery in 2nd Corps.

Taken from the retiring 2nd Corps artillery units that were on their way to Cove, Bilbrey had been given an abbreviated course in the handling, firing and maintenance of said 'ordnance' by the fussy inventor himself before loading the men and machines he would need for his new job onto barges to cross the Cumberland and begin an overland trek into the Central Highlands. The ox drawn carts and carriages were stable enough for most things, but not for something that could literally explode in their face.

An enterprising young engineer in Nasil had developed a new axle spring for the carriages and wagons however that was working pretty well so far. Based on old technology from before the dying, the design used heated steel and iron in layers beneath the axle to give a slight 'spring' to the vehicles, which in turn kept them from rocking quite so violently. Even so however it was a slow and painstaking business to move that kind of equipment and supplies forward at more than a snail's pace.

He was supposed to link up with an infantry regiment along the river and then stand in support of the River Guard as they patrolled the Cumberland against an incursion by Imperial troops. He had fired his new weapons exactly a half dozen time, twice with the special munitions they were designed for. They had performed flawlessly those six times, but that was before they had been subjected to this over land jostling. Would they still perform so well once they arrived and were set up along the river?

Bilbrey wiped the sweat from his face with an already wet rag as he imagined the carnage one of those things could create among his men if something went wrong. The potential was devastating to put it mildly. He could vividly remember seeing the effects of similar weapons on the battlefield after all, and to call it horrifying was far too lenient. Fascinating to be sure, but still horrifying.

Of course, if he happened to hit one of the Imperial boats should they venture down the Cumberland, then they would probably think a dragon had bitten them on the ass. He grinned in spite of his worry at that happy thought.

Be almost worth all this, he decided.

Meanwhile, he sweated.

-

"I heard you got a courier in?"

Bret Chad looked up to see Tom Hildebrand standing over him, a look of hopefulness on his face.

"Yes," he nodded. "We've been advised that we're 'on call' as a backstop to a force that's moving into the Highlands north of the river Cumberland. Protecting against an incursion by the Nor. No movement orders as yet, just telling us that we may be tasked to assist if they call for it. Nelson Pierce is in command. Been promoted to Brigadier, no less."

"Is he now?" Hildebrand raised an eyebrow. "Good for him!" Both had known Pierce for some time and thought highly of him.

"He knows we're here and available, so he may well call for us," Chad nodded. "We're closer than almost anyone else to his proposed HQ in Springfield."

"So, we might just get some action then," Hildebrand rubbed his hands together slightly. "Be a shame to miss out on all this good training though," he tried to look regretful and failed miserably.

"They don't need us yet," Chad laughed. "Which means the 'good training' will continue for now, sorry."

"Well, we can always hope," Hildebrand sighed as he sat down heavily on the bench across from his commanding officer.

"You realize that 'hope' would include another incursion by the enemy into our territory?" Chad asked, eyebrows raised.

"I know," Hildebrand nodded. "Terrible choice we have. Die in combat or die in training."

Laughter rolled up and down the table at that. Trust Tom Hildebrand to make light of the most serious situations.

-

"What do you think, Arlen?"

General Roland Raines was watching his artillery chief as he evaluated the new artillery munitions that had arrived from Nasil. The two men that had accompanied the supply train had taken great pains to explain and then demonstrate the new 'ordnance'. Raines like the sound of the word, he decided. Very military and very intimidating.

"I think they'll be a great asset if they don't blow up in our face," Brigadier Arlen Foss replied grimly. "The striking power is unlike anything I've even imagined. Coupled with pitch pine and the like it's almost impossible to imagine the carnage this can cause."

"It could help us beat back a determined attack," Raines nodded. His command had been weakened by the stripping of one of his cavalry divisions for use in the valley campaign, but the two militia outfits had been good ones, and helped greatly to replace the lost combat power. That didn't change the fact that he was still severely outnumbered. His best estimates of the enemy forces across the river placed him at a two, perhaps three-to-one disadvantage in numbers. There was no way to know for sure since part of that force was Tribal Warriors who didn't assemble or fight in anything like standard units the way the Imperials or Soulan Army did. Best guess was just that; a guess.

"It could," Foss agreed, albeit reluctantly. "Could also kill an entire crew if it blows up on the rails. Could set the bridge afire and destroy it completely, too."

"My orders allow that if it will prevent a major incursion into the delta by the enemy," Raines informed him. "I don't want to, since the Prince wants it intact if possible, but he did say that if it looked as if we were losing it to burn it."

"I suppose if the fire's not too hot the frames will be okay," Foss sighed. "We can always plank it and use it again. Probably," he qualified hesitantly.

"We'll worry about that if and when we have to," Raines decided. "And those mines will help us as well, so long as our crossbowmen can hit the mark. What about them? What did you think?"

"Immensely destructive," Foss said at once. "Shards and balls of iron propelled like that? In nearly every direction around them? Kill or maim dozens at a time every time you fire one off. We can have the bridge lined with them all the way out to the edge of where our men can hit."

"No," Raines shook his head. "No, we'll keep them in close, just in case. I don't want any of them being taken by the enemy and studied. We'll sacrifice some range in order to try and ensure that the enemy doesn't get a good look. And we can cover the mouth of the bridge on our side to saturate it if they make it this far. Firing them off as needed and conserving them against a renewed attack. This will be an archery engagement so long as we can keep it that way. Archery and artillery, keeping the enemy at arm's length as much as possible. We have to hold, and we need to conserve our strength."

"We need the enemy's cooperation to do that, sir," Foss reminded him.

"To a degree, yes," Raines admitted. "But so long as we maintain our discipline, and use our weapons to our advantage, we have the chance of making it happen. At least for now. We don't have to do this forever. We just need to buy the Marshal some time."

"How much time, sir?" Foss asked, his look dubious.

"As much as we can," Raines looked out across the river. "As much as we possibly can."

-

"How goes the resettlement, Winifred?" Memmnon asked over supper. The refugee 'trains' had been on the move for five days in most cases. Even now new ones were being formed as refugees continued to enter the capitol.

"We've had word that the first two have reached their destination and are working to get land cleared for planting. It's a race against the seasons, now," she shrugged. "Hopefully they can do it. Once the crops are planted, they will alternate between building shelters and laying in stores for the winter, such as wood for fires. If gas or oil pockets can be found then each group has workmen who can use those resources to provide lighting and other conveniences. It's all we can do."

"And your training program?" the King asked.

"Not bad for just a few days," she admitted. "Most of the women are young and strong and are used to working. It's a different set of muscles to use a bow all day but all it takes is conditioning. We'll work on that most of the first two or three weeks, even as we also cover the fundamentals of aiming and firing. We should have them sufficiently trained in two months that they could man the walls in case of an attack."

"That seems like a long time, but I'm actually surprised it's that fast, considering that many of them will never have used a bow before," Memmnon noted.

"It is," Winnie nodded. "They're doing well."

"And you, Doctor?" he turned to Stephanie. "How is your project going?"

"Very well," she replied. "As I suspected, many of the applicants were knowledgeable enough to pass the tests to let them go to the more advanced training. We'll see the first class graduate before summer's end, and many of those who just enrolled will be working in the area military hospitals as aides before then. By year's end they should be nurses as well. The male nurses we'll send to the front while the women remain in the hospitals here."

"I see," Memmnon nodded. "Excellent work, the both of you," he complimented. "If we can manage to win this war, the two of you will have been a large part of it," he told them.

"Don't kid yourself," Winnie said flatly. "We may contribute, but if we win the war there's only one person you'll have to thank for it."

-

"Who do I have to thank for this?"

"It was a group effort, my Prince," Tinker smiled brightly. "A little here, and a little there. This list I'm sure is in no way complete, but considering some of their positions in the Army, I thought it better to give it to you now."

"Indeed," Parno perused a list of suspected disgruntled officers. Men who had supported Therron and would again if the chance arose, despite the fact that it was now common knowledge that he was a traitor and that his twin had killed the King on his behalf. Standing suddenly, he made his way to the entrance of his wall tent.

"Get Colonel Willard for me," he ordered the guard, who saluted and hurried away, his place being taken by another of the men stationed around the Marshal's tents.

"What will you do?" Tinker asked, curious.

"Send them to Nasil I suppose and let Brock have a shot at them," Parno sighed deeply. "Unless we get the opportunity to kill them first."

"You have become quite bloodthirsty since our first meeting, my Prince," Tinker raised an eyebrow. "I find that it suits you, somehow."

"I assume that's a compliment," Parno snorted just as Karls walked in.

"Why is he complimenting you?" Karls asked.

"He approved my fashion sense," Parno told him. "Karls, you remember the Tinker, don't you?"

"Indeed," Karls nodded. "How are you, sir?" he asked the dark-skinned man.

"I am well, Colonel, and trust you are the same?" Tinker smiled.

"I'm passing fair," Karls nodded. "What's this?" he asked Parno as the Marshal passed him the list.

"Tinker has been working for me a while," Parno told him quietly. "Rooting out as many of Therron's followers as possible. This is what he's learned so far."

"Damn," Karls murmured beneath his breath. "Some of these-"

"Yes," Parno nodded. "Interesting, no?"

"Interesting yes," Karls nodded, still reading. "I see five brigade commanders, alone. And two staff officers."

"Start with them," Parno ordered. "Take them one at a time, place them in holding. Once they're all rounded up, send them to Nasil, to Brock."

"You don't want a crack at them first?" Karls looked surprised.

"I very much want a 'crack' at them," Parno assured him. "Which is why I'm sending them to Nasil. Brock is far better suited for something like this, and he's better at it as well. And I have more than enough to keep me busy as it is. Not to mention that I doubt I'd be able to hold my temper with all of them."

"True," Karls nodded absently. "Tonight, or wait for dawn?"

"Tonight, for those you can but if you think it best wait until tomorrow. I leave that up to you."

-

Brigadier Norton Fisk staggered to his tent after another day of the Marshal's ever-be-damned 'training'. Every muscle he had was aching somewhere or somehow.

"I'll be glad when the real Marshal is back," he muttered as he stripped off his jacket.

"That might take longer than you think," a voice said out of the dark and Fisk's hand flashed to his side where his sword would normally hang. He felt strong hands grip each arm, holding him fast.

"Norton Fisk, you are under arrest for suspicion of treason and sedition against his Majesties Tammon and Memmnon McLeod."

"What!" Fisk managed to look outraged thought what he really was came far closer to stunned.

"Don't bother," Karls Willard was now visible in the dim glow of a battle lamp. "You've all but convicted yourself you little bastard. Now you can explain your statements and your 'writing' to the IG. If you live that long," he added absently. "Take him. I'll have a word with the General. And if he resists, well. . .he's a small fry. Killing him won't matter one way or another."

The men hauled a still protesting Fisk away while Karls went to speak to General Graham.

-

"Fisk?" Graham was pale. "Are you sure?"

"Very sure, sir," Karls told him gently. "I can't reveal how just yet, as the investigation is still ongoing. Have to depend on your discretion with that last, sir," he added. "Couldn't be more secret to be honest."

"No, no," Graham shook his head. "Of course, I'll say nothing. We can't. . .I mean we simply can't tolerate this, but. . .damn it!" he swore suddenly. "That bastard was on my staff until just before the war! He was promoted at the Marshal's…" he trailed off, eyes narrowing. "Son-of-a-bitch," he muttered.

"Sir?"

"He was in on it," Graham said firmly. "I promoted him on Prince Therron's recommendation. Practically on his say so, in all honesty. I mean he was deserving enough, don't get me wrong, but if I had been left to my own devices that position would have gone to another man who was a bit better qualified and had more time in service. Prince Therron was quite insistent that Fisk get command of that brigade."

"Was he now?" Karls asked softly. "How about that?"

"Yeah, how about that," Graham almost growled. "Now I have to start thinking back to every promotion made with the Marshal's 'blessing'. There's no telling how many snakes I've put into positions to help him."

"Don't move against them," Karls told him. "Simply let me know and leave it to me. Anything you do will hurt the morale of your men. This is bad enough as it is. Let's not make it worse."

"All right," Graham was reluctant but understood the need. "I should not have followed so blindly," he muttered softly. "I should have been more aware."

"Sir, he was the Lord Marshal," Karls had a minor bout of sympathy for the man. "You should be able to follow him, trust him, without fail."

"That doesn't cut it, Colonel," Graham replied forcefully. "You should know that our job, part of our job, is to maintain order within the Army. That includes ensuring that those above us in rank are not abusing their position, including the Marshal. That's why we have separation of powers, after all," he semi-lectured. "The King is there for us to appeal to if we have evidence of wrongdoing on the Marshal's part."

"Did you have evidence, sir?" Karls asked kindly.

"That doesn't mean it wasn't there," Graham replied, though shaking his head.

"Then there was nothing for you to do, sir," Karls shrugged. "Prince Therron was very careful to avoid officers who might have opposed his grab for power. The fact that you aren't in on it speaks well of you I would think."

"What an endorsement," Graham snorted, then straightened, his bout of self-pity already gone. "Finish what you need to do, Colonel. Should you encounter difficulty with any of my men, you know where to find me. We can't have this. Go and get them. All of them. I hesitate to think what I might do should I see them myself."

"Good evening to you then, General," Karls bowed slightly.

CHAPTER TEN

-

Anyone who ever said there was no work for an army when it wasn't fighting has never served in an army. Any army, anywhere.

Even without the fighting there was plenty to do. In fact, if you cast out all of the combat related work an army performed, be it in the field or in barracks, you would still have a full schedule that left you wondering how they managed to find time to train or fight any enemies.

Horses had to be fed, groomed, exercised, their health seen to. Harness and trace and strap and cinch checked for wear and tear, bridles and bits and all the other rigging that a cavalry man needed to be about his work had to be cleaned, polished, ready to go at a moment of notice.

Latrines had to be dug, filled in, then dug again. Cooking pots cleaned and prepared for the next meals. Animals butchered for that meal or beans soaked to make them soft and clean them for boiling. Grain ground into meal for bread. Water boiled before drinking so that the men didn't die of dysentery from drinking contaminated water, something that was all too possible in a camp this size that had been still this long. That water had to be hauled from the river, or drawn from a well or a creek. There was always more work to do than hands available to do it.

Work was constantly being done to strengthen the fighting positions of the Soulan Army. Barricades hardened, bunkers erected and covered to protect archers and crossbowmen from the enemy's return fire. Artillery placements hardened against enemy artillery strikes. Trenches dug along the front lines, along with stake pits and other traps to snare scouts or attackers either one. Drill conducted to ensure that every man knew his position in battle and could get to it in the quickest time possible, ready for battle.

Atop all of that, the soldiers of the Soulan Army still needed to train. To maintain skills needed in combat. To keep their strength and endurance high enough to meet the threat to their kingdom. There are only so many hours of light in the day and the Soulan Army made it a habit to use every last minute of every one of those hours.

Night time saw soldiers too tired to do anything other than collapse into their blankets and sleep, grateful for the rest. Night time also saw about a quarter of the army standing to on the line itself, a tripwire against a possible night attack or raid. To sound the alarm and hold the line until the rest of the army could form up.

Parno McLeod made his way to one camp or another almost every evening, taking dinner with line troops and talking to them in a way their own officers really couldn't. Checking on their welfare, asking after any family or friends, bringing news of messmates that might be returning soon if he had been asked to check on them.

The soldiers took note of the Marshal making his rounds and nodded approvingly at their young leader. He had proven himself time and again to the rank and file professional soldiers, the backbone of the Soulan Army. These were the men who made things happen, who kept the Soulan Army moving, mounted, trained and ready. They all shared the idea that their liege was a soldier. A soldier's officer at that.

None of them mistook his care, his concern for them as weakness. They had learned all too well that Parno McLeod would not hesitate to order them to their deaths if he had to. But they knew that if he did, he would have no other choice, and that he would likely be right beside them. He had proven that once already at The Gap, and again in the pitched cavalry engagement just two days after he'd arrived.

They accepted his openness in the way it was intended; genuine concern for their wellbeing and how it affected their ability to do their duty. Not personal care and concern. He wasn't their friend, and he didn't try to be, or pretend to be. He was their Marshal. Their commander. And for the first time in a long while, their leader.

Because Parno McLeod led men. And because he led them, men followed. They followed even knowing that they might die. And while they accepted that they might die themselves, the Soulan Army would not die, would not falter, and would not fail. Parno McLeod wouldn't allow it to. Which meant that their deaths would mean something. Would count for something.

Sometimes that made all the difference.

Sometimes it was all the difference.

As the days wore on, these same professional soldiers, even as they watched their young Marshal make his rounds, kept a wary eye to the north of their lines where their enemy laid waiting, resting, licking wounds. The longer the enemy waited, the more likelihood that when they did move it would be a concerted and concentrated effort against them, which increased the possibility of their being overrun. The Nor didn't take prisoners and no one had any illusions about falling into the hands of the Tribal Warriors serving the Empire. Instant death was preferable to a drawn out torturous one.

Yet there was nothing else that could be done. The Soulan Army was too weak to drive the invader out, mustering just enough men to keep them at bay, at least for now. But the Nor wouldn't wait forever. Their General couldn't wait forever. The Imperial Army was eating their weight in food every week and they had no food to steal here in Soulan, which meant that food was coming from the Empire. At this rate there would be hungry bellies in the north come winter, just as there would likely be in the south. The men took a strange sense of pride in that by merely being where they were, it was possible that they might inflict upon the Imperial Army the same fate that the Imperial Army was inflicting upon them.

In the meantime, they could only do what soldiers the world over had learned to do as patiently as possible.

Wait.

-

The waiting was not one sided. While the southern soldiers worked and waited, so did their counterparts across the way. Imperial soldiers performed pretty much the same tasks as the Royal soldiers did, though their training was not quite so stringent as the southern army was. Still, the same chores had to be performed every day with reference to latrines, meals, water, cleaning and the like. And Imperial officers were careful to keep their men busy. While southern officers sought to take their soldier's minds from the overwhelming odds against them, their northern opposites were trying to get the thoughts of their own men off of two staggering defeats at the hands of the vastly outnumbered southern army.

Such defeats were bad for an army on a number of levels. First of course was the sheer losses. The casualty count from the two battles was worse than the rest of the war so far combined. Far worse. Their losses in men, horses and material had been staggering.

Aside from such material considerations were the effect of having had your ass handed to you regardless of the odds. In the space of two days, albeit spread over several weeks, the Imperial Army had been rocked onto its heels, and that had an effect on morale. No army in history had ever absorbed such losses and remained upbeat.

Another effect was that of the men's confidence in their leaders. Too many such defeats and the men would begin to wonder if their commanders were losing their edge. Soldiers who lacked trust and confidence in their leaders would not give that extra 'something' that often made the difference between victory and defeat on the field of battle. Soldiers who might otherwise have simply leaped into battle, following blindly on the belief that their commander knew something they did not, would now hesitate wondering if their orders were the right ones to be given.

They wouldn't refuse, of course. But they didn't have to refuse to negatively affect the battle. All they had to do was hesitate. Even a minute of waiting could change the outcome on part of the battlefield, which could affect the outcome on another part and so on, until a domino effect cascaded across the field resulting in the loss of the battle.

Twice now the Imperial Army had been thrashed. Just like wheat in a field falling to a scythe, the men referred to their defeat as having been thrashed. It wasn't good for an army to think of itself in such terms, so the officers were working to make them think of something else. Anything else.

Or nothing at all except how tired they were and how much they looked forward to a nice night's sleep once their duties were over. Mind numbing work that left a man too exhausted to think left him too unable to think about how handily the army had been 'thrashed'.

It never lasted of course. Guard details had to be stood and the lines manned. And when a man was on the line, or worse alone or in pairs on a distant picket post (a post where the only objective was to live long enough to sound a warning to others before being run through with a Soulan lance), then remembrance of where they were and who they faced came roaring back to them, undoing all the hard work their officers had put in. Or had the men put in, to be more accurate. In an army the size of the northern force, men would stand to about once a week on average. Which meant that just about the time they had forgotten, even if for a bit, what had happened before, their turn at the line or the picket outposts would remind them firmly just how bad things were.

Then the process would begin again the next day. Such was army life in camp during wartime.

-

Lieutenant General Gerald Wilson looked down at the body and fought to hide his elation. It was difficult, but he had to do it lest he be considered guilty in some way.

The body of Brigadier Charles Daly lay at odd angles on the floor of the bedroom in the small house he had 'appropriated' for his quarters. The graves of the former occupants, a woman and three small children, were in the back yard. Wilson managed to keep his tone business like and calm as he looked at his Provost.

"Any notion how this happened or who did it?" he demanded.

"Not as yet, sir," the man shook his head. "The thing is, his aide had left him last night at fifteen of ten, heading for his own quarters. The escort saw the Brigadier then, through the doorway, before he told them he was retiring for the evening. The escort guard detail changed at midnight, no sign of trouble or problems reported. Detail changed again at six this morning, again as usual. Off going detail reported a quiet night with no disruptions and no one calling on the Brigadier. When he hadn't appeared by eight for breakfast, half-an-hour past normal, his aide entered and found him here. They sent for me at once, and other than to check and see if the Brigadier was deceased, the aide retreated from the building and touched nothing."

"You believe him?" Wilson asked.

"I do," the Provost nodded. "His aide is the last man Daly should have had to fear. He has protected the man for most of his career and because of Daly's influence the man's never been in a line unit. Served as a staff officer his entire career. He also apparently took advantage of Daly's protection to be something of a bully toward his contemporaries and on occasion even those right above him in seniority and rank. He's already feeling heat as word of Daly's death spreads. He had nothing to gain and everything to lose in the event of the Brigadier's demise."

"Makes sense," Wilson mused. "So, any theories? I'll have to notify the Emperor of this right away. I need to be able to tell him something."

"He was killed with a single knife thrust to the heart, from the front," the Provost replied. "Doctor Freed was here and did an examination of the body. No other wounds defensive or otherwise, and no sign of struggle. There's also no indication of stealth or forced entry. Whoever did this, General, I think Brigadier Daly had to know them and allowed them into his quarters. The thing I can't figure at this point is how they could gain entry without the guard detail seeing that someone had come in, regardless of whether they knew who it was. That's the part that doesn't make sense to me."

"Could it have been a woman?" Wilson asked.

"Yes," the Provost nodded. "He wasn't overpowered so a woman could have knifed him as easily as a man. Easier I suppose, depending on why she was here," he added carefully. Daly's 'dalliances' were well known as was his affinity for certain distasteful acts, hence the small graves out back.

"Could the guard detail be in on this?" Wilson asked suddenly.

"And they're all being held for now," the Provost nodded affirmatively. "I have a hard time seeing all of them being in on it, but that doesn't mean they aren't."

"What if some of them were supplying him with women?" Wilson asked, looking for anything that might make sense. The Provost frowned at that, clearly thinking.

"It would be hard to get them into the camp unseen, but it could be done," he admitted finally, albeit reluctantly. "The camp is so large, no matter how well we patrol there are gaps. Someone determined enough could find them. Exploit them."

"I'm not blaming you or your men, Provost General," Wilson said formally. "I'm looking for a reason and a way that this happened. Nothing more."

"I can't imagine either at the moment, sir," the other man admitted. "Brigadier Daly was very unpopular but given his connection to the Emperor I can't imagine anyone attacking him just because they didn't like him. As to the way, other than what I've given you, so far there's nothing. We'll be interrogating the members of his escort over the next few days, looking for inconsistencies in their story. Their initial stories are just far enough apart to ring true, though."

"What does that mean?" Wilson frowned. Shouldn't they all be telling you the same thing?"

"That would mean they had gotten together to come up with a story to tell us," the Provost was shaking his head. "We all see and hear things slightly differently, no matter what it is. One man may pay closer attention, have a better angle of vision, or just not have cared enough to pay attention to begin with. All of that results in men telling a slightly different version of what happened even when they technically all saw or heard the same thing."

"Huh," Wilson grunted, having never considered such a thing.

"No reason for you to think of it, sir," the other man shrugged. "And it's something we learn at investigatory school. A technique for separating the wheat from the chaff, so to speak."

"Sounds like a good one," Wilson admitted. "Well, if nothing else I've learned something new today," he sighed. "I'll have to hear from the Emperor on what he wants done with the body. Have we a way to store it so that. . .well. . . ." he trailed off.

"I'll check with the Doctor, sir," the Provost promised. "I'm sure he can do something."

"Report to me daily on what you find," Wilson said, forcing himself not to laugh at the unintended pun.

"Will do, General."

Wilson caught himself having a slight spring to his step on the way back to his headquarters and chided himself for it. He had to keep his elation from showing for at least a few days.

It would be hard though.

-

"Done?"

"We're done and they're all on the way back to Nasil," Karls nodded to his Marshal. "Full company of the Regiment as guards in addition to the IG and Provost troops. Have you sent word to Brock as yet?"

"Yes," Parno replied. "He knows who and what to expect. Maybe this will get us somewhere in cleaning out things. A bit at least."

"Should," Karls agreed. "So what now?"

"Keep working with 1st Corps," Parno ordered absently. "The quicker they're in shape, the faster they're back on the line. They hadn't suffered near the losses that 2nd Corps had so their replacements should shake down faster. They weren't as tired, either."

"What did you think about what Graham said?" Karls asked.

"About making appointments based on Therron's 'recommendations'?" Parno turned to look at him. "Sounds right. No one, even a Corps Commander refuses a 'request' from his Marshal or his Sovereign. Therron casually mentions he'd like to see a particular officer in a particular post and the officer in question gets the post. It's worked that way since. . .well, ever," he shrugged helplessly. "Only so much changes, Karls."

"True that," the other man nodded. "I'm starting to think Graham may be okay," he admitted.

"I'm starting to think he's not a traitor," Parno semi-agreed. "'Okay' is another matter. For now, though, I'll take what I can get."

-

"What are we doing now, Mi-Tinker," Rosala asked as they sat in the Inn, alone for the moment.

"We carry on," he told her simply. "Our job is not done until and unless the Prince says it is done. We have made a good start. We will continue."

"Where does this end?" she asked him. "Where do we stop and go back to-"

"Go back to what?" Tinker cut her off, looking at her with a raised eyebrow. "Is your life not better here, at this moment, than at any time in the past since your fourteenth birthing day?"

"I was not complaining about being here," she said patiently. "Nor was I wanting to leave. You are correct in that this is the best I have ever had it, and the same is true of the other girls. We simply wonder how long this can last."

Tinker realized he had snapped at her, assuming this would be another in a long line of complaints. Rosala loved to complain. He was convinced she sometimes simply walked and looked for something to be disagreeable over. Perhaps her behavior was a cover for some insecurity.

"It will last so long as the war lasts, I am sure," he shrugged. "Regardless of how long this job lasts, the Prince has given his word that we will be taken care of. We will not lack for a future, assuming that the Kingdom has one."

"And we are to simply trust this nobleman to keep his promises?" she raised an eyebrow of her own this time. "I've yet to meet a man of so-called 'noble' birth who believes that he must keep his word to the likes of us. I find it difficult to trust him."

"Then trust me," he replied calmly. "The Prince has always done as he promised. If he promises to help you, he will. If he promises to support you, he will. If he promises to kill you, then he will. Whatever he says, he does. I have seen this too often not to believe it. So, trust in that if nothing else."

"If I didn't trust you I wouldn't be here," she snorted lightly, a faint look of amusement on her face. "I need you to speak with Bell," she changed the subject suddenly.

"About?" Tinker looked at her.

"He has been paying Briel a great deal of attention," Rosala replied.

"She is a pretty girl, he is a healthy young man," Tinker shrugged. "That should not surprise you."

"She is not for this life, Mi-Tinker," Rosala shook her head. "I will not have it."

"Nor would he," Tinker replied evenly. "If he is looking at her, interested in her, then it is not because of anything in this inn. If he is interested in her it is because he sees someone he might take as a wife."

"A wife?" Rosala's disdain was apparent. "One of the Prince's Own? Take one of us for a wife? Now I know you have taken leave of your senses. Why would one in the Prince's Service take a serving girl as a wife?"

"Why wouldn't he?" Tinker fought the urge to smile at what he was about to say. "Briel is a rare beauty as well as a fine young woman. Aaron is a fine young man and a good soldier. Before he was a soldier in service to the Prince, however, he was a highway man of sorts," he smirked at the look of shock that appeared on Rosala's face. "Left an orphan at an early age, he fell in with a poor crowd out of necessity. He wound up in prison because of it and that is where the Prince found him. In fact, the majority of the Black Sheep are former prisoners or wanted criminals. Of those who were actually soldiers to begin with, only Colonel Willard and small company of men were not rejects and washouts. On their last chance tour when sent to the Prince." He stood, still smirking at Rosala's expression.

"So, you need not believe that he is somehow offended by what you do to survive. If any man understands it, Aaron Bell does. He has done what he had to in order to survive for far longer than most. And as I said, he is a man of strong honor. If he is looking at Briel, he intends to ask for her hand. I will speak with him at some point, but that is what I will speak to him about."

"All of them?" Rosa's voice betrayed her shock, her worry over her niece at least temporarily forgotten.

"Most," he shrugged. "Three-fourths at least."

"And the Prince takes them into his service despite that?" she asked, clearly reevaluating her position on at least one 'noble' man.

"Yes. He promised if they served him, they would be free. After the battle of the Gap the King himself gave them all a royal pardon. Yet they still remain. Loyal to the Prince to a man. As I said, what this Prince says, he does. I will speak to Aaron when the time is right. If you truly wish for her to have a life away from something such as this, he is a good way for her to accomplish that. Should he live, he will do well in the Prince's service. Should he die, she will be cared for. The Prince takes care of his Own."

-

"I'm sorry, sir. There's just nothing to report as yet."

Gerald Wilson nodded slowly as the Provost Inspector reported. Word of Daly's death had gotten around the camp quickly enough, it being difficult to hide something like that in a camp, no matter how large. The details of his death were still being kept to only a few, however.

"Very well," he sighed. "Keep me informed of anything new. Report each day, even if it's nothing to report. I have to send a courier to the Emperor."

"Sir," the man saluted and departed.

Wilson spent nearly an hour composing his missive to the Emperor, telling him everything they had learned to this point and offering, he thought, just the right amount of sympathy to be thought correct. The Emperor hadn't cared for Daly much it appeared, but he was a member of the Imperial Family. Appearances had to be maintained. When finally finished he called his aide and handed him the message.

"I want this taken to His Lordship right away," he ordered. "Make sure it's a good man. This is important."

"Sir," the aide nodded, taking the envelope and hurrying away.

After that, Wilson turned to finding a new chief of staff. Maybe one that actually could get work done this time.

-

"Penny for your thoughts, General," Enri Willard said as Davies gazed at the map before him.

"They have to hit us again soon," he murmured, almost to himself. "Don't they?" he looked up.

"No sir, they don't," Enri shrugged. "They're defeating us by just sitting there and they know it. We're losing millions of acres of crop land while they occupy so much of our territory. We have to stay here and keep them at bay, but they don't have to attack."

"Our new weapons had to come as a shock to them," the younger man continued. "It hurt their confidence in themselves and in their commanders. Likely hurt their General's confidence in himself as well. They won't be eager to face that kind of destruction again, even if the shock value is gone now. Another defeat like that last one might break their army entirely."

"It might break us, too," Davies pointed out. "Our casualties were horrendous."

"That is true, sir," Enri agreed. "But we've got two fresh corps on that line now. If their scouts and spies are worthy of the title, they know we've been heavily reinforced. They do still outnumber us but not by enough they can absorb the losses it would take to just try and roll over us. They're just as stuck as we are for the moment."

"If they keep sitting there it damages their morale almost as bad as the battle did," Davies argued. "The men will think their commander is afraid to face us."

"Maybe not," Enri countered "He may well explain to them the exact thing I just noted. 'We're winning just by being here and we don't have to lose another man in doing it'. That would appeal to the rank and file and keep their confidence up in both themselves and their commander."

"Are they smart enough to do that?" Davies asked.

"That I can't say, sir. That I can't say."

-

"So, we just sit here?"

Several heads nodded at the question, interested in hearing the answer themselves.

"For now, yes," Wilson nodded. He was entertaining his assembled Corps Commanders for supper, explaining his plans to them. "When the boats arrive we'll look at what can be done with them, and I've sent Stone into the middle province to try and pull some of their cavalry away from here. Anything we can do to weaken them, we'll do. I've also sent a courier to General Andrews asking if he can step up the pressure at the River Bridge. Even an attempted crossing there while we sit in camp might convince the Soulanies that we're making our push there now. If they draw off forces from here to help meet that threat it can only help us."

"How long?" another man asked, even as several men murmured their agreement to Wilson's plan.

"As long as it takes," Wilson replied evenly. "We're winning the war just by being here," he pointed out. "This is their prime growing area and we're sitting square in the middle of it. They have two choices; throw us out or starve. I don't care which one they chose, to be blunt. So long as we can defeat them without risking our soldiers any more than we have to, that's what we'll do. Until I hear otherwise from the Emperor, that is our plan."

He didn't like having to explain himself or being questioned like this. But these men were his top commanders, each leading several divisions of his army. He needed them supporting his decision, and he needed them talking about it. Knowing that the Commanding General was concerned for the welfare of his troops would give the army a badly needed boost in morale, or at least he hoped it would. He had been careful to make sure that several enlisted men were gathered to serve the table and take care of the chores and had ensured they could overhear his concern for his army. It wasn't feigned, he meant it. But allowing them to hear would add strength to the 'rumors' of why they weren't moving. Stolen information was always more accepted than given. Just human nature to be distrustful of open information he supposed.

His plan was brutally simple. Preserve his army, force the Soulanies to either attack him or just sit there. Either way he was winning. Meantime he had Stone going to raise a ruckus in the middle of Tinsee territory, the boats were on their way down the river and Daly was out of his hair.

And now he seemed to have convinced his leading commanders that his idea was absolutely the way to go.

"I like it," he heard more than once.

"We need our army as intact as possible to occupy Soulan after the war," he decided to add. "This allows us to do both. It will take a little longer, but we've waited for centuries. A few months more won't hurt us. We will win."

Heads nodded all around the table and Wilson sat back, relaxing slightly. He had convinced them that his plan was better. Hopefully that would help rebuild the confidence of the army and buy him some time to get things moving again.

He had won for now.

The collected commanders remained for another half-hour or so before they began to drift away, usually in pairs as they discussed the next day's duty or training or some other nuance. Wilson himself waited until the room was essentially empty before returning to his own quarters, stopping to thank the staff on his way out for doing such a good job. He knew that would be repeated throughout the camp and hoped it would add to the morale of the army in general.

Ignoring the presence of his escort and aide, Wilson ambled his way back to the small house he used as his private quarters. He barely registered his aide telling him goodnight and took no notice at all of the escort and guards around the small dwelling. Stepping inside he stripped off his uniform belt and tunic, placing them on a chair. He had just reached for the small decanter of bourbon on his desk when.
. .

"Good evening, General."

Wilson spun on his heel, hand flashing to his side only to find his sword not there.

"That isn't necessary, General," the man seated by the window said quietly. "If I meant to kill you, you would be dead already. Do go ahead and have your evening snort," a hand waved in the dark. "I'm not here to interrupt your routine."

"Then why are you here?" Wilson demanded, for some reason not bothering to call out to his guards. "For that matter who the hell are you and how did you get in here?"

"How I got in isn't really important, General," came the sardonic reply as the man stood, little more than a shadow against the wall it seemed. "As for who I am, call me Smith, I suppose. Colonel Smith, Imperial Secret Police." He said it calmly, as if he was just asking for a favor or giving a report.

Wilson could feel the blood drain from his face at the revelation. It wasn't as if he hadn't been expecting it, though he had allowed it to leave his mind in recent days as he labored to get his army back in shape and moving again. Now the specter of the ISP was standing before him in his own quarters.

"Well, what are you waiting for?" Wilson asked calmly. "I assume my family has already been eliminated?" He didn't know if he expected an answer or not, it was just what came to his mind. He did not expect 'Smith' to laugh in reply.

"Your family is fine so far as I know, General," Smith assured him. "As I said, if I were here to kill you, you would already be dead. I'm here to let you know that I have sanctioned Brigadier Daly at the Emperor's command and request that you stop your Provost investigation. Conclude it, I should say instead. This should sum things up nicely," he laid a folder on Wilson's desk. "It explains that Daly suffered from a heart problem and has died as a result of complications from that. Ensure that your physician cooperates with that report. You may send a copy of the completed investigation to the Emperor by courier since not doing so will attract attention. His Imminence is, however, already aware of what I've just told you."

"What?" Nothing could have surprised, could have shocked Wilson more.

"Brigadier Daly was becoming a problem," Smith told him. "You don't need the details but suffice it to say that he was fomenting his own rebellion of a sort, beginning with you. Undermining your position as commander of the army, presumably to pave the way for his being placed in command. The Emperor has tired of his machinations and put an end to them. That really is all that you need to know."

"Replace me?" Wilson seized on the one thing that made sense at the moment. "He doesn't, didn't, have the rank or the seniority for that! He would have destroyed the army!"

"Hence his unfortunate demise," Smith nodded. "He felt that membership in the Imperial family was sufficient qualification for leading the army, but the Emperor disagreed. At any rate, none of that is your concern, General. See to it that the investigation is concluded, preferably tomorrow. Assuming nothing else of note needs dealing with we should not be meeting again. Good luck with the army, General. I think your plan shows merit, by the way," Smith added. "It should work, and it keeps you out of reach of their new artillery."

Before Wilson could formulate a reply, Smith was gone. He almost ran to the door and threw it open, looking around him wildly much to his guard's consternation.

"Sir?" the sergeant asked warily.

"Did you see anyone just now?" Wilson demanded.

"Not since you went inside, sir," the man replied. "Is everything alright sir?"

"You saw no one?" Wilson ignored the question.

"No sir. All is secure."

Wilson realized suddenly how it must look with him standing on the small porch in his shirt tail, looking for a phantom that no one other than he had seen.

"Very well," Wilson nodded, forcing himself to be calm. "Carry on, Sergeant."

"Sir," the man stiffened to attention. Wilson made his way back inside, closing the door securely before allowing himself to react to the last few minutes. Sagging against the door, Wilson tried to take in those few minutes. He had gone from surprise to shock to acceptance that he was about to die to being reprieved all in the space of about two minutes. No matter how well balanced a man was, there were limits to what could be assimilated in so short a time and he had reached his limit for the moment.

Slowly he began to calm down, his heart rate slowing to something approaching normal. For lack of anything better to do he walked to his desk and picked up the folder 'Smith' had left for him. Inside he found a report from an Imperial physician certifying that Daly had a heart problem along with various letters confirming the presence of the heart defect in garbled medical jargon. A report on the conclusion of the investigation into the death of a Brigadier found deceased in his quarters detailing that medical report and the report of the examining physician certifying death by heart attack. All expertly done on proper forms and already signed. All that remained was to call the doctor and the investigator in and brief them on the findings of 'their' investigation and let them know how things stood.

And the way things stood apparently included the Emperor not having time for petty back stabbing and back room maneuvering. Wilson was reminded again that the current Emperor was not like his immediate predecessors in that he cared only for results and had no time for anything that might stand in their way. Something he had just proven with the assassination of his own cousin.

Placing the folder back on the desk, Wilson decided that he would have an extra drink before going to bed tonight. Maybe even two extra. It might help him sleep and he had a lot to do come morning.

-

Bryn Wysin's hammer rose and fell with a steady rhythm that a smaller, lesser man could not have maintained. Rough cotton shirt bulging with muscle, the smith truly was a giant of a man. He was also one of the best smiths around and that meant he stayed busy.

"Ho, Mister Wysin," Aaron Bell said as he walked up.

"Lad," the smith nodded in reply. "Be just a minute more," he said.

Bell watched as Wysin finished the lance cap he had been hammering, removing it from the iron bar he had used to shape it. Giving it an inspection, he nodded in apparent satisfaction, putting the final touches on the piece by hammering out the eyes using the odd-looking form next to his anvil. Dipping the piece in a barrel of water to cool it off, he tossed it onto a small table where one of his assistants would get it at some point and polish it.

"What can I do for ya lad?" he asked then, resting the hammer on his great anvil.

"Just paying a visit," Bell replied calmly. "We had a bit of a fishing trip a night or so ago. Lot of fish sent home," he said cryptically.

"Aye," Wysin nodded grimly. "Lot o' talk about the fishing, as well," he told the younger man. "Heard officers and enlisted alike discussing it all morning, wondering what has become of the fish."

"Anyone in particular we should talk to about the fish?" Bell asked carefully.

"No," Wysin shook his head. "Wasn't no complaints as I heard it, just them taking notice and wondering about it. So far that's all they be doing; wondering."

"Maybe they'll lose interest in a day or two," Bell smiled. "We'll see I expect. Meanwhile, you need anything done or gotten?"

"Nah, lad, we're good here for now," Wysin shook his head again. "Busy as can be but not run to ground. Men are bringing in what nots as they come off-line to have us repair and replace stuff what's worn and what have you. Reckon ole Tinker is more busy than we are."

"He's working right enough," Bell agreed. "Him doing leather work gets a lot of attention. Well, I guess I better get on. Speaking of Tinker, can't have him thinking I'm shirking. Might cut my pay," he grinned.

"Or might cut down on the time you can stare at the pretty waitress," Wysin needled a bit, laughing as Bell's face went red. "You've a good eye lad. She's a fine girl. Make a man a good wife."

"I ain't thinking about such," a red-faced Bell objected, though he was and everyone knew it. "Anyway, I'll see you later. Need me just send word."

"I'll do that lad."

Soon Wysin's hammer was falling again as Bell made his way through the camp, eyeing everything and everyone.

And thinking about a dark haired, dark eyed serving girl.

-

"Are you still brooding?"

Stephanie looked up from her book to see Winnie standing at the garden entrance, looking at her.

"I'm not brooding, dear," she smiled. "This is called reading. One does this for entertainment or for learning. Sometimes both. You should try it."

"Funny," Winnie snorted. "So, you are brooding, then." The younger woman walked to the bench and plopped down beside her most unladylike.

"I'm not brooding," Stephanie sighed, closing her book. "It wouldn't do me any good which makes it a waste of time. I'm just reading. And it's a nice day," she added with a wave around her. "One of the few, of late, that I'm not constantly on the run as well."

"True," Winnie agreed. "Still, it looks like brooding," she pushed a bit. "You need to make this right, Stephanie," she said more softly. "The longer you let it go, the worse it will be."

"If I thought I could make it right I'd have already done it, Winnie," Stephanie sighed, marking her place and closing the book. Her brief break from reality was over with. "I did the worst possible thing I could have, well almost," she amended, "and there's a price to pay for that. I hate that Parno is paying it as well because it's my fault and not his. But I caused this," her voice rang with finality.

"I'm not interested in blame," Winnie told her flatly. "I'm interested in seeing two of the most important people in my life repairing the damage to their relationship and working things out. That has to start with you. Like you said, he may not see a reason to come here again or to try and work things out. That means you have to do it."

"I don't know how," Stephanie was growing weary of this discussion. Winnie was nothing if not persistent. "Now I really don't wish to keep talking about this," she said more stiffly. "I had managed to put it out of my mind for a brief time until now." She stood, brushing her clothes off. "I know you mean well, Winnie, and I love you dearly for it. But enough. I have to look forward. Looking back is painful and useless. I know him. Much better than you. He will not forgive me. It isn't in him." With that she turned and left the garden without looking back, leaving Winnie watching her go and unable to come up with a suitable reply before Stephanie was already gone.

Winnie frowned. That hadn't gone as she'd planned at all. Clearly Stephanie felt as if she had no options going forward. Winnie had to convince her to try, somehow. She stood, face set with grim determination.

She would need some help.

-

"I'm afraid she's quite correct, Winifred," Memmnon said evenly. "Parno is not the forgiving sort. He is patient to a fault, but once he reaches a certain point then it's as if he simply turns you off like a lamp. I suppose he developed it as a defense mechanism against the rest of us," he admitted with a sigh. "We were none of us ever very good to him and that is an understatement if anything."

"Why?" she asked, arms crossed beneath her breasts. "Why be mean to him?"

"Our mother died giving birth to him," Memmnon told her, his gaze falling on something outside the window. "We blamed him for it. All his life. All of us did, from father on down. Even the servants treated him harshly and we allowed it."

"That's horrible," Winnie almost whispered. "My mother died birthing me," she added. "I don't know what I'd have done had my pa blamed me for that. I can't imagine blaming a child for something like that. That's not just mean, Memmnon, it's cruel."

"I'm aware of that," the King of Soulan nodded slowly, his gaze still fixed on something outside the window. Or nothing. It was a vacant stare, really. "I am aware of that but cannot undo it," he finally turned to face her. "I have done what I can to make what amends are possible, Winifred, but that is all I can do. I do not expect his forgiveness and would never ask for it. I do not deserve it," he said simply. "I find it the height of irony that the brother I treated the worst is the one upon whom I am most able to depend. To count on in such hard days as these."

"But regardless of the reason why," he continued after a moment of awkward silence, "I'm afraid that Doctor Corsin is quite right in her assessment of my youngest brother. Parno is not the forgiving kind. He never has been. His anger burns deep and long and such fires are almost impossible to put out."

"Something. . .there has to be something that we can do," Winnie refused to back down. "She's miserable, Memmnon! And while she may have angered him, she didn't do it on purpose! She was just upset herself, that's all. Surely he would listen to her if she tried to apologize."

"I cannot say," Memmnon shrugged helplessly. "I do not know. I don't know what she said to him or what context it was said in, nor do I know what his reaction to it was. It is possible that he might listen to her. He holds her in high esteem. There is, or was, a great affection for her in his heart I believe. Whether it is enough to weather such as storm I cannot say. I simply don't know."

"If she wishes to send him a message, I will have a Royal Courier deliver it," he offered. "It will reach him in three days time, no more. And the courier can wait for a return message, assuming he sends one. Anything I can do to aid her I will do," he promised.

"I need to take her to see him," Winnie said suddenly.

"No," Memmnon shook his head. "No, that is out of the question. A battlefield is no place for a woman, Winifred. Not even one so capable as you, my dear. And Parno does not need such a distraction, either. It would not be fair to him, placing him in such a position."

"You said anything you could do," Winnie semi-accused.

"That is not something I can do," Memmnon shook his head again. "Parno is the Marshal of the Army which means he has the final say in such matters, and he will not allow women on the battle line. The Army is his to command, Winnie. He sets the rules. That is the way it has always been. There are laws to separate the Crown from direct control of the Army and for many good reasons. It is the reason I could not take over when Therron was exiled. The law does not allow it."

"What if Parno hadn't been there?" Winnie demanded. "What then?"

"We would have had to appoint a general from the ranks to take Therron's place. Unless and until I had a second son, who would take command upon his majority and his graduating from the War College. It would not be the first time," he added. "In such cases the King of course assumes a more direct command of the military, as the General will answer to him. But the role of the Marshal is to separate the military of Soulan from the Crown."

"Why would you want to do that?" Winnie asked, clearly confused.

"A weak or angry ruler in command of a great military can make ill-advised decisions that cannot be undone," Memmnon said gravely. "A ruler can also be black-mailed much easier, or have pressures put upon him in the form of threats against family and the like. A Sovereign who is so compromised and in full control of the military apparatus can do a great deal of harm and there is no one to stop him."

"So, who stops the Marshal then?" Winnie asked.

"Rivalry among siblings of the Crown is a fact," Memmnon smiled wanly. Sadly. "Consider my own brother and sister and the lengths they would go to rule instead of myself, or even our father. A King would not allow a sibling to use the military improperly, and a Marshal would do likewise for the King. It is a very old system. Almost as old as the Kingdom herself. One that has served us well."

"So, because Parno doesn't want women in combat we can't even visit the camp for her to speak with him?" Winnie asked, just short of surly. Memmnon considered that for a moment.

"Technically I suppose that would not violate the spirit of his ruling," he finally replied. "But it would mean stretching it beyond recognition," he added before her smirk could bloom fully. "And as I said, he does not need such a distraction at the moment."

"She's not a distraction!" Winnie shot back.

"She most certainly is," Memmnon returned more calmly. "Whether you like it or not, her presence at the camp, or your own for that matter, would absolutely be a distraction to Parno and to many others. Not to mention that your presence would disrupt the camp every time you 'visited'."

"Who said anything about me going?" Winnie asked.

"Winifred, please," Memmnon feigned exaggerated patience. "I know it's difficult for you but could you please not constantly treat me like I'm an idiot?" His tone was easy, even light, but there was also a bit of steel there even so.

"What?"

"You have learned to play me very well, my dear," Memmnon chuckled lightly. "And I go along with it because it pleases you, which in turn pleases me. But don't fool yourself into thinking I can't read you just as well. While I have no doubt whatsoever that you intend to help the good doctor regain her relationship with my brother, do not for a minute pretend that you haven't thought about the fact that this is an ideal way for you to go somewhere you've been wanting to go for some time now."

She had the grace to look embarrassed but didn't back down.

"I already know I can't do that," she told him, trying to keep her dignity amid a furious blush at being 'caught out'. "And I've stopped asking. This isn't about me, Memmnon. It's about Stephanie and Parno. He may not want to admit it but he needs her. Just as much as she needs him."

"Do not ever fool yourself into thinking Parno needs anyone," Memmnon replied flatly. "You have not and will never meet anyone who is more self-sufficient than Parno McLeod. Again, likely something that was forced upon him as a defensive mechanism to deal with our poor treatment of him as a child and even a young man. The only person he ever really and truly had to depend on in his life is now lost to him," he almost murmured.

"Not if we can get them back talking to one another!" Winnie declared just short of hotly.

"I'm not talking about the good doctor, Winifred," Memmnon sighed, rubbing his eyes as he began to feel a headache coming.

"Then who?" she demanded. "The Colonel," she answered her own question a second later, her voice falling to a near whisper. "You're talking about Colonel Nidiad."

"Indeed," Memmnon nodded. "Darvo practically raised Parno himself. And his daughter. Her mother also died in childbirth I believe, though I. . .now that I've said that I'm not sure it's true. I do know that she died before Darvo assumed his post as

Parno's retainer. Regardless," he waved the irrelevancy away, "Darvo was the only person Parno ever allowed himself to depend upon. Or trust. I suspect he had begun to do so with her as well before their rift. Perhaps that is why he has reacted so poorly to whatever it was she said to him."

"I don't know what she said to him, she's never told me," Winnie shrugged. "I do know that she was trying to pressure Parno into marrying her before he returned to the front so that she could try and conceive a child."

"Good grief," Memmnon allowed his head to fall back on his shoulders as he looked toward the ceiling in exasperation. "Tell me you're joking."

"I'm not. Why?"

"Winifred, why would you think that's a bad idea?" Memmnon tried to coach her.

"I don't think it's a bad idea," she replied. "Why do you think it is?"

"I just told you what kind of father. . .how our father, the King, treated Parno when he was a child. Parno may as well not had a father. Now, why would he agree to try and create a child only to leave his or her mother alone the very next morning, now knowing when or if he would return or if he could assure that child's safety?"

CHAPTER ELEVEN

-

Parno sat before his dying fire, gazing into the embers that glowed with the gentle breeze. The coals would rise and fall in light almost as if they had a heartbeat of their own, creating a small light show against the rocks that lined his fire pit.

He had been back with the army for almost three weeks. In that time, he had accomplished a good deal of work. 1st Corp was even now being retrained, as was 2nd Corps though they would be a week to ten days behind due to travel. Chad and his men were doing better than expected and would be ready for deployment in less than a month while the first regular army unit to attend Cove's training session was well into their own cycle. Another two months, three at the outside, would see the first full division of cavalry trained up to the new standards ready to take the field.

All of that should have made Parno happy. Yet he knew that as good as the news was, it paled next to the work that remained to be done. Until 1st and 2nd Corps had completed their training cycle and were back on the line, the Soulan Army was vulnerable. Even after that his army would remain weaker than the enemy, especially when he pulled either Herrick or Freeman's men off line for their turn at the new regimen. He poked absently at the coals with a stick, his mind far afield.

He'd received word from Pierce that his efforts had been hampered by bad roads and trails, but that also meant that any enemy force would face the same. Meanwhile Pierce had arrived at Springfield and established his command, patrols already out and Pioneers already working to close off trails and roads or at the minimum make them harder to travel. Among all that would be traps and pitfalls to make the enemy wary of approaching even open roads for fear of ambush or injury from those traps.

Additional messages had informed him that the River Guard was now patrolling both rivers and the special artillery unit was in place along the Cumberland, supported by an infantry regiment and a smattering of cavalry. If the Nor managed to move up river then there should at least be some warning. It was nothing but blind luck that the Imperials hadn't already tried something like that considering their extensive use of boats in their initial assault. Parno shook his head in silent recrimination of himself for not thinking of it sooner.

"What troubles you my Prince?" Cho Feng asked quietly and Parno managed to prevent himself from jumping. He was convinced that Cho did that just to startle him. He refused to give the older man the satisfaction when he could help it.

"Where would you like me start Master Feng?" he replied, leaning back in his chair and looking toward his teacher. "There's a long list of things that trouble me at the moment. Be glad to share them with you," he snorted.

"I see," Cho nodded as if Parno's reply had granted him some answer only he could hear.

"What do you see Master Feng?" Parno asked, curious as to the answer.

"You are thinking about her," Cho said calmly, taking a seat across the fire from Parno. Surprised by the statement, Parno couldn't stop himself from laughing. A raised eyebrow was the only response from Cho.

"I assure you Master Feng I was not," he managed to choke out after a minute. "In fact, she might be the one thing I haven't been thinking about as I sat here."

"I see," Cho raised his other eyebrow, a signal that he was more or less calling Parno a liar.

"Think what you want Cho," Parno shrugged, still chuckling. "It doesn't cost me anything for you or the rest to believe that I'm sitting here brokenhearted."

"Are you?" the oriental warrior challenged.

"I am not," Parno assured him. "At the moment you spoke I was somewhat angry with myself for ignoring the threat of the river for as long as I did."

"It was not your responsibility at the time," Cho reminded him.

"It has been for a while now," Parno rebutted, shaking his head. "I should have thought of it. Should have anticipated it."

"So, should others," Cho shrugged. "As I recall you have a military unit that is responsible for river security," his teacher reminded him. "They should have already had a plan for this scenario."

"Should have, yes," Parno agreed. "But as with so many of Therron's appointments, I'm afraid the Commodore is more qualified to support my brother than lead the River Guard."

"Then replace him," Cho said simply.

"If I can find a suitable replacement I will," Parno nodded. "For the time being I think the fear of losing his head will ensure that the good Commodore at least follows my orders. I doubt I can expect any kind of original thinking out of him but he can at least do what he's told."

"What else?" Cho asked.

"Thinking about how shorthanded we are, and how long it will be before we can have the entire army trained up and ready. And after that how long it will be before we can take any action that will begin to move the Nor out of our lands."

"It may be that you cannot force them back and will have to settle for a war of attrition," Cho suggested.

"No, we can't do that," Parno shook his head slowly, looking into the fire once more. "That way leads to defeat, Cho. They have more men, more support, more everything than we do. We have a few advantages but none of them are usable in such a war. We have to make them fight, but fight when and where we want. Where we have the advantage and can use it against them."

"You know your enemy and yourself," Cho nodded in satisfaction. "Yet you must also face the fact that your enemy may not allow you to select the battlefield nor the day of engagement. What then?"

"If they attack here, we hold here," Parno shrugged. "We have three more or less full corps here plus several independent commands as well as our new artillery. We've made a fairly impressive defensive line and have sufficient cavalry to prevent a flanking maneuver, even one in strength. We are outnumbered," he nodded slowly, "and that will hurt us. I estimate the enemy has us at least at a two-on-one disadvantage, and likely closer to three-to-one. But," he looked up at his teacher suddenly, "they have a choice to make as well."

"Oh?" Cho asked, leaning forward. "What would that be in your opinion?"

"They have enough men to defeat us here, probably," Parno said. "But their losses will be so great they can forget about conquering the rest of Soulan, let alone occupying it. The war will stretch on for years and they will never have any peace in these lands."

"A possibility," Cho nodded thoughtfully.

"So, they can't do both," Parno shoved his stick into the fire and left it, standing. "They have to decide what's more important; defeating us, or claiming our territory for their own. Looking at the time, money and material they have invested in this war, I think it's clear they want to conquer and hold Soulan for themselves. Add us to their 'Empire'. That means they need their army somewhat intact in order to pacify the Kingdom."

"True," Cho nodded.

"They lost a field army at the Gap, or at least so much of it that what's left is useless," Parno held up a finger. "They've lost two battles here that cost them heavily." A second finger. "It cost us too, but far worse for them. Semmes and his command managed to destroy their feint," he added a third finger. "Hurt their navy and exposed their ruse, not to mention inflicting serious losses on them. Our own losses were ruinous to be honest, but they accomplished their mission. Nor losses are adding up in a hurry and they had planned to take us by surprise. The war should have been long over by now had their plans worked."

"But they didn't," Cho leaned back, a faint look of amusement on his face.

"So now their plans are shot," Parno nodded as he began to pace slightly. "They have to face the fact that we will be able to cripple their army if they come at us. We may not win the field but we can spoil their victory. We can hurt them enough that they can't take over Soulan, which means their losses mean nothing." He paused, face contorted in a frown.

"Past commands have seemed callous or indifferent to losses," he said flatly. "One of the things that Darvo mentioned to me was the Nor penchant for simply throwing mass numbers of men at us with no thought for actual strategy or tactics. Just charge at us and overwhelm us with numbers. Which has always failed in the long run."

"But. . ." Cho prodded when Parno didn't immediately continue.

"But this time is different," Parno stopped his pacing and looked at his teacher. "This time the Nor aren't going about things dumbly. They're using their heads for once and that might make them dangerous indeed. Combining their strength with some intelligence could well be what helps them achieve victory. Or would have," he muttered.

"Were it not for you," Cho finished for him. "You, my Prince, have been the thorn in their side. Actually, more like in their eyes, to be more accurate. You have blunted their stroke to take your capitol," the oriental held up a finger of his own, "then led an attack against their position here that set them back several weeks and inflicted heavy losses." A second finger.

"When they had mustered a prepared attack on your positions you beat them back, again inflicting massive losses upon them," he added a third finger, and then a fourth. "And it was you who saw through the ruse out on the ocean, enabling you to bring the other half of your army to bear here. Something they sought to prevent until it was too late. From their standpoint, you are the problem, Parno McLeod," the older man grinned slightly.

"I doubt they even know who I am," Parno snorted. "Whoever that is over there probably just thinks Therron is lucky or else allowing his subordinates to command in battle."

"That may be true now, and was certainly true in the beginning," Cho nodded. "Remember however that your flag of truce offer was sent in your name?" Parno looked at him.

"I had forgotten that," he admitted, a bit shame faced. "So much for them not knowing who I am, huh?"

"A simple thing to overlook," Cho allowed Parno a bit of leeway. "But something to be aware of. The enemy at least knows who you are even if they know nothing else about you. Remember that. They now know you," he cautioned.

"They know who I am," Parno emphasized with a shake of his head. "That's not the same thing as knowing me. No one over there will know much about me because no one cared anything about me before now. Anything they know will have been learned before the war for the most part. Inept, drunken brawler, womanizer, the list goes on and on, right?"

"An important distinction and a good observation," Cho agreed. "But you have proven to them by now that you are not inept, whatever else might be true."

"That's true, yeah," Parno agreed. "But they won't know anything worthwhile about me otherwise. Nothing about my training or my education, things like that. It will be hard for them to anticipate me, at least for now. That will change the more we're engaged of course, but for now I'm still largely an unknown factor to them. Combined with the reverses they've suffered recently it might make them hesitant, at least for a bit."

"And that time will benefit you, not them?" Cho prodded, always teaching.

"No, it could benefit them as well," Parno replied after brief consideration. "But the longer they wait before resuming action, the better off we are. If they actually wait long enough for just 1st Corps to finish training and return to action then I'm confident we can meet any attack they can mount and survive."

"I see," Cho said yet again and Parno looked sharply to him.

"What does that mean?" he demanded.

"Perhaps you were not thinking of her after all," the older man smiled and Parno had to chuckle.

"Always comes back to that, doesn't it?" he asked. "You, Karls, even Enri seems to want to say something on occasion. And I'm pretty sure that Harrel has thought about it more than once."

"We are merely concerned for you," Cho shrugged, unapologetic.

"Don't be," Parno told him firmly. "It's better this way. I tried to make her see that before and couldn't. Apparently, this time I succeeded. I have put the good doctor behind me and you all need to do the same. We have more than enough in front of us without looking behind us as well."

"I will agree with that," Cho nodded slowly. "I am sorry to see you have such a loss, my Prince," he added softly.

"Ah, I'm used to it," Parno shrugged, returning to his seat and the stick he'd left poked into his fire. When he said nothing else, Cho rose and departed as quietly as he came, Parno not even noticing as he gazed into the fire.

"I'm used to it."

-

Parno woke the next morning with an idea. Messengers were sent out and orders issued. An hour later over a dozen high ranking Soulanie officers were assembled in the Marshal's command tent.

"It's time we start putting the Nor on edge," Parno told them without any preamble. "We can't just sit here and let them dictate everything, we have to set the pace. Before I had to send them on another mission, Generals Beaumont and Whipple were operating behind enemy lines, harassing lines of communication and supply, attacking smaller detachments and slowing larger ones where possible. We're going to replicate that on a much larger scale, now."

"I'm taking one cavalry division from both 4th and 5th Corps, placing them with the cavalry division I took from 3rd Corps, and forming a new if temporary unit. We'll call it 1st Cavalry Corps for now, I suppose. I will leave it to Generals Davies, Herrick and Freeman to decide the command structure according to their experience, but the orders are simple; get in behind the Nor line, deep into occupied territory, and tear it up. Destroy anything you can that might hurt the Nor or aid us in any way. Kill all the Nor you can wherever you can with an eye toward preserving your own command wherever possible. I don't want any suicidal or reckless attacks made so far from home. Every soldier and every horse we lose are lost for good so far from here, so make sure your losses are weighed against what you might accomplish. Understood?"

"Yes sir," a dozen or more voices replied, heads nodding all over.

"Very well. Make plans to head out tomorrow morning. You have the rest of the day to see to your provisioning. I expect you back here in no more than two weeks unless something is wrong or you find a reason to head back all at once. Be watchful for Tribal Warriors. We haven't seen them since the cavalry battle but they were here then so they are probably still in the area. If you get the chance to kill them take it, so long as doing so doesn't endanger your command. I cannot stress this part enough, gentlemen; do not endanger your command. I would rather you allow a ripe target to get by you than for you to risk great loss in trying to take it. Your primary mission is to keep the Nor off balance, so as long as you're doing that, everything else is a bonus. Any questions for me?"

"Prisoners, sir?" one man asked.

"None," Parno said flatly. "Black flag all the way, gentlemen. Anything else?" There wasn't.

"Then Godspeed you all and good hunting."

-

The 5th, 9th and 14th Cavalry division commanders were arrayed before the commander of 1st Army and the other Corp Commanders. There were a total of twelve full cavalry divisions in the standing Soulan Army along with numerous smaller, independent commands ranging from battalions to regiments to entire brigades. For reasons that had long since been forgotten there had never been a 7th or a 13th division. All three men were good commanders and among the best trained and educated in all of Soulan.

"General Allen, you will lead the combined command," Davies addressed the commander of the 9th Cavalry, part of Raines' 3rd Corps. The man nodded his understanding, remaining silent.

"Remember the Marshal's warnings," Davies stressed to them. "Do not endanger your commands. Your primary mission is to spread havoc among the heathen and be seen doing it. Reports of a large group of southern horse soldiers in their rear areas will likely cause a problem among their rank and file as well as panic their leadership. In the past that has always been how we hurt them so badly."

"You take no prisoners," he said grimly. "I know that is distasteful but consider that it's how they make war. And remember that many of our fellow subjects are now suffering the not so tender mercies of the Imperial Army. Let that harden your hearts when necessary or needful."

"If I may?" General Thaddeus Coe, commanding 5th Cavalry raised a hand. "Are we to allow some prisoners to live so as to let them spread the word? If we kill ninety of one hundred for example and then release the rest? To tell their tale to others?"

"An excellent tactic and one the Marshal has already approved of," Davies nodded approvingly. "Good thinking. You may certainly do so. Anything else?"

"The Marshal said unless we find a reason to head back sooner," General Wilton Vaughan, commander of the 14th Cavalry said. "What would qualify as such a reason?" Vaughan was a towering black skinned man whose family's military service predated the Kingdom itself. His ancestor had literally ridden with Tyree.

"Yeah," the other two men nodded in agreement.

"If you found yourselves in danger of being cut off, for instance," Davies replied. "If you realized that the Nor have found a way to entrap you or otherwise damage your command. If you came across actionable intelligence that there was an attack in the offing and your presence here could turn the tide. Anything of that sort gentlemen would be grounds for you to abandon your mission and return here as expeditiously as possible. In a way that does not further endanger your command," he added as a warning.

"Yes sir," Vaughan nodded, falling silent once more.

"Your combined strength is tallied at twenty-two thousand seven hundred and forty-two effectives as of this morning," Davies continued, consulting a note in his hand. "I assume you have horses for all of them?" Three heads nodded. "All in good repair and ready to ride?" Davies stressed, and again received three nods.

"Very well. General Allen, I will leave the rest to you. You know your orders and your mission. Godspeed, gentlemen, and may He go before you."

"Thank you General," Allen said, taking Davies proffered hand, as did his two temporary subordinates. The three men departed for their own commands, a hectic afternoon waiting as they readied their commands for the coming dawn.

"What do you think?" Davies asked after the three had gone.

"It's a good plan," Freeman said at once. "One that historically has worked well. Which of course is an argument against using as well as for," he conceded. "Still, the plan here isn't to try and win the war with this tactic, but just to stall the Nor. I think it can work."

"I agree," Herrick nodded thoughtfully. "I'd feel better about it if they were stronger, but I realize why that's not possible. We have to maintain enough strength here to be able to withstand an attack if it does come."

"We've stripped most of the Kingdom of men as it is," Davies nodded. "Raines has only one cavalry division left, along with some militia and mounted infantry. There isn't a cavalry force larger than a regiment that isn't committed to one front of the other aside from the men at Cove Canton. It's all we can do."

"So, it is," Herrick agreed. "Well, we've been away a good bit. Time to head back, I think, General," he nodded to Davies and took his leave.

"Reckon I better go as well," Freeman nodded in agreement. "No telling what that bunch of mine has been up to while I been gone," he chuckled.

"Take care," Davies shook Freeman's hand and watched the other man depart. Looking back to the map before him, he took a deep breath and released it slowly. It was a lot of territory to cover and there was a lot that could go wrong, but . . . they had to do something, and there was just as much that could go right as well.

It was a good plan. They'd just have to wait and see what happened.

CHAPTER TWELVE

-

Captain Anthony Chastain, commanding officer of the cruiser HMS Halifax, Soulan Navy Gulf Squadron, observed the small collection of buildings through his glass from the command deck of his vessel. As part of their anti-piracy patrols the naval presence in the Gulf would check on these outlying areas for the presence of pirates or raiders, or signs of their activity.

This particular settlement was actually not a settlement at all, but was rather a collection of buildings that belonged to the Royal Family. Rarely used even in peace time, the last thing Chastain had expected to see was signs of occupancy. Smoke rising and movement that he could make out from off shore had put that expectation to rest. Someone was definitely there.

"Something wrong sir?" his executive officer, Commander Jerome Hart, asked.

"I'm not sure," Chastain admitted. "Take a look," he passed his glass over. Puzzlement written on his face, Hart did as ordered, taking the glass and surveying the shore.

"Pirates again?" he asked, lowering the glass and then returning it to its owner.

"Could be," Chastain nodded. "Signal to Seadragon and Seasnake," he ordered. "Prepare to lower boats to send shore party ashore. All Marines to go ashore prepared for engagement." Seadragon and Seasnake were frigates, escorts for the heavier Halifax.

"Order Major Guilford to stand to with his men as well," he added. "We'll take all our men ashore in case this is a problem. Perhaps it's just a visitor, or a party from the Family seeing to the upkeep of the place, but in time of war I doubt it."

"Aye sir," Hart nodded and went to issue the proper orders. Leaving Chastain to turn his attention back to the compound on shore. It had been used by pirates more than once and Chastain had cleared it twice himself over the years since he'd been assigned to the Gulf. Nothing brought pirates and brigands out like war.

He'd see soon enough.

-

Captain of Inspectorate Dennis Johnson had never been happy with his assignment, and that had not changed in the time since they had arrived. Therron McLeod should be six feet in the ground right now for what he'd done (or better still burned to ash and the dust scattered across the Kingdom), and yet he was sitting here pretty as you please with a house full of servants and a life of leisure. Had it been any of them that had committed such treason they'd be lucky to be sentenced to hard labor for the rest of their lives.

But orders were orders, and General Brock had shown great trust in Johnson to give him this assignment. Sixty men in the guard force he commanded plus a dozen support staff for the Prince had not completely filled the billets around this place. Having been designed and intended as a retreat for the Royal Family, there was sufficient billeting for a complete household staff and a full regiment of cavalry each as escort, including sufficient stables for so large a force.

The place had an older couple as caretakers to keep it clean and pest free, but they didn't live here. Otherwise the place was deserted when not in use. Of course, it would be in use now, at least for the foreseeable future, as the home of Therron McLeod. He shook his head again at the thought of such a terrible punishment. This place had near ideal weather year around, save for the occasional storm. Yes, a real punishment to be living here. Fully stocked library, servants, fresh food, all the comforts of home. Must be nice, being the son of a-

"Sir," Johnson's musings were cut short by the word. He looked to see Lieutenant Smith standing beside him.

"Yes?"

"Sails to the west, sir," Smith reported, pointing in that direction and offering a glass. "At least three vessels. Approaching slowly."

Johnson raised the glass, looking to the approaching ships. He couldn't make out any flags as yet. Could be pirates, could also be part of the Gulf Squadron. He said as much to Smith.

"Yes sir," Smith nodded. "But did you notice they're launching boats?"

Johnson had not noted that and took another look. Barely visible even with the glass were a dozen small boats. He couldn't be sure at this distance but it did look as if though they were headed in.

"A dozen more or less," Johnson mused, lowering his glass. "Figuring ten men per, they'll outnumber us two-to-one or close enough it won't matter. Sound the alarm, mister," he ordered Smith, who snapped a salute and ran to carry out his order.

Dammit! Johnson sword mentally. He had told Brock that his short company wasn't enough for such an isolated post as this. And that was before he had learned from the caretakers that the place had been overrun by pirates at least twice in the last five years. Cleared each time by the Navy, they had managed to do a good deal of damage in the meantime, not to mention using the place as a base.

"Could be this is the Navy, and they think we're pirates," he mused aloud. "Or it could be pirates coming to take the place again," he sighed. He had sent word to Brock upon their arrival that he was too exposed here and needed at least as many men again as what he had, but had received no reply. In truth he hadn't expected any but the Army ran on paperwork the joke went. If something went wrong here, he had a written record of the fact that he'd asked at least twice for more troops. He knew there was a war on, but if you wanted to keep a seditious member of the Royal Family alive and yet separated from everyone you had to be willing to part with the manpower to get it done.

The bell in the courtyard began to ring, jolting Johnson from yet another reverie. Shaking his head, he made his way to the main house to tell the guard there to keep Therron McLeod inside the house until he could sort this out.

-

Inside, unaware that Captain Johnson thought so poorly of him (not that he would care or even notice), Therron McLeod looked up from his book at the sounding of the bell. Realizing what the bell meant, he closed his book and stood, walking to the window of the study and looking out at the ocean.

The house, indeed the entire compound faced westerly, placing the reinforced rear of the strongly made buildings toward the most likely direction of any storms. As a result, he could see the ocean clearly and in the distance sails. Ships!

Even as he turned toward his door it opened, then was filled with the large form of Lieutenant Hans Bruckner. Very large man was Bruckner.

"Beg pardon sir," the man's voice was predictably deep. "Ships approaching. Captain Johnson requests you stay under cover until he knows who it is. For your safety, sir," he added.

"Thank you," Therron nodded. "I will be here."

"Sir," Bruckner nodded and closed the door. Therron almost laughed when he heard the audible click of the door locking. So predictable. As if he was suddenly going to become a threat to nearly one hundred people. He returned his attention to the approaching boats, wondering who was coming to dinner.

-

"Activity on the beach sir," Major Guilford reported.

"Very well," Chastain nodded. "There wasn't much chance they wouldn't see us coming. Ready your men, Major."

The marine nodded and began flashing signals to the other long boats. Each boat had a crew of four and carried one dozen marines, a full company. Whoever was using the Royal Compound Chastain doubted their ability to withstand a full company of marines and a platoon of sailors.

He'd soon test that theory.

-

"All men standing to, sir," Lieutenant Smith reported.

"Very well," Johnson nodded absently, his gaze still fixed on the boats as they approached the shore. "They appear to be in uniform so it's possible this is a visit from the Navy."

"Yes sir," Smith nodded. "I would imagine activity here would attract their attention after what we were told about the pirates sometimes making their base here."

"Just so," Johnson nodded. "I'll take two men and meet them on the shore when they land," he said suddenly. "No point in having more, and if they are Navy boats then there's no reason to, either. Maintain the men at their posts. If we're wrong and it's an enemy force, then carry out your orders."

"Sir, you should let me-" Smith began but stopped at Johnson's raised hand.

"One day, perhaps even this day Mister Smith, you will find yourself in a position of command. When you do, command. Lead. But today is my day I'm afraid. You have your orders."

"Sir," Smith snapped to attention, nodding, and then hurried to his own place. Smith indicated the two nearby troopers to follow and then started for the beach.

"A good walk before dinner never harmed anyone."

-

Chastain allowed half the force to beach before his boat went into shore. With both himself and Major Guilford aboard he couldn't afford to let the boat be sunk or the occupants killed. He had not thought about that at the time or he would have put Guilford on another boat. By the time his boat made land there was a man in a Soulan Army uniform standing on the beach a short way from the boats, watching them carefully. Two other soldiers were standing behind him at rest.

"Major, this appears to be Soulan Army but we'll proceed with caution," he ordered Guilford.

"Aye, sir," Guilford nodded. "Dooley, Johansen, take a point. We are not hostile unless we are met with force. Understood?"

"Aye Major," the two men answered in near unison.

"Off with you then," he ordered. "Form squads and follow!" he ordered the others. The sergeants from each boat had already organized their men so it remained only to set them in motion. Guilford's three lieutenants watched this action with a wary eye, knowing better than to interfere with the NCO's work. Two of the junior officers, the men commanding the frigate detachments, were fairly experienced and more steady. His third lieutenant, a gangling youth of nineteen fresh from Officer Training School and on his first tour, looked both scared and lost. Guilford shook his head sadly and looked back to the soldiers in the distance. He'd thought having the boy with him on Halifax, training him up himself, would help the lad but thus far he could see no sign of that.

Well, he would learn. If he didn't then he'd die or be mustered out. There was no room in the Navy for useless baggage. This wasn't the Army after all!

"Forward," he waved. "One squad to flanks to cover, the rest five up, five back. Make it so, gentlemen."

"Aye Major," he heard three voices reply, one a bit hesitant but still loud enough.

"Caution is the word, Major," Chastain urged. "Mister Reed, you will remain here in command of the boat detachment. Be ready to come to our assistance if needful, but be also ready to make way in the event we need a quick retreat." Lieutenant Reed, Chastain's own Third and also on his first tour, nodded.

"Aye Cap'n," his voice was steady and firm. Chastain almost smirked. His Third was much better than Guilford's.

"Steady lads," the Major's voice brought Chastain back to the present and he turned to follow the marines up the beach.

-

Johnson watched the marines approach warily, fairly certain that he was facing Soulan forces now and thus friendlies.

"That's far enough," he said calmly when the marines were in easy speaking distance. "Advance, be recognized, state your business. This is Royal Land and property of the Crown."

A man in the rugged shipboard livery of a marine officer stepped forward flanked by two hulking marines.

"John Guilford, Marine Detachment Delta, Commanding," the man reported. "Stationed aboard the cruiser Halifax. We're charged with keeping this area clear and saw activity so we're investigating."

"Quite a party for an investigation," Johnson observed.

"Last time we lost nine men killed and fourteen wounded clearing this place," Guilford nodded, sounding in no way apologetic. "We investigate in force after that."

"Sounds like a good policy," Johnson nodded. "I'm Captain Dennis Johnson, Office of the Inspector General and commanding this detail. There is currently a member of the Royal Family present, convalescing. We're his protection detail."

-

". . .protection detail."

Chastain frowned at that. Since when did the IG do that kind of work? He stepped forward now.

"I'm Captain Anthony Chastain, Commanding Task Force 3 of Gulf Squadron, Soulan Navy. Also, commanding the cruiser Halifax. Forgive my ignorance Captain, but since when does the IG provide protection details for the Royal Family?"

"This is a special case, Captain Chastain," Johnson replied easily. "Normally we do not, you are correct. In this instance, however, we are."

"You'll forgive me if I ask for some kind of verification of that I hope," Chastain replied. "It would not be the first time that someone tried to make use of this place by pretending to be part of the Soulan Military."

"I can well understand your doubts, Captain," Johnson nodded. "We were informed of the history when we arrived. I was somewhat put out that I hadn't been given that information before hand, to be honest." Johnson walked forward, pulling a leather wallet from inside his coat which he opened. Removing a paper from inside he passed it to Chastain.

"My credentials," he offered. Chastain took the paper and inspected it. It did, indeed, identify one Dennis Johnson as a Captain of the Inspectorate. The description of Johnson matched the man he was speaking to and the seal on the paper was authentic. He passed the paper back, feeling a bit easier.

"Thank you, Captain," he said politely. "I appreciate that."

"Not at all," Johnson accepted his papers back and returned them to the wallet which he once again stored inside his jacket. "Do you need anything before returning to your vessels?" he asked.

"I would prefer the men be able to rest a short while before rowing back," Chastain admitted. "And if you have water that would be much appreciated."

"I think we can accommodate you alright," Johnson replied with a nod. "I assume you will want to send your men up in groups so as to maintain a guard on the boats?"

"I doubt anyone would try to take one with the ships just offshore, but yes," Chastain nodded. "Major, you may divide your command and send half to water now, the other half when they return. Mister Reed, you will do likewise for our own men and maintain command of the boat force, ensuring that all men are allowed the chance to get water and rest."

"Sir!" Reed barked and began issuing orders that weren't needed but had to be given nonetheless. Chastain watched for a few seconds as Reed worked, then nodded in apparent satisfaction and turned back to Johnson.

"If you would, please Captain."

"Right this way, Captain."

-

"What's the matter with you?" Beaumont demanded as he watched Whipple squirming in his saddle.

"I don't know," was the uncharacteristic reply. "I just get the feeling something is off, somewhere. I can't put my finger on it but I also can't seem to get rid of the thought, either."

"It'll pass," Beaumont promised. "We're making good time, too. You were right. This is better than trying to follow or anticipate Callens."

"We should be there day after tomorrow if nothing happens," Whipple nodded his agreement. "And well ahead of Callens, too," he added with a smirk.

"We'll see this put right soon enough," Beaumont agreed with a grim look on his face. "I'll be glad to see it behind us. It's a long ride back to where we belong. Sooner we can start, the better."

-

"I always forget how nice this place is," Chastain said as he and Johnson made their way onto the veranda of the main building.

"It is that," Johnson agreed. "Care for a taste?" he asked with a grin.

"I would indeed," Chastain grinned. He followed the man inside and then into a small office off the main hall. Johnson pulled a bottle and two small glasses from the shelf behind the desk and poured the two of them a drink.

"The Crown," Johnson held his glass up.

"Long may she stand," Chastain nodded, clinking his own glass against Johnson's before upending his glass. The fiery liquid burned as it traveled down his throat.

"Oh, that's good," he murmured. "I thank you kind sir," he smiled at Johnson as he set the glass on the desk. "Almost made the trip in from the ship worthwhile," he joked.

"Glad I could help," Johnson smiled.

"So, what are you really doing here?" Chastain asked. "I've never known anyone in the Royal Family to travel with less than regimental escort."

"I'm afraid I've revealed all I'm allowed to about that, Captain," Johnson told him.

-

Therron had been able to see the men disembark from the boats and recognized them as Soulan Navy. His mind immediately began fomenting a plan. This was an ideal opportunity for him to make is escape. If he could convince that Captain to assist him then he could travel up the coast, land in Norfok, the capitol of the Coastal Province Government, and head overland back into the Kingdom. He might even be able to get assistance from the CPC government. He'd always had a good relationship with them, or thought he had. The Coastal Province Coalition depended on Soulan for protection from Imperial aggression. He knew many of the higher-ranking men in the CPC military. It was small, but very good. A few of them to back his play would put him in a position to take power from Memmnon and his father.

But first he had to get a message to that Captain and make his escape. He could ensure his assistance once he was free.

"Now how to get attention from him," Therron mused as he glanced around the room. Movement drew his attention back to the window and he almost smiled as he saw the ship captain and half of his men coming toward the house.

Excellent. Now he had to think of a way to get the man's help. Moving to the desk, Therron used a pen and paper to write a short note. He dried the ink and then rolled the message tight, secreting it in his sleeve.

He could hear when Johnson had brought the Captain inside. Realizing that his chance was here, Therron hurried to complete his preparation. He would only have one chance at this. There was some risk involved, but the greater risk was in doing nothing.

-

"I understand," Chastain nodded. "Well, whatever you're doing here I wish you well. If it weren't so isolated it would be a great place. Well, it is a great place but would be better if it were less isolated," he amended.

"It is isolated," Johnson agreed. "Having to send wagons on a four- or five-day trip for supplies, men wanting to have furlough to try and find something to do, there's always som-" he was interrupted by the sound of breaking glass and then something heavy hitting the floor. They looked at each other and then Johnson started for the door. He had scarcely made his way into the hallway when he heard Bruckner shout from the study. Forgetting the naval man behind him, Johnson broke into a run.

He found Bruckner kneeling over a prone Therron McLeod who was turning blue. The shards of a lamp were scattered across the floor, as were books and papers than had probably been on the desk.

"Report!" Johnson shouted.

"Found him like this sir!" Bruckner was struggling to get the limp Therron onto his feet. As he did so he took the edge of his hand and hit the Prince's abdomen just below the ribs.

"What are you doing?" Johnson demanded.

"He's choking, sir!" Bruckner replied, hitting Therron again. With a loud plop a piece of jerked meat popped from Therron's mouth and shot onto the floor. This was followed by Therron gasping for air. As Bruckner managed to get the prince to his feet Therron looked around him in confusion.

"Wha-"

"Easy sir," Bruckner told him. "You were choking sir. I think you'll be okay now, sir. Just take it easy for a minute and get your bearings."

"Choking?" Therron asked, still looking a bit dazed. "What could I have. . ." he trailed off at that, noting the hunk of jerky on the floor and then an overturned chair next to the desk.

"I tripped," he said suddenly, as if he was trying to tell himself what had happened. "I can't even walk across the floor it seems. I tripped. I already had the jerky in my mouth, working it around. I do like a good piece of spiced jerky you know," he added. Johnson and Bruckner both knew this to be true and nodded. "Who are you?" he narrowed his eyes a bit, focusing on the man who was out of place in the room.

"Captain Anthony Chastain, sir," Chastain snapped to attention. "Pleasure to meet you, Marshal," he added, having recognized Therron.

"Wish it had been under better circumstances but it's a pleasure to meet you too, Captain," Therron extended his hand to the naval officer, much to the surprise of Johnson and Bruckner, and Chastain took it before either could object.

–

It was a simple sleight of hand to slide the note from his sleeve into his hand, and then into Chastain's hand. Gripping the other man's hand tightly, Therron looked into his eyes, trying to establish a silent rapport that would lend the note some validity.

He felt Chastain stiffen as the note was passed and used that eye contact to try and encourage him to wait and read it later.

Not realizing what was going on but knowing that Therron was not only the Crown Prince but also the Lord Marshal of Soulan, Chastain nodded slightly, smiling.

And slid the note into his pants pocket as he stepped back.

–

Johnson saw the contact but didn't know how he could have prevented it. He cursed himself mentally for not having told Chastain to stay put, and then again for inviting him into the house to start with. It was too late now at any rate.

"Remain here and see that the Prince is truly alright," he ordered Bruckner, who nodded. "I'll send for the surgeon to have a look at him, just to be sure. Captain, if you will," he indicated the door, showing Chastain out.

"Of course," the naval officer smiled and made his way out. Johnson followed and closed the door behind him.

"I'm afraid the Prince is not well," Johnson said gently, using the story that had been concocted when all this had began. "He was ordered here by the King to rest, but. . ." he allowed his tale to trail away, shaking his head sadly.

"A poor time for the Marshal to be down," Chastain mused, thinking of that note. "Perhaps he will recover soon. This is a good place for someone ill to recoup." He straightened a bit and smiled.

"I appreciate your courtesy good sir," he said more formally, though still smiling. "I need to get back and let my young lieutenant make his way up for water as well. Perhaps we shall see one another again."

"Look forward to it, though less all the drama would be good," Johnson snorted. "Safe travels Captain."

"Good fortune, Captain."

-

Chastain returned to the beach and sent Reed up the small beach to the compound. Leaning against one of the boats he opened the small note ensuring that no one was close enough to see it. It was odd enough as it was, getting a note slipped to him by the Lord Marshal.

The contents of the note were even more so.

Captain,

I observed you making your way up the beach. I must hope you are a loyal son of the Kingdom and place my hope and trust in you. I am a prisoner here, kept by these people against my will. The story they have spread is that I am 'unwell'. They do not specify what is wrong, but insinuate that I am addled in my mind. I assure you this is not the case.

I am convinced there is a coup attempt underway and this was a part of it. I must get back to Nasil as soon as possible. I have no idea who has taken command of the military in my absence, or what may have befallen my father.

I realize that I am asking a great deal of you Captain, but I have no choice. I need your assistance.

Free me and carry me up the coast to Norfok, where I can secure assistance to return and thwart this plot against the Crown.

Therron McLeod.

"Holy shit," Chastain breathed as he finished reading the note a second time. He glanced around him once more to ensure that no one had heard him, then turned his gaze up the hill toward the house.

He was tempted to cast the note into the ocean on his way back to the ship, and yet the message it contained had a ring of truth to it. He remembered Johnson's sad head shake and the insinuation that Therron McLeod would likely not recover. The way the two Inspectorate officers were treating him. And there was another thing; what was the IG doing providing protection to a man who had an entire regiment assigned for his personal protection? None of this made the least bit of sense.

Johnson's reluctance to inform Chastain what was going on, at least at first, also added to the weight of the small note. Under other circumstances he could understand. Knowing that the Marshal had fallen victim of some kind of breakdown during a war for survival would not be good for the troops, that was certain.

Taken with the note and Johnson's somewhat mysterious behavior, however, all things pointed to the Marshal being held prisoner as he had said. And that meant that Chastain had to do something about it.

He hadn't observed too many troops at the compound, perhaps half as many as his own. Not even half when taken with his boat crews, really. And the IG troops were jailers, not soldiers. Guilford's marines would be more than a match for them he was sure. He wondered if the men holding the Prince even knew what they were doing, or if they were following orders and believed what they had been told.

"Something wrong sir?" Guilford's voice startled Chastain from his thoughts and he looked sharply at the officer in question.

"We have an issue," he said softly. "Marshal Therron McLeod is up there," he nodded toward the compound. "Being guarded by troops who appear to be from the IG's office. He slipped me this when I met him earlier. Read," he ordered as he passed the message to his chief infantry officer.

Guilford gave him a puzzled look but took the paper and read. His eyes grew wider with each line until he appeared as shocked as Chastain felt.

"Good Lord!" the stunned marine looked up at him. "How can this be?"

"I don't know," Chastain said truthfully. "I do know that the behavior of that bunch up there is funny. Strange funny, not humorous. They evaded my questions about why they were here, and then implied that the Marshal was mentally ill. We're at war with the North and our Marshal is apparently a victim of a coup attempt."

"Beg pardon sir," Guilford said, "but did you talk to Johnson about this? Get his side?"

"No, I did not," Chastain shook his head. "I didn't read the note until I got back here. And Johnson was extremely reluctant to answer any of my questions anyway," he said again.

"Sir this makes no sense," Guilford returned the note. "There has to be another explanation!"

"Are you willing to leave the Marshal a prisoner during war time so that we can find out if he's really sick or not?" Chastain challenged. "What if we find out later that he's being truthful and we did nothing?"

"We can return for him once we've reported this to the Commodore, sir," Guilford pointed out. "It's the safer plan, with all due respect."

It was the safe plan Chastain agreed. But safer in war time wasn't always the best plan. And without the Marshal, who was leading the defense of the Kingdom?

"Who is leading us while the Marshal is being held here?" he asked. "Who are we getting our orders from? And, assuming this is a coup attempt, who's in on it, and how high does it go?"

"Sir, Marshal McLeod is second in line behind only the Crown Prince," Guilford stated. "Who would dare oppose him as leader of the entire Army?"

"There are only two people below him, and one is his twin," Chastain replied.

"You're seriously suggesting that Parno McLeod is somehow responsible for this?" Guilford didn't bother to hide his incredulity. "Sir, I'm sorry, but I can't see it," the marine shook his head. "That man doesn't have the sense to pour piss out of boot with the instructions written on the heel from what I've heard. No way he can pull something like that off. There has to be more to this than what we can see. Or read," he motioned to the note that Chastain still held in his hands.

"Doesn't mean he isn't a figurehead for someone else," Chastain rebutted. "Look, I don't like any of this Major, but like it or not it's been dumped into my lap. This whole thing reeks of something being out of sorts and considering how reluctant Johnson is to provide details I have to take the Prince at his word."

"Sir, what if Johnson is under orders not to provide those details?" Guilford asked. "You said yourself, during wartime is a hell of a time to find out the Marshal has lost it. He may well had reluctantly told you the truth because you happened to walk in on it and nothing more. I know if I was faced with something like this I'd damn sure try to come up with something else, hell anything else other than telling the rank and file that their leader has lost his gourd!"

"That could be," Chastain nodded. "The bottom line for me though is that I can't trust what Johnson is saying."

"Sir you have no proof he has lied to you in any way," Guilford shook his head. "Nothing but a strong suspicion and that built on a note slipped to you by a man who may well be nuts."

"Again, that could be," Chastain straightened, his face flat. Clearly, he'd come to some kind of decision. "But I can't risk it. If the Marshal really is off his rocker then we'll bring him back. He's asked to go to Norfok for some reason, so we'll take him there. I want your men down here ready to move in five minutes, Major. I'd like to take Johnson and his troops by surprise. I want to avoid unnecessary bloodshed. These men are likely just following orders and that may well include Johnson."

"Sir, this is a mistake," Guilford tried one last time.

"Are you refusing your orders Major?"

"That's a low blow Captain, and not one I deserve," Guilford drew himself to attention. He was a man of almost painful integrity and Chastain knew that.

"Then assemble your men, Major," Chastain ordered, aware that he'd probably just lost the loyalty of a good subordinate with that remark but unable to take it back. If he was wrong, then Guilford was following orders and he and his men would be protected. If he was right. . .

"Five minutes."

-

"Something's wrong, sir," Smith said softly.

"You'll have to be more specific, Lieutenant," Johnson snorted. "There are in fact a great many things wrong."

"Five of our men have abandoned their post in the last fifteen minutes, sir," Smith ignored the jab. "I've not been able to find them, either. I've set new guards, but. . .something is wrong."

"Sound the alarm, Lieutenant," Johnson resisted the urge to swear.

"I'd rather you not do that, Captain," Chastain's voice came from the doorway. Johnson looked to see the naval officer standing there as marines entered the building, flanking him.

"Captain, what do you think you're doing?" Johnson kept his voice calm. "You have no authority here. None. Take your men and go while you still have a career to go to."

"Funny, I was thinking that you were the one who was protecting his 'career'," Chastain replied just as calmly. "All sounding any alarm will do is get your men killed, Johnson. I'm taking the Marshal out of here and if you try to stop me-"

"I'll have to try," Johnson sighed. "I'm here on orders of the King himself. And you're about to 'free' a traitor, Chastain. I can't imagine how he managed to get you to aid him, but-"

"Save it, Johnson," Chastain replied flatly. "You've lied to me from the start and there's no reason to think you're being truthful now. The Marshal is being held against his will at a time when we're at war for our very survival. Whatever game whoever you're working for is up to, I'm putting an end to it."

"You idiot," Johnson sighed, drawing his sword and Smith following suit. "Therron McLeod is a traitor to the Crown. His own father sent him here into exile rather than execute him, fearful of what the news would do to the army. You've played right into his hand. Typical sailor," he snorted.

"If you resist, I'll kill your men," Chastain told him flatly. "I'd prefer not to since I assume they are merely following orders, but I will do it in order to free the Marshal. Your choice, Johnson."

"Sir?" Smith's voice was calm at his side. He was clearly going to follow Johnson's lead no matter what.

"You'd risk the Kingdom to do this?" Johnson asked, incredulous. "Risk your men in going against the Crown like this?"

"Sir," Guilford said at Chastain's side, and his tone was questioning rather than supporting. Clearly, he wasn't on Chastain's side fully.

"Quiet," Chastain hissed to the marine. "Johnson you've proven to be a liar already so anything you say is suspect. You've no one to blame for that but yourself. I'm not risking anything. I'll carry the Marshal with me, and if he's really in exile as you say then he'll be returned. If not, well then, we'll see to it he gets back where he belongs."

"Go ahead then, Captain," Johnson said suddenly, aware that all his resistance would do was get his men killed for no gain. "Go ahead. And when word of this reaches the Crown, you and all your men will be hunted down like dogs and hung as traitors. Remember that I warned you just as the noose tightens. You remember it too, Major," he looked at the marine. "Remember that I tried to help you."

"Take him and be damned for it," he returned his sword to its scabbard.

"Put it on the floor," Chastain told him.

"Come and take it you bastard," Johnson growled out. "This is all you get without bloodshed. Blood that will grease your entry into the part of hell reserved for idiots and traitors. Smith?"

"Sir?" the lieutenant was still with him.

"Go and tell Bruckner to let this traitorous son-of-a-bitch have what he wants, which is the other traitorous son-of-a-bitch. There's no sense in him getting killed to no gain."

"Yes sir," Smith replied, returning his own sword to its scabbard and moving to do as instructed.

"Major, go with him and retrieve the Marshal," Chastain ordered.

"Yes sir," Guilford was clearly reluctant but obedient nonetheless. He and several of his marines followed Smith to the study.

"You almost convinced him Johnson," Chastain mentioned.

"Too bad for him I didn't," Johnson shrugged. "He'll hang right beside you."

"You seem awfully sure of that," Chastain snorted.

"I took my orders directly from the Crown," Johnson told him flatly. "The King himself gave me my marching orders. You're defying the King himself in doing this."

For the first time since making his decision Chastain felt uneasy.

"Then why tell us he was sick?" he questioned.

"King's orders," Johnson shot back. "It was better than executing him for treason he figured. And before you say anything, yes there are several people in Nasil and the Army who are well aware of all this. At least one Provincial Governor has already been replaced and imprisoned as having been in on the whole thing. I suspect by now several others are rotting in a cell somewhere. But you won't rot, I imagine," Johnson smirked. "You they'll hang."

"We will see," Chastain refused to allow his unease to show. Suddenly Therron McLeod burst into the room, Guilford right behind him. Bruckner and Smith went to Johnson's side and stood by him.

"Captain Chastain, thank you," Therron smiled widely. "I knew I could depend on you."

"Marshal," Chastain nodded, feeling better about his actions now.

"Kill them and we can depart," McLeod ordered as he headed for the door.

"Sir?" Chastain looked shocked.

"Kill them," Therron repeated. "I can't leave them alive to tell the rest that I've gone."

"Marshal, I'm not going to kill men who aren't resisting and are just following orders," Chastain replied, unease flowering once more in his belly. "You're free and we will be taking you out of here. That's all that matters."

"Don't presume to tell me what matters!" Therron shot back at him, enraged. "Now kill them!"

"No," Guilford said flatly, replying instead of Chastain. "My men are marines, not murderers. There'll be no killing of unarmed men by marines under my command. Sir." Therron turned on him in a second.

"How dare you defy me!" he thundered.

"I dare when you defy the Rules of War we operate under," Guilford replied easily. "Rules you are supposed to enforce as Marshal. Sir." It was clear that he was adding the 'sir' as an afterthought at this point.

"Enough Major," Chastain tried to take control again, now almost certain he'd screwed up but too far along to do anything about it. "Take the Marshal to the boats and secure his safety."

"Aye, sir," Guilford nodded. A few short commands later his men were on their way to their boats with a still complaining Therron McLeod in their custody. Guilford made sure he was the last man to head to the boats, picking up an empty bottle as he went.

"That's the man you freed, Chastain," Johnson said once they were gone. "Make you feel better about yourself now?"

"Shut up," the naval officer growled, beginning to feel the enormity of what he'd done. "Don't try and follow us," he warned.

"Don't worry," Johnson laughed harshly. "I won't. I look forward to hearing how you fare. Like I said, remember that I warned you when you feel the noose tighten around your neck you idiot."

Rather than reply Chastain turned and left, his stomach now roaring at him with unease. His mind was racing as he tried to settle his mind that he had done the right thing. If only Johnson had leveled with him before now none of this would have been necessary, damn him!

"Sir," Guilford's voice came to him from the steady growing dusk. "We're making a mistake," the major tried one last time.

"We've already made it if it is one," Chastain shrugged. "And you're just following orders, Major. I'm the one this will fall on," he added fatalistically.

"Not if Johnson is telling the truth," Guilford shook his head. "It. . .it feels like Johnson was telling the truth, sir. I don't like the casual way the Marshal ordered us to kill the lot of them, either. "

"We didn't kill them and that's what matters," Chastain told him. "Now let's get to the boats. We need to be going. And not a word of our destination until we're on our way."

"Sir," Guilford nodded. He tossed the bottle he'd been holding back toward the beach and moved toward his boat even as he bellowed commands to his men.

Twenty minutes later the boats were on their way back to the ships. Chastain sat in silence the entire way, having been smart enough to place the Marshal in another. It would likely be bad enough that he had the man aboard Halifax before it was all said and done.

One hour later still all boats were back aboard and tired sailors heaved anchors up as others dropped sails. Marines lent a hand on the oars and soon the three ships were moving away from the coast and picking up speed.

"Captain, you shouldn't have defied me," the Marshal just had to come up on deck. "Those men are traitors."

"I remain unconvinced of that Marshal," Chastain replied calmly. "I've done my duty as I saw fit, which was to free you and support your return to Nasil. I will not kill unarmed men who serve the same flag I do when they're guilty of no crime other than following orders. Those same men would be executed for not following orders, so execution for following them is the height of unfairness. Your quarters are satisfactory I hope?" he changed the subject.

"They will do," Therron nodded. "Where are we bound?" he asked.

"You wanted to go to Norfok, Marshal, so we're bound for Norfok," Chastain replied. "Unless you'd rather head for Moble?" he asked, almost hoping the answer was yes.

"No," the reply was emphatic. "No, Norfok is better. I can secure transportation and possibly assistance from there and head back into Soulan through the mountains. So long as I can get through the passes before winter, I'll be fine. How long you estimate until we can reach our destination?"

"Depends on the winds, sir," Chastain shrugged. "We will catch southerlies this time of year at least part way and that will speed our voyage, but as the wind dies away we'll have to 'tack' more and more and that will slow us some. Using the oars will help, but we can't use them around the clock. We don't have the manpower. We will use them during the daytime hours so we can make the best use of that extra speed. If all goes well, we should be in Norfok in four weeks, give or take."

"Four weeks," Therron sighed. "I'd hoped for quicker," he said.

"We may make it quicker but I doubt it," Chastain shrugged. "We'll do the best we can, but we're at the mercy of the weather once we're northbound. And we have to be wary of Imperial Fleet presence."

"The Imperial Fleet is a joke," Therron scoffed.

"Large Imperial Fleet off the Sunshine Coast at last report," Chastain said evenly. "They don't sound very funny to me, sir. Word was that Admiral Semmes was taking the combined fleet minus the Gulf Squadron against them as soon as they could be assembled. Probably happened by now but we've been at sea for three weeks already and we'd had no word when we sailed."

"I saw the reports," Therron nodded. "Trust me Captain, the Nor do not have a fleet that can stand against southern ships."

"I'll have to it seems, Marshal," Chastain smiled dimly. "We're heading that way regardless."

CHAPTER THIRTEEN

-

General Gerald Allen reined in his horse at the top of the small rise, raising a glass to his eye to survey the valley below him.

His command had been in the field for six days now, two of which he'd spent getting in behind the Nor lines. He was now looking for a suitable target for his men. Scouts were out prowling the countryside even now to get the lay of the land.

"Looks clear, sir," his second, Brigadier Sam Walters said.

"So, it does," Allen nodded, returning his glass to its case. "Anything from our scouts as yet?"

"No sir, not yet," Walters shook his head. "What are your plans, sir?" he asked.

"Send runners to Generals Coe and Vaughan, Sam," Allen ordered rather than reply directly. "Pass the word we'll rest here for an hour. Men to take lunch and see to their horses. Pass that word as you go, please."

"Yes sir," the man nodded and kicked his horse into action, galloping down the line. Behind him, Allen pulled a map from his pocket and made some rough calculations in his head. If he was accurate then they should be about ...

"You wanted to see us Gerry?" Coe's voice broke his train of thought.

"Yes," he nodded, holding his map for them to see. "If I'm right, we're about here," he stabbed a spot on the map. "We're less than a day's ride from the river, about here," another stab. "What say we ride over to the river, send out scouts to see if the enemy is using it, and then make our way north from there for two, maybe three days ride?" he asked, looking at the other two.

"I'm for it," Coe nodded, examining the map. "Might see some action."

"I like it," Vaughan agreed. "The Marshal and General Davies are both concerned about those boats the Nor used at Lovil. If they're using them then we might see them along the river. Even if we can't do anything about it we can at least send a party back to warn the Marshal they're on the way."

"That's what I had in mind," Allen agreed. "I'd really like to know what's over there, too."

"It's not yet noon, hardly," Coe pointed out. "Might be we could make it before dark if we push," he suggested.

"I'd rather get an early start in the morning," Allen disagreed after a brief pause. "I'd rather us not run into something near or after dark. If we're on the move by first light then we can be there early afternoon, especially if we make a little more headway today. Maybe ride a quarter of the way today, and the rest in the morning, say," he looked at the other two.

"That would give us plenty of light if we did find something," Vaughan nodded. "And we're far enough from the lines that we shouldn't hit a force larger than we can handle if we have to."

"True that," Coe agreed. "Well, let's send out scouts in whatever direction you think best, give the men say, thirty minutes to eat and rest their horses, and then what? Ride until maybe two hours before dark? We probably won't want to make a fire so when it gets dark it's dark sure enough for us."

"Good plan," Allen liked it and agreed at once. "See to it," he ordered and Coe nodded before setting off to send the scouts out.

"Be nice to catch those boats out of the water somewhere and burn them to ashes," Vaughan said quietly. "Kill their crews too."

"It would indeed," Allen nodded. "And it would be a big help to the Marshal to know that at least some of the boats were out of play, too."

"Maybe we'll get lucky," Vaughan smiled suddenly, and Allen decided that he wouldn't want Wilton Vaughan smiling at him like that. No sir, he wouldn't want that at all.

"Maybe we will."

-

Captain Lucas Silven was disgusted. Technically it was now Commodore Silven, but Silven didn't much care and he had his doubts that the Navy would honor Stone's brevet promotion anyway.

His disgust came from how slow the going was as he and his men poled their way up the Tinsee. Or down.

"Damn this country," he cursed for the umpteenth time since taking to the cursed River Tinsee. Whoever heard of a river that flowed south to north, and damned if the southerners didn't have two of them only few miles apart.

The river was strong in places and while it wasn't so strong as the Ohi, at least for the most part, they were poling against the river all the time. At least on the Ohi they had been able to use the current somewhat in crossing. Here they were fighting for every inch. As a result, his timetable of three weeks to reach the Army was starting to look wildly optimistic.

And impossible.

"Lucas, we are not making any kind of time here."

"Tell me something I don't know, George," Silven resisted the urge to snarl. Captain George Stenopolous was a good man and a good sailor. It wasn't his fault that Silven's plan was going to hell in a hand cart.

"We've been at this for two weeks already and we're not even half-way there," Stenopolous persisted. "At this rate, it will be fall by the time we reach the Army."

"I am aware of the time, Captain," Silven ground out. His patience wasn't that good. "There's not a damn thing we can do about it except keep going. This current is a lot stronger than it looks and the river isn't always shallow enough to pole the boats."

"And sometimes we're having to carry them where the water goes from one extreme to the other," Stenopolous reminded him.

"I'm aware of that too, George," Silven sighed. "What would you suggest we do about it?" he asked with exaggerated patience.

"I'm not sure there is anything we can do short of having wagons enough to haul the boats overland. Which we don't have and can't get," he added tiredly. "I'm sorry. That's not much help, but I don't see a solution other than keep going, like you said."

"Is Major Greeley still bitching about how slow we're going?" Silven changed the subject. Major Wilhelm Greeley (and wasn't that a mouthful!) commanded the short battalion of cavalry that Stone had assigned to assist the boat crews and guard their train and supplies. He had complained from day one about anything and everything he could find. They were too slow; they had too much of a baggage train; his men were not guards; the boats crews obviously didn't know what they were doing.

That last one had stung Silven into a verbal altercation with Greeley just five days into the journey as the Captain (maybe Commodore) had told Greeley to feel free to show them how it was done. Greeley had responded that it wasn't his job to move the boats, to which Silven had replied 'then shut the hell up.'

Since that time the two had barely managed to coexist. Actually working together simply wasn't going to happen. Greeley wasn't going to cooperate any further than he thought necessary to keep himself out of trouble, and Silven wasn't going to listen to any more of his mouth.

Impasse.

The result was strained and barely correct relations between the boat crews and the horse soldiers as they tried to make their way down (up) river to where General Wilson was waiting for them. Probably somewhat impatiently by now Silven realized. But try as he might he could not speed things up. They were literally going as fast as they could possibly go.

"What is the hold up this time?" the unwelcome sound of Greeley's nasal whine cut into Silven's thought process. He looked up to see the cavalry officer sitting his horse, flanked by two men that followed him most everywhere. Bodyguards, Silven assumed.

"There's no hold up, Major," Silven replied evenly. "Boats are still moving, we're just fighting an especially strong current. Makes for difficult going."

"You're said that since we started," Greeley said/whined.

"It's been true since we started," Silven grated. "This river is flowing against us. Not a thing I can do about that. We're going as fast as we can and I'm well aware that it's not fast enough to suit you. Tough cookies. This is all there is for now. Hopefully we'll hit some wider, slower water further down, but until we do, this is what you get."

"It's a shame you aren't under my command," Greeley almost preened even as he sneered. "I'd have this rabble of yours beat into shape in no time."

"Yes, because you've done such an excellent job with your own that the only assignment General Stone could trust you with was to carry our luggage," Silven replied without pause. Greeley's face almost purpled in rage and Silven felt sorry for the horse as Greeley roughly turned the mount and spurred him savagely away. The horse lunged forward and Silven laughed as Greeley was almost tossed from his saddle.

"Gawd! I'd have give a month's pay to see that bastard hit the ground and his horse run away!" Stenopolous was guffawing right beside Silven. The brevetted Commodore allowed himself and his contemporary another minute to laugh at the inept cavalry commander then turned serious once more.

"We need to find a way to move faster," he told Stenopolous.

"Other than getting 'Greasy' to pull the boats with his horses, I got nothing," the other man shrugged helplessly. The nickname had arisen among the sailors because of the hair tonic Greeley coated his hair in every morning, resulting in it being slicked down on his head.

"I'd say we can forget that," Silven said ruefully. "Be thinking, George," he urged. "We need to pick up the pace."

"I will," Stenopolous promised. "I just don't see what we can do."

-

"We'll make camp around here," Allen declared, looking at the surrounding area. "There's water and it's fairly isolated. A good place to picket horses and make a cold camp. We set double guards tonight as well. We're in occupied territory so we can't afford to take chances. I want us in the saddle at first good light and moving toward the river. I'd like to be there before noon if we can, but certainly by early afternoon. We need time to establish whether we should stay or make camp elsewhere."

"We'll see to it," Coe promised.

The command was soon spread out over the rolling plains and woods of almost a thousand acres of Royal Reserve land that had been set aside in past years to produce grain for the Royal storehouses. Unoccupied and far from any settlement to speak of, it was the perfect place for so many men and horses to bed down overnight.

Allowing his subordinates to oversee setting up the camp, Allen returned to his map and his notes, studying the lay of the land around him and keeping a careful eye on known Imperial positions. A quiet man without much in the way of political ambitions, Allen had not risen to his position because of family influence but rather due to his intelligence and his ability. He was an excellent tactician, as any division commander must be, but he was also a fair strategist as well, something Davies knew and one of the reasons he had appointed Allen to command the temporary cavalry corps.

Looking now at his map, Allen saw all kinds of possibilities for his mission behind Imperial lines. Once they had attempted to verify the boat theory, he intended to do all he could to disrupt Nor lines of communication back to the Empire. If his men could hit even one supply train and destroy it, or better still capture it mostly intact, then that would get the Nor's attention in a big way and maybe even force them to send someone after him.

In addition, he knew from Beaumont and Whipple's expedition earlier that the Imperial Army had posts and substations all along the trade route they were more or less following as an invasion route. While their horses would be useless as war mounts to southern cavalry, they would do for other work such as wranglers, ranchers or pulling wagons or plows. And any beef on the hoof they could steal would not only be taken from Imperial mouths but also be put into Soulanie mouths.

By the time his command had settled in and night began to fall, Allen had stored his map and notes away, a sound plan already formulated in his mind. A good night's sleep tonight and an early start tomorrow would see that plan followed and whether or not it might bear fruit.

-

"How far you think?" Beaumont asked as he and Whipple galloped alongside each other.

"Not even a full day," Whipple replied, shaking his head. "We're very close. And I'm glad, too. A month in the saddle is about enough."

"True," Beaumont nodded his agreement. They had actually been 'in the saddle' in pursuit for just over five weeks in fact. Thirty-eight days they had spent on the long road to their destination. Three of those days had been spent on rest along the way as horses sometimes required more rest than an overnight. Beaumont had begrudged every second of that time but knew it had to be done. They had lost over a dozen horses even with those stops. Horses were almost as precious as soldiers nowadays.

"Be dark in a couple hours," Beaumont observed. "Not a bad road but I don't know the way in the dark. I don't suppose... " he trailed off, looking at his aristocratic friend. Whipple shook his head.

"Been there once, years ago," he admitted. "I'm all but certain I can get there again but in the dark? Not around here. There are gators in every wet spot and they're ill-tempered when you step on them in the dark."

"Yeah, seems I'd heard that somewhere," Beaumont replied sarcastically. "Well, I guess we need to find a place to camp for the night, then. We can get-"

"Scouts incoming General," one of the riders ahead of them called. Signaling a stop, Beaumont waited as a team of four scouts appeared escorting a fifth man.

"This is trouble," Whipple said softly as the man got close enough to recognize his uniform. "That's an IG outfit."

"Damn," Beaumont muttered.

"Sir, detail reporting with one dispatch rider from Key Horn," the scout sergeant reported.

"Who are you, then?" Beaumont asked.

"Lieutenant Smith, sir," the young officer replied. "I'm glad to see you but I'm afraid you're too late, assuming you've come to help," the man added.

"Too late for what?" Beaumont didn't want to know but had no choice but to ask.

"Marshal McLeod, the former Marshal," Smith corrected himself, "was taken by force yesterday evening, General," Smith reported. "I'm carrying a report from Captain Johnson to the militia station in Jayville, for a courier to take north."

"Taken by who?" Whipple asked, leaning forward. "There's no way they got here before we did," he was almost insistent.

"They who, sir?" Smith asked. "And he was taken by a Naval Task Force, sir," he added, realizing that Lieutenants by and large didn't question Brigadiers. "Captain Chastain of the Halifax and his Fleet Marine Force landed at Key Horn compound yesterday investigating our presence. Somehow the Marshal got a message to the Captain and convinced him to assist the Marshal in escaping. Sir."

"How bad where your casualties?" Beaumont asked.

"We had no casualties sir," Smith reported. "Chastain was a friendly, investigating possible pirate activity, which we know is common in this area, including the Royal Compound over the years. We allowed them to rest and refresh before rowing back to their ships. At some point the former Marshal managed to contact Chastain somehow and he took us by surprise."

"So, you didn't even fight back," Beaumont snorted.

"Captain Johnson was intent on making a stand, General," Smith's voice was cool. "Chastain outnumbered us three to one and threatened to kill all of our men if the Captain didn't surrender. Captain Johnson saw no point in losing his entire command when he could not affect the outcome of the situation."

"Why did he even allow this Chastain to land?" Beaumont bellowed.

"Would the general care to explain how sixty men could prevent two hundred men from landing if they were so minded?" Smith's voice held an edge now and he had remembered that as a member of the Inspectorate he didn't answer to Beaumont.

"Why not let's leave this for later," Whipple cut in before Beaumont could embarrass himself further. "Mister Smith, can you get us to the compound tonight? We're not sure we can find it in the dark."

"I can, but my orders-"

"We need to speak to your Captain before you carry that dispatch anywhere," Whipple explained. "We don't want word of this leaking out just yet. There's a good deal you don't yet know. If you will lead us to the compound, we can explain to you and the Captain in detail. In fact, we will likely require your assistance in the coming days."

"Very well, Brigadier," Smith nodded. "It's not that far, but you are right that it's treacherous after dark. Once we get within a few miles the road will be lit with torches, however. If we hurry, we won't have to ride far in the dark. And watch for the gators, sir," he added. "They really don't like being stepped on."

"So, I hear, Lieutenant," Whipple smiled. "So, I hear."

-

Captain Dennis Johnson was on the porch of the main house when he heard guard calling out. He had heard the rumble that only many horses could produce but had simply waited. Now it appeared that the horses were coming to the compound as he had assumed.

"We can't catch a break," he sighed as he stepped down from the porch and walked toward the main gate. It wasn't much as gates went, just a way to close off the roadway from casual traffic. A five-man guard was posted as a precaution against pirates more than anything else. But pirates didn't ride horses as a rule.

"Lieutenant Smith is with them, sir," the sergeant reported as Johnson arrived.

"Who is 'them', Patterson?" Johnson asked.

"General Buford Beaumont, Soulan Army," a new voice said from the dark. "My command is here to assume control of the former Marshal."

"Day late and a dollar short I'm afraid, General," Johnson sighed. "Figures that once they decided I really did need help it would get here too late to be of any use."

"Beg pardon Captain, but that's not all," Smith rode up from the dark and dismounted. "There's a lot more going on than what happened to us, sir."

"I see," Johnson noted how pale Smith looked. "Well, you may as well come in and make yourselves comfortable, General," Johnson offered. "There should be sufficient room for your command since this place is set up to accommodate up to three Royal regiments at a time. I'm sure your men are tired. Fortunately for you we just laid in stores so we have enough to feed you for a few days." He motioned to the guards to open the gate and stepped back as the horse soldiers filed through.

It was the work of nearly an hour to see to billeting, set guards and get food cooking for the men who were decidedly tired of eating cold rations in the saddle. Soon a large beef half was roasting over two different fires and several large cook pots were boiling beans and rice, traditional soldier's fare.

"Captain, you're losing the former Marshal has put us in a tough position," Beaumont's voice cut through the dark as he and Whipple made their way onto the porch.

"I didn't 'lose' him, General," Johnson replied calmly. "He was taken at sword point by a force that outnumbered me three-to-one. I had the choice of allowing my entire command to be slaughtered for no gain, or letting him go. The end result was going to be the same, mind you. There was no way for my men to prevent the marines and sailors under Chastain's command taking the former Marshal from here. I do think that Chastain regretted the action even before it was completed, but fool that he is couldn't just back down and say so. Regardless, do please enlighten me as to how you would have done it."

"I would have fought," Beaumont shot back.

"An easy claim to make with a brigade of soldiers at one's back," Johnson wasn't at all intimidated. "Try it with sixty policemen and investigators against a full company of combat soldiers and a half company of sailors. I'm sure you could do better than I did." With that Johnson turned his back on Beaumont and took his seat, lifting a glass from the table next to his chair and taking a drink of the whiskey within.

"We can see that you had a difficult position to work with," Whipple restrained Beaumont after he'd taken only one step in Johnson's direction. "As your lieutenant reported however, there is a great deal more going on than this renegade naval officer taking Therron McLeod from here."

"Well, do please take a chair and fill me in if you want," Johnson waved to other chairs on the portico. "We can dine here while General Beaumont continues to make himself feel good by berating a team of policemen who couldn't find a way to take on a short battalion of trained soldiers."

"That's enough, Captain," Whipple's voice hardened slightly.

"I'm just getting started, Brigadier," Johnson refused to back down. "The good General here has essentially called me a coward for not allowing my men to be murdered in cold blood by a traitorous psychopath, and I just naturally take exception to that." He paused to toss back the rest of his drink and then pour himself another.

"I asked before we ever departed Nasil for more men," he told the two soldiers. "I hadn't even seen this place yet but knew that such a small force could never manage to prevent a determined enemy from taking the Marshal. Once I got here and found out the local situation I sent a message to General Brock again requesting additional men, at least twice what I had. No reply. I know there's a war on but I thought that this little post might warrant some attention seeing as it held a man who had tried to seize the throne by force or subterfuge or both. Of course, I have been wrong before. Cheers," he lifted his glass and took another snort.

"And I don't answer to you, Brigadier, nor to you, General, and neither do my men," he continued after that. "So while I have extended you every courtesy, I'm under no obligation to do more than that. And you took it on yourselves to stop my courier who was carrying an urgent dispatch for my own superiors, then all you can do once you're here is question my decisions without knowing a damn thing about the situation and call me, and by extension my men, cowards."

"That was a rather unfortunate misunderstanding," Whipple tried to smooth things over. "I'd appreciate it if you can overlook that and write it off to a month in the saddle with little more than a nap every day."

"Done," Johnson said at once with a nod. "What brings you gents here, since clearly you aren't here to reinforce this post."

"Why do you say that?" Whipple asked. He took a chair across from the Captain and more or less shoved a still fuming Beaumont into another.

"We're at war and an experienced brigade of horse soldiers is a thousand miles from the front and headed the wrong way?" Johnson tilted his head to one side. "Bad strategy."

"Point," Whipple nodded. "Truth is we we're here for a different reason. The first thing you should know is that... "

"Good Lord," Johnson almost breathed as Whipple came to the end of his narrative and sat back. "I just thought I had problems. The King dead?"

"And the Crown Prince assaulted and nearly murdered. By Therron's twin sister, Sherron. And she is even now on her way here with Therron's regiment to free him, hoping to return him to Nasil and to power."

"Well, she's gonna be too late for that, since Chastain is already doing it," Johnson sighed. "I tried to tell the moron he was opposing the Crown but he wouldn't listen. I think in the end he realized he was wrong, but he was so deep into it he couldn't see a way to stop it, you know? I still won't feel sorry for him when he hangs, though," Johnson sat back again. "He left here knowing he was violating the law and exceeding any authority he had. He also knew the consequences of his actions, I made sure of that. He did it anyway. That's on him."

"We need you to carry on here as if Therron McLeod was still a prisoner," Beaumont said, his earlier ire now under control. "We need to lull Callens into a false sense of security. Depending on how much she slowed him during the trip, they could be here as soon as tomorrow."

"I doubt we'll see them in less than a week," Whipple shook his head. "By now Callens had told the witch it's his way now and stopped her from slowing him anymore, but they still lost a great deal of time on the way down. Our men will be rested when they get here and so will our horses."

"You expect to fight then?" Johnson asked, looking from one to another.

"We will destroy Callens' regiment, take him prisoner, if possible, along with the Princess, and return them to Nasil. Our orders are to kill them all if we cannot safely return them to the capitol." Whipple's voice was a bit cool as he relayed that.

"That ought to do it," Johnson nodded. "This Callens, he's commanding what used to be Therron McLeod's personal regiment?"

"An elite regiment of horsemen, yes," Whipple nodded. "We outnumber them substantially, but that doesn't mean we will have an easy time of it. Callens is a good commander and his men are well trained. They won't go easy, and those who know what Sherron and Callens have done will know that if they surrender there's nothing but a hangman's noose waiting for them."

"Don't you miss the days when people were loyal?" Johnson asked suddenly. "I mean, I'm the first one to admit there's a time and place to question authority and all, but the key is the proper time and place, and under the proper circumstances. War time not being proper at all," he added.

"A valid observation, Captain," Whipple was almost amused.

"Well, if we're to perhaps have a battle soon I guess I need to set a better guard," Johnson rose to his feet, slightly unsteady.

"Are you sure you're in proper shape to be doing that Captain?" Whipple's amusement was still evident.

"Oh, I'm not going to do it myself," the IG Captain assured the Brigadier. "Bruckner!"

"Well ladies, how are things going?" Memmnon asked. He had been joined by both Winifred and Stephanie for lunch, something his schedule rarely permitted.

"Things are good with the archery lessons," Winnie reported. "All of the women have stuck it out and are now shooting. Some are better than others, but all of them can hit a stationary target from at least fifty feet. That's nothing to brag about for someone already trained, but for a grown-up learning for the first time it ain't-it's not, bad."

"The new nursing school is up and running as well," Stephanie said next. "A total of seventeen people from among the first group of refugees and another thirty-nine from here in the city are now working toward a nursing certificate. I've identified five of those who will almost certainly be able to move on and become surgeons and three more that are capable of becoming outright physicians."

"We will need them I'm afraid," Memmnon nodded slowly. "I'm glad you've found so many capable people."

"Our educational standards are making themselves felt, your Highness," Stephanie nodded. "Your family's dedication to high educational standards throughout the Kingdom gives us a population that has a strong foundation for higher learning. We are reaping the benefits of that now when we need it most."

"Very kind of you," Memmnon smiled softly, "but not something I can take credit for. Those standards have come down all the way from Tyree. It was historically part of his attempt to preserve Ancient Technology after the Dying."

"We will be able to graduate our first class in just a few months," she promised. "We are also already looking for the next group of students. Ideally, we will always have at least one class waiting to start. If we're lucky we'll manage to have two."

"It's nice to have some good news for a change," Memmnon sighed happily.

"You've had bad news today?"

"No, not today more than any other of late," he shook his head. "But in a time of war it's seldom you get welcome news. I shall take what I can get."

-

General Gerald Allen was in the saddle and moving before sun-up, his men behind him and scouts before him. They were away on schedule and making good time already, just as he'd hoped. He wasn't sure why but he had a hunch there was something for them to find at the river today. He had nothing to base that on other than his gut feeling, but checking it out was within the scope of his orders so nothing was lost by doing so. And even if they found nothing on the river itself, there was always the possibility they would encounter something of value to hit.

So long as they were visible, 'made lots of racket' as Vaughan had put it, then they were doing their jobs.

-

"C'mon boys, let's go! We need to make today a good one so let's get to it!"

Lucas Silven was walking through his encampment shaking his sailors out of their bunks. He'd love to give them a day to rest but he couldn't spare the time. Poling against a current like this was exhausting and his men had been at it for over two weeks without let up. Every day from light until dark they were pushing their boats up river, and didn't have a great deal to show for it as yet. So in spite of the need to let them rest even a half day, he insisted they get up and get moving.

"Shake a leg, let's go!" his chief NCO was less kind than the commander as he walked along, kicking the feet of anyone who was still in their blankets. "On your feet Bailey! Thomas, get your ugly ass up and ready to go! Beale, didn't I already tell you once to get up and get moving?!"

It took the camp fifteen minutes to stir from its sleep and get packed. Another fifteen minutes to pack gear into company wagons to resume the trip south. Still another half-hour to get everyone fed, allowing for calls of nature and a brief time for hygiene.

Finally, one hour and twenty minutes after Silven had first begun his 'shaking out' of the camp, the first boat was ready to make its way into the river. It was forty-five minutes later than Silven had hoped for, and a fact that Greeley didn't allow to go unnoticed.

"If you people were more disciplined you could get your camp up and moving on time," the cavalry officer sneered. "But instead we have to wait and wait while you get going at a more leisurely rate. My men were awake and moving before sunup!"

"I'm aware of that, Major," Silven nodded. "I'm sure that riding a horse all day is exhausting work. Meanwhile poling our boats is easy by comparison so you're absolutely right. There's no reason we couldn't be up and moving ahead of your men, yet we deliberately chose to wait until now."

"You know you're lucky you don't answer to me," Greeley snarled.

"I remind myself every day how lucky I am not to be in any way subordinate to you," Silven assured the cavalryman.

"My men are combat soldiers!" Greeley hissed. "They deserve better than playing babysitter to a bunch of lazy ass sailors who act like they're on leave!"

"Well, perhaps you will get your wish once we get to General Wilson," Silven replied calmly. "I'm sure he will be able to find work for such a crack outfit as yours." He turned to walk away as Greeley spluttered behind him, unwilling to continue the conversation.

It was going to be a long day as it was.

-

"Something riding you, Gerald?" Allen turned to see Wilton Vaughan beside him, tall in the saddle. At times like this he was reminded of just how huge the black skinned cavalry man was.

"What you mean?" he asked.

"We're riding pretty hard this morning," Vaughan shrugged. "You seem almost like you know something we don't and are in a hurry to get there."

"I don't know anything," Allen admitted. "I just have a strong hunch. Nothing more than that."

"Fair enough," Vaughan nodded. "Nothing wrong with following a hunch. Think it's the boats? That the Nor are maybe using them on the river?"

"River flows north here," Allen mused. "I suppose they can use them, I just can't see how. I guess they could pull them with horses from the bank, but that's not an option everywhere. There are places you couldn't do that at all."

"Could pull them from the water and move them overland to the next good spot," Vaughan suggested.

"If you have enough horses to haul the boats, you have enough to haul supplies with," Allen replied. "Why use the boats?"

"They may not be hauling supplies," Vaughan shrugged. "Maybe they aren't hauling anything, just bringing the boats to where the Imperial Army is and then try to carry men past our positions and land them south of our position."

"Like the Marshal believes," Allen nodded. "What do you think of him?" he changed the subject suddenly.

"Seems to know his business," Vaughan replied. "He's not afraid to take risks, or to ask what others think. I haven't seen him trying to foist responsibility off on anyone else, whether for decisions that need to be made or for the results for those decisions. I think he's smarter than most of us gave him credit for, myself included."

"That is true," Allen nodded. "I'm hoping that his plans will help us turn things around. We are absolutely up against-" He cut himself off as there was a stir in the line ahead of them. In less than a minute a pair of scouts drew rein before Allen.

"Sir!" one saluted. "Sir, we've spotted a column of Imperial horsemen with a baggage train. They seem to be shadowing the river at the moment. And we've spotted a dozen boats on the river. We think that many at least. We can only get a glimpse of them through the trees where they are at the moment."

"How far are we?" Allen asked.

"No more than five miles as of half-an-hour ago, sir," the breathless scout replied.

"Any size estimate on the cavalry detail?"

"At least battalion strength, sir."

"Very well," Allen nodded, clearly thinking this over. It took him less than a half-minute to make his decision.

"Wilton, your troops are first in line, correct?"

"They are," Vaughan looked eager.

"Very well," Allen nodded. "Shake them out and take this outfit. I suggest you send one brigade south to cut them off from getting by us. Otherwise it's your operation. Tear them apart."

"Yes sir," Vaughan nodded. He drew his reins around and was soon conferring with his brigade commanders. Fifteen minutes later thousands of horses were thundering by Allen's position on their way to the river.

"Pass the word to General Coe to come up," Allen ordered. "And inform Brigadier Walters to join me as well." Sam Walters had taken command of Allen's division while he led the combined command. Soon the two men were with him, one on either side.

"I saw Vaughan's men take off," Coe mentioned as soon as he was there. "What's up?"

"Scouts found a small Imperial column, at least a battalion, moving along the river and some boats on the river moving with them or vice versa. Vaughan is taking his division and moving to attack. We need to be prepared in case something else pops up or in the unlikely even he needs assistance."

"Have to be way more than a battalion for him to need help," Coe nodded. "We can strengthen our flankers and push them out a bit more. I'd suggest putting some additional scouts out past our flankers as well. In both directions."

"See to it," Allen ordered, nodding his agreement. "Meanwhile we will continue on until we hear something else."

-

Lucas Silven had taken his turn at the pole of his boat and was now taking his break. Soon he would take the other pole and spare his tiller man after that. Most officers wouldn't perhaps be taking a turn, but he couldn't just sit and watch. It wasn't in him.

It also gave him the chance to excise his anger against that idiot Greeley instead of killing him as he really wanted to. He'd never met anyone he wanted to drown more than the pompous cavalry officer. There was no reason whatsoever for the man's animosity or his attitude toward the boat crews or himself. Silven was fair enough to admit that the situation that Stone had found when he'd arrived was grounds for some animosity but this was ridiculous.

And it wasn't as if he, Silven, had asked for Greeley to come along. He was following the orders of his own general officer, so if the man had an issue with those orders, he needed to take them up with Stone. But that required a level of intestinal fortitude that Silven just didn't think Greeley was capable of to-

"Captain, you hear that?" The soft-spoken question startled Silven out of his thoughts about Greeley.

"Hear what?" he replied to the man at the tiller of his boat, his senior NCO. "I don't hear-" He broke off as he heard what might have been distant thunder from somewhere west of them.

"Might be gonna storm, sir," the petty officer on the port side front pole mentioned. "Can't see for these blasted trees," he added, his gaze on the western sky.

"That would be all we need," Silven muttered to himself. "A good, driving downpour on top of everything else."

"Begging the Captain's pardon," the starboard petty was shaking his head. "I don't think that's thunder, sir."

-

Major Wilhelm Greeley was a rather arrogant man. His family were considered nobility among the Empire, his relatives having a distant kinship to the Emperor's family that was some generations old. Well off, well-educated and knowing it, the Greeley family held a great deal of land and power in the northern provinces of the Empire.

Military service having long been recognized as a political necessity in the Empire, there had never been much doubt that Wilhelm would be enrolled in the Imperial War Academy, and from there be inducted into the Imperial Army. Determined to make a name for himself in what might be the final ever war between the Empire and the Kingdom of Soulan, Greeley chafed at this escort duty.

He and his men had faced the Soulan army and been hurt badly in that engagement, then spent weeks with General Stone chasing shadows behind the lines that never materialized into anything. Now, with Stone riding into the central areas above the southern capitol, sure to find action more suitable to a cavalry engagement and against more favorable odds (where a man with a hard driven and well-trained unit could make a name for himself), here he was, stuck once more behind the lines, playing babysitter to a bunch of useless Naval types and their toy boats.

This was nothing but scut work and Greeley was furious at the time it was assigned to him and was no less furious now. In the just over two weeks this had lasted his men had seen not so much as a Soulan firefly, let alone an actual enemy combatant. There was no glory to be had in escorting a collection of lazy boat crews down the river! At this point he had stopped even sending out scouts or flankers, save only a handful of scouts ahead of him to find the best trails to use in shadowing the river.

His executive officer, a sound tactician if not an overly bright individual, had tried to maintain their flankers at least, citing regulations for moving in enemy territory. Greeley had argued that this was scarcely enemy territory, what with the Imperial Army controlling everything for hundreds of miles. The man persisted nonetheless until Greeley had threatened him with court-martial for his disrespect. Never a man with a great deal of moral courage, his first officer had faded away at that threat, leaving Greeley in peace.

That decision was about to come back to bite Major Greeley rather hard on his pompous ass.

-

"No sign of scouts at all?" Vaughan asked, frowning.

"None sir," the lead scout shook his head. "No flankers whatsoever. We have caught sight of what may be a few scouts to their front, essentially breaking trail it appears, but nothing else. And we've confirmed there are a number of boats on the river, sir. More than the original dozen. We aren't sure exactly how many more, but over fifty at a minimum."

"So, the Marshal was right," Vaughan nodded. It was a stroke of genuine luck for them to come upon the boats like this out of the blue. Allen's hunch had paid off as something finally broke Soulan's way in this war.

"Brigadier Charles, you will take Colonel Cambry's Brigade and move to intercept the front of this column. Attack when ready and we will base the rest of our attack on your timing. Try to pick a place where your archers can engage the boats if possible."

"Sir," Charles nodded. He and Cambry reined around and moved back to the latter's command. Just minutes later several thousand horsemen were on their way around to cut off the Imperial advance.

"Colonel Shelby, you will take your brigade and move to a point well back along their trail, then slowly come forward to envelop them, keeping a careful watch on both the river and your trail. Ensure that we aren't caught by surprise during the attack, and as with Colonel Cambry's men have your archers engage any boats that are in their range." Shelby and his second in command moved immediately back to their command, and were only two minutes later than Cambry in departing for their part in the attack.

"Colonel Moore, what say you and I take your men and see what havoc we can wreak on these heathen invaders of ours?" the huge general asked, his face splitting suddenly into a wide smile.

"That sounds like a fine idea to me, sir," Moore grinned back. "Gentlemen, set your commands in line and advance slowly to contact or until we hear Colonel Cambry's men engage." His three regimental commanders moved at once to deploy their men. It took ten minutes for them to be online in the broken territory, after which Vaughan gave Moore a nod. Moore raised a hand, looking right to left until all his commanders were responding in kind, then lowered his arm in a forward motion. In fits and starts the lines began moving forward, dressing as they went to maintain or reform lines. Vaughan watched as the lines moved forward, then turned to Colonel Moore.

"Let's see who these people in our neighborhood are, Colonel."

-

Greeley was still fuming from his exchange with Silven when one of his scouts came galloping up. Greeley absently noted the man's uniform was torn and bloodstained but ignored it as being a result of his pushing through rough country.

"Sir, we're under attack!" the man exclaimed even as his horse slid to a halt in front of his commander.

"What? Preposterous!" Greeley exclaimed. "Attack by who?"

"Soulanies, sir!" the man said breathlessly. "They'll be here in just a minute, sir. I'm the only one who managed to get away. There are thousands of them sir!"

"Stop your rambling and be accurate you dolt!" Greely demanded. "There can't be thousands of Soulanies this far into territory we control!"

"Sir, I'm telling you there are thousands of southern cavalry coming right for us!" the man insisted, bordering on panic. "We have to get ready or they're gonna roll right over us, sir!"

"Don't presume to tell me how to command my battalion you insolent jackass!" Greeley stormed back. "I'll have you tied to a wagon wheel and whipped until...until..." Greeley frowned, trailing off his diatribe as the distant sound of thunder came to him. "What is that?"

"Sir, I'm trying to tell you it's the Soulanies!" the scout stormed. "I'm getting out of here!" the man put heels to his mount and shot past his commander, heading for the rear of the formation.

"Come back here you cowardly scum!" Greeley shouted. "Sergeant, get that man back here!" he screamed at a nearby NCO.

"Begging the Major's pardon, sir," the wide-eyed man said evenly, slowly raising a hand to point a finger past his commander. "But we got bigger problems."

"What?" Greeley turned to follow the pointing finger, finding-

"My God," he breathed as line upon line of southern cavalry emerged from the woods to his front. At the sight of the Imperial horse soldiers a shout went up along the southern lines and suddenly the entire formation was barreling toward Greeley.

"Sir!" he heard the sergeant shouting but Wilhelm Greeley's mouth was suddenly too dry to answer.

"But we're in safe territory!" he managed to exclaim just before a southern lance tore through his chest, the men in front of him already dead or dying.

Wilhelm Greeley would not have to worry about his political fortunes being affected by his not having an opportunity to make a name for himself. He would be forever remembered as one of many who had not returned from the Kingdom of Soulan.

-

"What in the hell?" Silven muttered. He and his men could hear shouting from the shore, but it was difficult to see what was happening along this stretch as the trees were somewhat heavier and were blooming nicely in the waning spring.

"Sir, I don't like this," his chief petty officer said from the tiller. "That sounds a lot like-" He was cut off by shouts of consternation from behind them. Silven turned to look behind him and saw one of his men falling into the river with an arrow protruding from his chest.

"Son-of-a-bitch!" Silven cursed, shocked. Even as he watched a shower of arrows from somewhere on shore fell among his boats, some finding flesh and blood targets. His men were being shot, dying.

"Sir!" his chief petty officer exclaimed.

"Come about!" Silven shouted, motioning for the chief to turn their boat as well. "Move across the river with the current!" he cupped his hands and shouted to the other boats. "Pass it on!" Others took up the call down river, carrying the orders down the line. Boats began to turn away even as another volley of arrows came flying from shore. The quick turns of many boats placed them out of the target areas but not all of them had turned quick enough and more of his men fell victim to arrows.

"Damn it!" he exclaimed. His men were dying and he was helpless to stop it. All he could do was try and get them out of the line of fire because they had zero ability to fight back.

"Move with the current!" he called again. "Use the current to move across the river!" Another volley of arrows flew from the trees toward the boats but he couldn't see any of them strike home. Shouts from down river told him that might not mean none had, however.

"Use the oars!" he called out. "Pass the word to unship oars! Use them to get to the other bank and out of range!" The call was picked up and relayed down the river as oars appeared over the sides of boats in view. Satisfied that his men were doing all they could do, Silven turned his attention toward shore once more.

What the hell had happened to their escort? Had that incompetent idiot Greeley ran off and left them? He knew they were defenseless out here. That was the whole reason for Greeley and his men being there to start with!

"Where the hell is our escort sir?" his senior NCO echoed his own thoughts.

"I was just wondering that myself," Silven told him even as he worked to get one of the boat oars into the water. "That idiot Greeley probably ran off and left. . ." he trailed off as a horse with a rider wearing the uniform of an Imperial cavalry man plunging off the bank right out of the woods and into the river.

"What the hell?" he and the chief petty officer asked at the same time.

The cavalry man managed to stay on the horse until it hit the water. The horse had fallen perhaps fifteen feet into the river and hit the water hard. As Silven watched the rider was vaulted over the struggling horse's head and into the water. Three arrows were visible sticking out of his back.

"I think I know what happened to our escort, sir!" the chief petty officer called out as he fought the tiller under the influence of the current that now trailed and pushed the boat rather than opposed.

"No shit!" Silven called back even as he put his back into the oar he had grabbed. "Wonder if they got Greeley!"

"We're due some luck, sir," the other man shot back hopefully. "Something has to break our way sooner or later."

"Does. . .it?" Silven grunted between oar strokes. "I'm not. . .so sure!"

-

Wilton Vaughan surveyed the work of his division with a grim satisfaction. His men had done an excellent job of destroying the Imperial horse unit. A small number of them were headed north as fast as their horses would take them, thinking they were escaping.

"They should hit Shelby right about. . .now," Moore said, just as they could hear faint shouting to the north of their position.

"I don't guess we need to worry about leaving any of them alive since those sailors are headed north again," Vaughan mused, humor hinting at his tone. "What word on the boats?"

"They turned, used the current and moved across the river, General," Moore reported. "We managed to kill several of the sailors though we don't have a definite number, sorry, and at least one of the boats devoid of crew crashed into the bank on our side and we set fire to it."

"Are the boats still headed north?" Vaughan asked.

"Last word was yes," Moore nodded. "I have a squad tracking them down river a short way to see if they stop. Their orders are to go no further than three miles."

"Excellent," Vaughan nodded. "Sound recall and let's get this mess cleaned up then," he ordered. "I'd like it to look nice and neat when General Allen arrives," he semi-smirked.

"Yes sir."

-

"One hundred seventeen wounded still in the boats sir," one of Silven's officers reported. He nodded, still a bit shocked at what had taken place.

"How many lost?" he asked, dreading the answer.

"We're missing one hundred nineteen sailors, sir," George Stenopolous came up just then. "Presumed dead, I'm afraid. And two boats missing and presumed lost."

"Damn it," Silven muttered under his breath. "How seriously injured are the wounded?" he asked.

"Some probably won't make it to nightfall, sir," Stenopolous fielded that one as second ranking officer. "We have almost no medical supplies and no surgeon. There's really nothing we can do for them."

"We don't have much of anything I'm sure," Silven nodded. "We don't have any choice but to continue down river until we hit help, gentlemen." There was no point in putting off the decision. "We've lost our escort, our baggage train, our supplies and means to cook them, everything. Get everyone loaded and let's get under way."

"Shouldn't we bivouac here tonight sir?" on officer asked. "To care for our wounded?"

"Were you listening?" Silven asked. "We don't have a way to care for our wounded, mister. The only thing we can do for those who might live is get them back as quickly as possible. We'll be lucky not to starve as it is, not to mention the need to find safe drinking water since we've got nothing to boil the river's water in. Now get loaded I said!" he snapped out. "Every minute we waste here talking is a minute we could have been traveling. Get a move on!"

"Look," Stenopolous said softly, a hand coming up to point across the river. Silven looked that way to see a dozen Soulan cavalry troopers watching them calmly from the other bank, thankfully out of bow range.

"Bastards," Silven muttered under his breath.

"Can't really blame them," Stenopolous said quietly. "We are invading their country."

"I don't give a damn about their country," Silven spat. "All I care about are the men under my command!"

"Then maybe we shouldn't have brought them here," Stenopolous shrugged. "Because they damn sure don't look like they're giving up on the idea of killing us all just yet," he nodded across the river.

"All the more reason to get moving, George," Silven growled. "Now go!"

"Aye aye, sir," Stenopolous touched his hat brim and made his way back to his own boat. Silven watched him go then clambered aboard his boat, ready to cast off.

"Down river, chief," Silven ordered.

"Aye sir," the man replied and turned the boat with the tiller as the two front men pushed them off.

"And stay as far from the other bank as you can," Silven added, watching milling cavalrymen studying them.

"Was gonna do that anyway, sir."

It would be a hard and dangerous trip back to friendly territory. Not all of them would make it.

CHAPTER FOURTEEN

-

Wilhelm Greeley's would not be the only Imperial Cavalry command to find itself in dire straits that day. One hundred miles to the east, General Brent Stone was receiving yet another report of a blocked trail and destroyed bridge from his scouts.

"Is there a single trail in this cursed country that isn't blocked off?" Stone demanded in disgust. "I always heard the Soulanies kept their roads in good shape for trade!"

"Ah, sir," the lead scout, a nervous looking Captain stammered, "these trails are. . .that is the debris blocking them is fresh cut, sir."

"What do you mean?" Stone asked, unease settling instantly in his stomach.

"Sir these trails have only recently been damaged and obstructed," the young officer clarified. "It's been done deliberately it appears in order to slow or obstruct our advance."

"How the hell could they know we were coming?" Stone demanded. "We didn't know until maybe three weeks ago and we've only been across the river half that!"

"Sir it would appear that they have blocked the roads as a deterrent to a raid such as ours," the captain shrugged helplessly. "I don't think they knew we were coming, they were preparing for anyone who tried to come this way."

"That might explain all the deserted homesteads we've seen," Stone's aide remarked.

"So, it might," Stone nodded. "Can we get through it?" he asked.

"Which one, sir?" the scout commander asked.

"Any of them, Captain!" Stone almost managed not to sound pissed off.

"It will take a good while, but with axes we can cut our way through," the man nodded.

"Then get to it," Stone ordered. "We don't have any Pioneers with us so commandeer the first company in line and get them working to cut those roadblocks out of the way. Take the first two in fact and one can rest while the other works. Perhaps that will speed things up."

"Yes sir," the man saluted and moved to carry out the orders. Soon one hundred and eighty horsemen were moving south to the first blockage in the road they were following.

"Do the same thing to the other blocked roads," Stone ordered his aide. "Let's get these roads opened up good in case we need them."

"Sir," the man nodded and rode over to the nearest units, shouting orders to milling cavalry troopers.

"And get some security out!" Stone called out to no one in particular. "Sitting here in the open like this is just asking for trouble!"

-

'Trouble' was already watching the Imperial horsemen, Stone just wasn't aware of it yet.

"Looks like they're gonna try and cut the roadblocks out," one man said softly, rolling a wad of chewing tobacco from one side of his mouth to the other and spitting. "Reckon better let the General know that, Sam," he told his partner.

"Will do," 'Sam' nodded in reply. Backing down off the small ridge he'd been using to observe, 'Sam' mounted his horse and was soon spurring it toward General Pierce's field headquarters. The newly promoted Brigadier had spread his command out only slightly, using the 31st as the central unit, being the largest single command he had. Colonel Jared Whit was waiting with Pierce to see when or where his men would be needed. It would take 'Sam' just twenty minutes of hard riding to reach Pierce and report.

-

"Are the archers in place?" Pierce asked. The assembled commanders all nodded.

"One company of bowmen at every trail blockage sir," Whit assured him. "We're reinforcing that number right now, as planned." The plan had called for each block to receive a second archer company if the enemy was approaching.

"Excellent," Pierce nodded. "Have we had word from any other scouts?"

"Not as yet, sir," his aide shook his head. "It's possible that the Nor General won't divide his command this far into enemy territory on his own," he suggested.

"I suspect you're correct, at least for now," Pierce nodded. "Remember that we hurt their cavalry badly in that first engagement the Marshal led. I would imagine they're at little better than half strength overall." Pierce looked at his map for a minute.

"We'll leave things as they are for the moment, but," he raised a hand before anyone could speak, "I want our men here ready to ride on five minutes notice. If there is a breakthrough among our road blocks, we have to counter it at once before too many of their horsemen get through here."

"For now, all we can do is hope that our archers are up to the task."

-

"And here we sit, waitin' for the bloody Nor to come and kill us all," Rye March grumbled as he spat on the ground in front of him. "Is this really the best we could come up with you think? Felling a buncha trees to block the roads and then shoot from ambush when the Imps try 'n clear 'em?"

"If you'd rather shoot from out in the open, Rye, you go right ahead," Sergeant Mike Cado told him, rolling his eyes where the irritable old solider couldn't see him. "Me personally I like the idea of shooting from cover just fine." Several grunts of agreement went around their position as the others let their opinion be known.

"Ain't no fit way fer a man to be fightin' no war, that's all I'm sayin'," March shook his head stubbornly. "Last war, we rode right at the bastards and pushed 'em all the way back to their house."

"Last war you was maybe ten," Cado snorted. "You wouldn't know no more what happened than the rest of us would."

"My daddy rode with the Marshal back then," March sniffed. "Have you know that I know exactly what happened count o' I got it straight from my old man."

"And he was as truthful and unlikely to exaggerate as you are, right?" another man asked.

"Damn straight," March said firmly, not realizing or perhaps ignoring the sarcasm pointed his way.

"Lord deliver us from igno-" someone started.

"Quiet," Cado hissed suddenly, his right hand up. "Listen." Straining ears waiting and could finally make out hoof beats approaching.

"Here they come," Cado said unnecessarily. "Get set but remember; no one shoots until the Captain does. Got it?" Affirmative responses came from up and down the position as men moved into place, arrows nocked and ready.

Cado watched for the enemy to approach, also keeping an eye out for where his Captain was hidden, waiting for just such a moment as this.

-

The Imperial Army did not as a rule carry axes in great number outside their Pioneer companies. Units on the move like Stone's cavalry however would carry at least one ax per company, and often more than that if they were doing independent and unsupported operations. This was such a time.

Captain Wayne Barrows had collected axes from every company in the brigade his company was part of and acquired a few more elsewhere throughout the command until he had enough to equip his entire company with a tool. Normally he would not have had everyone working like this, but with a second company not far behind he assumed he would have sufficient security on hand that he could set all of his men to working on the brush and trees that were blocking the army's way.

He was about to learn that 'assuming' was the bane of any military man.

His men had been working perhaps five minutes when he heard someone shout. Looking up from his notebook where he was dutifully recording his part in this historic war effort to reunite the Empire, Barrows could see one of his men on the ground.

"Already?" he shook his head, making another assumption, this time that one of his men had already succumbed to heat exhaustion and passed out. He had warned them all about staying hydrated, esp-

His thought process was cut off by a cloud of arrows erupting from the tree line on both sides of the road. Right before his eyes his men began falling as hundreds of arrows struck the area where his men were working. Not all of them found a target but enough did that he could see right away that he was taking casualties.

"Fall back!" he called at once, his notebook forgotten. "Fall ba-" he was cut off by a hammer blow striking his chest and knocking the wind from him. Looking down to see who or what had dared strike him like this, he was shocked to see a crossbow bolt emerging from his tunic, the bulk of it buried in his chest.

"Med-" he tried to form the word medic but his mouth was suddenly full of blood that spilled out as he tried to talk. He was still trying to form the word when he hit the ground, dying.

Seeing their Captain on the ground, his men ran. Grabbing the nearest horse to them without regard for who 'owned' it, each man ran for his life. In their hurry to get away from the ambush they ran headlong into the supporting company that was almost on their position. Horses spurred on in a blind panic slammed into horses ridden by men who had no idea their companions were under attack until the arrows started falling around them as well.

"AMBUSH!" one of Barrows luckless men cried as he galloped by. "There's thousands of 'em! RUN FOR IT!!"

Without a pause the follow on company did just that and turned tail.

Behind them, Sergeant Mike Cado and his men were out making sure that all the Nor on the ground were truly dead, and if not then helping them on their way. Distasteful but necessary work.

"Ain't no fit way for a-" Rye March began to mutter.

"Shut up Rye," Cado told him sharply. "Last thing we need right now is that gob o' yours mumbling a crock o' that mess you're always spouting. Don't make me tell ya again," he warned when March looked as if he was about to complain. March took one look at his sergeant and decided he didn't really want to talk about it anyway and kept quiet.

Ten minutes later all the Soulan bowmen were back under cover, waiting to see who came calling next.

-

"Make sure our scouts are keeping a close eye on their main body," Pierce ordered as reports began filtering in from nearly a dozen such engagements so far. "They're almost certain to make a move of some kind after suffering so many casualties for no gain. I don't want any one place overwhelmed."

-

"What the hell is going on here?" Stone demanded as the third company in ten minutes came streaming back into camp, what was left of them at any rate, some men wounded and others babbling about 'thousands' of enemy archers in the trees.

"Ambushes set at the roadblocks, sir," his aide supplied.

"I can see that, Captain," Stone's tone was acidic at best. "There's no way in hell there are 'thousands' of Soulanies around here! Find me someone who actually knows their ass from a hole in the ground!"

"Captain Barrows and his first Lieutenant were both killed in action sir," the aide didn't react to Stone's temper tantrum. "Captain Sligo is wounded and his First Lieutenant didn't return. I don't know which company came in after-" he cut off as yet another group of Imperial horsemen came galloping back from the direction they'd ridden off just minutes before.

"Who is that?" Stone asked flatly, feeling a headache forming.

"I'll go and see, sir."

Over the next half-hour every single group sent to cut out roadblocks obstructing the roads and trails returned. Rather some of them returned. Many of them would not return at all.

"There can't be that many southern troops in this area," Stone refused to believe it. "Can't be. They've got every man jack they can scrape up confronting 1st Army in the west. This is just a bunch of locals trying to keep us out."

"They're doing a good job then," Brigadier Silas Weir noted, unafraid of Stone's volcanic temper. "These 'locals' have cost us better than three hundred dead and over five hundred wounded, we don't have a single kill to answer for it and the roads are all still blocked!"

"Which of these roads is most important to us?" Stone asked, ignoring Weir's comment. Silas Weir was his oldest and most able Brigadier and commanded Stone's 2nd Division. He was also the meanest and most prone to challenging someone to a duel. No sense poking the bear if it wasn't needful.

"This one I'd say, sir," his aide stepped in and placed a finger on the central road. "This one will take us through the heart of their central highlands area and straight to the river opposite their capitol, if we're so inclined. If we want to make sure the Soulan Army feels they have no choice but to come after us, I submit this road is the one we should be taking."

"Makes sense," Weir nodded in agreement. "And we are here to raise hell and get attention," he added, rubbing his chin. "What are your orders, sir?" he asked Stone.

"Shake out 2nd Division then and attack this roadblock," Stone ordered. "While you do that, I'll post orders for a strong demonstration in two more directions to try and confuse and split up whatever forces are out there, and hold the others in place. Roll over them," he ordered Weir.

"We'll give it a shot," the other man nodded grimly. "Half hour?"

"Half hour," Stone nodded.

-

"What do you think?" The scout post was now occupied by Pierce's chief of scouts, a young major who knew the area quite well.

"They're gonna hit the Nashboro Road," he replied, using the ancient name for the road that his parents had always used. "Gonna try and roll right over the roadblock."

"What about the other forces?" the young captain beside him asked.

"Feints to hold us in position," the major shook his head. "Still, we need to let the general know. If he don't reinforce those outlying roads then the Nor will be able to break through anyway. A feint that works stops being a feint." He scribbled a hasty note for his general in his notebook, tore the sheet loose and handed it to a young corporal he doubted had ever known a razor.

"Get this to General Pierce without delay, soldier," he ordered. "We'll remain in place and try to see what they do next."

"Sir!"

-

"Even if that's a really good guess, Nelson, it's still a guess," Colonel Jared Whit said softly as he read the note from the scouting unit. "If we devote everything to stopping-"

"We won't send everything, but we will send the greater part of our forces against them there," Pierce cut the other man off without rancor. "Get your boys in the saddle and get going. You've got extra arrows, yes?"

"Twenty per man," Whit nodded. "An extra ten per man for the others on post as well. What will you do?" he asked.

"We'll send a battalion of cavalry to each of these other spots the major thinks they will demonstrate before," Pierce replied. "I'll keep the rest of our forces here, able to move and react to any breath-through or any new threat." Left unsaid was that the 'rest' of their forces wouldn't quite number a full brigade of men.

"Very well," Whit was clearly unconvinced. "We're on our way."

"Good luck."

"Luck is for fools," Whit threw over his shoulder. "We're going hunting."

"Good hunting then," Pierce smiled. "And give them hell."

-

Silas Weir studied the debris ridden road before him through his glass, a doubtful look crossing his craggy features that he was careful to keep his men from seeing. He lowered the glass and looked at his assembled brigade commanders. After the debacle in the west a few weeks before his units were at barely three-quarters their nominal strength, with some individual battalions being well below even that. He shook his head in resignation. Stone had ordered this attack and that meant he had to carry it out, but it was doomed to fail and he knew it.

"Sir?" He turned at the questioning tone to find Colonel Terry Wiskowski sitting his horse beside the Brigadier, awaiting orders. The look on the Colonel's face showed all too clear what he thought of this operation, but professional soldier that he was, he didn't share it.

"Dismount your brigade and form regiments to advance in line against their position, Colonel," Weir spoke almost against his will. "The rest of us will come up on each flank and see if we can force them to turn. You'll have to hold their attention while we do that."

"You know we can't carry that position, sir," the younger man said softly so that no one else could hear. "I doubt the whole division will be able to if the enemy is there in any strength. That is a strong and well sited position with excellent cover and fields of fire. We're walking into a hornet's nest here sir."

"I know," Weir nodded. "But we have to try. Stone won't hear that this is anything other than locals trying to stymie our drive south. For my money we're at least facing well trained militia. No way a bunch of unorganized locals hit our men that hard in so many places." He looked at Wiskowski again.

"So, shake your men out and get moving, Colonel," his order held a grim finality to it. "We'll support you on either flank, so concentrate your men toward the roadblock itself. Let's see if we can't at least take the position from them. In the event that it is just a small number of locals, I'll sound the charge and all commands will center their attack on the roadblock itself. We'll bowl right over them."

"Yes sir," Wiskowski nodded, snapped a salute, and moved away to where his regimental commanders were waiting. It took twenty minutes for the bulk of the dismounted division to form lines and prepare to advance. The cavalrymen had trained to do this of course, but most of their training had centered on fighting from horseback. Fighting on the ground was as foreign to them as the ground they were walking on itself.

Looking over the lines and finding them satisfactory, Wiskowski signaled to Weir that he was ready. Weir looked to the other commanders and received similar signals from them. He nodded to the signalman next to him who raised a long, slender pole into the air with a red banner fluttering in the light breeze. As pennants raised along the line in answer, Weir raised his arm, then lowered it sharply. The signalman slapped the red banner down in the direction of the enemy position and the lines began moving forward.

Weir sat his horse behind the line, watching pensively.

-

"Looks like a division of cavalry, sir," Whit's aide reported softly, though Whit could clearly see that for himself.

"Are our men in position?" he asked, looking through his glass at the approaching enemy even as he spoke.

"Hernandez left, Richards right and Gates in reserve, sir," the aide reported, looking to each command as he called it off to reassure himself that he was giving his commander an accurate report.

"The group that was here first is supporting the center?" Whit asked. He had left the two companies that had engaged the enemy here first in place. They were all expert rated archers.

"Yes sir," the aide replied. "Two hundred twenty-seven effectives combined. All bowmen. They've been resupplied from the earlier engagement."

"Very well," Whit nodded. "Nothing for it but to wait, now."

His plan was simple. He wanted the enemy to think that they were still up against the few bowmen who had defended this position earlier. To do that he had ordered the original companies only to fire, leaving them in position and moving his regiments to either side of them. The first three volleys would be from that group only, which hopefully would trick the Nor commander into committing his forces piecemeal, or in some haphazard fashion that Whit could counter.

There was real danger here as few of his men were overly skilled archers. All of them knew how to use a bow of course, but very few of them could claim the title of military archer. Still, two hundred bows would put up a small cloud of arrows at least for a minute. That might be enough to suck the enemy in and get them to commit to something stupid.

"Sir, the enemy appears to be working to flank us," his aide mentioned. Turning his glass, Whit noted that the enemy was indeed spreading out, what looked like a full brigade to either side of the initial attack.

"Runners to Colonels Hernandez and Richards," Whit snapped out. "Reserve fire until enemy is within one hundred yards, or until the center fires their third volley, whichever happens first."

"Sir!" the aide replied and moved to inform two waiting runners of the new orders. Whit silently cursed the enemy commander for trying to force the flanks of a hilly position like this. It was unlikely he could carry Whit's position without suffering mass casualties first, but if the Imperial commander was willing to pay the price, he might well do just that, using his much greater numbers to overwhelm Whit's smaller command.

"Message to Brigadier Pierce," he said without lowering his glass. "Estimate under attack by one division of dismounted cavalry. Expect to be hit with far superior numbers but believe we can hold at least for a time. Advise if we should hold or fall back if the position begins to fall. May prove impossible to hold this position against a determined attack. Message ends."

"Right away sir!" Soon another runner was galloping away. It would take twenty minutes to reach Pierce, another twenty to get an answer, and however long Pierce debated on what to do. In all likelihood, the battle would be decided before he got an answer, but this was a stronger attack than he had anticipated.

All he could do now was wait. At least he didn't have to wait long.

-

"Why come we're stuck right here 'n the midst o' all this?" March was, predictably, complaining.

"Shut up Rye," Mike Cado growled. Unlike before when they were facing a fairly equal number of Nor cavalry, they were now outnumbered about two-to-one at least. The veteran NCO was understandably concerned and March's muttering wasn't helping his calm any.

"I'm just sayin' we done an' did ours!" March ignored the order. "Time we was getting' a chance to sit back like that bunch back yonder whilst the rest of this outfit gets them a taste o'-"

"Rye, if you don't shut your mouth, I'll shut it for you," Cado turned to look at the complaining soldier. "We need to be concentrating on what's coming and not worrying about your complaints. Now shut it!" the last order was more of a hiss than anything as Cado's patience ended abruptly.

"Man can't even complain 'round here," March murmured to himself as he shifted in place, but he fell silent under the withering glare of his sergeant. Cado gave him one more glare for good measure and then turned his attention back to the approaching enemy. An enemy that was getting closer and closer with each passing second.

"C'mon, c'mon," Cado muttered to himself. "Don't let 'em get right up on us for Gawd sake!"

"Easy Mike," another soldier said just as softly. "Reckon the Colonel knows what he's about."

"You reckon all you want," Cado replied without rancor. "We're the ones sat here in the way, mind."

"Look," the other man said in way of reply, pointing toward their left. Cado looked and saw the yellow banner standing tall at the center of the line.

"That's us boys," he whispered. "Pass it on, yellow flag is up. Nock and ready!" The message passed down the line in a hurry as the men prepared to fire. They didn't have long to wait as Cado looked back to the area where the signalman was standing in time to see the banner being slammed down forward.

"Fire! Fire! FIRE!" Cado shouted even as he rose to his feet and loosed his own first arrow. The battle plan was for the original force to fire three volleys before the rest opened fire. The first three volleys were to be ragged and uncoordinated to give the appearance of an unorganized militia rather than a military unit. Pierce had unknowingly played right into the Imperial thought process with that decision. No other order he could have given would help as much as that one was about to.

-

"I'll be damn," Weir said to himself as the ragged flight of arrows came out of nowhere. Even as some of his men fell to them, Weir felt himself smiling slightly. A second ragged volley came, far too long in coming for trained military archers and even more ragged than the first.

"Stone was right," he muttered. "Stone was right!" he said louder and his aide and runners looked at their commander in question.

"Did you see how ragged that volley was?" he demanded. "No trained military outfit fired that! Bugler, sound charge!" he ordered without waiting for an answer.

-

In front of him Wiskowski heard the charge sounding and grimaced. Weir was jumping the gun with that command the young colonel thought. Two volleys wasn't enough to establish anything except an enemy presence. But orders were orders and there was nothing for it now.

"Double quick boys!" he shouted and heard the order being relayed first by regimental commanders, then battalion and finally company commanders. His lines grew more ragged as his men began to jog forward. NCOs and junior officers tried to dress the lines but that wasn't easy with the entire brigade moving forward and another brigade advancing on each flank.

The third enemy volley was just as ragged as the first two and Wiskowski allowed himself a few seconds of belief that Weir and Stone were right. He was facing locals trying to protect their homes.

It only lasted those few seconds.

-

"All troops prepare to fire," Lieutenant Colonel Carlos Hernandez said calmly. The enemy was behaving just as Pierce and Whit had predicted. How often did that happen? he wondered.

"All companies answer ready, sir," his signalman reported at his side.

"Fire at will," was the simple command. He heard the sound of the pennant's pole hitting the brush in front of him, followed in seconds by the twang of thousands of bowstrings being released.

The battle was truly joined now.

-

Wiskowski took one second to curse Weir's over-eager orders as the first heavy volley of arrows fell among his brigade. Thousands of arrows, not hundreds, fired in disciplined volleys with concentrated fire that devastated his front ranks.

"Son-of-a-bitch!" he shouted. "Keep moving, keep moving, we have to join with them or those bows will eat us alive!" he ordered. "MOVE!"

His order notwithstanding the men of his brigade were still too stunned to do more than look at the holes in their formation in shock. Officers and NCOs harried and yelled, trying to get them moving. Movement was their only source of self-preservation at the moment. As close as they were to the enemy even running wasn't a good option since they would get several good volleys into the retreating formation.

Their efforts failed as the Soulanie troopers would not grant them the few seconds reprieve they needed to get their troops moving again. Even as Wiskowski shouted and yelled and cursed to get his men moving another cloud of arrows hit his men, felling still more of them, leaving his men in windrows on the ground before the enemy.

No amount of shouting or cursing could prevent what happened next. First it was individuals, then pairs, and suddenly it was entire squads, at least what was left of them, turning tail and running headlong for the relative safety of their line of departure. They didn't have lines of their own to run to but they had horses waiting. They were cavalrymen, trained to fight from horseback. Once more their inept leadership had led them to slaughter and it was too much for many of them. Leaving far too many of their comrades on the ground behind them, the men of Wiskowski's brigade broke and ran.

Their sister brigades didn't fare much better. With Wiskowski's men in headlong retreat, that withering fire soon was falling on them and they fared no better than Wiskowski's men had.

It took less than ten minutes to route an entire Imperial cavalry division.

-

Weir watched with anger that slowly turned to horror as he realized the reason his men were running was that they were being slaughtered. Even as he looked on yet another cloud of Soulanie arrows flew into his men, felling them by the hundreds on the field before that cursed roadblock.

Weir was about to castigate Wiskowski for losing control of his brigade in such a way when he realized that his other two brigades were now in headlong flight as well, their own losses almost as bad as Wiskowski's men.

"Sound recall," he told his bugler, chafing at the necessity but knowing there was no use in trying to maintain the attack. His men had been soundly beaten and the majority of the fault lay squarely with him. He had jumped the gun, eager to make something happen.

His men were paying the price for that overeager attitude right before his eyes.

-

"Cease firing," Hernandez ordered calmly, watching the withdrawing Nor troops through his glass. "Check for losses," he ordered his aide.

"None reported as yet, sir," the man shook his head, waving toward the runners who had just arrived with reports for him. "No damages, either."

"Good," Hernandez nodded. "We've either broken them completely, or they'll be back with blood in their eyes. One or the other. I'd give a month's pay to know what they're saying over there."

-

"What happened?" Weir demanded, angry at having been made a fool of.

"You sounded the charge and we walked into an ambush," Wiskowski said bluntly. "Sir," he added almost as an afterthought.

"I don't like your tone, Colonel," Weir growled.

"My tone?" Wiskowski was incredulous. "I just lost a quarter of my command following your orders and you don't like my tone, sir?"

"You're past the mark of insolence, soldier," Weir's voice was frosty now. "And insulting as well," he added dangerously. Everyone knew how touchy Weir was and how prone to dueling he was as well. Wiskowski knew it too, but was far past caring.

"Begging the Brigadier's pardon, sir," the younger man shot back, "but this clusterfuck can be laid squarely at your feet, not ours," he indicated himself and his fellow brigade commanders. "I told you we couldn't carry such a strong position if it was held in force. But rather than scout it out or approach with skirmishers you elected, sir, to order a charge by our men and them on foot. And charge we did, Brigadier, right into an excellently set ambush that has cost us heavily. And I doubt we inflicted a single casualty on the enemy."

Weir was about to explode when he noted the equally surly looks on the faces of his other two brigade commanders. They were just as angry as Wiskowski and had suffered almost as many losses. The look on all three faces staring back at him was about one step below mutiny and for once Weir managed to hold his temper in check as he realized how precarious his position was at the moment.

"It was a rash decision and I regret it," he nodded instead. "I listened to General Stone state there couldn't be an organized enemy force in this area and when I saw those first ragged volleys, I allowed myself to believe it. I ordered the charge because I felt that if you could get among them quickly it would limit our casualties. It was a mistake, but I can't take it back."

The three men facing him lost some of their belligerence at that, but looked no less hostile toward him personally.

"Remain here and see to your wounded," he ordered. "Stay out of bow range and under cover as much as possible. I'm going to report to General Stone. If he wants this position taken we'll need more than just our division it looks like."

All three nodded and walked away without bothering to salute or render any manners whatsoever. Normally quick to take offense to any oversight such as that, Weir decided to ignore this one. He told himself it was because he deserved it.

Not because the look given him by the three men was in any way unnerving. Not at all because of that.

-

"You're telling me your entire division couldn't sweep aside one measly group of farmers and lumberjacks? That's what you're telling me. Right?" Stone's voice had a biting quality that set Weir on edge. He had calmed down considerably on the twenty-minute ride to Stone's field headquarters and had managed to present his report calmly and concisely, only to have Stone talking down to him, refusing to accept that he had been wrong. Again.

"With respect, sir," Weir shot back, "you weren't there or you'd know it's not just a bunch of farmers and lumberjacks! There were thousands of bows behind that tree line and on that hill, sir. Clouds of arrows hitting my men and felling them like leaves, sir. And no, my entire division can not carry that position without support. We have no artillery and damn few archers of our own as you may recall, sir. I'm sure you can find a way around that, but I, sir, cannot. And my men are the ones suffering because of it."

Now it was Stone who bit his tongue to keep from responding to Weir's acidic tone of voice and edge of insolence. He had no desire to find himself facing Weir with a sword in his hand, which he would have to do if challenged because if he pulled rank to get out of it, he would lose what respect he had left among his men.

"How many men do you estimate they have, then?" he asked. "And what were your losses?"

"My losses were still being tabulated when I left," Weir replied. "As to how many, I can't but tell you it has to better than two thousand and that's conservative. They fired a mass of arrows packed so tightly there's no real way to estimate it. We could be facing an entire division for all I know, and them with every advantage."

Once again, the lack of mounted archers, or even cross training for his men in archery, was coming back to haunt Stone. His men had been intended to be an answer to southern cavalry. As such it had been determined that they wouldn't need archery skills, able to depend on archers among the infantry instead. A fine idea indeed. Except for forgetting that the infantry would by and large not be nearby during a protracted cavalry battle since such a battle would of necessity be fought on open ground with room for thousands of horses to maneuver freely.

The decisions made for his men were made by men who would never face the southern army in battle themselves. Stone was sure that from one thousand miles away that it looked perfectly fine to depend on infantry archers to support horse soldiers. From up close and personal that wasn't working worth a damn. And now

Wilson had sent him and his men into yet another nest of wasps without proper support, resulting in too many of his men being killed for absolutely no gain. You could bet that Wilson wouldn't be accepting any of the blame for this if his men failed here, either.

"Suggestions?" he asked Weir and his other two division commanders who had rode over after seeing Weir return.

"Go home?" one of them suggested, only half joking.

"We're supposed to be trying to pull troops from the west," the other shrugged. "Looks like we've accomplished that."

"No," Stone shook his head, ignoring the joke. "No, I can't believe for a moment that this bunch came from the group opposing Wilson. They were already here, which means that someone over there," he waved a hand to the southwest, "anticipated this very move and placed troops here to stop it. Damn that Wilson, I told him he was setting us up to fail!" he said before he thought. His men looked at him but said nothing. It wasn't like they could have refused after all.

"We either try and carry one of these positions so we can break through or we double back, head further east and try to find a way through there," Weir sighed, his anger finally bleeding away somewhat.

"Or we can stay here and demonstrate like we're looking for a way through," Terry Blake, commander of 1st Division, offered. "Like I said, we're supposed to be a threat so we act like a threat. Our orders don't actually say we have to reach their capitol after all. Just to threaten if we got that far unopposed. Which, we didn't."

"Unless we actually make some progress, we won't be pulling any troops from the west," Stone shook his head slowly. "We have to become a threat or we're not fulfilling our mission. That means we have to break through this mess somewhere and get in behind them. If we can get them on open ground then we might be able to take them. Even eliminate them. That would force their army to further divide itself in order to send someone to oppose us here. That weakens them in the west and makes Wilson's job easier."

"Because he's made it so easy on us," Weir snorted. Stone didn't snap at him, mostly because it was true.

"All right," Stone mused. "We'll take all three divisions and attack, but…"

Stone spent ten minutes outlining his on-the-fly plan. By the time he was finished his commanders were all nodding their agreement. Maybe the Soulanies weren't the only ones who could use sleight of hand.

-

"I think they're leaving."

The men hidden in the scout lookout were careful to stay hidden, lest they be caught, but even from their obscured spot on the wooded hilltop overlooking the temporary Imperial command post it looked as if the Nor were doing just that; leaving.

"Something's up," the young major shook his head. "This isn't. . .why come all this way to make one aborted attack and then run?"

"Maybe they didn't expect to find anyone here," the even younger lieutenant shrugged. "On the face, it would make sense that all of us was over yonder," he pointed west, "with the army. Right?"

"They would have to know we wouldn't leave the door to the capitol open," the major shook his head again, not realizing that the former Marshal had actually done just that. "This is something else."

The division that had been cut up by the 31st Mounted Infantry moved past the other two Imperial cavalry divisions on its way north. As it went by, the others fell into trail. By all appearances, the Nor were headed back the way they had come.

"Unless they're going to try and find a way around us, the only reason to head back that way is if-damn it!" he broke off as the Imperial horsemen suddenly wheeled right in the road and took off at a gallop.

"Hurry and get this to the Brigadier," the major ordered. "Tell him the enemy is headed down the Sadler road at a full gallop! Hurry!" he urged again. "The entire command, tell him! All of them straight down the Sadler road!"

The young lieutenant leaped onto his waiting horse and set the spurs to him, slapping reins around him to urge the big charger on. The major looked at his sergeant.

"Ride to Colonel Whit's position and tell him that the entire Imperial Cavalry Corps is on its way down the Sadler road," he ordered. "At a full gallop. If he doesn't move and move now, they may be in a position to cut him off. Go!" The sergeant snapped a salute and aimed his horse west, tearing away from the outpost as if scalded. The major looked back at the departing enemy and shook his head ruefully. The enemy general had put one over on him. Acting as he were withdrawing until all of his units were on the road, then wheeling in place with his line of march already set, to take off at a gallop toward his actual target.

The Sadler road position had been visited by ax wielding cavalrymen today as well, but had seen no other action thus far, so they had not been reinforced. Right now, all that manned that rugged fortification and the cut it commanded was a company of mounted infantry. Less than two hundred men against at least twenty-thousand and almost certainly many more. The major had never gotten a good count from so far away and with so much action among the enemy.

Pierce had to either get his command gathered and fall back, or rush everything down the Sadler road and hope that he was both in time, and that everything would be enough to hold.

The major was pretty sure that both were forlorn hopes.

-

"All of them?" Pierce asked the gasping lieutenant who had just blurted his message out to him.

"Yes sir!" the young officer nodded. "They acted like they was leaving until they was formed up and then came about right in the road and headed straight down Sadler, sir!"

Looking at the map before him, Pierce traced the Sadler road. It didn't lead to the capitol straight on but it would lead the enemy much deeper into their territory. That much closer to their objective.

"I had hoped we could hold longer," he sighed. His position had just become untenable.

"Runners to all commands, reform at the first alternate position," he informed his aide, who nodded and began issuing orders. "And I need a courier."

-

"Well, that didn't last too long," Jared Whit sighed as he mounted his horse. "I rather hoped we could hold out here for a while longer."

"Here we likely could have," Hernandez shrugged beside him. "They're hitting somewhere else though, and we can't be everywhere at once."

"Straight to the rally point gents," Whit told his scouts. "Spare the horses though," he warned. "We may need them before the sun sets."

The 31st Mounted Infantry rode away from a naturally strong defensive position that had just been made unusable by virtue of being flanked. Pierce didn't have sufficient troops to hold this entire line so they had to withdraw.

Privately Whit wondered if they would be able to halt the Imperial drive short of the river opposite the capitol of Soulan. They didn't really have terrain on their side except in a few places. Once the Nor found a way through them, as they had here, then the territory would open up slightly. Not much, but enough for a large group of horsemen to take advantage of their mobility and greater numbers.

They were going to need help to hold on, but Whit had no idea where that help would come from.

CHAPTER FIFTEEN

-

General Jackson Andrews reread the message from Wilson as he waited for his division commanders to report to his tent. Unlike Wilson's command, the western army wasn't formed into 'corps', having all division commanders answering directly to Andrews instead. Eliminating one level of command had streamlined Andrews control of his forces and the command structure of his army. The fact that his army was only about half the size of Wilson's helped make this possible, as did the quality of Andrews' troops. Mostly from the mid-western reaches of the Empire, the men here were a bit more hardy and accustomed to hardship than their eastern counterparts.

His mission here had always been one of feint and distraction, keeping the Soulanie 3rd Corps in place here along the river so that they could not spare any of their strength to help oppose the invading army in the plains. His orders did allow for him to force a crossing if he was able to do so without severely damaging his army, but so far he hadn't seen a way to do that. He had suffered moderate casualties every few days with half-hearted attempts to cross the bridge, such attempts always being repulsed by the enemy somewhat easily. He could only get a certain number of men on the bridge before adding more simply made it an abattoir. And that number was never enough to seriously contest for the bridge and force a crossing.

Now, however, Wilson was asking Andrews to try and force such a crossing anyway in hopes that doing so would pull troops from his front and weaken the forces opposing his drive into the heart of Soulan. His drive was stalled and nothing he had tried had worked so far.

Andrews looked up as his commanders filed into the large command tent, each followed by his second and an aide.

"You wanted to see us sir?" the senior man asked.

"I did," Andrews nodded. "General Wilson has sent me a request. He asks that we make a determined attempt to carry the bridge in order to put pressure on the Royals and hopefully force them to reduce the troops facing him in favor of reinforcing Shelby." He got the looks of shock and sound of silence he had expected and nodded.

"Comments?" he asked finally.

"Sir," Charley Riordan, commander of the 11th Imperial Infantry and Andrews' senior division commander, was the first to speak. "Sir, we've made several feints at that bridge and the enemy fire we've received in reply was highly effective. While it chafes to admit, sir, I don't think we can take that bridge without incurring substantial casualties. And by substantial, I mean ruinous." The other division heads murmured their agreement with nodding heads. Andrews looked thoughtful.

"Any of you have suggestions on how we can increase the pressure against the Soulanies without ruining our army to do it?" he asked finally.

"We need a distraction, sir," Rolf Skagaran, commanding officer of the 32nd Infantry offered when no one else spoke.

"We're supposed to be the distraction, Rolf," Andrews replied with a half grin. "But I know what you mean," he continued after everyone had a good chuckle. "How can we do that?"

"We need to get some men across the river somewhere else," one of the cavalry commanders, General Caster Urich, spoke for the first time. "A raiding party in strength to pull forces away from the bridge."

"I don't see how we can do that Cass," Andrews was shaking his head before Urich finished speaking. "That river is too fast, too wide and too deep to swim, even if that would work, and we don't have any boats that can make it across with one horse let alone more than that. And for a raiding party to have any chance at survival it would have to come from you and Atwell," he nodded to Atwell Haskins who led his other cavalry division. "No way infantry makes it more than a couple days."

"True," Urich nodded. "All I can think of is we have to move back north, cross there, and then come down the river on a deep raid, or at least reconnaissance in force. Force them to pull troops off the line to chase us down. Ultimately, we can join up with Wilson to refit, or make our way back north if the attack here fails."

"That might work, but there's no guarantee that the troops they send after you come from there," Riordan was shaking his head. "If they cut loose cavalry from their main army to chase you down, then we've. . .well, technically that would accomplish our mission," he broke off thoughtfully. "Our goal is to pull troops away from Wilson's opposition. If this was successful then either way it works. Either it weakens them here so we can get across the river or else it weakens them in front of Wilson, which is our objective anyway. This might be the best option," he told Andrews.

"It's also the most long ended," Andrews was dubious. "And takes far longer as well. You're talking about riding almost a thousand miles before you get into territory that we don't already control access to and when you get there you will be completely on your own," he told Urich. "All you will have in the way of supplies is what you can carry, and wagons are out in this kind of work. You won't have an adequate resupply point for two hundred miles at the least depending on where you are from Wilson's army. Every other depot will be behind him somewhere and even further away."

"That's another thing," Andrews' remaining cavalry commander, Nathaniel Haskins, spoke up just then. "Where the hell is Stone? Why isn't he able to get this done for Wilson sir? He has nearly twice our strength taken all together. His three divisions have over thirty-five thousand troopers. Cass and I together don't muster much more than half that. He got the larger draw because of his position as 1st Army cavalry commander, but we have to create a diversion for them?"

"Had over thirty-five thousand troops," Andrews said softly. "Stone had that many troops before he was soundly beaten by Soulanie cavalry in a major cavalry engagement within sight of friendly lines. He lost over ten thousand men killed and wounded in one engagement. An engagement where he was numerically superior, was supported by infantry on one flank and Tribal warriors on the other, and where his enemy was already tired from having stomped three infantry divisions flat that morning."

"What?" Urich was stunned. "How in the Emperor's name-"

"Apparently he was over confident, but southern archery played a part as well," Andrews shrugged.

"We tried to get training for horse mounted archers but were denied," Haskins sighed. "Southerners have used bows from horseback for generations. It's part of their standard training regimen. We were told we didn't need it since we'd have infantry support and could 'depend' on their archers. No offense," he glanced at the infantry officers in the meeting.

"None taken," Riordan spoke for them all. No infantry man wanted to be facing cavalry, especially Soulanie cavalry, out in the open on foot.

"Anyway," Andrews got the discussion back on point, "Wilson has sent Stone into the middle portions of Tennessee and Kentucky," he used the Ancient names for the two provinces. "His mission will be to work down along the highlands on an extended raid in an attempt to pull troops from in front of Wilson in that direction."

"That's the stupidest thing I've ever heard," Urich said flatly. "That country is a horrible place for horse warfare, sir! Those hills with narrow passes and rock ledges? Asking for horses to lose their footing and likely take their riders with them. Not to mention that almost every pass they come to will be ideal for an ambush."

"I didn't say it was a smart plan, Cass," Andrews refrained from either correcting his subordinate or agreeing with him. "I said it was the plan he had. And it's why Stone and his men aren't available." Haskins and Urich both shook their heads in dismay at what they were told.

"Back to our issues," Andrews cleared the air again. "We need to find a way to make something happen if we can. And I am not going to send our cavalry all over hell's creation for what might end up being a disaster," he added.

"All we can do is try to take the bridge," Riordan shrugged. "But I'll tell you right now I don't think we can do it without wrecking ourselves. We have numbers on our side that is true, but they have terrain. There's a narrow avenue of attack with only one approach and they have it locked up tight. The more men we cram onto that bridge, the easier it is for them to kill. Their artillery is sighted on that bridge and can kill dozens of our men with every shot. There's nothing waiting for us there but a massacre." The other division commanders again murmured their agreement.

"If our artillery could reach that far we could advance under a barrage," Skagaran noted.

"I'm afraid that's not a possibility, sir," Colonel Artemis Perry spoke for the first time. He was the commanding officer of the 15th Imperial Artillery Brigade and the senior artillery officer of 2nd Army.

"Agreed," Lieutenant Colonel Vance Norman seconded. Commanding the 5th Imperial Engineer Battalion, Norman would have to be considered a good back up for that statement as he was undoubtedly the best engineer in 2nd Army.

"The size of the engine needed to make any impact across the river at this point would be prohibitive," Perry continued. "The base would have to be enormous and even then, we'd be risking the whole thing tipping over if we got the counter weights wrong. And the war might well be over before we managed to get it constructed anyway," he added with a shrug.

"Not to mention that such a large weapon, if we could even build it, would be completely immovable," Norman chimed in again. "It would never leave here intact and would have a very limited field of fire. We're talking adjustments in inches at best."

"Other than leaving it for a future enemy to use that wouldn't bother me over much," Andrews admitted. "Having a giant trebuchet fall on me on the other hand is something I can do without," he added wryly.

"So, we're back to trying to carry the bridge," Riordan sighed. "Sir, we're supposed to be here demonstrating. We're doing that, keeping their men in Shelby tied down here. We've made several forays onto the bridge to no gain. I submit that Wilson's problems are of his own making, sir, and no reason for us to destroy our men to try and help him make his mistakes go away."

"You're assuming he has made such mistakes," Andrews pointed out.

"He outnumbered his enemy at least three-to-one, sir," Skagaran replied this time. "His enemy was unprepared, or should have been, and outnumbered. He should have bowled them over and kept running. In all honesty the war should be over by now."

"But it isn't and we have to do our part," Andrews' voice took on an edge. "I didn't ask you here to critique the war effort, gentlemen," he told the group as a whole. "I'm looking for viable solutions to this problem. So put your heads together and give me something I can use. Report back to me after breakfast in the morning and bring me something workable. Dismissed!"

Snapping to attention the men filed out in pairs, talking among themselves. Andrews waited until they were all gone before taking a deep breath and releasing it slowly in an attempt to relieve his tension.

Damn that stupid ass Wilson anyway.

"Oh, I am so glad you two are back."

Carl and Billy heard that phrase over and over as they walked through the Foundry, checking on what had happened while they had been away. They exchanged a glance, knowing why everyone was so-

"Stop messing with that you moron!"

"Oh I've missed that," Carl sighed. "We could always just go home and come back tomorrow," he suggested.

"Nah," Billy shook his head. "Too much to get done. Besides, if we're here then maybe he won't be so-"

"Who told you to do that?!"

"You were saying?" Carl almost smiled but couldn't quite muster the energy. It had been a long, hard journey from Shelby home to Nasil and both were tired. And neither had actually missed working for Roda Finn.

Well, that wasn't true as both men enjoyed the work they were doing. It was Roda's explosive temper and scathing tongue they could do without if given the opportunity.

"It's about time you two got back!" Roda yelled before Billy could reply, having caught sight of the two as they made their way over.

"Got back as soon as we could boss," Carl shrugged. "I take it you've had a hard time keeping up with things without us here?" he managed to get out before Roda could say anything else. Whatever screaming Finn had been about to do blew itself out as the impact of Carl's words hit home with the fussy inventor.

"As if I actually need you two for more than just glorified messengers," he scoffed instead. "I take it you managed somehow to ensure that the soldiers at Shelby are adequately trained? Between the two of you?"

"Almost," Billy fielded that one, working to keep a straight face as he did so. "I think we can expect them to get three, maybe four salvos off before one of them screws up. Not the best odds, I admit, but still it's better than noth-"

"WHAT?" Finn lost his taciturn stance at once on hearing that. "You were supposed to stay there until they were capable of using. . .oh, I see," Finn interrupted himself as he noted both his assistants struggling to contain laughter. "Funny man."

"Ah, you had to be there," Carl shrugged it off. "They should be set," he went on more seriously. "Test fires went off without a hitch and they all passed the exams on the first try after training. If a major attack comes, they're ready for it. We also supervised construction of a bunker to store surplus munitions in. It's well back from the line but not too far from the main battery. They had some very bright young artillery officers who grasped the concepts quickly and well."

"Good, good," Finn's anger was no longer in evidence. "I need you two to resume supervision of this bunch," Finn waved toward the factory floor. "I have a project I'm working on for the Marshal and another I'm still developing that I need time to perfect. Something that just might give us an edge in this conflict, and we can use one about now."

"That is true, sir," Billy nodded. "We'll make a round and make sure everything is ship-shape. Anything we need to know?"

"Everything is still running as it was when you departed- ARE YOU INSANE?!" he cut himself off to screech at someone. "Put that down before you kill us all!"

"How about we go and check on things while you work on your projects, sir," Billy suggested even as Carl ran to where a young woman, frightened nearly out of her skin by Roda's screech, had come close to dropping a prepared charge that would have severely damaged the Foundry and killed her and many of her fellow workers.

"I tell you I can't manage to turn an eye away for a second without someone almost killing us all," Finn sighed in exasperation. "What were you saying?" he asked Billy. "Just now?"

"I said let us handle this while you work on your projects sir," Billy repeated dutifully. "We can keep things going here and allow you to work on developing new items."

"Yes, that would be an excellent idea," Finn nodded absently. "I have a great deal of work to get done."

"Well you go ahead then, sir, and leave this to us."

There was almost movement of air around him from the collective sigh on the factory floor as Finn returned to his office and left his two chief assistants to carry on.

"So glad to be back," Billy shook his head. "Really I am."

-

Lucas Silven was standing in the bow of his boat, holding a burning torch to help illuminate the water before him. Leading the rest of the boats down river in the dark, Silven was doing his best to avoid the many obstacles that a river set practically in the wilderness could present to a detail like his.

They had apparently left the southern cavalry behind them finally after the horsemen had followed them for miles, occasionally lofting arrows at the boats when one veered to close to the western shore. Without food or water, let alone medical supplies for his wounded, Silven had little choice but to continue on down river in hopes of reaching help at some point before hitting the Ohi. Shirts torn into strips and soaked in the tar/pitch solution used to help seal boats and keep them water tight had been wrapped around a half-dozen sturdy limbs to make expedient torches to help the see and stay together. Silven had one in the lead, George Stenopolous had one in the drag boat, three more were distributed around the other boats and the last one lay next to him as a back-up to the one in his hand.

He again cursed Stone, Greeley and Wilson all as he looked for dangers lurking in his path. Twenty-two of his wounded had already died as they made their way down river and many more would undoubtedly perish before their trip ended. And there was exactly not a damn thing he could do to help them that he wasn't doing right that second. He couldn't even make them comfortable in their suffering.

From behind the moaning cry of a young man in serious pain floated across the water just then, reminding Silven of just how helpless he was where his wounded were concerned.

He hated this country. He hated the heat, he hated the bugs, and he most of all hated the fact that he was anywhere within two hundred miles of where he was right this minute.

I wish we never had come here, he thought bitterly. I think if I got the chance to kill the Emperor for sending us here, I'd do it and hang the consequences.

It might or might not have surprised him to know that he was far from the only Imperial officer having those thoughts that very evening.

-

Oh, I so hate this cursed country.

Brent Stone took of his hat and wiped his forehead with a handkerchief, then wiped the narrow cloth sweatband inside the hat before replacing it on his head.

Hot during the day time, and now that the sun has set its already getting cold, he shook his head in disgust.

Today had been disappointing to say the least. The butcher's bill had been high today yet again. The initial ambush had been nothing compared to Weir's losses in the main engagement. He had established a field hospital on a small abandoned farm, leaving two surgeons and a full company of cavalry to stand guard. Five hundred seventy-nine men dead, another seven hundred fourteen wounded, with at least one hundred of that number likely to die in the next two days or sooner.

His belated acceptance of the situation had led to their only tactical success as his men had raced down the road they had chosen to confront another brush and felled tree road block only to find it abandoned, the enemy already gone.

Axes flying, his men had made fairly quick work of the pile of trees and other detritus, clearing the road in two hours. Continuing down the road hoping to force an engagement, Stone had finally been forced to call a halt as the sun sank behind the trees and the lighting fell to dangerous levels for travel in strange territory. They had seen not a single sign of Soulan military activity since the ambush on the road.

Stone took a drink from the small flask he had taken from his saddlebags, allowing the very small sip of whiskey to burn his throat. He placed the cap and stored the flask without even thinking of taking another drink from it, no matter how bad he might want it. Drunk generals made stupid mistakes, and he was making plenty of stupid mistakes already.

The confidence he had worked so hard to instill in his men leading up to the war was now gone. The war had started well but in their first major cavalry engagement they had been soundly beaten in a battle they should have won but for southern horse archers. And the fact that southern war chargers were much larger and stronger than their own. Imperial cavalry horses were wiry, fast and tough, descended as they were in part from the hardy breeds of wild horses on the western plains, but they were also small. He had seen more than one Imperial horse and rider simply bowled over by a Soulanie cavalryman riding such a large beast.

His remarks to his men about their losses not mattering had been ill timed, but he had managed to do at least some damage control over that. He hadn't meant it in the way it had sounded, but he was sure that some resentment lingered even now and he couldn't fault his men for it. They deserved to be able to know that their general was not callous in his regard for them when committing them to battle. The Imperial Army had long had that very reputation and was at least partly responsible for the fact that Imperial Army had never, not once, won a war.

Not that anyone ever admitted to that, he snorted to himself. All that propaganda and pomp about the might of the Imperial war machine and how we were destined to rule the ancient land again. He had took part in it too. Had even allowed himself to believe it to a certain extent. But the truth was that all that propaganda was just that; a fairy tale invented by the Empire and her bureaucrats to convince the people that their great, grand military machine was worth having higher taxes and making do with less of everything that made life bearable.

This time was supposed to be different. So much time and money invested to make sure that it was different. Yet here he sat, in enemy territory, losses to his once proud 1st Cavalry Corps mounting and without a single victory to show for it. Not a single accomplishment they could call their own unless one counted having his ass handed to him twice now. Why shouldn't his men lose confidence in him considering all that?

Who could blame them for not wanting to follow me, or take my orders anymore? he thought bleakly. He sat for a moment staring into the small blaze before him, feeling his despair all the way to his bones.

On top of everything he was sure that the commander of the Soulanie units he was facing was sitting somewhere comfortable right then, laughing his ass off at how he'd made a fool of the Imperial cavalry.

On second thought I think I will have that second drink.

-

General Stone might have been surprised to find that he was wrong on at least one count.

"Not a bad day, eh General?" someone said as the officers of Pierce's combined commands met at his fire.

"No, not at all," Pierce's voice as deceptively mild. "Unless you count the fact that five days worth of fortification work was lost in the space of one afternoon, we're on the run from a force that outnumbers us at least five-to-one and likely more, and we're all that stands between them and their showing up across the river from the Palace!" The Brigadier's voice had gotten steadily louder and more stringent as he spoke until his last few savage words were just short of yelling.

"Sir, we inflicted well over five hundred casualties on the enemy without a single loss to ourselves!" one battalion commander objected. "Surely that counts for something!"

"If they couldn't spare that number and not miss them, I'd agree with you, Major," Pierce nodded. "Trouble is, they can. And we lost not only our initial positions but our fallback position as well. We're just damn fortunate that we were able to outdistance them so they couldn't force us to engagement. Had they done so, I doubt we'd be sitting here so pleased with ourselves this evening!"

That appeared to somber the group a bit at least, he was pleased to see.

"We can expect them to come knocking right after daybreak tomorrow gentlemen and I'd imagine they'll be some pissed at us after today, what do you think?"

"Probably," Whit nodded. As the senior officer following Pierce, he was technically the second in command. "And I agree, today was just short of a disaster for all that we won. There is such a thing as losing the war even when you win the battles," he reminded them.

If the group had turned more serious after Pierce's tongue lashing, they were downright macabre after Whit's declaration.

"Orders, sir?" Whit turned to Pierce, satisfied that he had helped put a period on the momentary elation of the lower ranking commanders.

"We have to wait and see what they do," Pierce sighed. "We don't have the strength to attack them directly so all we can do is try to react to what they do and try to slow them down. We're facing a losing battle here and that isn't going to change. If they do make a drive for Nasil, I don't see a way to stop them short of the city and the defenses there," he admitted. "In that event, we would bleed them as much as we could to buy time for the city to prepare, and then fall back on the city to add our strength to theirs."

"Can we get any help?" one clueless battalion commander asked.

"We're all there is," Pierce said flatly. "This attack is almost certainly meant to draw some of the army away from the front in the west. We were sent because we were all independent commands and not part of any larger unit. I have sent a message to one unit that might be able to lend a hand, but even assuming they can get here their numbers won't be a tithe of what we need to even things out. Still, whatever help we can get is better than nothing," he admitted.

"Do you think they're headed for Nasil?" Whit asked.

"Possibly," Pierce nodded. "Threatening the Royal City would almost guarantee a response from the Royal Army and that has to be the goal of this little foray. Remember they intended to use the army destroyed at the Gap to threaten the capitol. Failing that, I think now they're just trying to present a possible threat and get the Marshal to react to it."

"Will he?" someone asked.

"He already has," Whit replied to that one. "We're his reaction. It's our job to make sure this bunch can't do too much damage."

"Right," Pierce nodded. "And I could wrong in my assumption, as well. This may be nothing more than a raid, or a reconnaissance in force where they get a look at this part of the Kingdom to see what their options are. But I think they will threaten the capitol if they get the chance," he insisted.

"Why?" another officer asked.

"Because it's what I would do," Pierce shrugged. "Scouts out on all approaches, gentlemen," he said abruptly, standing. "No man to stand guard alone or for more than two hours. We need to be rested. I have a feeling we're about to be very busy indeed."

-

"I'm sick and tired of playing catch up to these people," Stone told his assembled division and brigade commanders. "We're going to put our heads together and we're going to figure a way to get some odds on our side for once," he said as he spread a map on the ground next to his fire, securing it with small stones to act as paperweights.

"If you've got ideas, usable ideas," he stressed, looking up sternly, "then trot 'em out. I want to get around this bunch before they can create another bottleneck like that last one. We need to get into an open area where our lack of archers won't hurt us so bad."

"Where around here is that going to be, sir?" Blake asked, frowning. "This entire country is nothing but hills and dales and winding trails. I've yet to see a single open area even large enough for us to make one camp in let alone fight a battle."

"Then figure me a way around that," Stone replied, gesturing to the map. "No more whining and complaining from any of you who aren't trying to solve the problem," he warned. Stone was feeling that second shot of whiskey and it had loosened him up a bit. "I'm damned tired of seeing my men cut to pieces by these people and it's going to stop, one way or another. You're either part of the solution, or you become part of the problem."

Everyone in the group caught the edge in Stone's voice and a few exchanged wary glances. This was a side of Stone they rarely if ever saw. He was savagely serious at the moment and they had to tread carefully here, lest they incur the wrath that he was currently expelling toward the Soulan Army.

Silas Weir was the first to speak.

"If you're really serious about this, then there's only one thing I can think of that will work." He squatted by the map and took a piece of wheat straw from his mouth, using it as a pointer.

"We move away from that bunch entirely, cut through here away from some of these hills and move back to this Trade Road. Soulan does maintain excellent Trades all over their Kingdom. We can use them to move better and be more open. And they will play pure hell trying to block that Trade Road like they block these backwoods hill routes," he said firmly.

"This Trade leads straight to their capitol, albeit on the wrong side of the river," he traced the road with the straw. "We take that road and head down it as quick as we can safely travel, tearing hell out of any and every thing we find along the way. In three, maybe four days, five at the very outside, we're sitting across the river from their 'Royal City'," he almost sneered the words. "That will give 'em something to think about." Murmurs of agreement went through the group and Stone nodded thoughtfully.

"Do we try and use any deceptive tactics?" he asked the group.

"No," Blake shook his head, falling in beside his fellow division commander. "No sir. We use our strength to our advantage for once and force them to play it our way. Our horses are smaller than theirs on the whole, but our mounts are fast, and tough. They've got staying power and can run all day if we need them to. I'm not advocating we do that, just pointing out that we can move much better if we follow Silas' plan and head to the Trade Road. If we move expeditiously, we can be around and in behind them before they realize we're even gone."

The murmurs were more excited this time as heads nodded around the campfire.

"When we reach the river, what then?" Stone asked. He was getting excited himself for a change and was enjoying this planning session. I need to do this more often.

"I think by necessity we have to play that one by ear, sir," Jerome Baxter, the youngest of Stone's division commanders and leading his 3rd Division. There were vague rumors about Baxter's relationship to the Emperor, but Baxter was mum on the subject himself so there was no telling what was true and wasn't.

"Why?" Stone challenged, interested in what the young man had to say.

"Until we get there, sir, we don't know what shape we will be in, or how close the enemy may be pursuing us. We may find a good spot along the river to turn and force and engagement that will favor us over their archers," Baxter shrugged. "There is one bridge across the river there, I believe," he added with a thoughtful look on his face. "I don't know that it's still standing. It's very old if it is."

"How do you know that?" Weir demanded.

"It's in history books," Baxter replied. "I read it."

"Are you suggesting we take that bridge into the Royal City itself?" Stone asked warily.

"No sir," Baxter shook his head. "I would advise against that in all honesty. That city will be a nest of vipers with a bow behind every window. A force no larger than ours would not fare well there to my way of thinking."

"Ridiculous," Weir snorted in derision. "If that bridge is standing, we should absolutely take it into their city and burn it down. Their army is all to the north."

"So, who killed your men this morning, then?" Baxter gave as good as he got. "All of the Soulan Army is obviously not opposing General Wilson, sir," he turned back to Stone before a spluttering Weir could reply. "The Soulanies believe in unorganized militia, sir. Their people who didn't already have training when the war started will definitely have it now. We do not want to face an entire city of women who can shoot a bow at least as well as any of us and are hiding behind walls and barricades," he stressed.

"That is a good point," Stone nodded thoughtfully. "So, we demonstrate across the river and try to throw them into a panic, or head further east after that, what?" he looked around the group.

"I think Brigadier Baxter has the right idea, sir," Wiskowski offered when no one else spoke up. "Until we see what our situation is, we can't really make a decision. I would suggest we plan for whatever contingency we can imagine between now and then and plan to counter that contingency."

"What do you mean?"

"Well, say we get there and find all of the Soulan cavalry there waiting for us," Wiskowski shrugged. "True, it would mean we've accomplished our mission, but that won't matter to us very much if they kill us all. So what would do in the event we find ourselves outnumbered and outmatched. If we're separated in flight, where do we try to regroup? If we're unopposed, which way do we travel? If there is a way across the river, do we take it, and if so, what then? See what I mean?"

"We generally do that anyway," Stone nodded. "Though I hadn't imagined getting there and finding their cavalry waiting for us," he admitted. "All right," he handed the map to his aide as he stood, brushing off his pants. "We move as soon as its light enough to see. We backtrack a little ways and then head west toward the Trade Route. From there it's straight on to the city or at least opposite it on the river. We destroy everything of value we find along the way unless we can take it with us. But," he raised a finger and slowly swept it around the entire group, "we do not kill civilians, gentlemen, that are not actively engaged against us. Our men will not turn into a rabble like those sailors we cleaned out in Lovil. Do you understand that?"

"Yes sir!" the groups answered in unison.

"Then brief your commanders and get some rest," Stone ordered. "Maybe tomorrow we start changing things."

-

"There is an old observation tower just north of here, perhaps five miles distant," Johnson told Whipple as the two were looking over the compound. "We can post men there who can signal with smoke when and if they see Colonel Callens approaching."

"No," Whipple shook his head slowly. "No, Callens and the Princess have both been here before and will know about the tower. Anyone we send there would end up killed. I won't sacrifice a man or group of men like that."

"I suspect from the way he talks that your General Beaumont does not share that sentiment," Johnson said stiffly. "And I would not do so either. It hadn't occurred to me that the two of them know this area so well. It should have, but I'm not overly familiar with it myself."

"I was here several years ago," Whipple nodded, ignoring the jab at Beaumont since Johnson was still somewhat put out by the former's attitude. "Came down with my family to visit with the King. I was just a boy though, and a lot has changed," he admitted. "No, my idea is somewhat different," he continued. "What I want is to…"

-

"That will almost certainly work better than just waiting for them here," Johnson was impressed and it showed. "And it adds the likelihood of preventing their escape, as well."

"And that is very important," Whipple said grimly. "Callens and his senior officers no doubt knew what they were doing from the beginning and should all hang. His junior officers and NCOs were likely roped into this without being aware, but. . .they have to know by now what they're doing is wrong. We can't take the chance that the rot has spread through the entire regiment. It's a waste, and at the worst possible time," he shook his head.

"Do you think he knew she would kill the King?" Johnson asked. It was still too new to him to not speak of it in a near whisper.

"Doesn't matter now," Whipple shrugged. "If he didn't know, then he certainly should have either stopped her, or failing that should have taken her into custody and turned himself in with her. That's what a man with any honor would have done. Instead he stood by while she next tried to kill the Crown Prince, and then took her out of the palace intending to bring her here and free her traitor brother. That's beyond what I can forgive him for."

"Me too," Johnson agreed. "Set the trap every day until they show up, then?" he changed the subject to something more appealing.

"We need to be in place no later than an hour after light," Whipple nodded. "Be prepared to wait until at least dusk, as well. I don't think they will travel after dusk, especially in this country. You lighting the last few miles of road at night will allow us to get back inside without trouble. Our biggest threat comes from discovery by scouts. Our advantage is that he doesn't know we know where he's going. Or that Prince Memmnon is now King Memmnon, for that matter."

"We'll get them."

-

"Hard riding the next two days will see us arrive the day after," Callens told his assembled officers. "Two more nights of discomfort and we can spend at least a couple nights in a bed," he grinned wearily. Some tried to smile back but most had a hollow-eyed look about them. Word had spread gradually through the entire unit about the King and Crown Prince. Those who had been roped into this were still stunned and not a little angry at suddenly being branded traitors and not even knowing it.

"I know some of you are concerned, and I understand," Callens said softly. "Know that we did the right thing. We need Marshal McLeod leading the Army in time of war, not that sniveling weasel, Parno."

"Beg pardon sir, but that 'sniveling weasel' has led the army to its only two victories," one young lieutenant said. More than one head nodded in agreement and Callens saw it.

"Using troops trained by the Marshal and led by men he chose," Callens nodded. "Even a blind squirrel will find a nut on occasion," he tried again to smile. "While he may have done well at the tactical level, his strategic thinking will be far too short sighted. We can't risk him being in command."

He could tell that most of them were unconvinced and made a note to mention it to his company commanders in private, but then several of them didn't look overly happy either. They had supported him freeing the Marshal, but not killing the King and Crown Prince. Too late they realized that they had crossed a line they couldn't return from.

"Let's get moving," Callens ordered, unable to think of anything else to try and persuade them with.

He walked to the carriage where Sherron McLeod was waiting, impatient as ever.

"Are we going now?" she asked in a huff. She'd been in one for two weeks or so.

"We are," he said simply. "We will stop briefly for lunch to rest the horses and allow for a break. Then back on the road until dark. If we make good enough time today, we should be there by noon, day after tomorrow."

"Good," Sherron crossed her arms in defiance. "When I see Therron, don't think I'm not going to tell him how you've treated me, either," she threatened.

"Do as you please," he sighed, mounting his horse. "I really couldn't care less." He spurred his horse forward, moving away before she could answer.

Sherron McLeod watched him go, a small smile tugging at her lips. Callens was a real man, she decided. It really was too bad that her plans didn't include him. She would have enjoyed it immensely.

CHAPTER SIXTEEN

-

Parno was standing on the observation tower looking north toward the Imperial lines. The Nor had been quiet and that was suspicious. He had learned enough from Darvo and now Cho to know that it had to be costing a literal fortune for the Nor to keep such a large army in the field. Holding it idle had to hurt.

So why weren't they moving, or trying to move at least? The answer to that eluded him save for one option; they were moving and he just couldn't see it. He had tried to cover everything as best he could, but his men were spread thin everywhere. He was gambling by trying to retrain two corps at once, but so far it was paying off. So far being the key phrase. He knew it couldn't last, but didn't know of anything else he could do. No one else seemed to know of anything either, or at least they hadn't brought it to his attention yet.

He stored the scope he'd been using and headed down, mind still turning over his limited options. There really wasn't much else he could do. There were places he absolutely had to defend, and that meant that his army was spread out. He didn't have the strength to attack, and might, barely, have the strength to hold his ground, but that was about it. There wasn't much left.

"Sir, we've got riders coming," Berry told him as he hit the ground. Parno looked to see two men riding quickly toward him. They slid to a halt, dust flying past as one dismounted.

"Cavalry returning, milord," one reported. "Be here in another half-hour or so, most like."

"Did they look beat up?" Parno was pensive.

"Looked tired but that as all we could tell, sir," the man admitted.

"Very well," the young Marshal nodded. "Thank you."

"Sir!" the man saluted and then was back in the saddle, the two returning the way they had come.

"Well, let's go and wait for them."

-

General Allen was both pleased and not with his mission. They had managed to stop the boat force, that was true. But in the remaining time he'd had for this mission he had not found another single worthwhile target. He didn't know if the Nor were limiting their supply runs or if they just didn't happen to see them, but his command had no luck whatever in locating another target. He was still thinking on that when he drew rein before the Marshal's tent and dismounted, joined by his division commanders.

"Go ahead inside, sirs," Sprigs informed them. "He's expecting you." The men did just that, finding the Marshal at his field desk, reading.

"Sir," Allen reported for them all. "Cavalry detachment returning."

"At east gentlemen," Parno said easily. "You all look hale. Everything go all right?"

"You were right about the boats, sir," Allen said without fanfare. "We had an amazing stroke of luck when our scouts located a group of boats moving down, well up river," he corrected, "escorted by a battalion of cavalry with their baggage train. We dispatched the cavalry and a good many of the boat crews. As a result the boats turned back north and fled with the current."

"Excellent!" Parno clapped his hands together once. "That is great good news, Generals!" he enthused. "Your losses?" he asked carefully.

"Forty-one wounded, eleven killed sir," Allen reported. "We caught them without scouts out and took them by surprise. General Vaughan and his men did I should say," he amended with a nod to the huge Vaughan.

"Good work," Parno nodded. "Did you see anything else of note?"

"No sir, and that seems to be noteworthy of itself," Allen admitted. "We seen nothing. Not a single train of any kind, not a patrol, nothing. Maybe it was the timing, sir, but it seemed damned odd to have an army in enemy territory and not at least have patrols out."

"So, it does," Parno mused. "Very well then," he stood. "Go and see to your commands. I'll expect your reports day after tomorrow. That should give you time to rest and see to your men properly. Please report back then, say about ten," he motioned at Sprigs who nodded and wrote the appointment down.

"Will do, Marshal," Allen nodded. All of them came to attention. "With your permission?"

"Carry on," Parno nodded. The men departed, leaving Parno feeling much better about his day and hoping it wasn't premature.

-

"Not a sign of them nowhere," the scout reported to Pierce. "Trail leads back the way they came. We followed it nearly ten miles but nothing. Still moving. We turned back to report, but figure you may want us to head back out and trail 'em."

"Yes," Pierce nodded his agreement. He silently cursed his own complacency that had saw him sit and wait with scouts deployed for the Nor to come to him the day before. They hadn't, so today he had dispatched scouts to take a look at them. They had just returned to report they had found nothing.

"This is bad," he told Whit after the scouts were gone. "Damn it! I sat here yesterday waiting, thinking they had to come after us, and they haven't!"

"Maybe they're going back," Whit shrugged, though his tone indicated he didn't believe that.

"You know as well as I do they aren't going back until they've done some damage," Pierce snorted. "They're taking a page from our book this time and running us ragged. Only they have the numbers to do it all over the place and we don't. Where in the hell are they?"

Whit had no answer for that.

-

General Roland Raines was watching the opposite shore of the Great River through his own glass from the observation tower at Shelby.

"How long has this been going on?" he asked the man commanding the observation point.

"Since light, sir," the young Captain reported. "At first it didn't seem like a big deal, but. . .it looks as if they have a large portion of their army moving out."

There were indeed many horses moving north away from the opposite end of the bridge and the encampment there, heading north. Not all of them, but a great many.

"I'd love to know where they're going," he said softly. "Good work, Captain," he said in a louder tone. "Let me know if anything else changes. Heading down."

"Sir," the Captain nodded but didn't salute. Raines almost ran down the steps to find his aide waiting below.

"Billy, get me Brigadier Simmons, please," he told the younger man. "I may have a job for him."

-

"Pretty morning," Winnie said as she and Memmnon dined on the veranda overlooking the palace gardens.

"It is," he smiled, nodding his agreement. "This time of morning is always nice. It's quiet still, without the hustle and bustle of everyone moving about as they will be by lunch. I'm glad you could join me," he added.

"It's my pleasure, my lord," Winnie grinned. "Have you given any more thought to what we can do for Parno and Stephanie?" she asked.

"There's nothing that I haven't already mentioned," he shook his head. "And so far she hasn't really indicated that she has any desire to fix it, honestly," he shrugged.

"What is that supposed to mean?" the redhead demanded.

"Just that she hasn't approached me even once to ask me for a courier, to talk about Parno, nothing," Memmnon shrugged. "I would have thought she would want any help she could get, but. . .so far she's asked for none."

"She's very proud," Winnie sighed. "And she's convinced that Parno will not forgive her so there ai- isn't any reason to try," she caught herself.

"She may well be right, I don't know," Memmnon shrugged. "There's really very little I can do," he repeated.

"You could order Parno to talk to her," Winnie suggested.

"Yes, because Parno takes orders so well," Memmnon replied dryly. "Winnie, Parno would be just as apt to tell me to mind my own business or ignore me completely as he would to brook any interference in his personal life, particularly by me. I'm sorry that's how it is, but there's almost nothing I can do to change it."

"It's worth a try," she pressed ever so slightly. "It's best for both of them. You know it as well as I do."

"I know what I think to be true," he allowed. "But I don't know what Parno is thinking. For all we know he has put her completely out of his mind altogether. That is how he works, more often than not," he pointed out.

Winnie sighed in frustration, falling silent. There was one more thing she could try, but it would probably leave both Stephanie and Parno furious at her. Was it worth it? She thought of all that both of them had done for her and decided that it was.

"I need a courier," she told Memmnon suddenly.

"Of course," he said at once. "May I ask why?"

"I need to send Lady Cumberland a message," she told him honestly.

"Ah," Memmnon nodded. "I see. When all else fails. . ." he smiled.

"Exactly."

-

"Sir, scouts are reporting a large body of horsemen approaching on the main road."

Beaumont looked up from the report he'd been writing to see his aide standing before him.

"Very well," he nodded, handing his book to the aide as he stood. "Store this for later I suppose. Pass the word for all commands to stand by and stay quiet. We want them to pass us by, and then we fall in behind them."

"Yes sir."

Beaumont felt the familiar urge to battle running through him as he tightened the cinches on his saddle and mounted his horse. All this way, all this time, all for this. He was ready for this assignment to be over.

-

"Riders approaching sir," Lieutenant Bruckner reported to Johnson. "In large numbers, it appears."

"Too early to be Buford," Whipple noted, nodding to the three runners that had stood when Bruckner approached. "Sound the word, gentlemen," he ordered gently.

"Sir!" the three snapped to and headed for their individual regimental commanders. Whipple stood and took his bow from the table.

The plan had been simple enough; Beaumont would take his cavalry and wait concealed for Callens and his people to pass him by, then follow. Whipple and his own men would wait in concealment in the compound itself and the surrounding area, laying an ambush for the traitorous regiment. Johnson and his men would maintain their normal routine though Whipple's men had replaced them on the gate and around the front to avoid placing the IG troops in combat they weren't really trained for.

Callens would be given the opportunity to surrender simply to avoid bloodshed among the loyal troops. Neither expected him to take the offer, but it was hoped that losses might be avoided among their own men at least. He would be given only the one chance, however, before the shooting started.

With Whipple's men firing on them from concealed positions and Beaumont pressing in from behind, they should be able to get the majority of Callens' command under thumb quickly enough.

Simple. Not easy, but straightforward.

"Shall we Captain?" Whipple asked.

"Suppose we had ought to," Johnson replied in his trademark laid back manner. The two started for the gate together to see what would happen.

-

Callens ought to have been feeling good. He was nearing the end of a six-week journey that would see his benefactor set free and on his way to being King of Soulan. He would also finally be rid of the responsibility of the Princess Witch (as he'd taken to calling her about week three), something he longed for almost as much as a decent bath, meal and bed, in that order.

Yet the closer they drew to the Royal Compound of the Key Horn, the more anxious he became. Why he didn't know. There was no reason for it that he knew, yet there it was.

"Something wrong, sir?" one of the men near him asked.

"No," he shook his head. "Nothing that a good beer won't solve," he tried to grin and mostly pulled it off. "That and a good soak followed by a week of sleep."

"Amen to that," another man muttered. All of them were in a state of general disrepair and ready for a break.

"Compound up ahead sir," a trooper before them called back. "Looks clear," he added. "Gate guard looks about normal."

"Then let's see about getting our Marshal back," Callens nodded. The regiment moved on, not slowing until they were mere yards from the gate, which had remained closed and barred.

"Open in the name of the King!" Callens called out.

"Identify yourself!" a guard called out from the small tower overlooking the gate.

"Colonel Callens, Prince's Own," Callens replied. "Now King's Own!" he added.

"Hell, you say!" came the reply and instantly Callens was on edge again. That was not at all the reply he had expected.

"I do say," he nodded. "Now open this gate before I have it torn down!"

"I'd like to see you try," came the mocking reply, but not from the tower. This reply came from the ground and Callens looked to find the speaker.

"This gate is pretty stout," Callens finally spotted a man in the garb of the

Inspectorate through the barred iron of the gate. "Doubt you could do it. And we've had no word at all that Therron McLeod was anything other than exiled for his crimes. So you'll excuse us if we doubt the veracity of your claim, Colonel."

"The King and Crown Prince are dead," Callens told him evenly. "Prince Therron is needed to restore order in the Kingdom. Right now all we have is that idiot Parno McLeod running things, and that way leads to ruin! Now open this gate and bring the Marshal to us!"

"The Crown Prince isn't dead you traitorous ass," a cultured voice said from out of sight. "He is in fact now King of Soulan and ruling even this very moment. And that 'idiot', Prince Parno, sent us to bring you to heel. Well," the voice became conversational, "that's not actually the whole truth. He sent us to kill you all, remove your heads and impale your dead bodies on pikes as mile markers along this road as far as they would reach. But that's almost the same thing."

Callens felt the blood drain from his face at that. Memmnon alive? And now King? He was conscious of the murmuring wave running through his command as the news trickled backward but was too focused on what he was hearing to worry about that.

"You'll understand if we don't believe that," he managed to sound calm though he was anything but.

"Couldn't care less," Horace Whipple walked into view as Johnson stepped back and away from the gate. "And, just to add insult to injury, Therron isn't even here. He took flight a week ago aboard ship with yet another traitor. You bastards came out of the woodwork when the war started, didn't you Callens?"

"I know you," Callens could see now. "Brigadier Whipple, isn't it? You're a noble yourself, are you not?"

"I've been called worse, but not lately," Whipple nodded cheerily. "Your point?"

"How can you stand against Marshal Therron when he has supported the noble families in all things?" Callens asked, hoping to woo Whipple to his side. "And what do you mean 'took flight'?" he asked, as if it only now registered on him what he'd been told.

"He convinced an idiot naval Captain that stopped here to help him escape," Whipple shrugged. "Don't know where he headed exactly, but we'll track him down. And when we do we'll kill him too!"

Before Callens could reply an angry voice cut into his hearing.

"What are we waiting for!" Sherron McLeod demanded. "Why are we still sitting out here! Get us inside so we can talk to Therron. I have to tell him what's happened so he can be ready to assume the throne!"

"That won't be happening, Sherron," Whipple replied for Callens. Having been stomping her way up the line of horsemen, Sherron faltered at that. She looked through the gate at the speaker and seemed to go a bit pale.

"Horace?" she almost stammered. "What are you doing here?" she demanded.

"Came to take you back to Nasil in chains, you bitch," Whipple's tone was friendly. Cheerful. "And kill your co-conspirators of course," he added as an afterthought. "However," he raised his voice now, "there is this one opportunity for you to surrender! Lay down arms, dismount, and prepare to be taken into custody! Doing so is the only chance you have at survival! This is also your only warning! Take it now, or die here. The choice is yours."

Before Callens could respond to that the sound of approaching horses claimed his attention.

"Many riders coming behind, sir!" a trooper called from well back. "At least two regiments!"

"It's actually a full brigade and then some," Whipple told him. "And you're facing another brigade of archers, among the best in the army, right here," he added. "So…what will it be, Callens? Gonna fight it out for good old Sherron there? Or throw yourself on the mercy of King Memmnon?"

Mercy? Callens remembered the last words Crown Prince Memmnon had spoken to him before losing consciousness and knew there would be no mercy from King Memmnon. He took a deep breath and release it in a sigh.

"My junior officers didn't know," he told Whipple. "They only discovered what was happening a few days ago."

"What are you doing?" Sherron demanded. "Kill him!" she pointed to Whipple.

"And all the rest?" Callens asked, snorting. "How do you suggest I do that, you witch? This is your fault, you know. Had you not insisted on stopping every five miles, we would have been here ahead of them, had Therron, and been gone again before they arrived. There's no one to blame for this but you!"

Sherron looked at him in shock for a few seconds. What happened next caught everyone by surprise so that no one reacted until it was far too late.

Sherron McLeod's face slowly turned a bright red as fury welled up at her treatment by Callens. Suddenly she yanked a dagger from her sleeve and shrieking in fury like the witch she'd just been called leaped upward toward the Colonel, plunging the blade into the inside of his thigh and twisting it savagely.

Without hesitation Whipple drew an arrow from his back and fired, catching Sherron McLeod in the side and knocking her from Callens'. She fell onto the road beneath him, knife staying in her hand and trailing down the horse's side, the razor-sharp blade carving a large chunk from the charger's flank. Scared and enraged by this injury, the horse reared just as other archers took Whipple's act as a signal to fire and launched a volley into the men below. Unable to control his horse, bleeding out rapidly from the severed artery in his leg, Callens was vaulted from his saddle to hit the gate, where he slid to the ground already all but dead.

The next few minutes were a wild scene as Callens' men reacted as if they were being attacked, which technically they were, and drew swords. Seeing that, Beaumont ordered his men to do the same and advance, believing this to be a sign that Callens had refused to surrender. Seeing the cavalrymen coming toward them convinced Callens' men that they were, in fact, being attacked and would not be given a chance to surrender. As one and with no need for a command, the rear most battalion in line wheeled and charged the brigade behind them, believing they had nothing to lose at this point and hoping they could break through and make a run for it.

The lead battalion was caught beneath a withering fire of some of the best trained archers in the south, and fell like row crops, many with six or seven arrows embedded in them and with more than one horse suffering the same fate. In the face of this onslaught the lead battalion melted before Whipple's men.

The center battalion faced a cruel choice. Again, believing that no surrender would be accepted, they were faced with either fighting that archery fire or braving he cavalry brigade behind them. In the end the group split almost evenly with the front half opting to try and take out the gate to the compound and get at the archers while the back half wheeled to charge Beaumont's men along with those behind them in line.

The battle was fierce, brutal at times. Men with nothing to lose always fought desperately. Men fighting for vengeance always fought savagely and without mercy.

Five long and terrible minutes after Whipple had fired his first arrow, the battle was over. Prince Therron's Own had ceased to exist save in the history books.

-

"And good riddance," Whipple almost spat as he and Beaumont looked down at the body of Sherron McLeod. His arrow had not been fatal in and of itself, but the horses that had trampled her as she lay on the road had finished the job nicely.

"I take it Callens didn't want to surrender?" Beaumont asked, wiping the sweat from his brow.

"No idea," Whipple admitted. "The Witch stabbed him before he could answer other than to tell me his junior officers weren't in on the plot. Based on that I think he might have, but when she stabbed him I shot her, and things went downhill from there," he shrugged. He looked at his friend.

"Losses?"

"Twenty-seven dead and fifty-nine wounded," Beaumont sighed. "Good men lost to that scum," he shook his head.

"Had to be done Buford, and our men died serving their Sovereign," Whipple pointed out. "We lost ten men killed and nineteen wounded, but our men had better cover. At least the wounded will have a nice place to recover in," he added, nodding to the compound where all their wounded had already been moved.

"So, they will," Beaumont nodded. "I've set details to get this lot taken care of. We'll bury our dead and burn theirs," he added. "Johnson agree to remain on and watch over our men?"

"If we leave a company of men to help bolster the position," Whipple nodded. "I can't blame him for asking for that, either. There's always the chance that Chastain will bring Therron back. Johnson said that Therron wanted Chastain to kill them before he left, and he refused."

"We'll leave a company of my men and a few squads of yours with them," Beaumont nodded. "If they do return, I want that Captain in irons."

"Good deal," Whipple nodded. "What do we do with her body?" he kicked Sherron McLeod's dead body, lying in an undignified heap at their feet.

"All we need is her head," Beaumont replied flatly. "Burn the rest just like the others. She gave up the right to special treatment the minute she killed the King."

"Works for me."

-

General Jackson Andrews watched as the division taking part in this mission made their way past him again. This was the third time in two hours that this same division had made the wide loop around to present itself once more that the bridge head.

"You think this is going to work?" he asked Caster Urich, whose division was making this theatrical performance for the benefit of their enemy across the river.

"No idea," Urich admitted. "None. And I think if we do this anymore, they'll start to get wise to it," he added. "This is three times, and it takes almost an hour each time. I'd say we go one more round and then stop. Let them go upriver this time for the rest of the day, make camp and then return tomorrow. The Soulanies will see them moving and probably send someone to keep an eye on them. Maybe that will fool them. I'll come back around from the west so they don't see us return. Our camps are back that way anyhow."

"All right," Andrews agreed. The idea had been hatched by five of his generals over dinner the night before. It was simple and promised the best possible return for the least risk.

Urich's division had spent the last three hours marching up river for nearly an hour before circling back to camp using a road that had been carved out of the wilderness to make traveling between camps easier. Three times they had done this, disappearing from sight but still moving north. The idea was for the Soulanies to see the men moving and assume that a large portion of the army was headed for Wilson's position, or else for a river crossing further north to conduct a raid into Soulan territory.

If it worked then it would actually be the opposite of what Wilson wanted of course, except that if it worked very well that would give 2nd Army the opportunity to cross the bridge and take Shelby. Even if they couldn't move away from the bridgehead, the Soulanies would have to reinforce the troops opposing them and try to retake the city and push the Imperial troops back. Those troops would have to come from somewhere, and the only place for them to get help was from the army opposing Wilson on the plains.

It took a long view but it was also a good idea. They would just have to see how well it worked out.

"I'll see you back here tomorrow, Cass," Andrews said. The other man nodded, sketched a salute and then stepped into his own saddle to join his men. Soon they were once more moving north, this time to go as far as the light would allow before making camp.

Now all Andrews could do was wait and see what his observers could make out from the other side of the river.

-

Brigadier Alan Simmons watched the Imperial troops moving north through his glass, trying to estimate the number of troops without conscious thought.

"At least a division sir," the man next to him estimated, and Simmons agreed.

From the look of things, the Imperials had just sent three or perhaps even four divisions of the troops facing them across the bridge back north. They had to either be heading to the battle along the Tinsee where the main army was, or else they would cross over into Soulan Territory further north to raid down along the Great River and cause whatever troubles they could. Either way was bad.

Simmons orders were pretty straightforward; take his separate cavalry brigade and shadow the Imperial troops moving north to see where they were going and what they were doing. Report back as soon as he knew something, and in the event the enemy troops were moving to the east and the battle there, send couriers to the Marshal and General Davies alerting them to the danger.

"Let's get mounted," he told his officers. The brigade had been resting for the last ten minutes as Simmons examined the Nor troops they were trailing. He wanted to get moving again before he lost sight of them. He and his men couldn't stop until the Nor made camp. He'd have to decide then whether to start sending messages to Raines.

Until then he would follow.

-

"Seemed as if the Princess knew you, Brigadier."

Johnson's statement was quiet as the two men sat on the porch once more, sharing a bit of bourbon as preparations were made for night.

"Seemed that way," Whipple nodded, nursing his glass.

"Would a man be out of line to ask how?" Johnson asked. "If so then we can talk about this lovely weather," he added with a smile.

Whipple sat quietly for so long that Johnson decided that the brigadier did not, in fact, wish to discuss it. He was about to actually start talking about the weather when Whipple decided to speak.

"My father," he said quietly, "is Tammon McLeod's second cousin. Whipple is my mother's maiden name. I took it when I joined the army to avoid any sort of favoritism. Very few know who I actually am, believe it or not," he snorted. "The Marshal isn't one of them." Pausing, he tossed back his drink and then poured another.

"I spent more than one winter here when I was a boy," he continued. "With her and her brothers, except for Parno, the current Marshal. He was usually left behind at the palace. None of them had any time for him. Hated him in fact. Damn shame really, since they hated him because his mother died in childbirth. That's a lot more common than it used to be I've read, back before the Dying. Don't know why," he shrugged.

"There was talk at times of Sherron and I marrying, believe it or not," he chuckled. "My father was all for it, claiming it was a good match. That was when I joined the army using my mother's name. She at least didn't like the idea of letting the witch get her claws into her little boy," he laughed gently, this time in true mirth. "My mother didn't have a real high opinion of Sherron even then."

"So, you're actually a member of the Royal Family?" Johnson asked cautiously.

"No," Whipple shook his head. "Not really. My grandfather I guess would have been in line for the throne somewhere. Fourth I think, or maybe fifth. There were a lot of them in that generation," he explained. "Nowadays our family is nowhere near the line of succession. For which I give thanks on a regular basis," he raised his glass in silent salute and then threw back another shot, refilling his glass once more.

"I'm sorry I brought it up, Brigadier," Johnson said into the silence.

"Ah, hell, don't be," Whipple waved the apology off as unnecessary. "It's not a big deal really. I just never wanted anyone to make an exception for me because of an accident of birth. I joined the army as a private and was selected from there to attend officer training school. Made grades good enough to attract attention from the War College and eventually made it into active service as a lieutenant instead of a buck private," he chuckled. "But I earned that," he added.

"So you did," Johnson raised his own glass in salute. "And I'm glad for you that you didn't have to marry such an unpleasant woman," he added, feeling his liquor a bit now.

"Lord, me too," Whipple said earnestly. "I'd have killed her inside a month." He said it straight faced and with a flat delivery, and it took Johnson a minute to realize that he'd said it at all. As it finally registered, Johnson chuckled slightly, seeing the humor in the statement despite the fact that Whipple had in fact killed her earlier that day. That chuckle turned into a laugh, which in turn became an actual belly laugh. Whipple joined him and soon the two were nearly howling with laughter over the very notion of anyone having to be married to Sherron McLeod.

They were still laughing when Buford Beaumont joined them almost five minutes later, demanding to know what was so damned funny.

His only reply was more laughter.

-

Nelson Pierce brought his horse to a stop when he saw two of his scouts returning. The two men skidded to a halt before him, already talking.

"We found 'em sir," a breathless sergeant told him without preamble. "They backtracked and then cut over to the Trade Route, sir! They're headed toward Nasil on the Trade! Been at it at least a day, looks like."

The news hit Pierce like a sledge hammer. One of the things he had been supposed to prevent was any incursion reaching the Royal City. He had failed completely to block the northern cavalry force and now they were in a position to threaten Nasil and the seat of Soulan's government. He sat in silent recrimination of the error in judgment he had made that had allowed this to happen.

"-way across to the Trade from here!" Whit's urgent tone drew Pierce out of his funk and he turned to see the Colonel asking the young Major who commanded the scouts and pioneers how they could move in order to get in front of the enemy. Whit held a map open in his hands and the Major was pointing to it.

"Sir, there's not much in the way of cutting them off," the young man admitted. "We can take this road here," he pointed, "and that will get us to the Trade Route they're on quicker than they made it, but depending on where they are, we like as not can't actually get ahead of 'em. Might not even be able to catch them before they hit the river opposite the City."

"There's got to be a way," Whit shook his head. "We just have to find it."

"There's not," Pierce said flatly, his voice carrying the tone of defeat. "They have a day start on us thanks to my sitting on my ass after our initial engagement. I expected them to come after us and instead they've gone right around us." He took a deep breath and expelled it.

"Sound officer call," he ordered his bugler. Five minutes later all his commanders were assembled before him.

"We have to move," he told them flatly. "The enemy has moved behind us and is now in a position to directly threaten the capitol. There's very little likelihood that we can cut them off or that we can even catch them before they arrive. Still, we have to make the effort." He paused, thinking.

"Major, cut us a trail out of here and back to the ferry we used to cross the river," he ordered finally. "If I recall correctly that ferry is actually east if the city by some miles?"

"Yes sir," the young man nodded. "Not likely to be seen by the Nor if they stick to the Trade Road. But sir, there's a bridge on that Trade Road that will carry them across the river not far from the Palace," he added.

"So, there is," Pierce nodded. "Colonel I need the three best riders we have, mounted on the best horses available. Five minutes ago. The rest of you have fifteen minutes to inform your men that we're about to be moving at a gallop for the rest of the day. We'll rest horses by walking ten minutes of every hour, but we ride the rest of that hour. Have the wagons and anyone with them to head for the river and the Guard Force there. Drop anything that will slow us down. The wagons can carry it or we leave it here. Anyone who falls behind gets left behind. Meals to be eaten in the saddle. Any questions?"

"Will we make camp at night?" one asked.

"We'll have to, but not until we literally can't see the road before us. We have got to make up as much time as we can. Anything else?" There wasn't. "Then use your time wisely gents. We move in fifteen minutes." There was a flurry of activity then as men hurried to return to their own commands. Pierce ignored them as he took his notebook and began to write furiously. He wrote out three different messages, then decided to write a fourth to be safe, ordering Whit to corral another rider. With five minutes to spare he handed messages to each man.

"You two are headed to Nasil," he told the first two. "These messages are for the Palace Guard. There isn't much in the way of actual troops left in the city so they will have to do it. Now go and remember what's at stake!" The two took the rolled-up papers, secured them, and bolted south as if demons were chasing them.

"You two are headed for Cove Canton," he handed messages to the remaining two men. "You know it? Good. Get this message to them as soon as you possibly can. Don't let anyone stop you for any reason, understand? Without their help we may lose the city. Godspeed and hurry!"

Again, the messengers paused only long enough to store the messages and then they were gone, spurring their horses and using reins to urge the horses on. Pierce watched them go and then turned to Whit who was still looking intently at the map and shaking his head.

"Forget it, Colonel," he ordered gently. "This is on me. I've let them steal a march on us and now a lot of innocent people are about to pay for it I'm afraid. Now let's get moving. We don't stop until we can't see to continue."

"Yes sir," Whit sighed, putting the map away and signaling for the column to get moving. It took about ten minutes for the column to fold in on itself and point back toward the ferry at least roughly. They would depend on the scouts to find them when they had the best trail worked out but until then they would head that way as best they could.

And hope they were in time.

-

Stone rode at the head of his column save for scouts and one battalion of men serving as the van for his forces. His satisfaction was evident to those near him. His troops were finally about to play the role they had been trained for, other than facing the southern cavalry in open battle. They were going to raid the southern capitol and wreak havoc behind the enemy's lines. With luck they would not only create panic among the south's 'rulers', but also cause such a ruckus that their army had to part with troops to send back to meet the threat that Stone and his men represented.

This was definitely more like it, Stone decided. Riding hard and fast at the head of his men, on his way to sow terror and reap distraction. Just the idea made him feel better, lifting the funk that had settled on him after recent setbacks.

A productive raid like this was just the thing to restore the confidence his troops had lost in recent weeks and to reassure people like Wilson that their cavalry was just as effective as the south's when used properly. They had stolen a march on the Soulanie troops opposing them and moved neatly around their blocking force without any difficulty. Now they were galloping toward the southern capitol unopposed and eager for battle. All that remained to do was to get into the southern 'Royal City' and burn it down.

He looked forward to it.

CHAPTER SEVENTEEN

-

Winnie was almost running as she hurried down the hallway toward Memmnon's office. She could tell by the amount of traffic in and out that something was happening but she had no idea what it was. As she rounded the corner before the hallway, she needed she met Stephanie coming from the other direction.

"Do you know what-"

"No," Stephanie shook her head as the two continued together, each trailed by their shadows. "All I know is that an arms-man summoned me from the school and said the King wished to see me at once. I was brought here even as he was talking in fact."

"I was with the refugee children," Winnie nodded. "Captain Case came to get me and literally drug me away." The conversation died there as they reached Memmnon's office.

"Ladies, do come it," Colonel Robert Moore told them even as he was headed out. "The King is waiting." With that he was gone, heading down the hall at a near run.

"What in the world is happening?" Winnie asked as the two moved into the office. Memmnon was at the window, his face drawn and pensive.

"Winnie, we need to assemble your archery students and bring them into the palace redoubts," he said without preamble. "Doctor, we will need to secure the wounded that are in hospitals around the city in the barracks here on the grounds. You will have some limited assistance with that, but only some. There is no time to-" he was cut off by the sound of a bell ringing somewhere overhead. He motioned to Stephanie and the door and she moved at once to close it while Memmnon closed the window. The bell was still audible but now at least they could hear.

"What is that?" Winnie asked.

"We're preparing for an attack here," Memmnon told her flatly. "There is a great body of Imperial Cavalry, perhaps twenty-thousand in number, headed this way down the Lovil Trade Route. Some of our men are trying to interpose themselves, but they are out of position and outnumbered. Barring a miracle there will be an attack on the city perhaps as early as tomorrow. If we're fortunate then we won't see them until the day after but we cannot count on that."

"My God," Stephanie breathed. "Sire, we can't possibly-"

"We cannot concentrate on what we 'can't', Doctor," Memmnon cut her off gently. "It must be done. This palace is constructed to function as a fortress, as are two other locations. All are reasonably well stocked for a siege and have their own water supply. The problem is that we do not have sufficient troops to man all three. We will instead concentrate on the Palace. Those non-combatants who are mobile will be shepherded south out of the city and hopefully out of danger. Sick and injured, those who cannot make the journey and those who simply don't wish to leave will be here, inside."

"Is there even enough room for everyone?" Winnie asked, stunned.

"Yes," Memmnon's voice as firm. "This palace is built in such a way as to function as a citadel. That was in fact what Tyree once called this city. You may have noted that there are walls and buildings surrounding the Royal Palace that create a large square?"

"Yes."

"Those buildings are crafted to withstand a siege," he assured her. "And with many people no doubt opting to leave, there will be more than enough room for the rest. I fear the city itself will suffer, however," he sighed, looking out the window. Outside, the bell in the palace has stopped ringing. As Memmnon opened the window again other bells could be heard in the distance as they picked up the alarm and passed it on.

"The bells will ring all through the city, preparing the citizens for heralds who will give them the news and pass on instructions for them. Meanwhile," he turned back to them, "we have work of our own, do we not? Winnie, your archers will be needed. I trust they will be able to serve?"

"Of course," the younger woman nodded at once. "They were scheduled for training not long from now. Hopefully they will still assemble after this," she added.

"They will hear the herald's instructions, I'm sure," Memmnon told her. "If they are like their teacher I'm sure they will flock here in hopes of serving," he raised an eyebrow as he spoke and Winnie felt her face burn as she blushed.

"Doctor, you will need to ensure that all medical supplies we could possibly need are inside the citadel when we close the gate. I've assigned all palace staff to assist you in moving your patients. I realize it's not much and almost certainly not enough but. . .you will have to make it enough. I need everyone else working to ready us for the siege. Time is precious."

"We'll make do, sire," Stephanie promised. "I need to go," she said then, looking at Winnie. "Be careful," she advised.

"I will. You too."

"Both of you," Memmnon nodded. "Off with you, now," he made a shooing motion. "I too have work to do. I expect both of you at dinner tonight to report on your progress. Until then."

-

"Rider coming!"

The call went forth through Cove Canton as the dinner bell rang three times, three chimes each time, announcing a likely courier inbound.

Dory Leman walked toward the gate at a dignified rate, trying to project the calm he needed to show as post commander, but this could not be good news. A rider coming that hard and fast toward them had to be bearing bad news. He waved to two nearby soldiers who ran to him.

"Find Colonel Chad and General Wilbanks if you please, gents," he ordered calmly. "Ask them to join me here if they would." The two snapped salutes and ran at once in search of the two officers. Before they arrived, the courier was through the gate and nearly falling from his saddle.

"Sir!" the man almost faltered as he passed over the stained and dirty page in his hands.

"Where are you coming from then?" Leman asked as he took the message.

"Brigadier Pierce's command, sir," the man heaved. "Message about an attack on Nasil."

Fighting the urge to panic Leman opened the message. In terse language Pierce informed the 'Commander of Cove Canton' that a large body of Imperial Cavalry had managed to move past his forces in the highlands and was now bearing down on the capitol. He was in pursuit but was outnumbered by a substantial margin so any forces that could converge on the city should do so without delay. Leman glanced at the sun and then pulled his watch from his pocket. If they left soon enough, they should be able to get off the mountain before dark-

"You wanted to see us Colonel?" Chad's voice broke into his calculations and Leman nodded, passing the note to Wilbanks as senior man present.

"Nasil is threatened by enemy cavalry," Leman told them bluntly. "Likely be in the city inside two days. There are to my knowledge only two regiments of troops inside the city, nowhere near enough for something like that," he nodded to the letter. "You two had better get saddled and ready. Colonel Chad your men are already finished and General Wilbanks your men are trained and within two weeks of finishing. You get early graduation it seems," he smiled weakly.

"So it would appear," Wilbanks nodded. "We'll be gone in an hour," he promised, headed to where his men were camped outside the walls.

"We'll be gone before that probably," Chad admitted. "You better keep scouts out, Colonel," he warned as he turned away. "This place will look good to a raiding force."

"Will do," Leman promised. "Let me know if you need anything at all."

"Thanks," Chad nodded and then went to find his men. He couldn't help thinking that Tom Hildebrand would be happy at last.

-

"It's not like this is your fault," Whit told Pierce as they walked their horses for ten minutes to allow them to cool down some.

"Of course, it's my fault," Pierce replied at once, though without rancor. "I'm in command, and this was my mission. Prevent this very thing from happening. How is it not my fault?"

"I'm just saying that it's not like you started the damn war," Whit shot back. "You were trying to stall a force that's easy five times our strength at least. They stole a march on you, yes. But waiting for them to hit you was about all we could have done. Had we tried to go and attack them we wouldn't have lasted twenty minutes and you know it."

"Perhaps," Pierce admitted. "Still, the responsibility was mine, thus the fault must also lie with me," he shrugged. "I should have made sure what they were doing, and I didn't."

Whit stopped trying to talk Pierce around as they stopped to remount. After that it was back to galloping for Nasil as fast as possible without killing horses, which made talk difficult.

He'd have to wait an hour to try again.

-

Tom Hildebrand looked at his commander with a stunned expression on his face.

"Say what now?"

"Get us ready to go Tom," Chad urged. "The capitol is threatened by a large group of Imperial cavalry and our forces are out of place. Us and Wilbanks' men are all there are. We have to ride and right now!"

"Right!" Hildebrand jerked into motion. "I'm on it!" He grabbed his own kit and headed away at a run. Chad turned around to find Leman coming toward him.

"I've turned out two companies of the Regiment that are ready to ride with you," he said without preamble. "They were recovered from wounds at the Gap and about to ride to the front to join the Marshal. They'll be going with you instead, since you're part of the Regiment now yourself."

"I'd honestly forgotten that for a minute," Chad nodded. He was now officially a battalion commander in the Prince's Own. Quite a step up for a militia commander. "We'll be glad to have them along but. . .are you sure you aren't going to need them here?"

"We have 2nd Corps and our own instructors plus the Women's Auxiliary. We'll be fine. And we'll have plenty of warning if they start up the mountain."

"Fair enough," Chad nodded. "2nd Corps?"

"I'm still checking but I doubt it," Leman admitted. "I'm sure they're willing but the initial training has been hard on them and they weren't in the best shape when they got here. Plus, one regiment from each brigade is making The March, so they're a day out at best. I'd expect them to follow possibly, but their strength is just about sapped."

"Wilbanks' division is full strength," Chad mused.

"But unblooded for the most part," Leman reminded him. "Still, they've been through the regimen. They're tougher than when they first got here. It will have to help."

"So, it will," Chad agreed even as a bugle sounded. "That's me," he nodded toward the field. "We should be on the road in twenty minutes. Take care Colonel," he offered his hand and Leman took it. The two had served at the Gap with the Marshal. That experience had bound all the survivors together into a brotherhood that nothing else could have formed.

"You take care, Bret," Leman ordered. "We'll be just fine right here. And we'll watch over your families," he promised.

"I knew that without asking," Chad smiled. "We'll see you when we see you." With that he took his saddlebags and ran toward the assembly.

Quartermasters and their assistants, including many of the dependents on the base, were busy handing out road rations to the men who stored them in saddlebags and sashes and packs against the hard days ahead. Even as that was being done Chad was speaking to his assembled company commanders, including the men from the original Regiment.

"This is how it is," he told them flatly. "There's a great big bunch of Imperial cavalry, better than twenty thousands looks like, headed for Nasil right now. General Pierce is chasing them but he's outnumbered at least five-to-one looks like and his men are a collection of several smaller units rather than an actual division. Plus, a lot of them are infantry that ride rather than cavalry. Be hard for them to engage trained cavalry, assuming the Nor give them the chance."

"I got no idea what we'll find when we get there," he admitted. "We might get there before them even. No way to know until we see. Assume the worst and that way we'll be pleasantly surprised if it's not the worst. Nasil is a fortress city and there are two excellent regiments there plus a smattering of Home Guard units and so forth so they're not completely helpless, but they are outnumbered."

"Wilbanks and his bunch will be right behind us, we're not alone," he reminded them. "That being said, I will be sorely disappointed if that bunch gets there ahead of us," he grinned and was glad to see it returned. "Get back to your men and make equipment checks. QM should be issuing arrows and bolts to archers and crossbowmen. If you need anything else they should have it nearby. Get it in the next ten minutes because fifteen from now I plan to be out the gate and on the way. Now go."

He watched them go, seven company commanders in all. He would have close to one thousand men with the addition of the ad hoc companies Leman was placing with him. Not bad.

And not a drop in the bucket to what he needed. But General Wilbanks had 1st Cavalry and they were almost ten thousand strong. A full strength, fully trained division, well mounted and ready to brawl. That would go a long way toward evening things out.

If they could all get there in time.

"I think we're ready, Bret," Tom Hildebrand reported a minute later as he handed Chad the reins to his own horse, saddled for him during the meeting. "Quartermasters are almost finished, I think. I started to issue lances, but. . .be a bitch to carry them so far. But a lot easier to draw some from an armory in Nasil anyway."

"So, it will," Chad nodded, swinging into the saddle and storing his own supplied behind him. "You wanted action, Tom. Looks like you get your wish."

"I wanted it while it would have gotten us out of some of that running," Hildebrand snorted. "I feel cheated now, having to ride my ass off running to Nasil after I've already finished the training. Damn Nor can't do anything right."

"Well, look on the bright side," Chad smiled.

"There's a bright side?"

"We're going to get to kill a bunch of Norland troopers with this new-found strength and what not."

"Oh," Hildebrand looked thoughtful. "I guess that is a bright side. Plus, we get to do it in these natty new clothes," he indicated his black and green 'Prince's Own' livery. "And we get our own Sheep, too," he pointed to where their color guard was casing a brilliant green flag with the now famous Black Sheep logo on it.

"Pretty bright after all, eh?"

-

"Milord have you sent a message to your brother?"

Memmnon looked Brock behind him, standing in the doorway to the office.

"No, I haven't," Memmnon admitted, turning to look out the window again. "There's no point."

"No point?" he could hear the amazement in Brock's voice. "Sire, we're about to be attacked-"

"What would you have him do, General?" Memmnon turned again to face his Inspector General. "He is barely holding on as it is against far superior numbers. He needs every man he can get just to hold what he has and prevent the Nor army from bowling through us like a wheat cutter. What do you expect him to do? For that matter, a courier sent from here, assuming he made it, would take a minimum of two days to reach Parno. It would take at least that long for him to send relief and probably three days. By that time, we will have either driven the attack off or we'll be dead." Once more he turned to look out the window.

"In either case, there will be nothing he can do. Parno has his hands full, General. We must look after ourselves this time. He has saved us more than once, starting well before the war even began. Surely we can protect ourselves just this once."

"Yes sir," Brock sounded a bit chagrined at that but Memmnon ignored it.

"How are the preparations going?" Memmnon asked, changing the subject.

"If we can get tomorrow to finish, we'll be set for the siege," Brock replied, his tone turning business like. "The only thing that will really hurt is the storehouses. We can't possibly relocate all those stores in the time we have. We're trying to bring those that are in the possible attack route inside the citadel proper but we can't get it all. Assuming the Nor bother looking for them, I expect to lose them."

"We will manage somehow," Memmnon didn't allow any trepidation to show. "Our people are the important thing. I assume many are heading south?"

"Perhaps not as many as you think but a good few are," Brock nodded. "A good many people are reporting here to help in whatever way they can. Their extra hands are going a long way toward helping us with preparations, including pulling stores from warehouses and getting them inside the walls."

"What are our assets?"

"We have the Palace Guard and your personal regiment," Brock reported. "Lady Winnie's female archers will help man the walls and there are nearly two hundred of them. I have one hundred seventy-one people of all ranks from the IG in the city. I've sent some of them with those fleeing to the south as guards and the rest will be here with us. There is also the city constabulary and of course the Royal constabulary. Those who aren't able to lend an effective hand in fighting will be able to help manage stores and carry supplies and what have you. Total effective fighting strength will be roughly three thousand two hundred and fifty, give or take. That includes Lady Winifred's archers and odd and end personnel in the city at the moment."

"So few," Memmnon sighed. "And Pierce has perhaps six thousand total?" he asked.

"Not quite I think, but around that," Brock nodded. "I doubt they all make it here, though, sire. Some were foot infantry if I recall correctly. No way they make this trip so quickly."

"So, at the absolute best we are at a better than two-to-one disadvantage," Memmnon mused.

"I'm afraid when you break those numbers down it's not quite that good, Sire," Brock corrected. "All of the Imperial cavalry will be fighting men. Most of them with experience. Far too many of our number here are not soldiers, and most of our soldiers don't have any real combat experience. People in my own command for instance will not be nearly as effective in open combat because they simply don't have the training. It isn't what they do."

"Can we hold the citadel at least?" Memmnon asked. He knew they couldn't hold the city proper.

"Sire, that's really a question for Colonel Stang to be honest," Brock admitted. "He would be better able to answer that than I."

"He's not here and you are," Memmnon shrugged. "You may not be a soldier but you're very intelligent or you wouldn't be where you are."

"I think we can hold here for a few days at least, and that should be enough," Brock nodded, not bothering to reply to the compliment paid him. "Pierce is coming, and so is help from Cove Canton. Their help will probably be worth more than Pierce's in the long run simply by virtue of their training and experience. How long it takes them to get here will be the key. The best we can hope for is three days, probably."

"So, we must hold for at least three days," Memmnon nodded. "Then we shall.

Is there anything we need to be doing that I can help get done?" he asked. Stephanie had restricted his physical involvement, citing his still healing wound and the damage that could be done by putting forth such an effort and straining himself.

"No, Sire," Brock assured him. "Everyone is working together quite well, in all honesty. We will be moderately well prepared even if they hit us tomorrow. If they give us until the day after, then our preparations will be much better and our odds of victory will improve considerably."

"Then let's hope we get that time."

-

"What the devil is going on?" Roda asked aloud, addressing no one in particular.

"Looks like we're getting attacked," Whip Hubel informed him quietly. "Look here, Roda. I'm gonna need to be headed up to the palace where my daughter is. I won't be down here while she's there through something like this."

"Of course, of course," Roda nodded, still shocked at what he'd been told. "But. . .we should be helping," the inventor said. "We should be there helping."

"Reckon they about got it covered, I should say," Whip shrugged. "Doubt we could be that much help, and anyways most of the workers from the Foundry are already on the way out o' town, by order of the King."

"We can help fight, Mister Hubel," Finn informed him flatly. "We may not possess the strength of the modern soldier, but remember what we do here. We can help and we must."

"I... I hadn't considered that," Whip replied, his face showing his surprise. "Plum slipped my mind to be honest. What you got in mind?"

"We need to find a team of horses, no... we need two teams of mules if we can find them and perhaps a team of oxen. And as many wagons with the new springs as can be found quickly." He was looking around him as he spoke. "Where are those two idiots?"

"Reckon they left with the others?" Whip asked.

"I doubt it," Roda shook his head. "Why would they leave when they could stay and make my life that much more miserable bef-"

"Hey boss!" Carl called just then.

"-before I die," Roda finished dramatically. "What is it?" he called back.

"Carl and me are gonna load some of the mines we were working on for the River Guard and take them up to the fort. Figured you might wanna go along."

"Did you get the flint tipped arrows that must be used to fire them?" Roda asked with deceptive patience.

"Of course," Billy looked pained at the question. "Already loaded."

"And do you have cross bows?" Road asked.

"We assumed they'd have some," Carl almost smirked at his thinking. Roda wiped that smirk right off by yelling;

"And what if no one up there has a crossbow you moron!"

"Why wouldn't they have a-"

"Because," Roda explained with a calm that was a danger signal to all who knew him, "they aren't a regular military unit, you imbecile! There may not be a crossbow in the entire place!"

"See, that's why we wanted you to go along," Billy broke in before Roda could work himself into a frenzy. "You're so much smarter and think of more stuff. You keep coming up with that while we load the crossbows we keep here on the wagon, sir, and whatever you come up with we'll see it gets done."

As always, the smooth work from the two long time assistants made Roda splutter and pop and as a result he fell silent.

"Reckon what we need them mules and such for, Roda?" Whip asked into the silence.

"We have two trebuchets on the test range that can be towed inside the citadel," Roda informed him. "And there are a good number of rounds for them already prepared and ready to ship here in the Foundry. We need to get those pieces to the fortress and get a good wagon to haul the ordnance up there. They might be a great help in the next few days. And there may be a few other ways we can be of assistance as well, but I will need to see what is happening first."

"All right," Whip nodded. "You start preparing to abandon this place while I work on getting what you need down here. We'll get 'er loaded up and get up there and see what's what."

"What do you mean, preparing to abandon this place?" Roda asked.

"Well, I didn't figure you would want to leave your plans and such laying around for the Nor to steal was they to come in here and find 'em," the archer shrugged.

"My prints!" Roda looked aghast. "My sketches! My books! Great stars above! I can't allow all that to fall into enemy hands! Good archer I must go and ensure that cannot happen! I leave the other details in your capable hands!"

"I'll see to it," Whip told the fussy inventors back as he waddled toward his office. He looked at Carl and Billy.

"Gather up ever body that's still here," he ordered. "We got a lot to get done and not a whole bunch o' time. I'm gonna see about getting some help."

"Right Mister Hubel," Carl grinned. "We're on it."

-

"My Lady is it true?" was the first thing Winnie heard as her archery students assembled.

"I'm afraid so," Winnie nodded. "We are pulling into the citadel around the palace to make our stand. Help is already on the way so all we have to do is hold until they arrive. We're going to help with that," she told them proudly.

"How long until we have help?" one of the older women asked.

"I estimate four days, but today is one of those days," Winnie padded the number in case their help didn't arrive on time. "If we are fortunate then the attack won't hit until day after tomorrow. If it does hit tomorrow, we will still be okay, we simply won't be able to save so much of our resources as the extra day will give us."

"What would you like us to do, ma'am?" a young woman about Winnie's own age asked.

"We are going to assist Lady Stephanie's people in moving the sick and injured from the hospitals into the soldier barracks inside the palace grounds," she smiled.

"They need assistance badly and we can help." She began issuing orders, dispatching teams of 'lady archers' to each hospital to help move either medical supplies and equipment or patients, whichever was needed. All of her students were healthy, solid women and more than able to assist with something like carrying patients or bundles of medical supplies, and she knew Stephanie could use the help.

They all could.

-

As it happened, the defenders of the Royal City would have their extra day. Not because Stone made a mistake because this time at least he was making very few missteps. No, the extra time would not really be 'extra', but instead was the result of Pierce's over estimation of how far the northern cavalry had gotten ahead of him. While true they were far enough ahead to prevent Pierce from catching them short of Nasil, they were not nearly so far ahead as he believed. As a result, the defenders of Nasil would spend the next thirty-six hours looking for and expecting an attack that wouldn't happen for another day at best. They would make good use of that time.

Four groups of people that afternoon, working or riding into evening, fates tied together though they had never met in person. Even as the riders had to finally stop to rest horses and men and take food, and because light had failed them completely, the people hurrying to secure the Royal City continued on well into the night. In fact, someone would be working all night long as work crews took turns at the warehouses, moving everything they could into the palace fortress.

It was very late when Winnie and Stephanie managed to return to report to Memmnon, who had ordered a very simple supper of cold meats, bread and cheese prepared. The two ate hungrily and in appreciation as they informed him of what they had managed to accomplish that afternoon and evening. He was nodding by the time they had finished.

"It sounds as though you both did very well," he complimented. "Winifred I must commend you on thinking to take your archery students to assist Stephanie's people in moving the patients. Well done."

"Thank you Sire," Winnie preened and bowed her head in acknowledgment.

"Doctor have we secured sufficient medical supplies for a siege?" he asked Stephanie.

"Yes, Sire," she nodded firmly. "I've taken everything from the hospitals we have abandoned, and pulled the more advanced students from the schools to help aid with patient care. Those less far along in their studies are assisting with food stores or gathering additional medical supplies. Everyone is working admirably together."

"I shudder to think what it would be like had Parno and Sebastian not unearthed that Imperial spy network some weeks ago," Memmnon shook his head. "Things are bad enough as it is. If we had to deal with traitors and saboteurs among us it would be much worse. There is still a threat of such of course, but not nearly so bad as it would have been."

"I think barring severe misfortune we will be ready when they arrive,"

Stephanie said. "Our weakest and most vulnerable citizens are already inside the walls here. Those still outside are the people capable of working even long into the night."

"What are you going to be doing?" Winnie asked.

"Once we've eaten, I plan to return to our new makeshift hospital and inspect it and the patients," Stephanie told her. "My parents are here and have agreed to help oversee the patient care. I tried to get them to leave but that isn't going to happen."

"So, stubbornness runs in the family then?" Memmnon asked playfully and even Stephanie had to contain a snort of laughter as Winnie's laugh peeled away.

"I'm afraid it does, Sire."

"Again, it sounds as if you two have done well for us," Memmnon repeated. "Winnie, what are you going to be doing?"

"I'll be with my students after meal time, getting a last bit of instruction in," the flame haired archeress said. "They should do okay but I can probably make that better just by spending a bit of time with them tonight building their confidence and talking about what's coming."

"I assume they all wanted to serve?"

"This is what they signed up for," Winnie nodded. "To be here to help in times just like this. They're ready to go."

-

"Made good time today," Hildebrand noted from his side of the small fire.

"So, we did," Chad nodded, poking the fire with a stick. "We'll need to tomorrow as well."

"No way we can make Nasil by tomorrow," Hildebrand said. "Too late a start today."

"At least we're off the mountain," Chad shrugged. "That will help. We should be there by noon, day after. No later than midafternoon, anyway."

"I hate to bring this up," Hildebrand spoke again after a minute of quiet, "but if we arrive alone, we won't last long against so many."

"True," Chad agreed, not looking away from the fire.

"So, what do we plan on doing?"

"I haven't worked that out yet," Chad admitted. "If Pierce is already there, we'll join on him. If not, we can harass the enemy flank and wait for Wilbanks. We can scout things out for when he gets there, and lend a hand anywhere the fortifications look weak by trying to pull enemy away. Once Wilbanks and the 1st arrive we can join on them. We'd still be outnumbered, but only something like two-on-one. We should be able to win that exchange."

"Should be," Hildebrand nodded. Unless something else happens, he didn't add. There was no real need. It wasn't anything that all of them hadn't thought about today already.

-

"What do you mean 'lost them'?" Raines was incredulous. "How the hell do you lose an entire division of cavalry? Four of them at that!"

"They disappeared from view and didn't return to it," Simmons shrugged, pointing on the river model to show where they had lost sight of the Norland force. "This stretch is heavily forested and it's nearly a mile across at that point in some places. Even with a good glass it's difficult to see over much. The road or trail or whatever it is they were using apparently ran behind a line of brush and trees and they never emerged. They could still be going north, or maybe west or back south now for all we know. We stayed around rest of the day trying to get a glimpse of them. Nothing. Rode another five miles upriver to see if they had emerged from the woods. Nothing. It was almost as if they disappeared. They didn't of course, but what direction they took we can't know. Sorry General," the younger man shrugged.

"And no sign of the others either?" Raines clarified.

"No sir," Simmons confirmed. "I don't know where they went, sir, but they didn't keep following the river. Of that we're certain."

After Simmons was gone Raines looked at his model and then looked at his maps. They knew so little about the other side of the river. His men had been stationed here primarily as a deterrent to Tribal raids in times past. This was the first time he knew of personally or in history that the Tribes had worked with the Nor. Seeing Imperial troops on the far side of the bridge had come as something of a shock to him when it had happened.

In times past, they had been reluctant to risk angering the Tribes, so information about the far side was limited. No scouting parties had gone over the bridge in many years. A few less than intelligent people had ventured across for one reason or another, but most never returned. There were no accurate maps that he knew of that showed any reliable information about the western shore and beyond.

For all Raines knew it was desert just beyond the trees that lined the river banks. Or it might be an oasis that all the Tribes shared among themselves, though that was doubtful. When there was no one else to make war on the Tribes tended to practice on one another. He couldn't really see them sharing anything much. Not for long anyway.

That thought made him wonder what the Empire had promised them to get the Tribes to cooperate with them and with each other. Had to be something special, but there was no telling what that was. He shook his head. That wasn't his problem at the moment.

His problem was the disappearance of four divisions of Imperial horsemen. That was something that could become everyone's problem.

-

"So, the problem now is that we don't have any idea where Therron has gone."

Beaumont, Whipple and Johnson were seated around the portico table, sharing a meal and beer. Whipple had just put into words the problem they faced now.

"He can literally go anywhere he chooses along the shore," Beaumont made a helpless gesture with his hands. "And there's a lot of shore."

"He's got to go somewhere he can commandeer troops and supplies," Johnson shook his head. "He's not going to let go of his chance to have the throne so easily, gents. He will try to take it again, somehow. And unless King Memmnon has done more to spread the word about his traitorous brother than King Tammon did, then he can likely spin a good tale and get that help somewhere."

"King Memmnon is spreading the word, but it can only spread so fast," Whipple said. "Arrest warrants have been issued for both of the twins in fact, as well as Callens and his senior officer, for Crimes Against the Crown, treason and the murder of the King. But until that word gets out to every post, it's a race to see who gets where, first."

"I think Moble would be among the last to get word," Johnson mused. "But it's possible that Jayville or Red Rivera would be later than them, too," he added, thinking of two major cities north of them. "Both have naval ports but no ships based there that I know of. Certainly not since the Keyhorn Squadron went north."

"What if he just left?" Beaumont asked. "What if he just gets this idiot, Chastain, to drop him somewhere in the Sea of Storms? Or in Berma, for that matter? There are any number of places within easy sailing distance that he could choose. Places where who he is would matter. He could claim to be a ruler in exile, forced from the throne by his family, all that sort of rubbish. Some would probably believe it."

"Might at that," Whipple nodded thoughtfully. "And he is a silvery tongued bastard for sure."

"He is that," Johnson agreed. "As it is though, I don't see any way for us to know wh-"

"Captain!" a shout from a running Lieutenant Smith made Johnson go quiet. The young lieutenant ran up the steps two at a time, gasping for breath as he plowed to a stop before his commander.

"Easy son," Johnson said, rising to his feet. "What is it?" Johnson wasn't nearly so worried at the moment about pirates or Chastain returning or anything else for that matter. Two brigades of troops could do a great deal to ease one's mind.

"Sir, look!" Smith gasped, thrusting a rough piece of paper into his Captain's hands. Johnson took it and opened the small roll, moving to the recently lit lamp. His mouth worked at first as he read, but then fell open as he finished.

"Well," he tried to keep his trademark calm as he lowered the note and looked at his guests. "I guess I made more of an impression on Major Guilford than I had realized, gentlemen." He passed the note to Whipple, who read it aloud.

"'Captain Johnson, I am unconvinced that we are doing the right thing, but I cannot prevail upon Captain Chastain to see reason. While you have no reason to believe me, myself and my marines are in fact loyal to Soulan, even before we are loyal to the Crown or the man who wears it. The Marshal has told us that he is being held as part of a coup attempt, and asked that we carry him to Norfok, where he hopes to gain assistance from the Coastal Province government. He believes they will lend him material aide in returning to his 'rightful place' as the ruler of Soulan. Please remember that I tried to help in the event he is insane. Major John Guilford, Marine Detachment Delta, commanding.'" Whipple lowered the note as he finished.

"I'll be damned," Buford was the first to speak. "Where did this come from, lieutenant?" he demanded.

"From this, sir," Smith held up a bottle that had the neck broken from it. "One of the men found it on the beach today during police and wondered what the note said. That's when we discovered the note, sir."

"Guilford had to have dropped this right under Chastain's nose," Whipple was shaking his head. "You did say he was reluctant."

"He was," Johnson nodded. "From the outset I believe. He tried more than once to get Chastain to stop but idiot that he is, the Captain kept plowing ahead. It's possible that Guilford felt that his men might side with Chastain if he tried to go against him, or that he's trying to play both sides against the middle. He warns us, but supports Chastain."

"Or he had a change of heart after hearing you out and was already in a bind," Beaumont mused. "Maybe this was all he could come up with," he shrugged when the other two looked at him. "Chastain is a Captain, but in a Commodore's slot, commanding a naval task force at sea. Puts Guilford in a bit of rough place, doesn't it? Hung for mutiny, or hung for treason."

"Hadn't thought of it that way," Johnson admitted. "But once they found out the truth, that should have stopped them. They should have backed down and left."

"Well, now we know where they're going," Beaumont said. "Makes cutting them off easier."

"We know where they told Guilford they're going," Whipple amended. "Doesn't mean they're going there. Or that they were and might change their mind. Still, it's a start. We can now send a courier to Savannah with this information. If Chastain is taking the bastard to Norfok, them the Navy will have time to get someone there to cut him off, assuming we still have a Navy."

"And we should probably send a courier to the Marshal, reporting what we know and asking for instructions," Beaumont nodded. "We can head for Cove Canton in the meantime. Be in a position to cut off Therron McLeod and any help he manages to get from the Coastal Provinces Coalition."

"I can't see them offering him any help," Whipple shook his head at that. "Therron is a good a talker, to be honest, but he's got nothing to bargain with. I suppose there may be something he can offer, but what it might take to get the CPC to aid him, I can't say. I can't imagine them helping him at all, especially with the Nor on the prowl. We're all that keeps them from being annexed by the Empire."

"True, but Therron likely has some contacts among their military," Beaumont offered. "If there's a way, you can bet he will find it."

"I will send two of my men to Nasil with a full report from me and you," Johnson said. "If you can provide an escort of maybe ten men to ensure they can complete the mission that would be a great help. And they can carry your, uh, evidence I guess, to the King as well. Not a job I would relish, to be honest. Long way to carry something like that in this heat."

"We can place it in formaldehyde, in a glass jar," Beaumont's voice was cold. "I wouldn't bother but orders are orders. They want to make sure there's no way for someone to say later that either one is still alive in the event they end up dead and can't be brought back for trial. Makes sense, distasteful as it might be," he admitted.

"We can do that," Whipple told Johnson. "Makes sense to let your men go as well. This is your post. We'll be leaving a reinforced company of men here with you for security while our wounded recover. And in case Chastain comes back or pirates try to take advantage of the war."

"I appreciate that very much," Johnson nodded. "We'll take care of your wounded. Once they're all able to travel, we'll see them home. I will arrange some ambulances from Jayville if nothing else."

"Better sound officers call," Beaumont sighed. "We need to be on the road when the sun gets up high enough."

"I was hoping for one more easy day," Whipple echoed that sigh. "Oh well. We can always sleep when we're dead I guess."

CHAPTER EIGHTEEN

-

Colonel Mason Stang had more jobs than he had people to give them to. That was a problem that wasn't going to change any time soon he knew, but that didn't make things any easier to get done.

Two days ago, a courier had entered the city riding hell bent for leather on a horse that was closer to glue than not, bringing news from a Brigadier named Pierce that a large Imperial cavalry force was headed for Nasil on the Lovil Trade Road. Trade Roads in Nasil were ancient roads once called 'highways', (why he had no idea). These roads ran all through the Kingdom connecting most major cities and allowing ease of travel on major trade expeditions. Many of those routes ran through to the north as well. The Tyree Dynasty had always made it a point to maintain these routes both for trade and for defense use. A fine idea save for times like this when it left a wide and well maintained road right into the heart of the Soulan capitol and the seat of government for the entire Kingdom.

As senior officer and commander of the Palace Guard, Stang was in overall command of the city's defense. Normally that job would fall to at least a Brigadier, but there wasn't one around at the moment. He wished there was one around, since he would likely also have a division of troops at his command and right now that would be a welcome sight indeed.

But there was no Brigadier and no division of troops. There was one coming and he had a force that was roughly equivalent to about half a division, but they were independent commands tossed together for this particular mission, which meant that their actions would not be nearly so well coordinated as an actual fighting division would be. It was possible that there would more help coming from Cove

Canton, in the form of part of Prince Parno's personal regiment and the 1st Soulan Cavalry Division, both of which were elite units and would definitely make a difference, assuming they made it here before everything was done and over with. But until and unless all of those units arrived, it was his regiment and Robert Moore's and a smattering of other small units and individuals pulled together on the spur of the moment.

Using the Royal Palace Citadel as the primary defensive position was the best decision possible in their circumstances, but it was not ideal simply because the fortifications there were meant to be manned by a full division of troops at a minimum. They had less than half that number available and not all of them would be able to use a bow, the primary weapon of defense in a position like this unless the enemy managed to gain the wall. Should that happen then the sword would become the weapon most needed for defense, and there were too many of the people arrayed for defending the position that had little to no training or experience with a sword.

Two thousand four hundred and nine professional troopers from the combined commands of the Palace Guard and King's Own regiments would be the bulwark of the defensive force. Their number was about one quarter of the minimum needed for defending the palace citadel, but there was no point in worrying about that now. What they had was all they had.

"Scouts are out, sir," a young lieutenant reported, shaking Stang from his thoughts on the problem at hand. "Orders are to move across the bridge and take post two to three miles up the Trade, depending on the best position they find. At first sign of the enemy they are to immediately return here with word, stopping for nothing."

"Thank you, Lieutenant," Stand nodded. "Please inform all battalion commanders to assemble here in twenty minutes."

"Yes sir," the young man nodded and hurried away, waving for nearby enlisted runners to attend him. Stang spent the next twenty minutes going over his plan. He could wish for more men, but there was no point and no time to waste on it.

He had what he had. It would have to do.

-

"We should hit the capitol by noon tomorrow," Silas Weir said as he walked his horse beside Stone. "Do we have a plan as such, or will we just burn and pillage and then try to cut out before they can muster a force against us?"

"We'll play it by ear until we see what's there to oppose us," Stone admitted. "I'd like, ideally, to do a good bit of damage if we can. Even if it's not damage that would directly affect the war effort, significant damage to their capitol could at least be bad for morale and force them to pull troops permanently away from the front. Anyone we can pull away from the troops opposing Wilson will only help when he starts moving again."

"Will he start moving again?" Weir asked. "He's been slow in moving since he hit major resistance where he is now."

"I don't know," Stone admitted. "I don't know what he will do or not do. He doesn't share with me. He does seem to be getting very good at laying blame for his failures anywhere except on himself."

"I've heard that's a trait among generals," Weir snorted. "Assuming we can wreak havoc here and get away without a major engagement, what next?"

"I'll wait and see do we get away, first," Stone replied dryly. "I think we can deal with whatever we face here, so long as we don't linger. We need to do what damage we can as quickly as we can and then make with the getting the hell away from here part of the plan."

"Are we going to try and hit their Royals?" Weir asked. "Hit their palace or whatever?"

"I don't know," Stone sounded thoughtful. "Depends, I guess. If they concentrate their defense there to protect their King, then that leaves everything else open to attack. If they try to defend the entire city then attacking the royal residence should pull defenders away from other targets to defend their King. We'll wait and see what we see I guess." He stopped then and pulled his horse forward.

"Mount up, Sergeant Major," he said to his chief NCO.

"Sir!" the man nodded and looked at the bugler. "Mount and stand ready," he ordered. The bugler blew the call and it was picked up and carried down the line. It took about five minutes for over twenty-thousand men to mount and dress ranks.

"Forward, gallop!" Stone barked and the bugler dutifully sounded that call next. The smooth way the entire column began moving was a testament to how well trained and experienced the Imperial Cavalry was compared to past efforts. Five more minutes saw the entire command once more galloping toward Nasil and whatever waited for them there.

-

"Take a break," Winnie ordered her students. "Rest, eat, make sure your families are safe if you have them. Work assignments for this afternoon will be available through Lady Stephanie's chief orderly. We will continue to assist with the hospital until and unless we are attacked." She looked at the assembly. Her initial students had been joined in the last two days by another fifty-two students. Some would never amount to much as archers went, but at this point every little bit would help.

"You're all doing well considering how short a time you've been at it. In the event we find ourselves fighting, remember your training and you will do fine. Stay calm and keep your focus. And remember this; this is an opportunity for us to prove that women can help defend this Kingdom. Make sure we make the most of it, right?"

Many of the voices, mostly of younger women, added their agreement to her statement.

"Dismissed then," Winnie waved, and the assembly began to break apart. She watched them go, resisting the urge to shake her head. If only they had begun this earlier. Several of her students showed a good eye-hand coordination that with time and training would make them excellent archers. But time and training would be hard to come by in time for what was coming.

"Winnie gal!"

Hearing her father calling her broke Winnie from her regretful rumination. She turned, looking around her until she spotted her father riding a wagon being drawn into the center of the palisade.

"Pa!" she waved and started forward but he held up a hand.

"Wait right there, girl!" he ordered firmly and turned to the wagon's driver, whom she recognized as one of Mister Roda's assistants, Billy. After speaking to him, Whip jumped down from the slowly moving wagon and made his way to his daughter.

"How is things moving here, gal?" he asked without preamble, embracing his daughter as he spoke.

"It could be better," she admitted. "I should have been training these girls a long time ago instead of trying to get myself sent to the front to fight alongside the others."

"That bad?" Whip asked, ignoring his daughter's admission that she'd been trying to make her way into combat. It wasn't as if he hadn't known about it.

"It could be worse as well as better," she amended. "Many of them show great promise, but there ain't-there isn't, time to develop their potential right now. Assuming we live through this, I'm gonna make it my mission to train 'em up to make a defense force for the city. Assuming it works, we should be able to do it for ever major city in the Kingdom."

"Sounds like my girl is startin' in to thinkin' like a Queen to me," Whip teased. "That sounds like a good idea Sweet Pea. I think it'll work out fine if'n you was to do it yourself."

"I would, though I'd take some of my better students from here to help," she nodded. "And, of course, was a certain grizzled old archer to offer to help, I'd likely accept it," she teased back.

"Well, the only grizzled old archer I know of around here close by is plumb busy at the minute, but if I can get the time, I'd be proud to help," Whip promised.

"What are you doing?" she asked, and he pointed toward the gate in answer. She looked to see a team of oxen pulling a trebuchet inside the walls, with another behind.

"We're bringing the stuff Roda uses to test his what-nots before sending 'em to the Army," Whip told her. "Ain't like having a great bunch of artillery but it's a help I reckon, since we brung along most of what he had ready to go. We can shoot so long as them two pieces hold on," he told her.

"Does Memmnon know?" Winnie asked, trying to keep her excitement down.

"You know, I doubt he does," Whip mused. "We just decided yesterday evening to do this here, and been working at it pretty much since then. Got a whole bunch o' Roda's goodies coming, assuming we get the time to put 'em where we can use 'em. Mind you it takes a good shot to set off some of 'em," he eyed her warily.

"We need to poll the regiments and find any high skilled archers among them I suppose," Winnie bit her lip as she thought. "Some probably are okay with a cross bow. Comes to that, some of that River Guard that's still around should be good with an arbalest since they use them so much."

Whip tried not to preen too much as he watched his baby girl making such plans and figuring far in advance. She had grown a great deal of late and while he was tickled that she would someday sooner than later become Queen, it was her ability to lead and to plan that his pride was complete in. She was a force to be reckoned with, even at her young age. How could a father not be proud of such a daughter?

"Sounds like you got work to do too, baby girl," he winked at her. "I better go and see to this here other. Roda'll be like to have a spasm o' some kind soon and some of us needs to be 'round to keep him from running off the help. Love you gal," he kissed her forehead lightly and hugged her tight.

"I love you to Poppa," Winnie said softly. "Come eat supper with us tonight if you can," she said.

"Will if I can," he promised.

-

"Stephanie, you look tired, dear."

Stephanie looked up to see her mother hovering over her, concern etched on her face.

"I haven't had time to be tired, mother," she smiled wanly. "There is too much yet to do if we are to be prepared for what is coming."

"Stephanie, you are one of the few physicians here in this city," Madelaine Corsin told her only daughter. "You cannot allow yourself to fall into poor health at a time like this. Come," she ordered, holding out her hand. "I have a small lunch waiting for you in the office your father is using. We will sit quietly for a few minutes and eat while you rest. And all of this will be waiting here when you are finished, unless of course someone else comes along and takes care of it in the meantime. Now come."

Stephanie thought of resisting but decided it would waste more time and energy to argue with her mother than to simply acquiesce to her demands. Leaving her inventory where it was she followed her mother to the small cubbyhole of an office in the back of the barracks where there was indeed a small meal of fresh fruit, bread and cheese waiting along with wine.

"So," Madelaine said once they had settled and took a plate. "I received a very interesting letter from Edema Willows of Cumberland not long ago," she dropped this tidbit out of the blue. Stephanie had been about to take a bite of apple and froze with the fruit still poised for that purpose.

"Close your mouth dear," Madelaine smirked. "That is in no way an attractive look for you." Red faced, Stephanie went ahead and bit into the apple, though unaware of the taste now.

"Edema tells me that you and Prince Parno have become very close," her mother continued. "I must say I was surprised to hear that from her rather than you, considering that you have been here over a month now at least. Of course, you haven't really taken the time to visit us much, now have you?" her tone was more amused than disappointed, but the words still hit Stephanie hard.

"I've been rather busy, mother," she temporized. "Not just in caring for the King, but in starting new training programs. Also I am serving as the official Chaperon for

Winifred during her courtship with the King. That takes a great deal of time as well."

"I'm sure it does," Madelaine nodded. "And I'm glad to see you doing such a thing as well," she added. "It's good that the poor girl hasn't been thrown into this life without anyone she can depend on to help her adjust. She's fortunate to have you, dear."

"Thank you," Stephanie bowed her head slightly at the compliment.

"That does not explain, however, how it is that I have to learn of your. . .arrangement, with Prince Parno by letter from an old classmate," Madelaine continued, her eyes literally dancing with mirth. "I wish to know all there is to tell from you, daughter."

Stephanie felt tears welling in her eyes despite her best efforts, but she managed to keep them at bay and force her voice to be firm if not strong.

"I'm afraid there is no longer anything to tell you, mother," she said calmly. "The Prince and I did indeed have an arrangement of sorts, assuming he lived through the war, but I'm afraid that in my haste I pushed him too far, and then responded to his concerns with derision and anger. As a result, I do not believe that such a relationship exists between us any longer. Indeed, he departed the next morning before I could take the opportunity to make things right between us. I'm afraid that my final words to him the evening before could have been interpreted to mean I had no desire to see him again. That was not what I meant, at least not really, but it could have been taken that way."

"My poor dear," Madelaine said after a moment of silence. "You never have learned to get a handle on that mouth, have you my daughter?"

"That's very helpful, Mother, thank you," Stephanie replied dryly. "What would I do without your insight?"

"Don't sass me, Missy," Madelaine shook a finger at her daughter. "What have you done to correct this mess you've made?" she asked.

"Nothing," Stephanie replied flatly. "There is no need. Parno McLeod is many things, Mother, but forgiving isn't one of them. I made a terrible hash of things and put him in a terrible position out of pure selfishness. And then accused him of selfishness when he wouldn't accede to my demands. I... I said a great many things in anger and disappointment that were designed to hurt him, and it apparently worked. As you said, I must learn to control my tongue better."

"So, you're just giving up, is that it?" Madelaine asked, her tone and facial expression indicating what she thought of that plan.

"Mother, this city is about to come under attack in the next twenty-four to thirty-six hours," Stephanie resisted the urge to roll her eyes. "I really do have more important considerations at the moment than my failed love life!"

"I see," her mother nodded slowly. "Don't have the courage to face him then. Well, I'm not surprised," she sighed theatrically. "I blame your father for this, really. He was a lot like that when we married. Always trying to avoid anything that might be a conflict."

"If you talk to anyone at Cove Canton then you'll know that there was no shortage of 'conflict' between Parno and I," Stephanie said acerbically. "And there is a difference, Mother, between lacking the courage to do something and knowing there's no point." She rose from her chair, only a few bites of her food eaten.

"I am indeed fortunate to have so many people around me who know so much better than I what it is I need to do, or to say, or what I am lacking in the way of courage, strength, or whatever else you can come up with. Now if you will excuse me, I have work to do." Before her mother could respond Stephanie was out the door and gone, fighting to hold back the tears that her mother's words had threatened to release for the first time in many days.

It was really too bad that her parents had decided to remain here and help out.

-

Edema Willows bit back a curse as her carriage struck yet another obstacle in the road causing it to bump and buck. Traveling to Nasil was normally a much easier and more comfortable task, but apparently the war was delaying work on the normally well-maintained roads between Cove Canton and the capitol. She had also requested that the trip be made as quickly as possible, which was not conducive to comfortable travel.

"Benson, do you think the driver could miss at least some of the bumps we encounter?" she asked dryly.

"Sorry milady, but the road is a bit of a mess," her foot man reported from his post beside the carriage. "At least we'll soon be in Nasil, milady. By noon, most like."

"Excellent," Edema smiled in spite of the harsh traveling conditions. A courier had reached her home just five days ago with a message from Winifred Hubel explaining how things had suddenly deteriorated between Parno and Stephanie Corsin. She frowned for the umpteenth time as she recalled Winnie telling her that Stephanie had reportedly pushed Parno into a corner on something private and then spoken harshly to him when he had resisted her.

Of all the childish things to do, she thought not for the first time since receiving that letter. She should know better than something like that! After all that boy has been through, pressing him on something he's uncomfortable with is a bad plan from the very beginning.

She broke out of her train of thought as her carriage began to slow.

"Benson, what's going on?" she demanded out the window.

"I'm not sure, milady," he admitted carefully. "We're coming into the edge of the city and…well, it appears almost deserted. Abandoned, even."

Edema felt herself growing cold at that pronouncement.

"Benson, listen carefully," she ordered as calmly as she could. "Order the driver to head directly to the palace and do not stop for anyone not in the Dynast's colors. No one. Hurry now!" she urged.

"Of course, milady," Benson nodded and moved his horse even with the driver. Seconds later the carriage began to pick up speed and soon was rocking through the streets at speed that was far in excess of safe.

There were few reasons for the normally bustling Royal City to look and feel abandoned, and none of them were good. She needed to reach the palace as soon as possible.

It took another fifteen minutes to do so, and when they arrived, she was more than surprised to see the palisades around the palace closed up tight, gates closely guarded.

"Halt!" one of the men standing at the gate they approached called. "State your name and business!"

-

Captain Jeffrey Winters was making rounds outside the palace citadel looking for weaknesses in the defenses at the request of Colonel Stang. As a member of the Black Sheep, Winters had true combat experience where most of the rest did not. Stang didn't hesitate to take advantage of that, either.

Winters didn't like the idea of trying to defend so large an area with so few men, but he had to admit that the structures and walls themselves were in good condition. Built for something just like this, they were strong enough to withstand a determined attack so long as they were adequately defended. It remained to be seen if the few men they had would be adequate. It all depended on how many troops were actually coming, and how smart their commander was.

As he approached the gate he had started from, ending his tour back where he began, he noticed a familiar carriage at the gate being challenged by the guards. Being a naturally curious type, Winters approached the carriage's off side to take a look at who would be visiting at a time like this.

"Lady Willows?" he asked in stunned surprise, seeing the elegant blonde sitting in the carriage as her driver argued with the guards.

"Lieut-no, Captain Winters, now, isn't it?" Edema smiled beautifully. "How are you? I am pleased to see you well."

"Thank you, milady," Winters nodded slightly. "What in the world brings you here, today of all days?" Before she could reply he looked at the guard.

"Is there a problem here?" he demanded brusquely.

"Trying to get inside," the guard replied. "No one expected her and she ain't from the city. We ain't-"

"You can't possibly be that stupid," Winters told the man flatly. "Do you not realize who this is?"

"No, sir," the man looked a bit wary now. "Beggin' your pardon, sir," he added, realizing who Winters was now.

Edema couldn't hear just what Winters said to the young and surly lieutenant that had been arguing with Benson and her driver, though she did catch Parno's name. She hid a smile as suddenly it was more than fine for her carriage to enter the palace grounds and welcome to the palace and so forth. The carriage moved slowly as Winters stepped back to her window, walking alongside.

"I'm sorry about that Milady," he apologized. "Truth is we're expecting an attack here within the day and everyone is a bit on edge. I'm afraid Lord Parno isn't here at the moment, milady. He is currently at the front with the Army."

"Attack?" Edema felt her face pale. "Here?"

"I'm afraid so, milady," Winters nodded. "I would advise you to leave but fear there may not be sufficient time for you to get clear. It may be that you're safer staying here now."

"I can't head back with our horses tired out," she nodded. "We'd never do well should we have to run for it. I'm afraid you're quite correct, Captain. We shall have to ride the attack out here with the rest. Perhaps we can be of some assistance, at least."

"I'm sure Lady Winifred can find you something to do," Winters chuckled. "You can bet that if she can't, Lady Stephanie sure can. I have to report in, milady. Be safe," he knocked twice on the carriage door and then was gone, leaving Edema digesting what he'd just said.

The Royal City to be attacked, and apparently, Winnie and Stephanie were playing quite the part in preparing for that attack. Interesting.

Very. Interesting.

-

"Poppa is bringing in two trebuchets from Roda Finn's testing range," Winnie informed Memmnon as the two met briefly for lunch. "That and some of Roda's more potent 'gadgets' as he calls them should be a big help. I hadn't realized he had noth-er, anything like that close by," she caught herself yet again before using slang. Memmnon stifled a grin as he knew it bothered her.

"I never have seen these gadgets in operation, but Parno assures me they are a sight to behold," he told her. "And your father is assisting?"

"He's been helping Roda test his new stuff for some time now," she nodded. "Him and Mister Roda's assistants are working on it. Won't be like having a sure enough artillery presence Pa said, but it will help."

"We shall take whatever we can get," Memmnon nodded. "And be grateful to those who provide it."

"Lady Winifred, Lady Cumberland is requesting an audience with you," a young staff girl announced.

"What?" Winnie looked stunned for a second, then recognition dawned. "Oh, no," she covered her eyes with one hand. "I had sent her a message asking for her help with. . .well, you know," she uncovered her eyes and looked at Memmnon. "And now she's here, now of all times! She had to have left as soon as the courier arrived!"

"Too late for her to try and leave now," Memmnon shrugged. "Show her in Amelia," he said kindly.

"Yes, Highness," the girl curtsied and left. Seconds later Edema was ushered inside.

"Lady Cumberland I am so sorry," Winnie began at once. "I didn't know we would be in such straits when I asked for your help!"

"Quite all right dear," Edema smiled brightly. "Quite all right. I had four men accompanying me that I have sent to the hospital to help out Stephanie. Is there anything I can do otherwise? Memmnon, dear, I am glad to see you up and about," she kissed his cheek lightly.

"Thank you, Lady Cumberland, and no, at present there is nothing," Memmnon replied. "When Winifred sent word to you we were unaware of this impending threat. We in fact received warning just day before yesterday that they were headed this way. We expect them today or tomorrow. My money is on tomorrow, now, as it is well past noon."

"That makes sense," Edema nodded thoughtfully. "This is the very thing Parno was concerned over. The Nor adopting our own tactics against us."

"So, it is," Memmnon nodded. "We are preparing as best we can, but I'm afraid we have few resources in the city at present. That being the case we have withdrawn everything and everyone we cannot send away into the palace fortifications. We will concentrate our defenses here. The city will suffer but we will do all we can to avoid loss of life."

"Is there help coming?" Edema asked.

"Yes, but not enough to ensure victory," the King told her. "It is unlikely that a cavalry force will remain in enemy territory unsupported for long, however. If we can endure for a day or three, we should be fine. We can rebuild damage to the city, so long as we can protect and preserve our people."

"Three days," Edema repeated to herself. "That seems like a very long time for something like this."

"If it lasts so long then it will be," Memmnon said grimly. "Still, all we can do is all we can do. I'm sorry your visit here coincided with such an event."

"Oh, what's life without a bit of excitement now and again?"

-

Dusk began to fall in Nasil at the usual time, but seemed far sooner for those hurrying to make ready for the expected arrival of the Imperial Cavalry raid. Gas lamps were lit along the streets and malls of the inner city and the palace grounds were completely illuminated the same way as people still working used that light to complete their preparations.

No one believed that they would have more than a few hours of light on the morrow, if that, before they came under attack. That lent urgency to their actions even as they were thankful for that little bit of extra time.

Everyone who could flee the city had done so by now. Watchmen and Constables patrolled the city in an effort to make sure that looting wasn't a problem. There would be some theft everyone was sure, as scavengers would take advantage of the emergency to try and pad their pockets at the expense of others. Two companies of the King's Own were likewise dedicated to patrolling the city to combat such thieving activity. With a state of war declared, the King's Own and other military units could be used in such a manner, and should the thieves be killed as they attempted to flee, well. . .it was war. How was someone to know that this wasn't a saboteur or enemy combatant of some type?

Cooks were hurriedly smoking slaughtered beef and parching or dehydrating vegetables for use by troops manning defensive positions in the coming days, as it would be unlikely they would have the chance to sit at table to take mess.

Soldiers and those who would be helping with the fighting spent the evening preparing weapons that had not yet been sharpened or otherwise prepared. Narrow barrels were filled with arrows and placed in strategic places around the defenses along with spare swords, pikes and even axes and lances. Any weapon might be the one needed, or the one that would help save a life or even the palace itself.

Ministers that had refused to abandon the defenders of the city went from place to place praying with and for the defenders, seeking a Divine guidance for the coming storm and His protection for their defenders and their strength, courage and even their aim. Some might have found it odd that a man of God might pray for such a thing, but Soulanie ministers realized and recognized that any free people required the services of men willing to commit violence to protect that freedom when needed.

Surgeons, of which there were few, prepared the implements of their trade as nurses hurried to amass bandages and clear areas suitable for operating on and treating wounded. Stephanie Corsin's expertise, along with her parents, was much appreciated in this most trying of times as they offered last minute suggestions and assistance for ensuring proper care and treatment. A wounded trooper in service to Soulan had a far better chance of returning to that service that an Imperial soldier or Tribal warrior, thanks in no small part to the work of such families.

Hardy men and women who would not be much help in battle worked through the night shoring up positions for defenders to occupy and adding supports to the walls and gates of the palace citadel. Their work would be priceless should those same areas be hit with overwhelming numbers of enemy troops come daylight.

Fall back positions were created inside the main walls, areas of 'last stand' strength in the event that they were unable to hold the enemy outside. Places where the struggle could be continued in smaller confines that might enable survivors to hold out just a little longer, waiting for help they knew was coming, just not how long it would take to arrive or how much help it would be.

Day break would find many sleeping where they had finished their work, waiting to see where else they might be needed. Soldiers would sleep where they were to fight, so as to be nearby if needed quickly. Patrols of Constables and Watchmen began to collapse their routes as day neared, even as teams of scouts made their way toward the edge of the city to watch for their enemy's approach.

They would not be ready, but they would at least be prepared.

-

In the midst of all this preparedness hustle and bustle came Roda Finn, wading through the fortress leading a small wagon burdened with his precious books, sketches and blueprints. He had been assigned a small secure area inside the palace proper at the order of Winnie Hubel and had a man and two women of the palace staff to assist him in securing his very valuable property from harm or theft.

As he passed two men, he was able to catch part of their argument, just enough to know that there was a problem with the Royal Storehouses. Something about being 'left to the enemy devices'.

"Could you please continue on and see to this?" he asked the man leading the mule that pulled the small wagon. "I've just heard of a problem that needs my attention. I dislike leaving this undone, but we are so pressed for time." Roda had learned to treat others kindly in times of need, especially those who didn't work directly for him. He had yet to manage not to yell at his employees, as they usually deserved it, at least in his eyes.

"Of course, professor," the man nodded.

"Please, please ensure the safety of these items," Roda almost begged. "They are quite irreplaceable in some cases, and all are very valuable."

"We'll make sure they are safe, sir," the man promised.

"Thank you ever so much," Roda smiled, bowed to the two women, and then rushed back to the two men.

"Excuse me?" he cut into the argument. "Did I overhear you to say that our storehouses would be subject to the enemy's intrusions?"

"Who are you then?" one demanded, but the other held up a hand.

"Master Finn," the man bowed slightly. "Yes, that is a concern. We are currently moving everything we can into the fortress, but a great deal will have to be left behind. I'm afraid there is no help for it."

"Do we assume that they will destroy these storehouses?" Roda asked. He didn't recognize the soldier who recognized him, but did recognize the black and green livery of the Royal Regiments.

"Once they have taken what they want, that is probable, sir," the man confirmed. "Something on your mind?" he asked.

"I might have a way to make the enemy pay for that," Roda mused to himself more than anyone else. "I'll need some help, and I suppose. . .yes, I should definitely get permission. I shall have to see the King, I suppose."

"I can't help you with that, Master Finn," the soldier grinned.

"That's quite all right, soldier," Finn returned the smile. "I know someone who can."

-

"I can't just be taking you to the King just like that, Roda!" Whip shook his head. "Man ain't got time for jabber jawin' with ever Tom, Dick and Harry around here!"

"Good Archer, I am not either of those three gentlemen, and nor do I engage in such activity as. . .'jabber jawing', did you call it? I have an idea that will help defend the city but I absolutely need the King's permission to carry it out. It may be he would rather not, and in this case it will definitely be better to get permission rather than try for forgiveness later on."

"And your own daughter is soon to be King," he pointed out. "So yes, you can carry me to see the King. And I would not ask were it not important," he added.

Whip looked at the fussy little inventor for another minute before sighing. Shaking his head, he turned to the men he had working for him.

"You fellas, you carry on while I get this done. Be back soon 's I can be, yeah?" The man nodded in reply, never slowing as they unloaded the wagon. Whip turned back to Finn.

"Well, come on, then!"

-

"I estimate we're no more than two hours ride from Nasil," Stone told his division and brigade commanders. "We will be moving as soon as there is enough light to see, and we will ride until we're just beyond sight of the city. Once that far we will stop for fifteen minutes to check gear and make nature calls, hydrate our men and get reports from our scouts. Scouts will make their way further into the city for reconnaissance as the main column heads for the river bridge here," he pointed to his map, "just across from the main thoroughfare of their city. Assuming we can cross the bridge and attack, we will follow that road with flankers and vanguard out until we encounter resistance or hit their palace, whichever comes first."

"Intelligence reports over the years had always indicated that the Soulanie Royal Palace was heavily fortified and could function as a fortress in times of attack. We've never been able to do this before," he told them, looking at each man in turn.

"We're about to make Imperial history, gentlemen, by being the very first Imperial forces to reach the Soulan Royal City and attack it. It would be even more historic if we could actually do a great deal of damage when we get there. But," he raised a hand and looked at them all once more.

"But," he continued after making eye contact with each one. "We are not pirates, we are not rapists, we are not Tribal scum. We do not kill civilians or molest them, am I understood? Kill anyone who actively attacks you with a weapon in hand, but an angry, screaming woman with a rolling pin in her hand in not an enemy combatant. An angry, screaming woman with a bow on the other hand, is."

"Don't make me have to say this again, gentlemen," he warned. "Keep your men under control. Even a hint of what we found outside Lovil with those swabbies among our troops and I will have someone's head, starting with the guilty party's commanding officer and working my way down."

"We have worked too hard to win some respect to throw it away with such behavior," his voice softened finally. "Our men are well trained and disciplined, and I want them acting like it. If we behave as professionals, we will be considered professionals, by our enemies and our own people alike. If that isn't important to you then I've probably got the wrong people serving in my command. Do I make myself completely clear on that?"

"Sir!" every voice agreed, every head nodded. Some even smiled proudly.

"Our goal is to do as much damage as possible for as little cost as possible," Stone continued. "We will reduce every militarily important building we come across, or else burn it to the ground. If we have to burn it and there are enemy inside, we will offer them the chance to flee unmolested so long as they throw down arms and aren't trying to kill us. We don't have the ability to take prisoners and I'm not a murderer. But we will not leave a single resource for our enemy to use that we can help. Understood?"

Again, all heads nodded.

"Very well," Stone stood. "Brief your men and get some sleep. And gentlemen, know that I'm proud of all of you," he added softly. "I'm proud to know you, to serve with you, and to be your commanding officer. Please make sure your men know that as well. Good night."

He watched them go in silence, making their way back to their commands, brigade commanders clustered around their division leaders for still more instructions and pep talking.

Tomorrow would see them do something no other Imperial Army command had ever accomplished, but he was under no illusions that doing so would be easy. The Soulanies would fight like a mother wolf over her cubs to protect their 'kingdom'.

How many of his men would gather around their fires tomorrow night, looking at empty places where their friends and mess mates were sitting tonight?

He tried not to think about that as he got ready to turn in. Tomorrow would be a long day, and be here far too soon.

-

Not so many crow flight miles from where Stone was getting ready for bed, Nelson Pierce was staring into the open flames of his own fire as his men bedded down and cared for their horses by torch light. They had ridden until it was literally dangerous to keep going along the darkened back roads they were taking to try and arrive at the Royal City as soon after the enemy as possible.

"We're doing the best we can, sir," Whit said quietly as he walked to Pierce's fire.

"Men are doing fine," Pierce nodded. "Couldn't ask for more, or for better from them."

"They won't be there too far ahead of us," Whit tried again.

"Any ahead of us is too much, Colonel," Pierce sighed. "Still, it's all that can be done. Once I let them get by us, it was predetermined that they would be able to inflict at least some damage. I just hope our riders got through with a warning."

"They were our best riders, mounted on our best horses and each leading a remount," Whit reasoned. "There's no reason to think that our men, who know these hills as well as any man living, didn't get there well ahead of the enemy, sir."

"I hope they got to Cove Canton as quickly," Pierce added with a nod. "Whatever help they can send may well make the difference."

-

"We could keep going," Hildebrand said quietly. "Might make the city by or even before daybreak."

"I thought on it," Chad nodded in the dark. "But if we did, and then can't get inside the defenses, our men and horses will be too tired to fight out in the open. It would be hard on them even from behind the defenses."

"It might have been once," Hildebrand pointed out. "But in case you haven't noticed, none of the men are suffering from hard travel, Bret. They're holding up well and so are their horses for now. I will admit that their horses will likely be tired if we ride all night, but assuming they pull everyone into the fortress, then if we can get inside it won't matter about the horses. Our men would be well able to stand to fight after just one night's ride."

Chad considered that. It was true that the training they had only just finished had left them in excellent physical condition. There was every reason to think that as slow as they would have to proceed in the dark, moving by torch light, their men would be more than able to fight come morning. Even the horses would likely be in decent shape, though that in no way meant they would be able to spend a day carrying a rider in combat.

Still, if they could make it before the enemy raid, and get inside the fortifications, that would go a long way toward stiffening the city's defenses and boosting the morale of the people inside. Would their contribution from inside those defenses be any better than if they were outside the walls, fighting on horseback? Hildebrand had been right in that their men alone, unsupported, wouldn't be very effective against so many.

But inside they would become force multipliers, wouldn't they? Well trained, combat experienced men who were all experts with sword and bow and lance. Conditioned to be able to fight for hours or even days on end with little in the way of rest, food or even water. To fight on foot or from horseback against a numerically superior foe and do so with every expectation of victory.

They'd done it before, after all.

"Call a fifteen-minute rest," he ordered suddenly. "Pass the word for officers call at the end of that break."

"Yes sir."

-

A half-day's ride behind Chad, Preston Wilbanks cursed the onset of dark as it had forced his men to halt. Making camp, his men were sitting at ease, in no way tired after two days hard ride so far. He shook his head in amazement at how much difference their conditioning had made.

If only they had some light! His men could easily continue on into the late evening and still be able to function the next day. He longed for the hunter's moon to be shining above them, but knew he might as well wish to already be in Nasil ready to defend the Royal City. The road through here was strewn with rocks and uneven patches that simply waited for the chance to hobble horses and men alike in the dark. Even torch light would be insufficient.

So regardless of his men's ability to continue on, they had no choice but to stop for the evening, still well over a day's ride from their destination. As he sat dejectedly by his fire, he wondered how Chad and his men were doing.

Maybe they were further along. He hoped so. Because there wasn't a damn thing he could do tonight to get his men any closer until morning.

CHAPTER NINETEEN

-

Scouting was dangerous work in the best of times. In times of war it was inherently more dangerous. At night, it was infinitely worse. Every sound could be an enemy. Every movement made noise, but it could be an animal as easy as a man. Experience would enable a man to tell the difference, but fear and anxiety could take that experience away when it was needed most.

With work likely to be going on right up until the moment of attack, Colonel Stang had expressed to his scout parties how important their mission was. Warning of any imminent attack in a timely manner was absolutely imperative to the safety of work parties outside the walls as well as the people within those walls so long as the gates were still open.

His most inexperienced scouts were to the east of the city, the direction least likely to see an enemy approach in the hours before daybreak. It was also the most likely direction that help would appear from, and the young men stationed on that side of the city knew this.

Carl Sweet was sixteen years old, just old enough to have been inducted into the militia ahead of the military buildup in preparation for the war. Still technically in training, he had remained in Nasil as part of the City Guard when the rest of the military had gone north. He had been happy and sad at the same time. Sad because he wasn't doing his part, happy that he might live to be a year older. It was a paradox he didn't have enough life experience to understand yet, but he still knew it was there.

Being sent to the least likely area to see enemy presence had presented him with another paradox, this one a bit of shame faced relief that he would not have to potentially face a horde of enemy horsemen as they rode into the city bent on death and destruction. Yet, he didn't want to be seen as cowardly or be thought of a someone who would allow his fear to prevent him from doing his duty.

He spoke of these things to no one, not realizing that he didn't have to, as every man around him had almost the same feelings. And many of them the same concerns, not wanting to allow their desire for self-preservation to stand in the way of their serving their kingdom or their fellow man.

He needn't have worried over much, since at sixteen no one really expected him to have everything figured. It was completely natural to feel fear, and at sixteen even more so. He was just beginning to live so fear of dying was only natural.

So, Carl Sweet lay atop the roof of a three-story building on the eastern side of Nasil, shivering in the pre-dawn cold as he stood his watch. He wished for a source of heat, even if it was just a small barrel burning sticks and twigs, but he even if it wouldn't have been a risk of fire, the light would be visible for miles in this darkened area of the city. So, he huddled wrapped in his blanket as he listened more than looked for anyone approaching his post.

As dawn came closer the air seemed to grow correspondingly colder, forcing young Carl to retreat further and further into his blankets for warmth. It also made him sleepy, and it became a struggle for the young man to stay awake, a struggle he was gradually losing.

And so it was that the group of horsemen were right on top of him when the sound of their approach jerked Carl wide awake and saw him on his feet before he'd even thought about what he was doing.

"Halt!" he cried at once, never thinking about what he would do if this were an enemy.

Below him a half-dozen bows were instantly trained on his position. The horsemen were illuminated by torches burning all down their line and Carl knew a moment of fear as he wondered if this was the enemy, come to burn the city.

"Identify yourself," he called more calmly, his heart still racing and the beat sounding like war drums in his ears.

"I'm Colonel Bret Chad," a voice floated calmly up to him. "Prince Parno's Black Sheep, Third Battalion."

"Sir?" Carl blurted as the words sank in. "Are you serious?"

"I'm rarely not serious, son," the voice sounded mirthful despite the reply. "Who might you be?"

"I'm Private Carl Sweet of the City Guard, sir!" Carl almost snapped to attention even in the dark. "This is Scouting Post number Eleven, sir!"

"Well, Private Carl Sweet of Scouting Post number Eleven, can you pass us into the city or do we need an escort, or what?"

"Sir, I'll be down in just a second and take you in myself!" Carl promised. Grabbing his gear, he bounded down the steps in rear of the building where his horse was tethered. It was the work of only a few seconds for him to tighten the straps on his saddle and then Chad and his men could hear the horse moving down the alley.

"Are you sure it's okay for you to leave your post, soldier?" Tom Hildebrand asked.

"Sir, in the event of help arriving, or of my getting sight of enemy approaching, I was to return to the city and report in person. No reason not to take you gents with me. I'm sure I'll be sent back as soon they take my report."

"Detail two men to stand guard here for one hour," Hildebrand ordered a man behind him, who nodded and went to do so. "They are to come in when Private Sweet returns, or at the end of that hour. Let them know what his orders were."

"Let's go then, Private," Chad said after Hildebrand was finished. "We've been riding all night and we're tired and hungry and our horses need to be fed and rested."

"Sir, yes sir!" Sweet almost yelled and took off at nearly a gallop toward the palace, his fear forgotten with a battalion of the Prince's Own now alongside.

-

"Sergeant of the Guard!" the call was soft for all that it carried. "Water Gate reports movement to the east. Horses coming. Many horses!"

"Right then," the Sergeant stood. "Go and get the Captain, then start passing the word to prepare to stand to. Don't wake the lads until the last minute, but get the on-watch troops awake and aware. Go on now," he shooed. The half-dozen men took off for each destination as the Sergeant made his way to the Water Gate, so called because the road that ran through that gate lead to the river. He could hear the horses himself by the time he got near the gate and waved to the sentry as he tried to make a report. The two waited together as the gas lamps in the city streets illuminated the front of the column, showing a large body of troopers behind the front rank.

"Sergeant, those are Dynasty colors," the sentry said softly.

"Really?" came the sarcastic reply. "I had thought sure they were the Emperor's Bloody Guards!"

The sentry muttered under his breath at that but otherwise remained silent. He was just trying to help. He'd let the damn sergeant figure things out for himself from now on.

"Column halt!" a quiet command went up along with a raised hand. The column slowed and then halted not a spear's throw from the gate.

"Sergeant of the Guard, reporting from Scout Post Eleven," a very young voice came from the dark. "Reporting arrival of Prince Parno's Own Third Battalion, along the East Road!"

"Thank the Maker," the sentry murmured softly.

"Amen," the sergeant agreed. "Approach and be recognized!" he called. Carl Sweet road forward with Colonel Chad and four troopers as escort.

"Sergeant," Chad nodded his head. "I assume you have room for my men and horses inside? We've ridden a long way and could use a meal and some rest in case we're attacked this morning."

"Yes sir!" the sergeant saluted. "Open the gate! Pass the word to stand down! Captain Winters to the Water Gate!" he called out to the night behind him.

Ten minutes later the men of Parno's Own were stripping saddles from tired horses and hoping that they got a hot breakfast cooked by the palace kitchen.

"Colonel!" Captain Winters exclaimed as he entered the stables. "Man, am I glad to see you, sir!" he extended his hand and Chad took it.

"Captain," he nodded. "Looks like you all have been busy of late."

"That we have, sir," Winters nodded. "We're about as prepared as we can be at this point. Having your command inside will sure make things stronger. We hadn't counted on any help before maybe this time tomorrow at the best. By tomorrow I don't mean this morning, either," he amended.

"We rode through the night by torch light," Chad told him. "We were already down to the better roads and we weren't tired, so we pushed on. Lost a man and three horses, but we might have lost more than that just trying to get inside tomorrow if we'd gotten here too late."

"True," Winters nodded. "We've no idea as yet how strong a force we're facing, just that the Brigadier in command noted it was 'considerable'. They had blunted the enemy's advance in the hills north of here, but that meant the way around their flank was open. Nor stole a march on 'em and was a day gone before they realized it. If the time is right the way we've got it, they should be here today."

"General Wilbanks will be no more than a day behind us with his division, just out of training at Cove Canton," Chad remarked. "So assuming we can hold out for today, we should get some relief tomorrow at some point."

"Probable that the force following the Nor will arrive by or even before then as well," Winters informed him. "They were trying to cut the enemy's time down by going through the back roads and such, but that means they won't be able to ride even until dusk. In those hills that's just asking for men and horses to die."

"So, we've got help coming, but not until-"

"Captain!" Mason Stang's voice cut Chad off. "I understand we've had-" he stopped as he noted the activity around the stable area.

"Colonel Bret Chad, Prince Parno's Regiment," Chad said simply as he offered his hand. He didn't have to brag and he knew it. He wouldn't have anyway, but knowing it wasn't needful was satisfying.

"Damn glad to see you, Colonel," Stang shook his hand heartily. "How in the world did you make here so quick, and in the dark to boot?"

"We ride longer than this in training," Chad shrugged. "The distance wasn't that great. The darkness was a challenge, but we came in by torchlight. What's the situation, Colonel? I have seven companies of effectives, just under nine hundred men. All combat veterans."

Stang tried not to gape and was barely successful. He had been openly doubtful of Winter's statements concerning the Prince's Own and their ability to move and fight above and beyond regular units but. . .if Chad and his men had made the trip from Cove Canton…

"When did you leave Cove Canton, Colonel?" he asked politely.

"Two mornings past, now," Chad said after reminding himself this was the third morning. "We left twenty minutes after we got the message."

"Very impressive, Colonel," Stang complimented.

"It's normal for us," Chad shrugged easily. "Any idea of the force we face?"

"Not as yet," Stang admitted, deciding to pass over the 'normal for us' statement.

It was probably true and there was no question these men were here, after all. "We hope to get at least some idea of their strength as they come into the city. I expect them to separate at that point so we may not get a chance to evaluate their numbers after that."

"Like as not," Chad nodded, thinking. "Are you planning to oppose them outside the walls at all?"

"No," Stang shook his head. "We need every man just to man the walls. Your arrival will help us do that, but we are still woefully undermanned. This place is meant to be defended by a division of troops, and we have a short brigade, many of whom are City Guard, Constables and what have you. The Palace Guard and King's Own are the only professional soldiers in the city, and few of them have seen combat."

"All of my men have," Chad said again. "Let us eat and rest for a bit and we'll be ready to stand posts. I'd prefer not to have to until we have enemy contact if that's all right. We've been in the saddle for almost twenty-four hours."

"Of course," Stang nodded. "Let's see to getting you a hot meal."

-

Roda Finn, Whip Hubel and a half dozen others were not there to see Chad and his men entering the palace fortifications. Instead they were visiting their ninth storehouse since the King had approved Roda's plan.

"And this will deny the enemy the contents of the storehouses?" he had asked.

"Yes sir, but in doing so will almost certainly destroy them," Roda had replied, on his very best behavior for this meeting. "But killing some of their people in the meanwhile, Sire," he added.

"How do you plan to do this?" Memmnon was curious.

"I will implant a number of devices at each place that are linked to the doors as a trap spring of sorts, which will fire the charges set along-"

"Roda, give 'im the short version!" Whip all but hissed.

"I am going to plant mines inside the storehouses and lace them with the magnesium sulfate that I've been experimenting with," Roda semi-glared at Whip before returning his gaze to the King. "The mines will kill or severely injure anyone close to them and with the proper materials around them will start a fire as well. The magnesium will prevent them from putting the fire out. It will also have a terrible impact on anyone it hits. Someone who escapes being killed might well wish to have died instead should they find themselves coated in burning magnesium sulfate."

"The enemy will likely burn the storehouses anyway," Memmnon mused. "At least that is what I expect."

"That was my understanding as well, which is what made me think of this, Sire," Roda admitted. "If they're going to be lost no matter what, why not make use of it?"

"And if they do not enter the warehouse, would you be able to prevent the explosion and fire later?" Memmnon asked. "Disarm the trap, so to speak? That we might be able to make use of the storehouse and the stores within safely?"

"I can," Roda looked surprised. "I hadn't considered that a possibility to be honest, but . . . it will take longer to do, and you must make sure that no one other than myself or my assistants enter those storehouses until they are cleared, but . . . yes, Sire. I can."

"Mister Hubel, do you think this will work?" Memmnon asked his father-in-law-to-be. "Is it worth doing?"

"Aye, milord, it is," Whip nodded. "Roda is a little fussy at times, and temperamental as an old mule come harvest time, but . . . his gadgets are something fierce to behold. If you think the enemy'll be firing the storehouses, might as well let him do it. They'll at least pay for everything they get."

"Then you may proceed, Mister Finn," Memmnon said after a moment of silence. "Show me what it is that you do, assuming the enemy behave as we believe."

And so it was that Roda was setting the 'spring' for his ninth trap that evening, now into the wee hours of morning. Whip was watching anxiously as the little inventor was beginning to show signs of strain and fatigue, and this really wasn't a job you wanted to be distracted in.

"And there," Finn stood, his back popping and cracking as he did so. "All finished. If they open these doors, and they shall have to open at least one to gain entrance, then the mines will go off. Where to next?" he asked.

"Back to the palace," Whip said flatly. "We're finished, Roda. You're too tired to keep doing this and you just sent Carl and Billy both away to see about placing mines around the palace itself. We're done. Can't risk you getting yourself blowed up. Prince be like to take my fool head off for allowing it."

"But we aren't done!" Roda protested. "There are at least six more storehouses are there not?"

"And when any of these go off, they probably won't bother trying to get into them," Whip was shaking his head. "We got all of the ones between us and the bridge, and around us out to the edge of the city. They're either empty, or you done set a trap in 'em. And you're just flat too valuable to lose to something like this, Roda. Now stop arguing and get up in that wagon. We're finished I tell ya. You done good, mind you," he slapped the smaller man on the back. "You did real good."

"Thank you," Finn mentally checked his back for broken vertebrae. "If you insist then we shall return. I admit I am weary."

"Then load up, and let's get outta here," Whip ordered.

-

The two Imperial scouts stood inside the tree line overlooking the target bridge leading into the Soulan capitol. They had ridden the last ten miles in the dark, picking their way on foot to get here just at first light. Behind them the rest would be already in the saddle and riding toward them.

"Is it just me or does that place look deserted?" one asked, sweeping the city with his glass.

"It's creepy," the second agreed. "Like a ghost town."

"You know there has to be people down there somewhere," the first remarked after a minute of continued sweeping.

"Got one man, riding away, left side to the bridge," the second reported.

"Headed for their palace it looks like."

"That's the palace?" one asked. "How do you know?"

"General said it would be the biggest building in the city," two shrugged. "That's definitely the largest building."

They continued to watch but saw no one else. After ten minutes they exchanged a glance.

"I have to assume they're all in that. . .that palace, then," one decided.

"I don't see anyone anywhere else," two agreed.

"We better go tell the General."

-

Not everyone was in that. . .that palace. There were several men hidden around the bridge with orders to stay hidden and make no movement that might attract attention until and unless they saw something themselves.

One of them observed the two Imperial cavalrymen riding out of the tree line and back down the Trade towards the north.

"Time to go lads," the senior sergeant told his men. "Our job to sneak back and let them know what we've seen. The others will remain behind to sound the alarm when the time comes."

Ten minutes later the group of five were walking their horses toward the palace, waiting to mount up until their movements would be shielded by buildings. They avoided the Water Gate and instead made their way to the Eastern Gate, riding inside the fortress from a direction that could not be observed from across the river.

"At least two scouts looked us over sir," the Sergeant was reporting a total of twenty minutes after the fact. "Slipped out and away afterward, straight back down the Trade. No idea if they twigged to anything or not, but they did watch over us a bit. May have been others we didn't see, but them two was dressed as Imperial soldiers."

"Very well," Stang nodded. "Rest your detail and get fed. You won't be called to duty unless there's an attack, so if you can get some sleep, do so."

"Sir," the sergeant saluted and went his way. Stang pursed his lips for a second in thought then turned to his aide.

"Order all scouts other than the Eastern Road and the bridge detail inside," he said. "We know they're coming, and where from. No sense anyone being caught outside."

-

Stone listened to the report in silence, allowing his subordinates to ask questions as they saw fit. Finally, as they grew quiet, he spoke.

"You saw no one other than the one rider?"

"No sir," the senior scout shook his head. "I'm sure there were people there, sir, as we could see smoke from cooking fires and what have you, but there was no movement in the city. That palace was too far away to be able to note people moving."

"It looked deserted you say?" Stone wasn't liking that.

"Yes sir, though as I say we could see smoke from fires."

"Very well," he nodded a dismissal. When they were gone, he looked at his division heads.

"It sounds as if they know we're coming," he said without fanfare.

"I don't see how, but I also don't see how it matters," Silas Weir shrugged. "Their army is far to the north, at least three days hard ride. That bunch we were facing back there," he waved in the direction they had come, "could be here, or at least close by, but if they had the strength to face us in the open, they would have done it then."

"I would expect no more than two, perhaps three regiments in the city," Blake said. "They have Royal regiments, but they're mostly for show."

"I wouldn't place too much faith in that," Baxter was shaking his head. "Their Royal Regiments are elite guards, General," he said to Stone. "Chosen from among their very best. They may dress flashy and serve as guardsmen, but they didn't start out that way."

"How do you know all that?" Blake demanded.

"I. Can. Read." Baxter grated the words out, tired of being asked that. "There are intelligence briefings available on this kind of thing, and history books speak of how Soulan is organized, at least so far as we know. We know more about their social structures then their military, but we aren't completely in the dark."

"Enough," Stone decided to head that argument off before it officially started. "Even if they are 'elite' regiments, if there really are only three or so, we'll have the numbers on them." He paused, clearly thinking things out.

"We're going across, assuming the bridge will carry us," he declared suddenly. "It's just too good an opportunity to pass up," he raised a hand when Baxter appeared about to object. "If they have withdrawn into their palace, then they're all in one place. We can have the run of the town and do as much damage as possible. Even just the morale boost of knowing we attacked their 'royal city', plus the damage it will do to southern moral, is enough reason to attempt it. We've never been this close before, and may not be again for some time. This is a perfect opportunity to show the Emperor we've been worth the money spent on us, and to show that infantry general that we can get the job done when he uses us right."

All of his division heads agreed with that sentiment, including Baxter. Wilson's disparaging had struck deep among the northern horsemen. This was a chance to prove him wrong.

"Scouts out, flank and van into position!" Stone called once he was mounted again. "Flankers and vanguard will cross over ahead and form a bridgehead for the rest of us. Exercise caution and do not be led into a trap. Wait for the rest of us before you try to seek out the enemy. Let's go!"

After days of hard riding, losses and no small amount of ridicule, Norland 1st Imperial Cavalry Corps was about to make a definite impact on the war effort.

-

"You know, there's a chance they won't even hit the city," Hildebrand remarked as he and Chad made their way to the ramparts over the palace walls to take a look.

"Why wouldn't they?" Chad asked, more to pass the time than anything. Two-

and-a-half hours of sleep had just made him more irritable than rested.

"Well, think about it," Hildebrand shrugged. "If they're in this part of the country to draw forces away from the main war effort, then attacking and running won't do that. If the attack is over and the enemy is already moving out of the area then what good is sending troops here?"

"Point," Chad nodded. "But until and unless we verify that the enemy has in fact moved out of our territory all together, then they remain a threat to us. Which means we still have to dispatch units to make sure they're gone, or to run them to ground."

"We both know that unsupported cavalry can't operate indefinitely in enemy territory," Hildebrand argued.

"So long as they can raid our stores and use them against us, they can keep going for a good while," Chad shrugged. "I don't know how much they managed to save, but there are over twenty storehouses in and around this city alone that will be filled with grain, smoked meats, dried fruits and vegetables, even corn and oats. Feed man or beast with almost any of it and keep them going for a good while."

"I had overlooked that," Hildebrand sighed. "So, I guess they can pretty much stay here until the food runs out."

"No," Chad shook his head. "Wilbanks has about nine thousand men, all trained to Black Sheep standards. Add in our group and the two Royal regiments and we're looking at about thirteen to fourteen thousand men, plus however any that Brigadier, Pierce, has with him. Those are good odds for us on our own ground. When he gets here, we drive them out or kill them. We just have to make sure we preserve our fighting strength as much as possible to add to his while protecting the palace and the King until Wilbanks and his men can get here."

"Easy then," Hildebrand snorted.

"Exactly."

-

Stone's cavalry were across the bridge and into the city in good order and short time. The scouts still deployed along the river almost waited too long to escape, running from the van of Imperial troops just as they entered the city.

Seeing the enemy before them, the Imperial troopers gave chase, forgetting their orders for a moment. They followed the southern troopers right up to the main palace gate, where the scouts wheeled suddenly and fled around the palace walls. Thinking they had their enemy trapped, the Imperial troops tried to follow.

-

"Here they come," Chad said gently. "Ready to fire on my command and not before," he ordered as he walked the ramparts behind his men and selected others from inside, including Whip and Winnie Hubel.

Stang had asked Chad to head that part of the wall and command the first encounter as he watched the overall battle develop from the bell tower. Moore, meanwhile, had spread the remainder of his and Stang's troops along the remaining walls, supported by Winnie's auxiliary archers, the City Guard, Constables, Watchmen and any and everyone else that could shoot a bow even marginally well.

In the center of the palace grounds were two companies of Chad's men and three more from the two palace regiments. Five hundred men in the reserve along with another seven hundred civilians who might last two to five minutes in combat.

With them were Roda Finn's two trebuchets and his 'gadgets'.

Something else Roda had brought to the palace were a wagon full of his mines. Production of the mines was running wide open when news of the attack came so there were a surplus of them available. The squat clay containers ringed the palace grounds now and each wall had twenty sharp-eyed troopers with crossbows loaded with the flint tipped bolts, waiting for the order to fire.

Stang had doubted the mines ability to make a difference but both Winters and later Chad had been extremely happy to hear that the fussy inventor had them and assured the Palace Guard commander that they were well worth the effort to place and fire. He had acceded to their advice even as he clung to his belief that the mines and trebuchets would be useless in the coming battle. The trebuchets were normally used against infantry, or against fortifications, using large stones as ammunition. The iron balls that Roda had brought would probably do some damage he admitted, but nothing like enough to deter a cavalry charge. Still, it didn't take that many men to man them, and any help was appreciated, so again he allowed it.

Stang was extremely conscious of the fact that his King was standing beside him in the bell tower, observing the action below. Of course, the King's attention was focused primarily on the front gate where his betrothed and her father had joined the defense.

And the argument which had preceded that decision would be long remembered in the palace.

-

"You can't do that," Memmnon said flatly. "I refuse to allow it."

"Excuse me?" Winnie's eyes narrowed. "I thought I heard you say 'allow'. But that can't be right."

"I did and it is," Memmnon refused to balk. "There is no reason, none, for you to engage in this battle unless we are faced with being overrun. Placing you on the fortifications is dangerous and unnecessary and I will not allow it."

"You know, we aren't married yet," Winnie told him flatly. "I've been training those women for weeks, and my father will be there as well. Most of those men up there I either taught to use a bow, or taught them to use it better. There is no way that I will allow them to stand there and fight while I do nothing. I have listened to you, to Stephanie, to Parno, to Edema and everyone else about how us women didn't belong in battle. How we were a distraction. Weaker, more delicate, unable to cope with hygiene issues and the list just goes on and on and on."

"Well, this time we're facing an attack right here at home! And something you men seem to forget is while you may think us women can't handle a fight, we can damn sure still die in one at the hands of an enemy. Do you think them Tribal Warriors who are fighting with them heathen Nor will care a damn that we're women? From what I hear they be more like to enjoy the fact that we're women, not to mention that we can't fight back cause we're weaker and more delicate."

"You done as much as admitted that we prob'ly can't hold this place for more 'n a few days unless we get some help. I might as well fight now as fight when we're all but beat. And since you ain't my husband as yet, it ain't your place to tell me what I can and can't be doing. You could have asked me not to, and I might have listened to that. But you can't make me stay here and not fight when you already done got women standing on the wall, bow in hand. Even a King can't deny his people the right to protect themselves!"

"Are you aware that your accent really comes to the fore when you're angry?" Memmnon smiled suddenly and was rewarded with a furious blush from his bride-to-be.

"Don't try and be all cute and get around me," she all but growled, trying to keep her gruff determination in place.

"So, you admit you think I'm cute?" Memmnon asked, his smile widening. "I don't think you've ever told me that."

Winnie's face had grown even redder at that but she would not be distracted or deterred.

"Stop that!" she bellowed. "Don't change the subject! The simple fact is that the only person in this whole place who's a better shot than I am is my Pa! They need my help, and the fact you don't like it won't change that!"

"And what do I do if something happens to you?" he asked her suddenly, all pretense and humor now gone. "Have you thought of that?"

"Reckon you find someone better suited to be a Queen than I am," Winnie shrugged, suddenly uncomfortable with his attention. "That's all."

"That's all, is it?" Memmnon nodded absently. "Well, if it means so little to you then by all means, do go and join the battle, Miss Hubel. You are quite correct that even the King cannot deny someone the right of self-defense, nor would I if I could."

And just like that it was over. Memmnon walking away, leaving Winifred Hubel to watch him go, gawking at the sudden change in his behavior.

"What's wrong with you now?" she demanded to his back.

"Not a thing," he replied without turning. "I was wondering where things stood, I suppose, and now I know, don't I?"

She didn't think of anything else to say before he disappeared into his offices, the doorway firmly blocked by four heavily armed troopers.

Now dejected despite her 'victory', Winnie went to the apartment she shared with Stephanie and changed into her buckskins, collected her weapons, and headed for the main gate to be with her father.

-

"Open fire," Chad said calmly as the pursuing Imperial troops rode into range.

Almost one thousand bows released an arrow into the oncoming battalion that rampaged down the avenue toward the palace. Having seen the only opposition so far in the city, they were following with a little too much zeal and not near enough caution. Despite the warnings of their commanding general and their division commander, they were being very careless.

The front ranks took the brunt of the first volley as only a few archers thought to loft their arrows over the foremost riders. Several Imperial horsemen hit the ground with multiple arrows in them. Many of their horses suffered just as badly with some taking as many as a dozen hits.

The battalion commander was not in the front rank, his horse not being quite as fast as the men of the leading company. Seeing his men being torn to ribbons, he immediately began to scream orders to his men.

"Pull back! Fall back! Take our wounded with us and fall back!"

His men didn't have to be told twice. Grabbing fallen comrades who were still showing signs of life, they began to try and get clear before the next volley. They almost made it.

The second volley was lofted higher this time, Chad taking the time to order such before releasing the second round. Arrows once more flew down the street and again many of them found targets. More men falling, dying, screaming in pain and fury. More horses injured, though not so many as before, more bloodshed in the streets of Soulan.

"Retreat!" the battalion commander gave up on the notion of an organized withdrawal, electing to try and save as many of his men as he could. "Everyone pull back now!"

One final volley of archery fire caught the rearmost ranks before they could pass out of range, felling still more and ensuring a route of at least that one battalion.

"Cease fire," Chad ordered, his voice calm but carrying. "Cease fire! Report damage and casualties."

There were none. This time. The Imperials had been caught flat footed and it had cost them, but they wouldn't be caught like that again Chad knew.

From here on in, things would get messy.

-

"Is it me?" Stone looked from one division commander to the next. "Do I not speak clearly enough? Is that the problem? Because it's obvious there's a problem or my men wouldn't continue to die doing the very things I tell them not to!" By the time he finished he was screaming at nearly the top of his lungs, clearly excised.

"Did I not say to advance cautiously, with an eye toward the enemy having set an ambush for us?"

"Yes sir," the three men all nodded.

"And did I not say that if they were in that palace that we would sack the town rather than try to attack fortified positions manned by archers?" Stone pressed, his anger not easing in the least.

"Yes sir," the trio acknowledged.

"And yet, here I am, receiving a report that my vanguard battalion is a complete wreck that has suffered over thirty percent casualties in the very attack that I said we weren't going to attempt!"

"Many of that number are only slightly injured sir," Jerome Baxter tried to help the situation. "And we can place those who lost horses on the mounts of those who have fallen and regain some of th-"

"How does that make it better!" Stone cut him off savagely.

"I just meant that the losses would end up being somewhat less than first thought, sir," Baxter fought the urge to sigh. It hadn't been his me so he wasn't really in any trouble for this, just a co-recipient of an ass-chewing.

"Which still leaves-, never mind," Stone made a sudden slashing motion with his right hand. "Enough. What's done is done. Get scouts out around the city. Find any militarily important buildings, storehouses, armories, sundries and the like. Get a report on what's here and what we can do to it. We need to be moving as soon as possible, but I want to do as much damage as we can before then. Go!"

They went. Leaving a still seething Stone looking at the palatial fortress in the distance. Mocking him.

-

"Tom, you may well have been right," Chad noted as he watched the activity of the Norland cavalry through his scope.

"Huh?" Hildebrand looked at him in surprise. "What did you say?"

"I said you may have been right about their intentions," Chad repeated, not seeing the look on his second in command's face. "I don't believe they intend to attack us. Likely that battalion was acting on their own, possibly even against orders." He lowered the glass and looked at Hildebrand. "What?" he asked, finally noting the look Hildebrand was sporting.

"I'm still recovering from shock," Hildebrand told him.

"What?"

"Shock at your saying I might have been right," Hildebrand delivered straight-faced. Laughter rolled down the line from men of Third Battalion at their XO's antics.

"Well, it is a rare thing," Chad replied dead pan, and the laughter grew. "But as I was saying, even a blind pig will find an ear of corn on occasion, and you appear to have found one. I think they're going to do as much damage to the city as they can, but not attempt to carry this place."

"How much damage can they do that will affect the war effort I wonder?" Hildebrand mused, his comedic routine shelved now. "I don't know what's out there," he admitted.

"Nor do I," Chad nodded. "But I have to assume that Stang or Moore does. We'll have to wait and see."

-

"We'll have to wait and see what they do, Sire," Stang said. "They appear to be scouting the city at the moment. It is entirely possible that they will simply sack the city and run."

"That's bad for the city but it would mean very few casualties for us," Memmnon nodded absently. There were undoubtedly some people still in the city, diehards that would have refused to leave home or hearth for any reason. Whether the Nor would spare them or not he had no idea.

"They will likely destroy the stores we couldn't move," Stang sighed. "That will be a loss."

"It will, but we can move supplies north from other areas," Memmnon nodded again. "It will hurt us, but with the new settled areas of refugees and our opening of the Reserves for planting and harvesting we should be able to offset the loss. It will likely mean hard times in the immediate future, however, as well as a lean time before next spring."

"We can take the men outside the walls and try to-" Stang began but Memmnon held up a hand to silence him.

"No, Colonel. Under no circumstances. Parno mentioned something that has stuck with me these last weeks and most especially since this event began. It is easier to grow grain and other food than to replace a solider or horse lost in combat. They will damage the city, but she has seen damage in the past. They will steal and rob and burn, but we will rebuild. We will persevere because we must. Taking your men outside these walls would be tantamount to suicide. You would be outnumbered at least ten-to-one, and those odds are too great."

"Let them do what they will," he ordered. "They cannot remain here long, and we have men coming. So long as they do not try these walls, let them do as they will."

"Yes, Sire," Stang nodded his understanding. "It will be done."

CHAPTER TWENTY

-

The occupants of the palace fortifications watched all morning and into the afternoon as the Nor cavalry poured through town, looking into everything they could find. It was a systematic effort, the military officers noted, with no looting or wanton destruction of any kind visible from their vantage point. Instead it was as if the enemy soldiers were taking an inventory of the enemy's capitol.

Which it turned out was exactly what was happening.

"Reports, gentlemen," Stone ordered his division commanders as they assembled with him after lunch. He was still angry about the morning debacle and his terse speech showed it clearly.

"We have located fourteen storehouses, or warehouse type buildings so far," Weir began. "Five of them are empty, doors left open and not enough inside to feed a rat if one was inside. The rest are closed up tight still."

"Over two dozen sundry stores carrying everything from seeds to tools to clothes," Baxter went next. "None of them have anything of especially high value, just a lot of the regular kind of things that people need for everyday living. We also found a slaughterhouse out on the western edge of the city. There are twenty-nine head of cattle there and a handful of pigs, apparently awaiting slaughter."

"There are a number of high-end places that sell dresses, liquor, books and such like," Blake tallied the last bit. "Again, there's nothing really special about any of it at first glance, though it does all seem to be high quality. Some of the dress shop also have a good bit of high-priced jewelry as well. And there are at least nine banks in the city proper that we've found so far. Three of them are pretty impressive looking and might have gold stores inside, though without going in we can't really tell. They definitely look prosperous though."

"A few deserted armories around, probably militia oriented," Weir added. "Some are attached to what look like police offices or constable stations, whatever they call them. Clubs, swords, a few shields, but nothing really high quality. About what you would expect a city police force to be providing to new recruits."

"Same for blacksmiths," Baxter was looking at a piece of paper in his hand. "Seven of them, two that also appear to make swords. I found one beautiful sword hanging in the shop of the second one we visited. As good or better as anything I've ever seen to be honest. Lots of horseshoes, lance tips, arrowheads, the usual run of things that you see in such a place."

"No less than four schools," Blake reported as if he couldn't believe it. "I had always heard they had a thing for education down here, but I didn't really think it was true. Apparently, it is. These are big outfits. One is obviously a college of some kind, but the rest are-"

"How do you know it's 'obviously' a college?" Weir demanded, cutting him off.

"Might have been that sign out front that said 'college'," Blake's tone was acerbic at best.

"Will you two stop that shit!" Stone demanded. "Enough! Going down the list the storehouses are item one. Open them up and let's feed our troops on their stores, then burn them to the ground. Weir, Blake, your men on that. Baxter, your men on the banks. If there is gold there, we want it. See what's there and get it if we can use it. Keep scouts in place as we have been. I don't want to be caught off guard. Now get moving. I want to be settled in well before dark so we can see where we are and what's around us."

-

"Looks like they're preparing to break into places, sir," someone called from down the line.

"Going to sack the city then," Chad sighed. He wished there was a way to prevent it, but there was literally no way for so few to fend off so many outside these walls.

"Wish we had the strength to go out and meet 'em," Hildebrand said softly. "Arrogant bastards."

"Reckon they 'bout to get cut down a notch or two," Whip Hubel was looking through his own glass as he spoke. "They just about the try and force the door into-"

His sentence was cut off by a distant thunder that actually seemed to shake the ground slightly. Men and women not familiar with Roda Finn's experiments ducked instinctively, while the Sheep all raised up slightly to see the expected damage.

"Well, there goes that storehouse," Whip said calmly. "And at least two dozen Norland troopers I'd hazard, though it's hard to get a count from this far out."

-

"What in the hell was that?" Stone bellowed, though at no one in particular.

"Sir, it came from there," his aide pointed. Stone followed the point to see a column of smoke rising in the air.

"What's over there?" he demanded, already taking the reins of his horse from his enlisted runner.

"Sir, General Weir was examining a Soulanie stores house in that direction," the aide reported. "Could this be the 'witchcraft' that the infantry were all talking about?" he asked.

"There's no such thing as witchcraft," Stone snorted. "Something exploded, that's all. Probably grain dust. Happens once in a while back home as well. Grain breaks down and creates something called methane, which is highly flammable. Just a spark is all you need to set it o-"

He was cut off by a second explosion and a new column of smoke and fire rising into the air, this one some distance south of the first.

"Yes sir?" the aide asked as Stone looked on, shock evident on his face.

"Let's go," was all the general said.

-

"Pass the word to all commands, don't enter any buildings!" Weir was shouting as Stone arrived. "They may all be rigged like this! That's two already and nearly fifty men dead! Get moving!" Two dozen runners headed in all directions to carry the warning to the troops before anyone else fell victim to the traps the Soulanies had left behind.

"Silas! What the devil?" Stone demanded as he rode up.

"That's what it is alright," Weir replied grimly. "They've done something to these buildings, Brent. My men opened one and the damn thing blew up right in our faces. I thought it was a methane build up, like the grain bins back home in the cities?" He paused to see Stone nod in understanding.

"Then the next one went up the same way a minute later," Weir continued. "Had to be sabotage. Had to be. Two buildings doing this? One I would have chalked off to bad luck, but two has to be som-" he was cut off by a distant boom that rolled over them, accompanied by an equally distant new fire. The runners hadn't made it to everyone in time.

"Make that three," Weir sighed grimly. "This whole city is a damn deathtrap."

-

"How many buildings did you fix that way?" Hildebrand asked Whip as he watched a third column of smoke rising into the sky.

"Nine total," Whip answered, lowering his glass. "The hope was they'd hit them first and think all of them are like that."

"Looks like they hit them first anyway," Chad nodded. "That Roda just keeps surprising a man, doesn't he?" he asked with a grin in his voice if not on his face.

"He does that, Colonel," Whip nodded. "He does that."

-

"It would seem that I owe Mister Finn an apology," Memmnon managed to sound calm despite the excitement he was feeling at the trio of explosions in the distance. "He had indeed managed to hurt the enemy at no cost to us so far."

"I'd say three storehouses full of supplies is a cost, Sire," Brock murmured.

"Stores we had lost in any case, General, and houses the enemy would have almost certainly burned to the ground once they had taken their fill. It's entirely possible they will avoid the rest now for fear of getting similar results in all of them. That will save the remainder."

"And they might just burn them all and be done," Brock replied.

"Are they any less lost than they would have been the other way?" Memmnon asked, turning to look at his Inspectorate.

"No," Brock replied almost grudgingly. "No Sire, they aren't."

"Then grumbling about it is useless, wouldn't you say?" Memmnon's voice was still pleasant but there was now a hint of steel underneath. "We will have to observe what happens now."

-

Stone looked at the bodies of his men laid out in the street, covered with saddle blankets and ponchos. Men burned and disfigured beyond recognition in some cases, identified only by personal effects, or by process of elimination.

The wounded were worse, if only because their screams carried everywhere. Men burned, blinded, limbs torn from bodies, hair and clothing on fire and skin nearly melted off of bone. Clothing and metallic objects melted onto the skin in some cases, with no way to separate the two.

Damn this country, Stone thought savagely. Damn this cursed country and every person in it straight to hell.

"Report," he said dully as his division commanders assembled around him.

"We didn't find anything like this in the few buildings we had entered, but it was just three buildings of little consequence. Small sundries stores was all." Baxter knew that he and his men had dodged a very large bolt with their assignment.

"Lost seventy-three dead and one hundred six wounded, some who are sure not to live out the night," Weir reported bitterly. "Some of the burns. . . ."

"Forty-four dead and thirty-seven wounded," Blake sighed. His men had opened the final storehouse to explode. "And some of mine, perhaps a dozen, also probably won't live through the night. Not if God is merciful anyway," he added, his voice as bitter as him compatriot.

"What were they using that could do that?" Baxter asked into the silence. "It was like it made the fire burn hotter. I didn't know that was possible."

"What? Something you don't know?" Weir's sarcasm was thick.

"You know General, no one really likes a smart ass," Baxter growled. "If you don't want my input, feel free to ride away or close your ears. I'm sorry that you're an ignorant, poorly educated ass who was promoted based on something other than ability, but that does not mean that the rest of us-"

"I swear, the next one of you who starts an argument like this, dies," Stone interrupted tiredly. "I'm sick of hearing you three pick and peck at each other, and it either stops here or it stops here. Get me? You don't get other options. You stop doing it, or I'll stop you from doing it, permanently."

"Yes sir," Baxter said, actually contrite it seemed or at least chagrined. Weir just changed his glare from Baxter to Stone but said nothing.

"Pile combustibles around the storehouses," Stone ordered. "All of them. Burn every stinking one of them to the ground. Every store, every stable, every shop. Pull the doors from the banks with horses and see if they explode or burn or whatever. If they don't, then see if there's anything of value in there. Burn everything else."

"Everything," he repeated again, his eyes like coal. "Make them pay."

-

"There goes another one," Hildebrand noted as the fourth building in one hour went up in flames. "They're being a lot more cautious and careful than before, but they're going to burn the town."

"Even if they didn't mean to the fire will likely spread out of control anyway," Chad sighed. "If Wilbanks were here, and Pierce, we could muster against them and drive them out. As it is, this is all we can do."

The troopers and civilians of Soulan lined the walls of the fortress and watched as Imperial cavalry continued to ravage their kingdom's seat of power.

-

"What have you found?" Stone asked Baxter. The young general shook his head.

"Nothing, sir. The banks are empty save for furniture and a few personal effects of those who work there. The safes were emptied. Also the jewelry on display in some of the shops isn't real. Just cheap costume junk. The real jewels are gone. There's nothing of value left in the town save for what's in those storehouses."

"And we can't risk opening them," Stone sighed. "Very well. Burn it all," he ordered. "Banks, shops, everything. If we can't get anything out of this forsaken place then we won't leave anything for those who live here. They can spend the summer rebuilding."

"Yes sir," Baxter nodded. "Sir, has it occurred to you that by doing this we risk inciting the ire of these people? Angry people fight harder," he pointed out.

"I'm angry right now, General Baxter," Stone shot back. "And this is how I fight. Burn it."

"Yes sir," Baxter sighed. "Do you want it burned now? And if so where will we make camp? We don't want the fires to threaten our camps."

Stone took a minute to think that over, looking at the sun overhead.

"It should be dark in what? Three hours?" he looked at Baxter.

"Roughly, yes sir," Baxter nodded.

"Send runners out and have all commands return here," Stone said finally. "You're right, we don't want this place burning down around us. We'll make camp, then set fire to everything in the morning before we head north. Sound good?" he asked solicitously.

"Always your call sir," Baxter replied diplomatically. "Will be nice to rest a bit before dark. Maybe we can find something decent to eat."

"Corral those cattle we found this morning, slaughter some of them and get them over a fire," Stone ordered. "We'll eat their beef tonight."

-

"Why did we leave those cattle there instead of sending them south with the rest?" Memmnon asked. "They're feeding our enemies right now."

"And most will be sick by morning," Gideon Philo smirked. "Those few cattle were left there because they're ill, Sire," he explained. "They would have been harvested for their hides and the meat destroyed had we not had this incursion. They were isolated from the other herds in the city for that reason. The yard they found them in is one used by the tannery. I hope they all eat hardy," he almost spat. "By tomorrow they will be experiencing dysentery as well as fever, chills and rash. Good riddance."

"What ails the cattle?" Memmnon asked.

"They have Triggin Syndrome," Philo almost gloated. "Advanced at that. We caught it through the blood test required for slaughter animals." Triggin Syndrome was uncommon but not unheard of. A disease left from before the Dying, the original name had long since been lost to the ages as Triggin Syndrome became the 'official' name. Parasites in the infected animal would be passed to the humans who ate it. Not even cooking the meat thoroughly would prevent it and the effects on humans could be fatal if left untreated. Extreme dysentery alone accounted for many of the deaths related to the disease as people died of dehydration.

"A good call, assuming they would take them," Memmnon complimented.

"Thank you, Sire," Philo bowed slightly. "We could not risk placing the infected animals with the others to move them, so left them where they were. If they had anyone among them who could recognize the signs they would see that the cattle are ill. If they do not, well," Philo raised his hands. "Then they will be very sick come morning."

"Excellent."

-

"Meat's ready sir," Stone's aide mentioned. The general looked up from his report and nodded. The aide handed him a plate and cup, already prepared. Along with the slab of fresh beef there were beans and a piece of hardtack.

"Makes a nice change from jerky and parched corn," Weir noted as he dug into his meal with relish.

"Does that," Blake agreed, doing the same.

"I don't. . .this isn't right," Baxter was shaking his head, smelling the meat.

"What now?" Weir rolled his eyes.

"I'm just saying there's something off about this beef, General," Baxter kept his tone calm. "Sir, I'm not sure we should be consuming this," he said to Stone.

"Why?" Stone asked around a mouthful of said meat. "Tastes fine to me," he added.

"There is a smell to it that's. . .off, sir," Baxter insisted. "I can't place it exactly, but I know it from somewhere."

"Let me guess," Weir snorted. "You read a smell." The derision in his tone was plain.

Baxter sighed, falling silent. He stood, taking his plate and leaving the fire, heading for his own command which was just now eating.

"Don't serve that beef to my men," he ordered the cooks, who were just troopers who happened to know how to prepare simple food on a large scale.

"Sir?" one of the men looked up.

"I don't want the men of my division eating that meat," Baxter repeated. "It's tainted."

"Ah, perhaps the General will explain that to his men before they come through and threaten to tear into us?" the cook asked hesitantly.

"I will," Baxter nodded. Soon he was speaking to his assembled brigade and battalion commanders.

"I know we were all looking forward to a slab of beef, but that isn't going to happen," he told them flatly. "This meat," he held up a plate, "is off, somehow. It smells off, I mean. I know that smell if I could place it, but I can't. If we eat this we'll all be sick come morning."

"Sir, the men were looking forward to-" one brigade commander began.

"I'm aware of that," Baxter cut him off semi-gently. "And I'm sorry. But make sure no one takes that beef. If they do, they'll be sick as a dog by morning."

"What about the rest?" another asked.

"I told General Stone, but he was already eating and said it tasted fine to him," Baxter shrugged. "I'm telling you it isn't. So pass the word; beans and hardtack with jerky tonight. I'll make it up to them when we're back in our own camp."

"Yes sir," the assembled officers replied and headed off to break the bad news to their men. Behind them, Baxter again lifted the tainted beef to his nose, trying vainly to remember where he'd smelled that off-putting odor before.

-

"We could push on, sir."

Wilbanks considered it for a minute, then shook his head, reluctance in every movement.

"No. As much as I'd like to, we can't. If we had gotten down the mountain before dark that first day we'd be there by now, or close enough to make no difference. But we didn't. We were too slow."

"Sir, it'd take a lot longer to mount and prepare an entire division than a battalion," his aide mentioned. "Chad and his men were able to make better time because there were fewer of them. That's all."

"And they're likely already in the city while we're about to have to make camp," Wilbanks sighed. "There's no help for it though," he added seconds later. "We can't make it in the dark. Still, we're no more than two hours from Nasil. Three at the outside. I want us in the saddle at first light, even if we have to use torches to see the road. Pass that word, and advise all brigade and regimental commanders I want to see them once their camps are established."

"Yes sir," the aide nodded and rode off to deliver his messages. Wilbanks dismounted and handed his reins to one of his escort, stripping his saddle off before the man lead his horse away to be cared for.

For at least the tenth time he wished there was a full moon. He was all but certain the enemy was in Nasil by now, and here he and his well-trained division were, just miles away and forced to stop for the night due to darkness.

It was enough to make a man drink.

-

"We're very close, sir," Whit said even as Pierce drew to a halt and signaled his men to do the same.

"How close?" Pierce asked.

"Two hours from the city at most, sir," Whit answered, knowing as he did that was too long-

"We can't make it before dark," Pierce sighed. "Hell, we can't even complete the ferry crossing before dark," he slapped his hat against his leg in disgust. "This territory is hell on horses in daylight. At night it's deadly. Pass the word to make camp, Colonel. We will continue the crossing by torch light in needed."

"Yes sir," Whit nodded and began issuing orders. Pierce conferred with his scout commander and soon the young major had riders out in all directions ensuring that no surprises would find them as they labored to get their men and horses across the river.

Pierce once more cursed his own complacency at having waited for the enemy to come at him rather than moving against them first. Had he at least tested them at some point, or tried to, he would have known that they had pulled back. That had cost him a day. At that time, he'd been thankful for that day, since it was a day for his men to rest and for him to plan.

Or a day for the enemy to gain a march on him.

"Damn it," he murmured.

All he could do now was urge his men on silently as tired troopers and tired horses worked to get across the river as soon as possible. Just to have a night of fitful rest and another hard ride the next morning with a battle almost certainly waiting for them before lunch time.

A battle where they would be hopelessly outnumbered if help from Cove Canton didn't arrive. Even if it did, the odds would still be severe.

For the first time since the war began, Pierce wondered if Soulan would survive.

-

"All your men back in camp, Cass?" Andrews asked. The Imperial ploy was completed, though they had no way yet to know if it had been successful.

"Yes sir," Urich nodded. A freak thunderstorm had made what should have been an overnight trek a two-night camping expedition. Heavy rains, mud and swollen creeks had forced his men to stay put most of one day, and cover had been scant. Men and horse were soaked to the bone and miserable by the time they had made camp. Wranglers and men from other cavalry units had been drafted to care for the horses while Urich's men had stripped off wet uniforms and feasted on hot soup that seemed like a delicacy after two nights of rationed hardtack and jerky.

"Sorry you had such a rough time," Andrews offered.

"Ah," Urich waved it away. "Wanted an easy life I'd have joined the Navy." Both men laughed at the old joke. Life at sea was anything but easy.

"Were you followed?" Andrews asked.

"I'd say at least a brigade tracked us up river," Urich nodded, accepting a small glass of whiskey from his commanding general and downing it appreciatively.

"They may have turned back once we ducked into the woods, but my scouts saw them continue up river a ways before riding to join us. They're at least wondering where we went."

"Well, that's a start then," Andrews mused. "We'll just have to see how it plays out I suppose. No reason for your men to have any duty of any kind tomorrow after being trapped in that mess. Let them rest."

"They will appreciate that sir."

-

"Still nothing," Davies grunted as he surveyed the Nor lines before dark with his glass. Or at least the direction of the Nor lines. He couldn't quite make out the enemy, concealed as they were in most places by trees and brush. The occasional flash of fire or color let him know someone was still there, but that was about it.

"Our scouts report no movement behind either, sir," Enri Willard agreed. "We have men across the river watching behind them there, and men moving around their right flank at all times, assessing their movements. Which right now are nil."

"They're up to something," Davies lowered his glass.

"I agree," Parno spoke quietly, startling both men. He had climbed the tower without either hearing him.

"Sorry milord," Davies said. "Didn't hear you come up."

"It's fine," Parno half raised a hand and let it drop. "And I agree they're up to something, but what it might be I can't know. Maybe the boats being stopped has thrown them for a loss or perhaps the cavalry raid in their rear has made them wary. Either way, I honestly expected some kind of movement out of them by now."

"I'm not complaining, so long as this isn't the build up to some disaster or other," Davies shrugged. "It does give us some badly needed time. If they let us continue like this a while longer, I won't complain."

"Nor will I," Parno nodded. "But it does make me wonder, General."

"What about, milord?"

"If they aren't doing anything here, what are they doing elsewhere?" Parno said gently. "What are they doing, and where are they doing it? And how much damage will they be able to do before we find out about it, and can stop it."

Neither man had an answer for him. But he hadn't expected one. They would simply have to wait and see.

-

"Lights ahead, sir."

Lucas Silven had seen the light actually but it hadn't registered on him. He had been awake for too long and under too much pressure.

"Several of them sir," another voice reported. "I think it's town!" he added a few seconds later, excited.

Sure enough, it was their starting point from weeks before. What had taken two weeks against the current and stopping at night had taken only four days of not stopping except in the most dire of circumstance to return. Moving with the current had made all the difference.

"Begin landing as far down as possible," he ordered his senior NCO. "Pass the word!" he cupped his hands and called back to the boats trailing. "Landing ahead, port side! Boats to land in line! Wounded to be given first priority in all things!"

There were only fifty-two wounded sailors remaining, the others having perished on the trip back. Silven bit back a curse at that thought, knowing it was useless. There was nothing more he could do. His men were starving and his wounded dehydrated. It would be at least two weeks before his men were able to try something like this again. Probably longer for some if he required a physician to sign off on it.

He was brought back to his immediate needs by a jolt when his boat beached beneath the lights of the small town where the garrison force they had left was stationed. Guards were already summoning help after getting a look at the boat forces, and Silven stumbled ashore, directing freshly arriving men to help off-load his wounded first of all. He found George Stenopolous doing much the same from the opposite side of their landing area as he walked the stretch where the boats were sitting.

"Made it, Lucas," his friend smiled tiredly.

"So, we did," Silven nodded. "Buy you a drink?" he asked.

"Only if it's next to a steak," the other man smiled tiredly.

"I can agree to that," Silven nodded. The two men started up the hill, having nothing to unload. All of their personal gear was in the hands of the enemy or destroyed.

But they were alive and mostly unharmed. A few good meals and plenty of clean water and rest would see most of them put right in a week or so. At which point they would almost certainly be ordered to try again.

Until then, it was definitely time for a drink.

-

General Wilson sat on the porch of the small home where he made his quarters, eating his supper and enjoying a cool glass of tea. Made with water from a nearby well rather than boiled river water, it was almost sweet to the taste and he enjoyed it.

Usually he dined with some of his officers of an evening but once in a while he enjoyed his own company, and tonight was one of those nights. Before him sat a plate with an excellent cut of steak, heaping pile of potatoes and assorted other garden vegetables and a slab of fresh baked bread slathered in southern butter. Being a general had a few perks, and having his own cook was one of them.

Another one was being able to command the field around him. The boats should be here in another week to ten days assuming Stone's estimate was accurate. And Stone should be well into the central part of the province by now, raising hell and attracting attention. McLeod would have to pull at least some troops away from the front to deal with Stone, and it would almost have to be cavalry, historically his most effective units.

He had yet to hear back from Andrews, but it was a long way to his camps and his couriers would take weeks to reach back here, assuming that the 2nd Army's commander graced him with a reply. Wilson was reasonably confident that Andrews would reply, as Wilson wasn't asking that much of him really. Just a demonstration against the bridge that might make the Soulanies draw off some of the forces facing him.

A few more weeks, Wilson thought as he savored the finely cooked beef, chewing slowly and enjoying every bite. A few more weeks and we may can get things moving again.

Just a few more weeks and the war would be all but over and the occupation of Soulan beginning.

This really was excellent beef, he decided.

CHAPTER TWENTY-ONE

-

"Move, move, move!"

Preston Wilbanks watched as junior officers and senior NCOs harried his troops into action, forcing slower troopers to get a move on whether they wanted to or not. There was already a faint line of light to the east and in a few minutes, it would be light enough to ride. Torches were already lit and being carried by men of every company to help illuminate their trail in the remaining dark. Scouts had departed a half-hour before, already moving ahead of the army and checking the path before them.

"Ready to go, sir," his aide surprised him and Wilbanks realized he'd drifted away for a minute. The light to the east was definitely higher now.

"Get us on the move," he nodded. It took about ten minutes for the long column to get moving good, brigades shaking down in marching order, but then the entire division was moving, and as Wilbanks had desired, doing so just as the coming dawn made it almost light enough to see.

If nothing went wrong, they would hit Nasil before lunch.

-

"We're mounted and ready, sir," Whit reported. As senior brigade commander, he had been the natural pick as Pierce's second, but Pierce tried not to lean on him over much as he was also still the commander of the 31st Mounted Infantry.

"Very well," Pierce nodded. "Move out!" he called as he moved into line with Whit and a few other officers, enlisted and aides. It took a few minutes but over the last two weeks or so the various commands had learned to work together much better and their shakedowns were going quicker. It still took longer than a unit their size should, but for a combined command of several it wasn't bad, Pierce decided. He was pleased with them.

Ten minutes after dawn, they were on the move, and on the right side of the river. And almost finished playing catch up, too.

-

Stone had commandeered a small house on the northern side of the city as his quarters for the night, pitching his bedroll on the floor. He had slept reasonably well despite his anger and self-chastisement over his various and sundry mistakes. He was about to burn the Soulan Capitol to the ground come morning, after all. Surely that would make up for some of the problems they'd endured.

Just before first light his eyes had popped open as his stomach began to cramp. He just managed to make it to the chamber pot in the small bedroom before his bowels erupted. As he sat there, he noted that he was chilled and put it down to a cool morning, but as he wiped his forehead he came away with sweat.

A cold sweat? From what? What the hell?

As his stomach went through another bout of anger at him, Stone recalled Baxter's reluctance at eating the stolen beef the night before and groaned. The little bastard had been right after all-

That thought was cut off as the urge to vomit suddenly hit and left him looking for something to use as a bucket.

It's going to be a long day, he thought even in the midst of his misery. I wonder how many of my troops are sick as I am?

-

A lot of them. Most of two divisions worth in fact.

Weir and Blake had held no reservations about the beef taken from the southern stockyard and had eaten hardy along with the majority of their men and their commanding general. Both were now in a similar position to that commanding general, stuck on a toilet and puking into a bucket.

Their men were taking refuge wherever they could, having erected no temporary latrines for what was supposed to be a one-night camp. Men scurrying everywhere that morning had been forced to drop trousers in the best available spot, less they embarrass themselves and render their uniforms unwearable, or at least their undergarments.

Fully two-thirds if not more of both 1st and 2nd Division were unfit for duty as the effects of the tainted beef ravaged the troops of those two commands along with most of the command staffs and the commanding generals as well. Men were literally forced to stay in a crouch as they would barely finish with one bout of misery before another hit. Add to that the effect of having to also throw up as they had to squat to relieve themselves and you had a large number of very miserable men indeed.

Baxter had to ride hard rein on his men who were laughing outright at the others suffering from such malady. They had been plenty pissed at their own general the night before, with many muttering threats against him under their breath as they turned in without having the promised beef that the other divisions had shared.

This morning however, seeing that their general had been right in refusing to allow them to partake of meat he suspected to be tainted, they were once more loyal soldiers to their general and deriding the troopers from the other commands for not having someone as smart as Baxter commanding them.

Baxter finally ordered his brigade commanders to start busting anyone found stirring such trouble back to private and assign them to help clean up the mess. Hearing that, the harassment stopped, though they continue to joke among themselves. Baxter said nothing about that, as he decided they had to let go of their humor somehow.

Seeing the state of their men this morning made Baxter very glad he had convinced Stone not to burn the town the previous evening. The buildings gave at least some of the men cover to cower behind as they wondered if they would live out the morning or not.

-

"Looks like a fun time in the Nor camp this morning," Whip Hubel grinned. "Think they ate something what didn't agree with 'em."

"I had heard that myself," Memmnon smiled as he and Whip shared a small breakfast on the balcony overlooking the courtyard. "Philo outdone himself there," he added.

"Bunch of right sneaky people 'round here," Whip nodded, chuckling. "They'll prob'ly still burn the city as much as they can, Sire, but they gonna pay for it and pay hard, looks to me like."

"Please, Whip," Memmnon looked pained. "When we are alone, call me Memmnon."

"I'll give it a try," Whip promised.

"How are things on the walls?" Memmnon asked, ignoring the question he really wanted to ask.

"She's fine," Whip answered it anyway. "Little mouthy, but that's normal for her," he grinned. "Think she's not as impressed with it as she thought she would be," he added after a minute.

"I am relieved she is well," Memmnon sighed. "I tried very hard to get her to remain here with me, or at least not to go on that wall. She would not have it."

"Have to learn to let her be her, son," Whip told him gently. "Reckon I done the best I could raisin' 'er, but she's as wild as a deer, that one, and free as the wind. Give her time and she'll like as not come around to your way o' doing things, for you if no other reason. But don't expect her to go changin' all to once like. It won't happen. And all it does when you try to make her do something or not is set her dead on doin' or not whatever it is, even if it's the last thing she does do."

"That much I have learned on my own," Memmnon said dryly. "Nor do I want her to change, least of all for me. I just. . .I did not want her in harm's way," he shrugged. "I desired her to be safe. I have no qualms of her serving, or I would not have asked her to train the women archers. I just preferred she not be on the wall. I refuse to think I was wrong in that," he said stiffly.

"Ain't no wrong in a man wantin' to protect his woman, son," Whip assured his son-in-law to be. "You ain't done nothing wrong, and don't let her convince you ya have, either. But you can't expect her not to go and be and do. She's done it all her life so far, and I've rarely said no to her cause she ain't never really wanted to do nothing wrong. How you handle her, well, that you'll have to figure out on your own," he smirked slightly.

"Thank you so much," Memmnon's voice grew even drier if possible.

-

"We should probably move those bodies," Winnie suggested. She was standing on the walkway over the main gate into the palace fortress. Below them were over one hundred bodies of Norland troopers who had fallen in the aborted attack/pursuit to the palace. They were already swelling in the heat, and would no doubt begin to smell soon as well as attract scavengers.

"No," Chad shook his head slowly. "Be nice to have them gone I admit, but not with half an army within sight of us. If the enemy wants to come and collect them, we'll allow it, but we won't be going outside these gates until and unless our reinforcements arrive. And even then, moving bodies will not be our priority."

"It's going to smell," Winnie objected. "I don't want to smell that." Winnie was becoming used to getting her way and meeting resistance made her want to hammer at it.

"Occupational hazard, Miss Hubel," Chad was unsympathetic. "This is what war is like."

Winnie had a sullen look on her face at that reply, but didn't push the issue. She assumed that Chad had learned of her desire to participate in the fighting and was using this as a sort of 'I told you so' moment for those who had told her repeatedly that combat was no place for a woman.

"I haven't seen any movement outside their camp," Hildebrand remarked. "I would have expected them to be up looting the town by now."

"Well, let's not look a gift horse in the mouth," Chad shrugged. "Maybe they're just getting off to a slow start."

-

Stone finally managed to stagger out of his temporary quarters, disheveled and in need of a bath. All it took was a simple look around to see that he was far from the only victim of the tainted beef they had enjoyed for supper.

"Repo. . .report!" he stammered, looking for his aide or anyone else who could let him know where things stood.

"Morning General," Baxter was calm but obviously not sick. Stone looked around him and saw troopers, all wearing Baxter's insignia, trying to help those who were sick.

"Morning?" Stone trued to growl but couldn't. "What the hell's good about it?"

"Didn't say good morning, sir," Baxter shook his head. "Just morning. How are you feeling?"

"How the hell do you think I'm feeling you jackass!" Stone shot back.

"Judging by everyone else, you're not feeling overly well," Baxter shrugged. "My men are doing what they can to take care of the sick and are pulling all the guard duty for now. Also assisting with the horses. A good majority of both 1st and 2nd Divisions are laid low by whatever ails you, sir. Neither can muster anything like a single full brigade that is fit for service."

Stone wanted to scream at the young general. He had warned them the beef was off and no one listened. He had every right to be smarmy this morning, but he wasn't. He was doing his job and being efficiently military and Stone hated him for it.

Hated him.

"Have some of your men get our horses saddled and ready," Stone ordered as briskly as he could. "And have a couple regiments begin firing the city. I want this entire place in flames as we ride out of here."

"Sir, I must advise against that," Baxter tried again. "If we burn their capitol, their Royal City, it will ignite a hatred that will make them fight all the harder. Let us burn the militarily important buildings and leave the rest. That action will be understood for what it is; a smart military move."

"I'm not interested in your advice, Baxter," Stone snapped. "You have your orders, so get to them!"

"Yes sir," the younger man sighed.

-

"They're going to burn the city," Stang said bitterly. "We're stuck here unable to stop them and they're going to burn the city."

"We can rebuild it, Colonel," Memmnon sounded far calmer than he felt. Beneath that calm exterior he was furious. Never had Soulan stooped so low as even to invade the north, let alone destroy their treasures. The Imperials had no such compunction it appeared.

"Schools, libraries, hospitals, none of those are of any military significance," Stang shook his head. "This makes no sense. They have to know this will incense our people."

"Then we will stoke that fire and keep it burning, Colonel," Memmnon remarked. "And they will pay."

-

"Schools, hospitals, libraries are off limits," Baxter told the colonel whose brigade he had selected to carry out the burn order. "If they get caught in the conflagration that's one thing, but I will not be a party to it otherwise, and neither will men under my command. Understood?"

"What about General Stone, sir?" the colonel asked. "He won't be pleased."

"He's too busy shitting himself to death to care," Baxter said coldly. "Had he listened to me he and the rest would be hale and hearty this morning like we are, and no one the worse for it. Now go on and get started. We need to be riding out of here as soon Stone and the rest of those idiots can sit a horse. I'm sure our speed will be cut to nothing with them stopping every mile to find a tree as it is. We can't afford to linger here any longer with so many of our men unable to fight. We're lucky not to have faced them before now. Which reminds me; keep scouts well out between us and them. If they get even a hint of how bad off we are, they'll attack for sure. And while our men could stand it, most of the rest cannot."

"Yes sir," the colonel saluted and rode off to brief his men. Baxter watched him go, convinced he had made the proper call. The last thing he would be remembered as was the man who destroyed a school or library, or most especially a hospital.

And Stone be damned if he didn't like it.

-

"Smoke in the distance sir!"

Wilbanks had not been looking at the horizon, but did so now as his aide pointed. Sure enough, there were a number of columns of gray smoke making their way into the air, just about where-

"Coming from Nasil, sir," his aide supplied. "They're burning the city."

"We're no more than an hour out," Wilbanks said. "We'll pick up the pace. Maybe we can get there before they've destroyed it all."

-

"Smoke," Whit said, pointing west. West toward-

"Nasil is burning," Pierce sighed. "I have completely failed now. I estimate we're no more than an hour out. That sound right to you?"

"According to the scouts, yes sir," Whit sounded angry.

"Then let's tarry no longer," Pierce ordered. "The ground here is better for movement so we will take advantage of that. Pick up the pace and let us see if we can save at least some of the city!"

-

Stone managed to mount his horse with difficulty, but he still did it unaided, which was more than many of his command could claim. He shook his head wearily as he contemplated how this would look. Even with the damage to the Soulanie ruling city, there was no way Wilson would view this as anything but a failure. Not to mention laughing at his men and himself for their sickness.

Silas Weir had managed to get mounted and made his way over to where Stone sat waiting for the rest to be ready.

"Guess I'll have to stop making so much fun of Baxter, huh?" he tried to smile but it came out as a grimace. "I don't know that I've been this sick before," he admitted.

"I've felt better myself," Stone replied. "Damn Soulanies left diseased cattle for us to steal and eat, damn them. They had to know this would happen."

"Not like they owed us a warning" Weir shrugged. "We are invading their country."

"Are you on their side?" Stone demanded.

"You know better than that," Weir shot back at once. "But if they were inside the Empire, would we not do anything and everything we could to stop them? To kill them? If we would do it, we can't expect them to do less, can we? That's how we get caught like this and surprised."

Stone didn't have a ready reply for that, but nodded his understanding as Weir's words made sense. It didn't make him feel any less disposed toward the people of this city, or want them any less dead, but he acknowledged that yes, were the circumstances reversed the Empire would overlook nothing in an attempt to repulse their invaders.

"Well, we'll see how well they do with this city in ashes," he finally said bitterly. "Are your men mounted?" he asked Weir.

"As many as will be leaving," Weir nodded. "Many of them are too sick to ride. We'll have to leave them here. Some of them may not live out the day anyway. Whatever was wrong with those damn cows has hit some men harder than others, that's for sure."

"Don't leave a single man we can get across a horse," Stone ordered. "Get them on a horse if we have to drape them across the saddle and tie them to it. We've lost too many as it is."

"Yes sir," Weir nodded and rode back to where his men were trying to prepare the division to move.

Blake rode up next, looking pale but otherwise much better than either Weir or Stone.

"I've got less than one brigade's strength able for duty, sir," he said tiredly. "The rest couldn't fight their way into a brothel, let alone accomplish anything inside. Be lucky if we don't lose some of them before the day's out, to be honest. Worst dysentery I've ever heard of, let alone seen."

"Get your men mounted as best you can," Stone ordered. "I've given Weir the same orders. We're leaving as soon as we've got everyone on a horse. Baxter's men are okay and they'll be helping. He's also setting fire to the city. I want us out of here within the hour. We're weak and vulnerable now thanks to that damn meat."

"We'll be ready," Blake promised.

-

"I don't think they're burning everything," Chad mused. "Just select buildings so far."

"Fire will probably spread and get the rest," Hildebrand remarked sadly. "They know it, too," he added.

"Could be," Chad nodded. "But I'm seeing a lot of men barely able to sit a saddle," he added. He lowered his glass and looked at Hildebrand.

"You thinking what I think you're thinking?" Hildebrand tried to keep the excitement from his voice.

"I think so," Chad grinned. "What say we ride out and knock a few of them out of those saddles?"

"Hell yes!"

-

"What the hell do you think you're doing?" Stang asked as he noted Chad's men saddling horses. They had already drawn lances from the palace armories.

"We're about to go and see just how sick those Imperials are," Chad replied calmly. "Looks like most of them are barely able to sit a horse at the moment. With their able-bodied troops mostly off burning the city, this is a good time to hurt them. We aim to do just that."

"No, Colonel, I can't allow that," Stang was shaking his head. "The protection of this fortress has to take precedent over everything else."

"Well, Colonel, that's your job," Chad replied, no trace of anything in his voice. "Yours and Moore's I suppose," he amended after a second of thought. "But I don't answer to you, Colonel," Chad smiled. "I answer to two people, neither of which is here. And our number one marching order is to kill Nor anywhere we find them, any way we can. From the Marshal's own mouth. And right now is a good chance to kill several of the bastards and maybe, just maybe, stop some of the damage they're doing." He swung into his saddle as Hildebrand gave the order to mount up.

"Which is exactly what we're going to do," Chad finished. "Good day, Colonel," he nodded politely even as Hildebrand led their men toward the gate. Without waiting to see if Stang had anything else to say Chad followed.

His work inside these walls was finished so far as he was concerned. Outside the walls was where he needed to be.

-

Baxter's decision to have scouts out and watching was about to pay off. Two of them, watching from a tower that collected both rain water and well water that was pumped from the ground, had considered themselves fortunate to have such easy duty. Right up until the gate to that palace place opened and began disgorging troops. Hundreds of them, all carrying lances, the favored weapon of Soulan cavalry.

"Well that's the blasted banshee wailing for sure!" one grabbed the other by the shoulder to get his attention. "Look!"

"At least a battalion," his calmer partner nodded after taking a look. "And they're still coming. C'mon," he said, heading for the ladder down. "We gotta get this to the General and fast!"

"Should one of us stay here?" the other asked.

"If you want to get cut off in this town after we burned down most of it, be my guest," his partner replied. "No way in hell am I going to place myself at their mercy." With that he was taking the ladder steps as quickly as he could. His partner waited perhaps ten seconds, weighing what he'd been told, before taking hold of the ladder himself.

"Makes sense."

-

"How many?" Baxter asked, heart racing.

"Looked to be near a regiment already and still coming sir," the lead scout reported, deciding that 'battalion' wouldn't sound good enough to leave his post. "Straight down the main roadway there," he pointed.

"Take that to General Stone at once," he ordered them and both raced away. He turned to his aide.

"Have assembly sounded, and keep it going so they can form on us here," he ordered. "We need to have at least a brigade formed to meet them or their archers will chop us to pieces. And send me a runner! Stone has got to get out of here and quickly. If they empty that place, we'll never stand against them alone. Damn that idiot," he continued to himself. "I told him burning this city was a stupid idea."

-

"Companies A through E will engage with lances and then draw swords!" Chad called out, waiting for the word to be passed. "Companies F, G, and H will engage the enemy with bows until we mix it up, and then may also draw swords if targets are not available. Stay together and remember your training!"

They could do this. They had the tactics and the training to do this. They had done it before. His men were well rested after their brief battle the morning before and their horses had enjoyed a full day of rest and good eating. The Imperials were sick, at least some of them were, and their horses had to be tired.

Plus, Wilbanks and Pierce should be close by. If Chad and his men could hold this bunch in place, then those two might just finish them off.

-

"Scouts report city in sight, sir," Pierce's aide turned his horse in beside the Brigadier. "Several fires are burning, some appear to be out of control," he added, his voice subdued.

"Very well," Pierce sighed. "Time to the city?"

"No more than twenty minutes at this speed I estimate," the aide informed him.

"Pass the word to ready bows," Pierce ordered. "We'll use archery as much as possible to offset their numbers. Cavalry battalions may engage with swords instead," he added. There were three independent cavalry battalions in his command. No sense in hobbling them with the necessity of a bow. Many likely didn't have one in any case.

"Yes sir," the aide dropped back to pass the orders.

-

"City is in sight, General," a scout told Wilbanks. "Fires in numerous places and a few are spreading pretty quickly. Some Nor visible through the glass, and at least one Soulan cavalry unit has left the palace barricades to engage the enemy sir."

"Has to be Chad and his men," Wilbanks decided. "We're what? Ten minutes away?"

"About that sir," the scout agreed. "Have to bend on the horses a bit to make the battle. Won't be able to pursue if the enemy runs."

"We can't abandon a burning city anyway," Wilbanks shook his head. "Pass the word," he told his aide. "Battalions to divide companies evenly between bow and sword. Swords to point and flanks to protect the archers while they whittle down the opposition for us. Two minutes and then expect forward at gallop!"

Runner were dispatched to Brigade and Regimental commanders with his orders and Wilbanks forced himself to wait until he received word that all was in readiness. No sense barreling in unprepared.

"We're ready, sir," his aide reported after five minutes.

"Bugler, sound gallop," Wilbanks ordered at once and spurred his horse. His escort and staff followed suit, and soon the entire division was increasing speed as regiments fell into stride.

-

Chad held a hand up, head cocked to one side. Chatter and talk fell away as their commander strained to hear.

"I hear a bugle call," he said finally. "A Soulan bugle call," he grinned. "Has to be Wilbanks. If he's close enough we can hear his bugles, he's close enough to support us soon."

"Enemy may hear it too," Hildebrand mentioned.

"Just make them think we're a part of a larger attack," Chad declared. "Which technically we are, I suppose. Are our men ready?" he asked.

"Lancers front, archers behind, lines dressed, though we're awful cramped here," Hildebrand complained. "We can't get more than thirty men across in this boulevard, sir. Lances may not be the best choice here."

"If not, we'll drop them," Chad promised, "but if we can employ them effectively it will give us an advantage at least initially. And we need all the help we can get wouldn't you say?"

"I would that," Hildebrand sighed.

"Forward at a walk," Chad ordered. "We'll move forward until contact before we charge. They know we're coming and we know where they are. Pass the word for the archers to watch the high points as we worry about what's down here."

The entire battalion began moving in disciplined unison that only an elite outfit would demonstrate. Eager for enemy contact despite knowing how outnumbered they were.

They were the Marshal's Own, after all.

-

"Approaching enemy is wearing the Soulanie Royal Colors, sir," an aide informed Stone.

"So?" he demanded, still surly and still suffering.

"Sir, survivors of Brasher's command reported that many of the men there wore these colors," the aide supplied. "We may well be facing the same men who destroyed his force at the Gap."

A sharp retort died on Stone's lips as he thought about that. If true, then they were about to face off against possibly one of the best units of the Soulan army. At a time when nearly half of his forces were sicker than dogs and couldn't fight a group of schoolgirls.

"Make sure that General Baxter is aware of this, since his men are assembling to face them," he ordered finally. "Tell him our column will be moving back to the bridge in ten minutes or less. Advise him to give us fifteen total minutes and then follow. It will be up to him to buy us the time to get across." And won't that smarmy little bastard just love that, Stone thought sourly.

"Will do, sir!" the runner took off to find Baxter.

"Stop stalling and get mounted!" Stone bellowed to those around him. "Ten minutes and we're moving! If you're not mounted by then you can catch up or be a guest of the southerners! Your call!"

-

"Canter!" Chad ordered and nodded to Hildebrand. His XO moved to the left of their unit to take command of the left wing. There was an open area around the bridge and Chad was hopeful that they were going to be able to catch the Imperials there rather than in the street.

It looked as if the Imperial General was going to oblige him. His men were forming their lines well back into the open boulevard where the street would open into a plaza. While still not ideal for combat from horseback, it was far better than the narrow street they were on right now.

"Lances!" he called and heard that call relayed to his front ranks. As the last call echoed back, lances in the front ranks fell in unison. Behind those lancers, archers drew and nocked arrows and prepared for battle. Satisfied, Chad returned his attention to the enemy before him.

The Nor seemed to be in good order for all that they were harried and hurried. Their number was much lower than he had expected, even with the apparent illness running through the Norland camp. There was no way to know how many of them were sick, but he couldn't see how from such a large number this was all they could be facing.

The enemy had no lances, though he knew they used them. His own men had not brought lances with them because carrying them so far on horseback was a tough job and they were pressed for time. Soulan would not have left lances behind on a raid into enemy territory, but apparently the Nor had done so.

So much the better for us, he thought to himself. They don't have lances, they don't have archers, that leaves swords.

Swords could of course do a lot of damage, but it was hard to reach a lancer or an archer with a sword. They were outnumbered, but they were better armed, better rested, and likely better trained.

It would balance out.

-

Baxter watched his men form even as the harried aide informed him that his men were now all that stood between the Soulan troopers and the likely destruction of their entire force.

All he had to do as listen to me, Baxter thought savagely. It was obvious that beef was tainted, but no, we're going to eat this southern beef and laugh that they're feeding our men in their own back yard.

And now Baxter and his men were about to pay for that arrogance. He could count and knew that his men outnumbered the forces against him at the moment, but he had heard the bugle calls to the east as clearly as had his enemies. He knew that these forces fronting him were not the only he was about to face.

And to top it all off, the enemy not only had lances, they also had archers. Regardless of his temporary advantage if numbers, this was not going to go well.

"Draw swords!" he ordered, and heard the call repeated down the line. Sun flashed on steel as his men drew their weapons. He could tell they were worried. They could see those lances and bows just as well as he could. But they held their ground despite that fear. By now they knew they were being left holding the bag as the rest of Stone's men ran for it.

He promised himself right then that he would not simply stand here and allow his men to be wiped out to save Stone, Weir, Blake or their men.

-

"Ready left!" Hildebrand called to his commander.

"Ready right!" Chad replied. "Draw!" he ordered and archers drew their bows, raising them above the lancer's heads as they guided their horses with their knees. Chad hesitated for a handful of seconds as he made sure all archers were ready, before he cried;

"LET FLY!"

Hundreds of arrows flew through the air, seeking enemy flesh.

-

"Ready!" Baxter called as he saw the archers draw back. There was nothing else he could do. He had no archers of his own and charging that wall of lances was a non-starter. His men would have to take the volley and hope they got a chance to strike back.

Hundreds of arrows flew toward them and they could do nothing but wait.

-

"Fire at will!" Chad ordered as the first volley left. His archers would now fire so long as they had arrows or targets. While they did it was time to get other things going.

"Lances! Cantor!" he ordered. His front ranks increased speed, careful to keep their lines tight even as following lines began to divide spreading to the flanks.

It was a battle now.

-

This battle wasn't the incredible cavalry battle that Stone had sought. It wasn't the nick of time, save the city battle that Pierce had wanted. It was not the first major test of his newly trained division that Wilbanks had driven so hard to get to.

It was instead a small battle, set in the smoke and destruction of a beautiful city that had been left ablaze by an angry general. It was a dirty and close fought action between two units that could not have been more different.

The Imperial Cavalry units were disjointed by the haste with which they had been assembled for this action. They were handicapped by a lack of lancers and archers in their ranks. They were a long way from home, in enemy territory, and they knew they were being left to fight a battle that rightly belonged to all three divisions and not just to themselves.

The Soulan Troopers were disciplined, well trained, and a bit angry. They were also motivated. Veteran troopers that had seen battle already and had no problem seeing more. They knew some of them would die, some would be wounded, some had already been wounded once in fact. They knew this could be their time, but that didn't matter.

What mattered was making sure that these Imperial invaders paid the price for being on southern soul.

And pay they did.

The first volley of arrows didn't have the punch that a larger unit might have had. Just over three hundred bows releasing against the enemy arrayed against them. A second volley was in the air before the first struck home, tearing gaps in the already ragged lines of the Imperial troopers.

As the third volley rained down, the Imperial commander knew he had to do something, and he only had two choices. He could either flee, or fight. If he fled, his men would be run down and killed. If he closed and fought, they would take more losses but at least have the chance to hit back. If they could hit hard enough, they might be able to escape, some of them.

And so, the northern horsemen jumped forward on their wiry horses, swords ready. They were met by a double rank of southern lances that tore through their ranks again, emptying saddles and in some cases killing horses. As lances shattered, men drew swords and arrows flew again over their heads.

But dropping a shattered lance and drawing a sword takes time, and that time gave the Imperial horsemen time to close and finally strike back. To draw blood themselves.

And they did so with a vengeance.

The battle lost any semblance of lines at that point as it devolved into individual battles between handfuls of men.

Green and black clad troopers began to fall, but be replaced by those behind them. Men who thrust their horses forward to block the smaller mounts of the northern cavalry and whose swordsmanship was among the best in a kingdom known for excellent swordsmen.

The Imperials' temporary surge was very temporary as the Black Sheep lived up to the name they had made famous at the Gap, slamming back against the enemy and maintaining their line even as they continued to force their way forward.

There was never a point where the outcome was seriously in doubt.

-

Baxter allowed the battle to run for only a few minutes. He wasn't sure how long but less than five. Already too many of his men were on the ground, victims of southern arrows or southern lances. It was enough.

"Fall Back!" he called. "Sound the Recall!" he ordered his own bugler. The orders he had given were to head for the bridge when the recall was sounded. If Stone and his bunch weren't across by now, that was too bad.

His bugler lifted his horn and began blowing the call that would pull what was left of Baxter's division from all over the city to the bridge, and whatever safety that might bring with it.

-

"They're running!" Hildebrand shouted ecstatically. "Do we pursue?"

"No!" Chad shouted, shaking his head. "See to our wounded and get men on these fires!" he ordered. "We'll see that bunch again and when we do they'll remember this. For now, we have to save what of the city we can!"

"Right!" Hildebrand nodded and began issuing orders. Chad did the same, ordering his bugler to sound the call for Reform, which would bring any of his men that were pursuing back to formation. As much as he might like to punish them, the Imperials were not nearly so important as the city.

-

Memmnon looked over the city from his private balcony, sadness on his face that he would allow no one else to see. He had projected calm and steadfastness through the entire emergency, but now that the enemy was being driven from the city he felt a bit of despair seeing his home, the seat of his government, left in such a state. He had been born here, had grown to manhood in this city. Loved every square inch of it, some more than others he would grant but all of it nonetheless was special to him. What he saw now hurt.

At least a dozen large fires burned out of control within sight of his balcony and he knew there were others not visible from where he stood at the moment. It wasn't just storehouses and armories, either, he thought sadly. The Nor had fired private businesses, homes and other buildings, and those fires had spread.

He had already ordered every available man out to battle the blazes, those orders making the libraries and hospitals the highest priorities. For some reason the thought of fire hadn't occurred to him before now and he'd take no special precautions for the libraries around the city. He had assumed that the Nor would limit their damage to militarily important targets and places like here, the palace, where they could strike directly at the Royal Family.

He couldn't remember just now why it was he had felt that. It wasn't as if the Nor had any real respect for anyone or anything.

"Memmnon?" he heard a soft feminine voice and turned to see Winifred Hubel behind him, bow in hand, looking at him.

"Winnie," he nodded. "I'm glad to see you well," he was almost stiff in his speech and wished he didn't sound that way. He didn't seem to be able to stop it.

"Are you all right?" she asked, moving out onto the balcony with him.

"Fine," he assured her with a nod. "I'm surprised to see you. I had assumed you would be with the forces giving chase to the enemy."

"Why?" she acted surprised.

"It's what you wanted," he shrugged. "As I said, it was merely an assumption. Your father was here a bit earlier but he's made his way down now, I believe."

"I didn't come to see my father," she told him. "I came to apologize," the words came hard for her.

"For what?" he turned again, looking at her.

"You know what for," she almost huffed before getting herself under control. "For making such a scene before. For saying what I did."

"Ah. That," he nodded, once more turning his attention to the view before him. "There's no need to apologize for expressing your true feelings," he assured her. "If that's truly how you feel then it's better I know it now, wouldn't you say?"

That statement caught Winnie by surprise.

"I just wanted to help," she tried to keep any anger from her voice. Her temper was a failing she was all too aware of. "I wanted to help protect this place."

"You did," he nodded, still not looking back. "Was it everything you had hoped it would be?" he asked solicitously. There was no rancor in his tone, no trace of anything other than simple interest.

"I didn't hope for anything," she told him flatly. "I wanted to help."

"Are you at least satisfied that you did so?" he turned once more to look at her.

"Do you feel that you've finally made the contribution that you wanted to make?"

"Why are you being like this?" she asked rather than answer. "I told you I came to apologize. I shouldn't have said what I did, Memmnon, and I'm sorry for it."

"What am I being like?" he looked and sounded puzzled. "I just asked a question, that's all. And if you feel you need my forgiveness then of course you have it," he nodded. "I do not see that you need it but won't argue the point. How did your Ladies Auxiliary do?" he asked. "I noted at least a few on the front wall along with you."

"They did fine," Winnie said softly. "Scared but did their duty. Some were a little green faced after the dead Nor were left in front of us all day," she admitted. "I didn't care for it myself."

"I suppose after this we should extend that training to everyone," he turned again to look at his burning city. "If they can attack here, they can certainly attack anywhere else. We'll need to create a training program for that sort of thing in all the major cities that the Nor might reach with such an attack. Many of the efforts taken here would be useful in those cities as well I should think."

"Is it going to be like this from now on?" Winnie asked.

"I don't know," he shrugged. "They have never done anything like this. Never had the horsemen capable of raiding into our territory so deeply without their main army to sup-"

"I don't mean the war, Memmnon," she cut him off slightly sharper than she actually meant to. "I mean us. Are we going to be like this from now on?"

"What are we being like?" Memmnon turned a puzzled face to her. "I don't understand."

"I feel like you're punishing me," Winnie admitted. "For going against your wishes."

"Would that do any good?" he asked her. "I can't see that it would myself, which means there's no real point. And I'm not much of the punishing type to be honest," he shrugged. "Just not my way, I suppose. You did as you wanted, and I suspect you will do so in the future regardless of any request I might make of you. As for punishment, I don't see what I've done or am doing that you would think of as punishment." He turned yet again to the sight below him.

"At the moment I'm watching the city I grew up in burn," he told her. "That and the loss of so much is really all that I was thinking of at the moment. Grateful for the fact that I've had no reports of any losses to our people other than minor injuries to be sure. That is the only bright spot I can see. As bad as this is," he waved his arm at the scene before him, "it could have been much worse. I am thankful that it was not."

"Are you telling me you aren't angry with me?" Winnie asked him then.

"I was never angry," he told her. "I was afraid. Terrified would probably be a better word, really. Terrified that something would happen to you and there was nothing I could do about it other than try to keep you safe, which you would not allow," he shrugged. "I wasn't angry then, nor am I angry now. Do not seek to project your reactions on to me, Winifred," he told her flatly.

"My reactions?" she huffed despite herself.

"When things don't go your way, your respond with anger," he nodded. "I can't afford to do so. I am not allowed to be angry, or anything else for that matter that might affect my judgment or my ability to rule. That includes being angry at you for placing yourself in harm's way, no matter how it may affect me. I watched my father rule in anger, and allowed it to influence me far too much. I know what an angry monarch can do, what damage he can cause."

"Thus, I cannot allow myself to be angry," he explained. "I was angry with my sister and issued orders that will likely see her and Therron both dead if they are not already. Justified? Yes. But still done in anger. I believe now I know why my father's heart was so weak," he admitted. "Stress."

"I've caused you stress?" Winnie asked.

"Of course, you did," he replied honestly. "How can I think of you down there, on that gate, and not be stressful over your safety? To even suggest otherwise is completely ridiculous. But if we are to be married it is something I will have to learn to live with," he shrugged. "And I will."

"If?" Winnie felt her heart seize. "If we're to be married?"

"You came here expecting a confrontation, and I have refused," Memmnon told her. "If you follow the pattern you have established thus far, you will become angry, or at the very least indignant, and then you will blame me for that. After which you will try and use my affection for you to force concessions from me for whatever it is you believe I have done, real or imagined."

"So, I will cut to the chase, so to speak, and simply ask you what you want." His tone was still as friendly and open as when he started.

"You think I came here just to ask something of you?" she demanded angrily, not realizing she was doing exactly as he had just predicted.

"Anger," he held up one finger but said nothing else.

"And whose fault is it if I'm angry?" she shot back, only to see a second finger raised in silence.

"If you thin-" she started, then stopped abruptly as she finally realized what she was doing. Memmnon raised a single eyebrow and looked at her.

"I think. . .what?" he asked.

"I…I'm sorry," she said softly, her face having fallen into a look of almost pain. "I didn't know I did that," she admitted. "Never paid no-any, intention," she sighed. "Why do you put up with me anyhow?" she asked, eyes now damp if not wet with tears. "Why?"

"Because I love you," he shrugged, as if that was all the reason he needed. And for him, it likely was.

"I'll do better," she promised suddenly, laying her bow aside and wrapping both arms around one of his. "I promise I'll do better."

"Don't make promises you can't keep, Winnie," Memmnon stroked her hair softly, rubbing the back of her head. "I'm not asking for any, you know."

"I'll keep it," she said so solemnly that it caught him by surprise. "I will."

-

Wilbanks and his men hit the battle field just as Baxter's men were pulling across the bridge. He desperately wanted to pursue, but one look at the city burning all around them made him realize where his duty was.

"Third Brigade!" he called out, "Secure the bridge, scouts out! The rest of you on the fires! Be watchful for enemy wounded and holdouts!"

His men fell in, assisting those already pouring from the palace fortifications to fight the fires. Soulan had specially fitted wagons that could be operated by hand to pump water onto the fires and these were now brought from their stations all over the city to areas where fires were raging out of control.

Oxen, draft horses, even war mounts were pressed into service to haul tanks of water from the river to feed these pumps. Soon nearly ten thousand men and women were fighting fires all over the city.

This was the scene Pierce and his men rode into roughly twenty minutes after Wilbanks arrived. Pierce sat looking at the city for a moment, wallowing in his complete and total defeat.

"Sir?" Whit pressed in. "Orders?" Pierce just looked at him.

"Sir, do we assist with the fires?" Whit asked, trying to keep any of the men from seeing him like this.

"Yes," Pierce nodded. "We'll head down to the plaza, there," he pointed. "Someone there is likely in charge and will know where we can do the most good. Let's be about it!" he said firmly for all around him to hear. He sounded calm and sure, but was anything but as he looked at the devastation around him.

This was his fault.

CHAPTER TWENTY-TWO

-

It took a day-and-a-half to get the fires under control. Not out, just under control. There were still fires burning in a half-dozen places as night fell the day after the Nor had departed. Four were fires centered around storehouses, the other two were business district buildings that had once housed dry goods merchants. Those fires had spread to the blocks around them thanks in part to the debris placed around them by Imperial soldiers. Soaked in any kind of accelerate the enemy troopers had been able to find, they had kindled quickly as the fires had spread even after they had abandoned their efforts.

As night did fall, weary troopers made bivouac inside the spacious palace grounds in the empty barracks and in some cases on the grounds. Uniforms were washed clean of soot and grime, horses cared for and men were able to bathe.

The King's Own and Palace Guard along with hundreds of civilians were all still working to put out the fires, but the combat units were exhausted and had to rest.

"Report?" Chad looked at Hildebrand who had been to the hospital.

"Forty-two dead, one hundred twelve wounded," the normally upbeat major sighed. "Thirty-eight will likely not serve again. Twenty-nine are slight enough to ride north with us in three days time. The rest are varied, but should be able to return to duty at some point."

"Not bad considering the odds," Chad's own sigh echoed his second's. "Enemy losses?"

"Three hundred ninety-one left on the battlefield where we engaged them," Hildebrand consulted his notes. "Another two hundred and change left scattered around the city with dysentery and what not from eating tainted meat left for them by the Agriculture Minister," he smirked. "All dead now," he added darkly. The Black Flag was still in effect, and after this it was sure to stay that way.

"I'll get a report written up, we'll need a courier by light," Chad mentioned.

"Royal Courier will be leaving at sunrise," Hildebrand nodded. "I'd recommend against that at the moment," he added after a pause. "We don't know where that bunch is and for all we know they can cross the river somewhere. Anything vital in those dispatches would fall into enemy hands."

"Marshal has to know what's happened," Chad shook his head. "We'll have to chance it. We'll send a squad if we have to, but I've always heard that the Royal Couriers are better mounted than we are. Might just slow him down."

"Probably," his second agreed. "I'll finish the tally and have it to you in a few minutes, then see when and where to meet the courier in the morning."

-

"Colonel, you've been a great help to me these last few weeks," Pierce told Whit as he accepted Whit's report. "I thank you for that."

"You sound like we're done here, sir," Whit frowned.

"Oh, I suspect you and your men will remain to either protect the city or the approaches to it so nothing like this can happen again, but I expect to be relieved. No matter how you view this, I was responsible for preventing this and I didn't get the job done. Like it or not, this is on me."

"Sir, I can't see it that way," Whit shook his head. "We did everything right, sir. Sometimes the enemy gets it right too, you know. And your timely warning sent here prevented the city from being caught completely unaware, saved no telling how many lives, and protected the Sovereign. That's not nothing, sir."

"Nor is it likely enough," Pierce smiled tiredly. "But I do appreciate it, Colonel. Are your men getting everything they need?" he changed the subject.

"Food and a chance to clean up and rest was about all they needed, sir," Whit nodded. "Other commands are doing the same. We could be ready to ride by morning, sir," he hinted.

"They have two days on us already, Colonel," Pierce replied. "That's a long chase."

"They also have a great many men who are too sick to ride far at a time, sir," Whit reminded him. "We could still catch them and do them harm."

"I will consult with the others and see what the consensus is," Pierce promised. "I am to meet with General Wilbanks and Colonel Chad in a few minutes, as well as representatives of the King's General Staff. I'm sure it will be a lively discussion."

-

"We made good time today," Whipple said as he and Beaumont shared a fire.

"Not bad," Beaumont agreed. "Figure three-and-a-half weeks, give or take, to put us at Cove Canton. By then the courier chain should have reached the Marshal. Might have orders waiting for us by then."

"You think he'll want us back to raiding, or waiting to see what happens from the east?" Whipple asked.

"You know that kind of thinking better than me, Horace," Beaumont shrugged. "I honestly don't know. I don't see what the CPC can do for Therron in all honesty. Wasn't for Soulan, they'd be part of the Empire anyway."

"Therron is a silver-tongued devil, Buford, don't ever forget that," Whipple warned grimly. "If there's a chance in hell to get help out of the Coasties, he can find it never doubt."

"I don't," Beaumont nodded. "Nothing we can do about it right now, though," he added. "Messages to Admiral Semmes and the Marshal are about all we can do. And not knowing how bad the Fleet got hurt before, there may not be anything Semmes can do about it neither."

"We'll know soon enough I should think," Whipple agreed.

-

"We should send every man we can muster after the enemy at first light!" the aging general at the head of the map table insisted. "We cannot allow this to go unpunished."

"It hasn't," Stang shook his head. "Over half their force are near dead with dehydration and dysentery according to the men left behind. And there was plenty of evidence of it left as well," he grimaced. Several buildings that had escaped the fires set by the enemy had to be destroyed because of that 'evidence'. Heathen bastards.

"That isn't enough," Brock shook his head. "We need to run these bastards down and kill them while they're weak!"

"General, need I remind you there are fires still burning in this city even as we speak?" Memmnon spoke calmly but firmly. "That there are thousands of people that will be day after tomorrow be flooding back into this city and that many of them will no longer have a place to live or to work? That we lost fully half the stores that had been stockpiled here for both the war effort as well as feeding the people here? We have plenty enough problems without sending our most able men off to chase a sick and retreating enemy."

"They have achieved a victory here, but we need not give them more of one," he ended flatly.

"I don't see how chasing them down and killing them is giving them anything other than the taste of southern steel!" the old general spoke again. General Turnbow had been among Tammon's most trusted advisers, and was not taking his loss of that status well. Memmnon did not listen to him as Tammon had. Or Therron.

"General, I think I have made myself clear on this," Memmnon looked at him sharply. "We have sent a scouting party in pursuit to make sure they are headed out of our territory. Messages received from them so far indicate that our enemy is suffering. Many of them no doubt will perish without medical attention they won't be able to get short of returning to their own lines. Our men are tired. Some have been in the saddle for days before arriving here and immediately fighting either the enemy or the fires, and in some cases both."

"We do not have so many soldiers and horses that we can afford to throw them away in chasing after an enemy that is already beaten. And many of the men now here are needed far more desperately at the front than they are here." He paused, looking around the table.

"I propose to send Brigadier Pierce and his men back into the central province north of the river day after tomorrow to resume their patrols and interdiction. They served us well in this instance and will continue to do so I believe. General Wilbanks and Colonel Chad will at the same time be taking their own commands to link up with the army and my brother. With two Corps out of the line for refit and training he can use all the help he can get."

"We will increase the training of unorganized militia here in the city, and will also be spreading that initiative to other cities as well. Every able-bodied man and woman who can draw a bow will be taught to do so, and shoot it. Every city will erect a fortification such as this one for their citizens to retreat to in the event of either a raid or an actual attack. This will take time of course, but the time will pass regardless of how we use it."

"In the meantime, we will mobilize what we can here to rebuild the city and replenish our stores as we can. We must look to the winter and be prepared. Our army must be kept supplied or we will fall. That is not an option, gentlemen."

"I do not believe Brigadier Pierce can be trusted with such orders," Turnbow shook his head. "Had he done his job in the first place, this attack would not have been possible. It was obviously a mistake to give him such a command and he should be replaced immediately. I propose-"

"Please show us, using this map General Turnbow, how you could have taken perhaps six thousand men and used them to completely block twenty-five thousand from making their way here," Memmnon's hand gestured to the table as he cut the older man's tirade off. "I'm sure we will all be able to learn from your greater experience and ability."

Turnbow's face reddened at that and he fell silent, glaring at his young king and then at the young brigadier in question.

"As I thought," Memmnon's voice was cutting suddenly. "I grow weary of such posturing, gentlemen. I will warn all of you one last time; stop. Any more of it will see you looking for work yourselves. I have read Brigadier Pierce's report and am satisfied, despite his ability to portray himself as being at fault, that he did all he possibly could to prevent what happened here. I would remind you that his force was placed where it was to prevent raiding activity, not a full-fledged attack by more cavalrymen than we have ever seen the Nor manage to put together in anything like an effective fighting force. Yet he held them at bay for two days, and then managed to get couriers to us with two full days warning, arrived himself just a day after the enemy despite their being able to use a Trade Route while he was forced to use back roads and trails, then cross the river by ferry."

"You have served Soulan well, General Turnbow, but please explain to me how you could have handled this any better. And if you cannot, then kindly keep your opinions of the men we are asking to defend us to yourself, hm?"

Chad watched in amusement as the King dressed the old general down, wondering if he was going to push the old man into a stroke. Suddenly Memmnon ignored Turnbow and turned to the rest.

"Rest and refit your commands tonight and tomorrow, gentlemen," he ordered. "Day after, you have your orders. Godspeed and good luck. And with that I believe we are done here. Good day." With that the King departed, his step firm and his back straight.

Glances were exchanged around the room except for a stunned Pierce, who had entered this room certain he would leave in disgrace. Instead, he had been complimented by the Crown and was retaining his command as well as his original mission.

Whit would get to say 'I told you so' tonight.

-

Admiral Raphael Semmes read the message in his hands for a third time, his face a mask. The only other man in his office was Commodore David, commander of the Key Horn Squadron, or what was left of it. Semmes looked up at the waiting commodore.

"Do you know this man, Chastain?" he asked. "I know him only barely, met him once. He falls under the command of Admiral Shirley at Moble."

"I've met him, sir," David nodded.

"Would he do something like this?" he handed the letter to David, who read it. The stunned look on his face as he finished was answer enough.

"Sir I... I can't imagine what the hell he was thinking!" David exclaimed.

"I don't really care," Semmes said grimly. "For the moment I'd like to assume that his subordinate Captains aren't in on this, but I don't think I can do that just yet. What of your squadron can you put to sea with?"

"Sir I have two cruisers and three frigates that can be away in two days time," David reported. "Three days would be better, ideally, as we are still repairing damage to spars and caulking seams. We also need to load stores and... I should have enough able bodies from ships that cannot make sail to crew them. We would need marines-"

"Get with Commodore Rhodes and poll the available sailors and marines from all three squadrons to ensure that your ships are fully staffed. Chastain has had twelve days already, so I need you to put to sea as soon as possible to stop him. You will stop him no matter what it takes. Is that clear?"

"Yes sir, Admiral," David came to attention. "Will the Admiral be joining us?"

"No," Semmes wanted to scream as he lifted his arm. "I am not fully released from the good doctor's care. With my ribs the way they are, I would be a burden to you, Anthony, as badly as I feel the need to be there. So go, stop this idiot, and return Therron McLeod to this base in chains. Or dead. After reading this warrant I don't care which and don't think the King does either."

"Yes sir."

-

"Report!" Stone called out as his men tried to make camp.

"We've lost another forty men to food poisoning or to dehydration, sir," Baxter reported flatly. "There are approximately fifty more that are likely to expire before morning."

"Damn those bastards!" Stone growled, not for the first time. "We need to make camp and get some clean water into every man in this command. More than that we need a doctor. Hell, we need a dozen doctors! I want you to send riders further north and bring back any medical assistance you can," he ordered. "We'll maintain this route all the way back into territory we control, so anywhere they can meet us is fine. Our destination will be Lovil, on the Ohi. We have to have time to refit and rest, get our men back on their feet."

"I'll see to it, sir," Baxter managed to reply evenly.

"How did your men fare at the bridge, Brigadier?" Stone asked.

Now you want to know about my men you bastard?

"I lost nine hundred and forty-two men dead, wounded or missing," Baxter told him flatly. "We were forced to leave many behind as we made for the bridge ourselves."

"Losses are still being figured for the others," Stone nodded. "I'm sorry," the older man said suddenly. "Had we listened to you, we wouldn't be in this mess. That's on me."

"Yes sir," Baxter's voice was neutral. "I'll round up some couriers, sir."

"Very well," Stone returned his salute and Baxter forced himself to walk calmly away instead of kicking Stone in the teeth as he deserved.

My time will come, he told himself.

-

One of the problems with long distance communications was the time it took for messages to reach their destination. A good courier, well mounted, could make fifty or more miles a day assuming fresh horses available to him along the way. Nights when the moon was full or near so would allow him to make a few more. As a result, it took time to receive long distance information by couriers. Still, it was all that was available for now.

Parno McLeod was about to eat a solitary supper when the first courier rode into camp. It had been a month almost to the day since so many of his changes had been started, and they took time to bear fruit. He hoped he was about to get good news from one of his projects, but this was not the case.

The message was from Raines. They had observed what appeared to be four full Imperial Cavalry divisions leaving the enemy positions on the western banks of the Great River, headed north. Scouts had tried to follow along but had lost them two days ride north when the trail veered away from view. There was now no way of knowing where they had gone.

Parno spent his supper looking at a map, trying to imagine how far an Imperial cavalry unit could make it in one day, and how far that would let them be by now. He spent a near sleepless night worrying over it, and then spent the next day ensuring that there was adequate scouting to his own west to prevent those divisions from showing up unexpectedly.

He also reexamined Raines deployment. With so many men now removed from that field, could he afford to take any of Raines men and bring them here to face the larger army? For the moment he was hesitant to do so, but it might have to be done.

Three days after that courier had arrived, a Royal Courier had come from his brother. This courier bore reports from three of his commanders as well as a letter from his brother.

Nasil had been attacked! The city was still burning when the courier had departed!

Stunned, Parno had collapsed in his seat, staring at nothing.

All of his precautions for nothing. All the movements, posturing, forced marches, all for naught as the very thing he'd sought to prevent had happened. Fully half the stores stockpiled in Nasil gone, either stolen or burned. At least a quarter of the city in flames. Chad's men had arrived in time to help drive the Nor away, but Wilbanks had been a little too late to assist and Pierce had gotten there only in time to fight the fires.

He read Pierce's report, angry at first that he had failed to protect the city, but as he read, despite Pierce's determination to take the blame on himself, Parno could see that the man had done all he could to prevent what had happened. He had too few men to confront such a force as the Nor had sent against him. That wasn't his fault, though he took full responsibility for it.

Chad's report was next, detailing how he and his men had arrived in the wee hours and manned the wall against the only attack the Imperials had mounted against the fortress directly. He had added that when it was apparent that the Nor cavalry had taken ill from eating the tainted beef left for them by the Agriculture Minister, he had taken his men out to confront the soldiers setting the fires and was able to drive them off. He noted that Wilbanks' arrival had likely played some part in that as his own men had been heavily outnumbered despite their success.

Wilbanks' report was likewise full of self-recrimination as he castigated his failure to get off the mountain before dark, forcing him to camp on the ridge and head down at first light. Parno made a mental note that something would need to be done about that in the future and then snorted to himself.

Future? At this rate Soulan wouldn't have a future!

"I heard you got a courier in milord?" Enri Willard's voice brought Parno back to the present.

"Oh, yes," he nodded, handing the sheaf of papers over. Enri took them with a puzzled look, sharing them with General Davies who had joined him. The two read silently and then swapped, each reading all the relevant reports.

"Milord, I don't see how Pierce could have done more," Davies remarked, apparently feeling the need to defend one of his most promising young leaders.

"Nor does the King," Parno assured him, passing over Memmnon's more lengthy and detailed report. "Pierce has been commended by the Crown and he and his men will have by now returned to their sector to continue their work. He did the best he could with what I gave him to work with," Parno admitted.

"The loss of stores will hurt," Enri Willard said gently. "But quick action and quicker thinking held casualties to a minimum. And smart move on Philo's part likely put the Imperial Cavalry out of action for some weeks as well," he added.

"I wouldn't be surprised," Parno sighed. "Which makes me think; make damn sure that all our cattle we're butchering to feed our men are being checked. I don't mean one in five, or one in three, but every single one. The last thing we need is to have something like that sweep through this camp."

"I'll make sure it's being done now, sir," Enri nodded and departed to do just that. Davies finished reading the King's own report.

"Milord, this isn't nearly so bad as it could have been," he said finally.

"No thanks to me," Parno sighed, leaning back. "I have no business being the Marshal of the Army, General. None. I told my father that, and I told my brother that as well when they put me here. This fiasco should prove that effectively I imagine."

"That's a load of horse shit, milord," Davies replied bluntly and Parno jerked his eyes upward to the older man.

"You are young, milord, and you are still inexperienced, that is true," Davies fell easily into lecture mode. "But you have a natural talent for this, milord, that cannot be taught or learned. You either have it or don't. It can be nurtured, grown, expanded upon, but if the base ability isn't there, then you can only rise so far before you're finished."

"Despite your age and inexperience, you have led this army to two victories, milord. Before that you scored an incredible defensive victory against a foe that should have been able to march over you in a day or less. It was your vision for the future that put weapons like those that Professor Finn has created in the hands of our soldiers and they have killed more Nor than any groups of swords in this army thus far."

"You have used a natural instinct for things to lead our men to victory. You have used every advantage you can wring from the world around us to do so, and you continue to do so. You may think this," he held up Memmnon's letter, "is a failure, but who sent Pierce there to start with?"

"You had the idea as well," Parno pointed out.

"I've been doing this since before you were born, son," Davies' eyes crinkled. "Had Pierce and his men not been there, following the orders you sent with him, then what do you think would have happened?"

"I'll tell you what would have happened," he didn't give Parno the chance to answer. "Twenty-five thousand Nor cavalry would have rode down on Nasil with about five minutes warning and destroyed the city and everything in it. Possibly killing or capturing the King and anyone else of importance in the city as well, leaving us in a real pickle instead of just in a bind like this," he shook the paper again.

"It's not my place to speak to you so, I realize, but milord you are doing a good job. You seem to have forgotten something however that is taught in every level of War College."

"What's that?" Parno asked.

"Sometimes the enemy gets things right too," Davies told him. "Sometimes, no matter what you do, or how well you do it, the enemy manages to get one over on you. When that happens, you have two choices; roll over and quit, or get up and hit back. I honestly can't see you as the roll over and quit type, milord. You'd never have survived so long if you were."

"Too true," Parno snorted, and a ghost of a smile lit his face for the first time in days. "Thank you, General," he said sincerely.

"Sometimes even generals need a good kick in the seat, milord," the older man winked. "I would have to imagine the same is true for Marshals."

"Did you talk to my brother like this?" Parno asked suddenly.

"I rarely spoke to your brother, in all honesty," the older man replied after a brief hesitation. "He had his favorites, and the General Staff was loaded with the men he listened to and whose advise he heeded. He may have listened to Graham once in a while, but again I doubt it. Arnold isn't a bad soldier, but he's not a brilliant tactician by any means. Nor is he prone to kiss enough ass, despite his reputation, to suit certain people. Same for Herrick and Freeman. I'm sure that your brother felt they would be amenable to his plans and that's why they were put in those positions, but I assure you neither of them would ever contemplate treason. Would as likely laughed in his face to be honest."

"I'd like to believe that very much," Parno nodded. "I need to be able to believe it. There is so much else to worry about without having to worry about who I can trust in positions like that."

"Milord, you let some of the rest of us worry about that," Davies told him. "Graham is now my subordinate, which makes him my responsibility. And I don't believe he will give you any trouble. Assuming he survives training alongside his men," he added. "Which I hope you don't expect me to do, by the way," he added. "I'm far too long on tooth for that kind of behavior."

"I couldn't spare you that long even if you wanted to go," Parno shook his head. "And truly, there's no reason for the Corps commanders to do it, if we're honest."

"You did it," Davies shrugged.

"I'm twenty years old, too," Parno chuckled. "But anyway. No, I don't expect you to do it, General. As I said, I can't spare you that long. We do need to think about our organization, but we'll do that tomorrow. I need. . .I need to think about all this. See what we can salvage."

"Very well," Davies nodded. "Send for me if you need me, milord," the older man said. He was almost to the tent opening when Parno's voice stopped him.

"General?"

"Yes, milord?" Davies turned.

"Thank you."

"You are quite welcome, milord."

-

Two days after that news Parno was once more at his fire. It was growing warmer so that the fire was more a source of light than anything, but the nights could still be cool. And besides that, Parno found comfort in the fire. He supposed there was some part of man that had always found fire comforting at night, as protection to ward off predators and other enemies.

"So, you have suffered setbacks I understand" Cho Feng walked into the firelight. He had been away for three days working to help train 1st Corp in their hand-to-hand combat skills. Parno had missed him.

"You could say that," Parno nodded. "Lost about half the stores we had set aside in Nasil, and lost over a quarter of the city by last reports. Chad lost over a hundred men dead or wounded and Wilbanks' men didn't get to the fight in time, nor did Pierce's. On the bright side, most of the Nor cavalry are sick as dogs and some have died from it according to scouting reports. Pity all of them didn't," he muttered darkly.

"You feel responsible for this," Feng said.

"Of course, I'm responsible," Parno snorted. "I'm the damn 'Lord Marshal of the Army'," his sarcasm was heavy. "You know there's supposed to be a baton of some kind that goes with this job," he said suddenly. "For official ceremonies and what not. Bet Therron stole it," he muttered.

"You know, once in a while the enemy will do something correctly despite all you can do to prevent it," Feng sounded more amused than anything.

"Davies said the same thing a few days ago," Parno nodded.

"I have always been impressed with his intelligence," Feng nodded, his voice dry as a desert.

"I'm glad you guys can take all this so lightly," Parno's tone was almost surly. "I've got Imperial cavalry raiding the capitol, more Imperial cavalry disappearing in the west to come up God only knows where, I've lost a great deal of supplies and stores that I had counted on to supply my army, we're outnumbered at a minimum of two-to-one, we're being attacked on two fronts, and now they've at least temporarily opened a third one, and my traitorous sister has murdered my father and now wants to free my traitorous brother and set him on the throne. Now where in all that do you guys find any room at all to relax, crack jokes, and make fun of my inexperience? I mean, just so I'll know for the future, in case I manage to live that long."

It was one of the longest diatribes Parno had ever made in Feng's hearing, and to the oriental sword-master it showed just how pensive his young warlord was.

"Is the city lost?" Feng asked.

"No, just burned," Parno exhaled it in one long breath, his exhaustion showing. "And they're already gone. Maybe most of them will die from food poisoning," he muttered.

"That was a good idea," Feng nodded. "Very sneaky."

"Better than any of the ideas I had apparently since it probably killed more Nor than what I had done," Parno said bitterly.

"How long do you plan to wallow in your self-chastisement?" Feng asked. "For while you sit here, castigating yourself at length for the enemy finally being smart enough to get past you, once, there is still a war to be fought and your army still must be led." The sword-master's voice was flat and yet cutting at the same time. Parno looked at him.

"What the hell does that mean?" he demanded.

"It means exactly what I said," Feng told him. "You are sitting here wallowing in self-pity because a capable enemy who is hundreds of miles from here managed to steal a march on you while you were distracted by an army that is easily twice the size of your own and camped solidly on your own ground. I said before; the enemy sometimes does something correctly as well, young warlord. You have known loss to this point, but not defeat. It could not last forever."

"Now, you know defeat, and yet your defeat is not near as damaging as it could have been. One, because of plans you yourself made and provisions for attack that you devised on your own. And two, because others are finally playing a part in this struggle. It is not for you alone to defend your realm, young lord. Others must do their part. Clearly they are beginning to do so."

"So, stop this ridiculous pouting, for that is all it is, and get back to work," he finished firmly. "You have done well up to now, Parno. Had you not, I would have told you so. I promise you I would have. What has happened here is an act of war. Simple as that. And it is nothing less than what you have planned for them. Now, perhaps, you will have the spark you need to justify the plans you have for the future."

"Unless of course you want to call if all off now and step down as Marshal, committing ritual suicide to atone for this unforgivable failure," he added dryly, a raised eyebrow punctuating the statement.

For a few seconds Parno sat staring at him. Then he threw his head back and laughed. Laughed as he hadn't in long weeks. For over a minute the 'young warlord' laughed from his belly so hard that tears ran down his cheeks. Wiping his eyes, he finally managed to get his laughter under control.

"Thank you, Master Feng," he gasped at last when he was able to breathe again. "As always, you make me see clearly that which is ever before me." He shook his head as if to clear away the last of his laughter.

"What can you do with what has happened?" Feng demanded, always looking to teach.

"Honestly, I don't know," Parno admitted, looking away into the dark. "I suppose I could send someone after the Nor cavalry, but . . . it seems a waste to try and catch men who are already dying from dysentery among other things. They should be out of action for at least two to three weeks, and many of them longer. I don't see the point in wasting the resources to go after them."

"Your losses in this latest round of engagements?" Feng pressed.

"Almost nil, really," Parno admitted. "Just over one hundred total casualties. That's not to say I don't hate every loss, because I do. But from a numbers standpoint we did well."

"All good commanders feel the loss of their men, be it one or a hundred or a hundred thousand," Feng nodded. "Your enemy did something you did not expect?"

"Not exactly," Parno mused. "He just did it in a strength I didn't anticipate. They came in much stronger numbers than I had thought."

"The boats?" Feng prompted him. Parno thought about that, the engagement that Allen had led.

"I had thought they might use the boats to try and slip past me, or else to raid into Nasil," he said finally. "It seems they were going to try and use the boats against me here, and sent their cavalry against Nasil. Probably wanting to draw off any troops they could from here."

"So, if that was their plan, it failed," Feng pointed out.

"True," Parno admitted.

"What will they try now?" his teacher asked.

"Until I know where that cavalry that disappeared from the west went to, I don't know," Parno shrugged. "Four divisions maybe of cavalry is a lot. Actually, a stronger force than what hit the capitol. We've no idea where they went or what they plan to do."

"Do you even know if they left? Or did they merely appear to leave and circle back?" Feng asked. "For that matter, do you know if they even had four divisions worth of cavalry across the river to start with?"

"Raines noted in his report that might be the case. The circling back I mean," Parno told him. "We know so very little about that side of the river there's no way to know what they might have done or where they may have gone. They could already be back in their camp while we're worrying over where they got to. As to whether they had that many to start with? There is absolutely no way to know. It's too far to see even with a good telescope, and we have no intelligence at all concerning the force across the river. Until they showed up there, the last thing I expected was to see Nor coming from the west. Until now the Tribes have never worked with anyone for any reason."

"So, at this point what can you do?"

"All I can do is keep a lookout for them while I continue to let 1st and 2nd Corps rebuild and retrain," Parno replied. "We are stretched thin, and that isn't going to change any time soon. The loss of so much in supply will hurt in the short run until more stores can be brought up from the south. And I will have to keep stores further south I suppose to prevent what happened in Nasil from happening again. We can't afford to lose another round of stores like that. We're going to face a shortage as it is before the coming winter is over."

"You are going to have to learn to depend on others for things like that, Parno," Feng chastised gently. "You must concentrate on winning your war. They must see to it that you have the means to do so."

"If I thought I could do so, I'd love to," Parno said dryly. "So far I've had a slim run of luck finding people I can trust."

"You must start somewhere," Feng insisted. "Your brother is a good King, Parno, and this is his realm. Ultimately, he has the most to lose. You must trust that he will do all in his power to support you or else his realm will fall. Does not his own training and education teach him how to make such decisions?"

Of course, it did. Memmnon had been trained since a young age to assume the role of King. Therron had as well to a lesser extent. But Parno had grown to manhood unable to trust anything about Memmnon and it wasn't easy to simply overlook-

"You must let go of your distrust, young warlord, if you are to save your people," Feng told him as if reading his thoughts. "Even if you cannot bring yourself to trust your brother on your own behalf, you must at least trust him to make the best possible decisions for your kingdom. It is to his own benefit as well as yours and everyone else. He will certainly do that which is best for himself, and now for Miss Hubel, will he not?"

Parno hadn't considered that. Memmnon had struck up a courtship with Winnie now. He would definitely be thinking about the future even as the war raged around him. If he was to have a kingdom to share with the red head archery maiden, then he would have to support his brother as he defended the kingdom for him.

Parno knew, intellectually, that Memmnon would of course do all he could to support the war effort. But a lifetime of distrust died hard. Parno had been learning to trust Memmnon when his older brother had essentially abandoned him before their father when Parno honestly had a right to expect Memmnon's support, and that sliver of trust that had been building had been shattered forever.

"I'll never be able to fully trust him, Cho," Parno said finally. "Regardless of what he says or does, and knowing that he will do what is best for the kingdom I still won't ever be able to trust in him the way I should be able to." The way I want to, he left unsaid.

"But, you're right," he added before Feng could argue. "I should be able to trust him that far. He wants a future with Winnie, and he'll do what's necessary to secure that future. The thing is, there are so many people beneath him that I can't truly depend on, and it's my men that will suffer when those idiots fail us."

"They are his men as well," Feng pointed out. "His subjects. They defend his realm. You must trust that he will do all he can to take care of them as they protect his kingdom. You cannot do otherwise, young warlord because you cannot do it all."

No. He couldn't do it all.

"I'll try," he settled for saying. "For now, I'll do my best to let it rest. Hopefully we won't get any more bad news."

-

"Edema!" Stephanie exclaimed when she saw Lady Cumberland entering the hospital ward. "I had no idea you were here! You chose a terrible time to visit, Lady Cumberland."

"Yes, I did," Edema nodded. "I must wait a few more days before returning home, as it may not be safe to travel the countryside. Colonel Stang has promised me a small detachment as an escort but it will be several days before they can be available. In the meantime, I must try and make myself useful. Tell me, dear girl, are you too busy for lunch?"

"I was about to try and get something in a few minutes," Stephanie admitted. "There's no reason I can't do so now."

"Then please join me," Edema extended an arm. "I've arranged for a table in the palace garden that will allow us some privacy."

-

"Would you care to explain to me what has happened between you and Parno?"

Edema didn't beat around the bush. As soon as the food was served and the steward gone, she launched right into it.

Stephanie blinked at that, unaware that Edema had even known.

"Did Parno tell you about that?" she asked, unable to believe that he would tell even her.

"He did not, nor have I spoken or corresponded with him," Edema replied tartly. "Winifred informed me, asking my assistance in trying to mend the damage between you."

"Then I'm sure she told you what happened," Stephanie's voice took a chilled tone. "I have told her more than once to keep out of my personal life. I would ask the same of you, Edema."

"You don't take that tone with me, young lady," Edema's voice cracked across the table. "You wanted his attention. I was the one who convinced him to give it to you. I placed my own credibility with him on the line to vouch for you, Stephanie. I was tired of his all but ignoring you and seeing you so sad and nearly depressed over him. I thought you would be good for him, and told him so. Now I have to hear that on the eve of his possibly returning to battle, you corner him, making demands of him that you know he cannot meet, and then have the gall to speak to him so hatefully as you leave him alone?" Edema's voice was far beyond frosty and Stephanie had to work to keep from recoiling from the older woman's verbal assault.

"How dare you do something like that to him," Edema almost snarled. "Do you have any idea the trust issues he has? The life he has led in this arrogance infested place with a hateful father and hate filled siblings? In you he had perhaps found someone he might finally place that trust, and then you, in a fit of temper that is completely unworthy of you, rip that trust away from him at a time when he most needs it? And then you think you can simply tell me to butt out? Stay out of your business?" Edema's voice was steadily rising.

"That boy's wellbeing is my business, young woman," she fairly growled. "I care that!" she snapped her fingers, "for what anyone in this infested palace thinks of him, and I can easily add you to that list if your attitude continues as it has in the last few minutes. Now did you or did you not come to me at Cumberland House, seeking both mine and Dhalia's aid with him?"

"Yes," Stephanie didn't even consider not answering. "I did."

"And did we not assist you?" Edema ground on.

"You did," the young doctor replied.

"The last I had heard was that the two of you had an arrangement between you, an understanding of betrothal, provided we win this war and he survives the process. Was that or was it not the case?"

"Yes," Stephanie kept her answers short, still reeling under this assault by a woman whose voice she had never heard in anything other than gay entertainment.

"So what, may I ask, prompted you to put such pressure on him in the first place?" Edema demanded. "And don't even think of telling me it doesn't concern me," she snapped when Stephanie began to do just that. "That boy may as well be my own son and I could love him no more dearly if he was. You have hurt him I wager, though I'm sure he would die before admitting it even to me."

Stephanie took a minute to try and gather herself, still reeling under this unexpected assault from Edema Willows. She had always known that the Duchess was formidable, but she had never seen her like this.

"I wanted a child," she said quietly, her face flushing at the admission. "I wanted him to marry me that night and hopefully I would be able to conceive in that one evening before he left the next morning. Should anything happen to him, then I might at least have that."

"I can see nothing wrong with such a desire," Edema surprised her. "However, you are aware that since. . .things occurred," she settled for saying, "that Parno now occupies the position of Crown Prince, and will until and unless Memmnon fathers a son?"

"Yes," Stephanie did her best not to grate the reply out.

"Then surely you realize that he cannot simply marry you on a whim in the dark of night and then slip away to the front," Edema's softness evaporated in an instant. "The marriage of the Crown Prince must be done as a public event whether you like it or not, and I can assure you he does not. But there are protocols at work here that are centuries old, Stephanie. Parno cannot simply ignore them, much as he might care to."

"He said that," Stephanie nodded.

"And still you persisted?" Edema asked.

"I told him I as sick of hearing it," the younger woman admitted. "That I was tired of him using it as an excuse, and if he had no desire to marry me he should have merely said so and been done with it. That he as being selfish," she added softly.

It was the look on Edema Willow's face that did Stephanie in. Not her scathing words or her biting tone, not her condemnation or her mother hen demeanor. It was the look on her face at hearing what Stephanie had said that broke the young physician.

"Anything else?" Edema's voice was brittle.

"He tried to reason with me but I was angry and wouldn't listen," Stephanie felt a tear trickle down her face but refused to wipe it away. "I decided I had heard enough and would retire for the evening. It surprised him that I was leaving, and he asked me if I was seriously departing, knowing he had to ride with the rising sun. My last words to him were that the sun could not come too soon and to have a safe trip."

Edema Willows was able to hold her tongue only by a supreme effort. While she prided herself on her mature behavior and calm decision making, the anger that enveloped her at this moment was greater than anything she had known save the wretched time when Edward was under the influence of Therron McLeod.

For her own part, Stephanie Corsin sat stoically, waiting for the explosion she expected, and felt she deserved. Hearing herself speak the words again simply reinforced her own opinion of what she had done, and that opinion was far from favorable.

Edema finally trusted herself enough to speak.

"All I can say is that I am very disappointed in you, Stephanie," she settled for an opening statement. "He had made it clear to you that he felt the war must at least appear winnable before he could consider marriage, and that was aside from all the pomp and circumstance he would need to endure as Crown Prince. And that decision was based on his desire to protect you and your reputation, you know," Edema added. "I had so hoped that you would be the stalwart buoy he needed to steady himself in this ocean of madness. To help him find his way when he seemed or felt lost. He is under an incredible amount of pressure, to assume such a post as so young an age."

"He had opened himself to you in a way I wasn't positive he was capable of, to be honest," she continued. "When he did my heart was glad and I had such hope for the two of you. I felt that you would be good for him and he for you as well." She sighed deeply, her eyes downcast.

"Edward has told me I meddle too much in the affairs of others," she admitted. "I didn't see the harm in just trying to help, but. . .perhaps he was right after all."

"Has he written you back at all?" she asked suddenly, catching Stephanie by surprise.

"Back?" she asked.

"When you wrote to him," Edema nodded. "Has he responded?"

"I haven't written him," Stephanie replied softly. "I didn't see that it would be fruitful at this point. I do not expect him to forgive me, and I certainly don't deserve it. But Parno is not overly forgiving, Edema. You know that as well as I. And as you said, I hurt him. I cannot see that he will view what I said, what I did, as anything other than a betrayal. And he is not forgiving of betrayal most of all."

"You haven't even tried to make this right?" Edema almost goggled. "Why would you not at least make the attempt, Stephanie? Even if you think he will not forgive you, even if he doesn't respond at all, that is no reason not to try!" Her eyes narrowed suddenly.

"You don't care for him as much as you thought, do you?" it was almost an accusation. "You don't want to marry him anymore, do you? So, you just allow this to go. To fester and die on its own."

"Of course, I do," Stephanie didn't retort in anger, she merely answered. "Remember, Edema, that I wanted him before he was Crown Prince, or Lord Marshal, or any of these other titles he now has to wear. I could care that!" she snapped her own fingers in mimicry of Edema's earlier demonstration, "for titles or status or anything else that goes with being a member of the Dynasty. I care about him," she stressed the word. "I love him. More than I ever imagined I could care for anyone, let alone the infamous Playboy Prince," she snorted delicately. "And yes, I pushed him. He is far too prone to placing himself in danger and. . .and if he. . .if he didn't come back then perhaps, if fate smiled upon me, I would have his child to raise as evidence of that love."

"But as you said yourself, I hurt him. I worked so hard to win his trust and confidence, practically chasing after him like some love-struck school girl trying to get his attention. I would like to think I'm not vain, but I'm not exactly unattractive either, you know. I come from a good family and I am a well-known and respected physician. A title I worked hard to gain, mind you, and one I wear with some pride. I am the first woman to hold the position of Royal Physician in so long that it would take a search of the records in the Royal Archives to allow us to say for certain when the last might have been."

"And yet I threw my pride and my dignity right out the window to chase a man who is years younger than I because. . .because he is the most amazing man I have ever encountered. A selfless man who works tirelessly for his people, who in many cases are unworthy of his sacrifices. They mock and scorn him, treat him with contempt and assume the worst no matter what, and yet, he still does it. And all I could think to do was call him selfish," she ended with another tear trickling down her cheek. This one she did wipe away carefully.

"I'm sorry dear girl," Edema spoke gently. "I'm often told I'm too protective of those I care about, and I suppose that is true. I had thought. . .well, it doesn't matter," she waved it away. "And there's no point in my making you feel any worse over this, since you're doing a fine job all on your own," she smiled sadly.

"First of all, no; Parno is not overly forgiving. He's never been able to afford that luxury. Has he told you anything of his younger years? How he was raised?"

"Not to speak of," Stephanie replied. "Just generalities. I know that he and The Colonel were close." The capitalization of The Colonel as a proper name was almost audible. Anyone who had been there when the regiment was formed would forever think of Darvo Nidiad as The Colonel.

"They were more than close, dear girl," Edema sighed. "Darvo raised Parno himself, alongside Dhalia. One reason that Parno dotes on her as he does. She is his real sister, blood or no, and she always will be." She paused, collecting her thoughts.

"I was there when Parno was born," she said finally. "His mother was one of my most cherished friends, and she had Parno against the wishes of your uncle, who advocated for. . .well. Margolyn had been told that more children was out of the question after the twins. She was a slight woman, bless her heart, and Sherron and Therron were overly large. Tammon tried to force her to listen to Physician Smithe and, well, terminate the pregnancy, but she would not hear of it."

"As a result, she lived only a few minutes after his birth. She held him close those few minutes and that was the last affection from his family he would ever know. I would have taken him away from here if I could, but that was of course impossible."

"The family treated him horribly and the staff here followed suit, blaming him for his mother's death. It was no wonder he became the drinking, brawling, womanizing and what have you, man that he did, for he had no reason to believe that good behavior would in any way be rewarded."

"And yet, when the Kingdom was in peril, who was it that managed not only to ferret that out, but then also to blunt an attack aimed directly for this city. Which cost him the only person he ever really had been able to trust; Darvo Nidiad."

"Then his father shows up, all puffed and proud of 'his' son, and declares that

Parno is now the Lord Marshal as he had led his men to victory and perhaps, he could do the same in the west, as Therron had been unable to do so, and so on."

"He accepted the position on the condition that his surviving men be freed, but I'm sure you know that," Edema went on. "In any event, knowing these things might help you understand how Parno came to be as he is."

"I knew some of it," Stephanie nodded. "That still doesn't explain why he would be so averse to trying. . .I mean, how would that…"

"Stephanie dear," Edema looked at her sadly. "Why would someone who effectively grew up without a father risk leaving a child of his own to do the same?"

CHAPTER TWENTY-THREE

-

Unaware that Edema Willows was inserting herself in his romantic entanglement, or at least what remained of it, Parno had managed to spend a day reviewing troop deployments and scouting reports. There was still no sign at all of the cavalry units that had been seen moving north on the western shores of the Great River. They could be back in camp or half-way to the lines opposite his own army here on the plains. That many additional trained cavalry would create a situation that could easily turn desperate in mere days if not minutes.

There were now sufficient stockpiles of Roda Finn's weaponry that all artillery units along the Soulan lines could now be supplied with them, and all of Soulan's artillery men had either already been trained to handle and use them, or would be within another week. 4th and 5th Corps were both firmly entrenched now in the lines facing the Norland army now as well. Should the Imperial Army try another massive attack against Royal Army positions, they would face over sixty thousand fresh troops backed by fully staffed and trained artillery well supplied with the destructive might of Roda Finn's 'wizardry'.

"We should be able to hold," he told himself, looking at his maps. That had become an everyday thing for him. Pouring over maps for hours on end, checking troop placements and suspected enemy placements, then reading reports. Reports on readiness, supplies, suspicions of enemy intention, progress on relocation of refugees, forecast of harvests and for herds that supplied the army with leather and beef, textiles for everything from blankets to uniforms to canvas for sails and tents, the lists were endless and all of them every one, mattered. Everyone figured in some way on Soulan's ability to wage war and defend her land and people.

"Courier, milord," Sprigs announced after lunch.

"From Memmnon?" Parno asked, dreading the answer.

"No, milord," Sprigs shook his head. "From General Beaumont."

-

The couriers sent from Beaumont and Whipple had not traveled together. The information was so time sensitive and so important that it was vital that it arrive to at least one member of the Royal Family, and do so as soon as possible. Traveling over a thousand miles by horseback was dangerous enough as it was. Doing it as quickly as said horse could manage was something else altogether.

Despite having further to go, the courier bound for the Army made it within hours of the courier arriving at the Royal Palace in Nasil. The courier was shocked to see signs of battle there but didn't allow it to deter him from his mission.

So it was that Memmnon and Parno learned of the developments on the Key Horn at roughly the same time.

-

"Sherron is dead," Memmnon said flatly as he, Winnie, Whip, Sebastian Grey, General Brock and Howard Govan sat in his office a few minutes later. "Perhaps a dozen of Callens' men survived the battle," he sighed. "An elite regiment that we could have used to defend this Kingdom, lost to the pursuits of my sister."

"What of your brother, Sire?" Govan asked hesitantly.

-

"So Therron managed to talk a ship Captain with more rank than brains into helping him escape," Parno seethed as he stomped about his headquarters tent. Enri Willard, Karls, Cho, Davies and Sprigs were all present. "Now they believe he is on his way to Norfok to enlist aid from the CPC to put down our 'coup' and put him back on the throne."

"Coasties?" Davies frowned. "How the hell can they help him. Assuming they even would?" he added.

"They will," Enri Willard said grimly, his face tight.

"Explain," Parno ordered curtly.

"Therron has a very good relationship with the Coastal Defense Minister, and the Minister of Finance as they call it," Enri explained. "They will at least give him an audience. And if he can convince them it's in their best interest to assist him, they just might do it."

"With what?" Davies was incredulous. "They need us to protect them from Norland for Crown's sake!"

"Their army is small, but very well trained and equipped," Enri nodded. "And while they couldn't defeat either us or Norland, we're at war already right now. If they sent a large force over the mountains, what would we oppose it with?"

"Perfect," Parno sighed, shaking his head. "Do you know how many times I thought about killing Therron when we were kids, let alone after we were grown? But no, I just went and got a stiff drink instead. Darvo always said my drinking would be my downfall."

-

"I can't believe the Coastals would assist him in grabbing the throne, Sire," Govan looked stunned. "They have everything to lose in such an effort, should it not go their way. And they would have no way of assuring that Therron would honor whatever agreement he might make with them, even if he was successful."

"I know that he has a good working relationship with their Defense Minister," Memmnon mused. "But he does not govern the Coastal Provinces of course. That does not mean he wields no power among them mind you, but it would not be something he could do alone. He would have to convince their Governor that it was in the best interest of the CPC to assist Therron. And frankly, I don't see how he can do that."

"We need to beat him to the punch," Brock spoke finally. "Have you sent a messenger to the Coastals informing them of the change in rule, Sire?" he asked Memmnon.

"Yes," Memmnon nodded. "A courier was dispatched five days after the fact. Before my father's funeral in fact."

"So they will already have received word of what has befallen Tammon, then," Brock continued, eyes narrowed in thought. "Did you inform Governor Princeton of the circumstances?"

"Yes," Govan fielded that one. "While we thought we knew where she was bound, there was the possibility that Sherron would try to flee there if pursuit was too close or she couldn't get to Therron. It was decided that Princeton should know all the facts, at least as we knew them at the time."

"Then he will now that there was no coup, and that the 'attempt' that Therron will try to convince him of was in fact orchestrated by his twin, in an effort to place him on the throne illegally."

"Unless our couriers didn't make it," Memmnon nodded. "We sent three, by different routes, as usual. Surely one made it through," he said it almost like a prayer.

-

"Regardless, unless Semmes can stop this idiot, Chastain, then there's not much we can do," Davies shrugged. "He's at sea and a long way from here. Any help the Coasties would send will have to come through the mountains, and they will have to start now readying an expedition that would make it through the mountains before the first snows fly."

"And they have to pass Cove Canton to get here," Karls reminded him. "The southern roads would add hundreds of miles to their journey and allow even more time for someone to see them and report their presence."

"True," Parno mused, looking back to the note. "Beaumont and Whipple are taking their commands to Cove, in fact, in case I wanted them there to interdict such a move." He paused again, clearly thinking.

"What are you considering, young lord?" Feng asked for everyone in the room.

"Beaumont and Whipple are a good team, and think fast on their feet," Parno told them. "And while I really need them here, Allen proved that he's more than capable of doing the same work they did. He, Coe and Vaughan did a fine job earlier, and there's no reason to think they can't continue to do so. That still leaves us two cavalry divisions here at all times, and 1st Corps is less than an hour's march back. Far less for their own cavalry. There is minimal risk involved in allowing Allen and his 'command' to continue to harass and interdict behind enemy lines for now."

"And they make a good reaction force to go after that Nor cavalry if it really does show up here somewhere," Davies nodded in agreement.

"So, Beaumont and Whipple will stay at Cove for now," Parno decided finally, standing. "They can go through the conditioning training which can only make them more formidable, and be on call to go after any incursion my traitor brother managed to wrangle from the Coasties, assuming they really will help him."

"I still have to wonder what they would want in order to lend him their assistance."

-

"Your cook is excellent, Captain," Therron complimented as he wiped his mouth. "That pork might be the best I've eaten."

"I shall inform him of your compliment, milord," Chastain raised his glass. "I'm sure he will be delighted to hear it from someone of your station." He fell quiet for a moment, considering his next question. Therron saved him the trouble.

"You're wondering why the Coastals would assist me," he smiled slightly.

"Not why as much as if," Chastain admitted. "We're in the middle of a nasty war with the Empire at the moment, milord. What profit is there for them in aiding us at all?"

"First of all, they won't be aiding us, but rather aiding me," Therron steepled his hands before him, bracing his elbows on the table. "I have an excellent working relationship with their Defense Minister, Picon Charleston. I've helped him considerably over the years since I became Marshal and his position in his own government has improved greatly because of that."

"Second, they want to ensure they stay on the good side of the ruling family because Soulan is all that keeps the CPC out of the clutches of the Empire. They know that any successful coup will not be good for them in the long run. We can trust them to do what's best for them, much as anyone else would."

"And finally, Governor Princeton is somewhat taken with my sister," Therron smiled in a way that made Chastain's stomach want to send the excellent food he'd just eaten back the way it had come.

"So, I shall dangle dear Sherron before him as an enticement," the Marshal finished. "Governor Princeton is only marginally intelligent, but he is prone to allow his nethers to do his important decisions making. If necessary, I shall have Sherron 'take one for the team' as the old saying used to go."

"Well, that does sound as if it would work," Chastain managed to keep his voice calm for the most part.

"I'm sure it seems distasteful to you, Captain," Therron smiled again. "The truth is, however, that such arrangements are all too common at our level. Sherron has expected something like this and planned for it all her life. It will not surprise her in any way. I'm sure she'll be running their country inside five years," he laughed. "And in any case, it's not as if it will be a hardship. Thanks to our protection of their cities, the CPC is quite wealthy. She will not be lowering her standard of living any, you may be sure of that."

"Of course, milord," Chastain nodded. "If I might beg your pardon, milord, but I need to check the watch. I try to observe the watch change every few days without warning. It keeps my men on their toes."

"Excellent practice Captain," Therron approved. "Please, don't let me keep you from your duties."

Five minutes later Chastain was on the observation and command deck of his cruiser, looking over his ship. He really did observe his men every so often without their knowledge to make sure they were not shirking in their responsibility, but tonight he knew that if he had waited any longer to get some cool sea air, he would not have been able to keep his supper down.

I have made a monumental error and I have no way at all to undo it. None. I have tied, no I have chained myself to this revolting man and have no way to free myself from him. My career, indeed my continued living, now depend entirely on his whims. What have I done?

That less than happy thought was all that was on his mind as his men went through their watch change minutes later.

-

"There's nothing we can actually do at the moment," Memmnon decreed finally as his chief advisers continued to pass the problem around the room.

"Sir, this is a direct threat to your rule!" Brock insisted.

"More direct that a half-million Nor soldiers?" Memmnon's voice was light but his meaning was clear. "Therron cannot possibly be more of a threat to us at the moment than the Imperial Army. Regardless, we can't do anything about it at the moment, as I said," he shrugged. "He's at sea. If Semmes has anything that can put to sea and try to stop this moronic Captain, I'm sure he will try, but remember that the Navy essentially destroyed itself protecting our shores and enabling Parno to consolidate the army against the invasion. If they cannot stop this Chastain person, then it will be difficult to hold it against them, wouldn't you say?"

"True," Brock sighed. "My man Johnson will be remaining behind with the wounded until they can travel, then coming north for reassignment. He told us repeatedly that he needed more men and we didn't heed him. If we had, if I had, we wouldn't be having this discussion in all likelihood."

"And if my father hadn't insisted on a cock-and-bull story about Therron being 'ill' instead of the traitorous snake that he is, Johnson wouldn't have been there needing more men to start with," Memmnon shrugged easily. "There is where the true blame likes, General. With Therron, and with my father. Johnson acted to save his men. From what I have read, all he could have accomplished was to ensure the death of every man in his command for absolutely no return. He did nothing wrong. Thanks to him we still have his men to serve where they are needed."

"Thank you, Sire," Brock nodded, clearly relieved.

"Now, we have enough to do rebuilding this city and making good the losses we have suffered without adding additional worry about my brother. Today's worries are sufficient unto themselves. Let us turn our attention to them instead."

-

"Stephanie, you cannot leave this to linger any longer," Edema said firmly. She was preparing to depart the next morning, the current emergency past. "You must try and salvage your relationship with Parno. At this rate, you won't even be friends."

"I'm not sure I would want to be just friends," Stephanie sighed. "I don't know that I could stand that."

"And you can stand this?" Edema asked, sipping her tea quietly.

"I haven't had much time to dwell on it," she admitted.

"Nor has he, which is a good thing," Edema nodded. "The longer you let it go, the harder it will be to repair."

"I can't go see him, and writing seems to be such a... a cheap way of telling him how sorry I am," the young doctor lamented. "I don't have much in the way of options."

"Why can't you go and see him?" Edema frowned. "Is Memmnon still unwell?" she asked, concern on her features.

"No, not at all," Stephanie shook her head. "But women aren't allowed at the front. You know that," she chided gently. "You were the one who told me I had no place there, remember?"

"As a participant," Edema corrected her. "I said nothing at all about visiting him personally to try and make things right between you."

"He won't allow it at any rate," Stephanie shrugged. "And Memmnon won't try and force him. I think Winnie tried to get him to make Parno do something similar and Memmnon just scoffed. Said something like 'yes, because Parno always does what I tell him to'," she chuckled dryly and Edema joined her.

"Well, you need to get away from here," Edema told her. "You're welcome to come with me. You need a few days that aren't filled with court. And being here all day, every day can't be helping."

"No, it isn't," Stephanie agreed. "Were it not for Winnie needing me, I'd already be gone," she admitted.

"Well, she seems to be doing fine on her own, and I'm sure your mother wouldn't mind watching over her a few days," Edema mentioned. "I plan to leave an hour after sunrise," she stood, and Stephanie stood as well, embracing her. "I shall hope to see you there, packed and ready to go."

"We shall see."

-

"You look like a man who could use a drink," Karls offered Parno a bottle of beer. He took it and drained it in a single upturning of the bottle.

"That's good," Parno nodded.

"I didn't mean all at once," Karls chuckled.

"I'm in a mood to drink and raise a bit of a ruckus," Parno replied. "I'd ask you to come bar hopping with me, but there are no bars, and you're an engaged man," he grinned.

"We aren't," Enri Willard said from the doorway and Parno turned to see both

Enri and Cho Feng standing there.

"And I happen to know where there's a bar," Enri added mischievously.

"Really?" Parno looked interested.

"Place called the Boar's Head," Enri nodded. "No," he corrected himself. "Hogshead. Yeah, that's it. Hogshead Inn. Got pretty serving girls and everything."

"Ah," Parno recognized that as Tinker's headquarters. "Heard of it," he nodded.

"Well, you're welcome to come along with us," Enri shrugged and Feng nodded. "Can't hurt. Food ain't bad, either," he added.

"I had heard that as well," Parno said truthfully. He had stayed far from Tinker's operation, but with things perhaps winding down there, it might not hurt anything. And anyway, an occasional visit once in a while would enable him to visit the Tinker without the spy having to come here. This might be fortuitous, really.

"You know what?" he said suddenly. "Why not. It's not like a few drinks can make my life any worse than it is at the moment, right?" he grinned.

"That's the spirit!" Enri grinned back at him.

"Parno," Karls tried to add some caution but Enri cut him off.

"Don't worry, little brother," he slapped Karls' back. "Master Feng and I will take good care of him, won't we?"

"Indeed," Feng fought a grin. "They do have good food and excellent beer," he added to Parno. "And the female company is quite attractive I must say."

"Talked me into it," Parno decided. "Karls, I promise to be on my semi-best behavior," he said to his friend. "See you in the morning."

Karls could only watch as the three men walked out. Minutes later horse could be heard departing, heading out toward the rear areas of the camp.

"I got a bad feeling about this," he muttered to himself.

-

Tinker was surprised to see the Marshal enter and even more surprised that he didn't come to see him but instead took a table with two other men he recognized as the young lord's chief Staff officer and his senior adviser.

"Good evening milord," he went to the table, smiling like a host. "How are you?"

"Tinker!" Parno smiled. "Heard you had some good beer on tap and decided I needed to check on the quality first hand."

"And the food," Enri reminded him.

"That too," Parno agreed.

"We have a very good roast brisket tonight, milord," Tinker smiled. "And I must modestly admit that the beer is in fact not bad," he added.

"I'll have both," Parno said at once. "Got some bread and potatoes to go with that?" he asked.

"I'm sure I can find something along those lines," Tinker promised.

"Same for me, please," Enri raised a hand.

"Myself as well," Feng made it unanimous.

"Brie!" Tinker called out. A young dark-haired beauty came to the table.

"These men want beer and brisket, with potatoes and bread on the side, Brie,"

Tinker told her.

"Right away, milords," she curtsied of a sort and hurried away.

"Pretty girl," Parno noted.

"Yes," Tinker nodded. "Being pursued by young Mister Bell," he added, just so there was no misunderstanding.

"He's a good man," Parno nodded. "Is she running from him, or staying just out of reach?" Parno asked. "I'm sure Bell's intent would be honorable," he vouched for the young soldier.

"I am convinced of the same, and they seem to have an agreement between them," Tinker grinned again.

"Ah, love!" Enri grinned broadly and instantly regretted it. His face fell as he glanced at Parno.

"Sorry, milord," he murmured.

"Stop that," Parno told him. "None of that foolishness. Not tonight, and not ever again! It's not a problem and it's certainly no reason to put a damper on our good evening. Hell, I envy Bell, myself. She's a doll. I'll have to make sure and give them a proper gifting should they marry. Be sure and keep me aware, will you Tinker?"

"I will, milord," Tinker grinned, thinking of Rosala's reaction to that. "If you need anything else please let me know." He left them to enjoy their beer as Brie returned with it.

"Food coming shortly gentlemen," she smiled and hurried away.

"Not bad," Parno took a swig from the bottle. "Not bad at all in fact. Enri, not a bad plan, this! You are to be commended."

"I thank you, milord," Enri nodded back, raising his own bottle in toast. He and Feng had decided that Parno needed a night out and so had hatched this little plan to give him as best a one they could.

Soon the food was before them, though they were already on their second beer by then, and their fourth before they were halfway through.

"This is great food," Parno said around a mouthful of beef. "Might need to do this more often."

"I actually was thinking the same thing," Cho Feng replied. "This food is most excellent."

Parno had consumed eight of the fairly strong beers by the time they had eaten and was feeling his oats pretty well.

"I think it's time we headed back, milord," Enri noted. He was feeling his own alcohol intake pretty well, too.

"Guess so," Parno had become more morose with each beer until he was now almost completely down. "Good idea though," he told them again. "Might's well head on back I reckon," he staggered to his feet, pushing off attempts to assist him. "I can make it," he told them.

As the three headed for the door after Parno had paid for their meals and included a good tip for Bell's girl, what was her name again?

He happened to glance at the stairs.

A raven haired, dusky skinned goddess was watching them, her dark eyes following him with particular interest. When she saw him looking at her, she smiled, and Parno perked up at once.

"Milord," Enri tried to grab him but Parno was already moving.

"Well hello," he said smoothly despite the amount of alcohol in his system.

"Good evening milord," the woman bowed slightly. "Have you enjoyed your meal?"

"I have indeed," Parno assured her. "Haven't had dessert yet though," he smiled impishly and the woman actually blushed at that.

"What's your name?" he asked her, leaning against the wall in front of her.

"Jaelle," the woman smiled again.

"Hi, Jaelle," he gave her a goofy grin. "I'm Parno."

"I know who you are, milord," Jaelle practically giggled. "Everyone does."

"Great," Parno muttered. "But now look here, Jaelle," he told her. "You can't believe everything people say about me, okay? Some of those people are probably making stuff up. Well, a few of 'em anyway," he frowned. "At least one or two," he amended again after some thought.

"I have heard many good things about you, Marshal," Jaelle laughed.

"Now I know they're making 'em up," Parno muttered again. "Still though, if people are telling nice lies about me, well that's okay then," he smiled again, which made him look younger, closer to his actual age, and also took away some of the worry from his face.

"Milord, we really should be getting back," Enri came over and placed a hand on Parno's arm.

"Not now, Enri," he brushed it off. "Can't you see I'm busy?"

"Sunrise will come early, milord," Enri tried again. "And it's a good ride back to camp," he reminded him.

"Ain't this an inn?" Parno demanded. "They probably got a room or two here. I bet I could stay here if I asked Tinker. He's a good guy."

"Asked Tinker what?" Tinker appeared as if summoned by his name. "Jaelle, what are you doing?" he asked, almost frowning.

"She's talking to me," Parno answered for her. "That's okay, ain't it?" he semi-demanded.

"But of course," Tinker smiled. "Carry on then, by all means," he encouraged.

"I need a room, Tinker, if you got one to spare," Parno told him. "Ol' mother hen Willard here is getting concerned that I'm not gonna get back to camp if I wait much longer and maybe he's right. Got a place a man can lay his head for a night?" he asked, looking back to Jaelle.

"Wouldn't mind talking to Jaelle here some more to be honest," he said as he looked at her. "She's the prettiest thing I've seen in a good few days, and that's just the plain truth."

"You could stay with me, milord," Jaelle said almost shyly and Cho Feng noted the frown on Tinker's face. He drew the man aside.

"Is the woman a problem?" he asked softly.

"Problem?" Tinker frowned. "Oh," he realized what was meant. "No, she isn't.

I just. . .it was almost as if she were leading him on. I don't think that's it, but that she's simply star struck to be honest. I just didn't like her almost waylaying the Prince like that."

"Let her," Feng told him gently. "If she is a good and trustworthy woman of yours, let them do as they will. I will take responsibility for this. He needs a night when there is no worry upon him, even if it's just one. She is. . .healthy, I presume?" Feng asked carefully.

"Absolutely," Tinker took no offense. "And completely trustworthy."

"Then allow it," Feng told him. "Do not encourage it, but allow it to happen if it does. As I said, I will be responsible."

"As you desire," Tinker nodded. "I would not allow him to be taken advantage of," he added.

"I know this, or I would not have asked your opinion," Feng assured him.

"If you wish to stay with Jaelle, milord, she is finished with her chores this evening and has no duties left to perform. She has a room upstairs of her own and may take there who she will. I ask that you be kind to her," he said formally.

"Tinker," Parno sounded hurt. "You know I'd never do nothing like that."

"I do and say so merely as a formality, milord," Tinker smiled. "Jaelle, mind your manners," he warned laughingly. "This man is my friend."

"Aye, Tinker," Jaelle promised. Reaching out, she took Parno's hand in hers.

"Would you like to come upstairs, milord?" she asked almost shyly.

"I would indeed Miss Jaelle," Parno smiled charmingly. "I would indeed."

"What are you doing?" Enri demanded of Feng once they were gone.

"Do not concern yourself," Feng told him flatly. "I will remain, as will his escort. A warlord must once in a while relieve himself of the burdens of command and concern. Tomorrow he will be better in all likelihood. You may return to camp. Advise his escort they will need to trade off shifts tonight. I will be here."

"Cho, are you sure-"

"Yes," the oriental nodded firmly. "Go your way, Brigadier, and do not be concerned. He will be well."

-

Stephanie had warned Captain Winters that she might well be going with Lady Cumberland the next morning and thus his company was prepared for that eventuality.

"You're leaving?" Winnie asked, looking as if she felt betrayed.

"Just for a few days, dear, I promise," Stephanie assured her. "And my mother has promised to fill in for me as your chaperon and make your life as miserable as possible while I'm away," she added with a tiny, sadistic chuckle.

"Funny," Winnie growled, now slightly angry as she learned that Stephanie wasn't abandoning her.

"I should be back in a week to ten days," the doctor promised as she set her 'doctor bag' in the carriage. "Meantime, mind yourself," he mock warned.

"I will," Winnie snorted. "Be careful and I hope you have a good time. Farewell, Lady Cumberland," she added.

"Goodbye for now, dear girl," Edema smiled. "We shall see one another again before you know it. I look forward to calling you 'her Majesty' one day," she teased and was rewarded with a full faced blush that disappeared into Winnie's neckline.

The carriage started and Stephanie settled into her seat across from Edema.

"I'm glad you chose to accompany me, dear," Edema told her.

"I appreciate your asking me," she replied.

The two chattered about insignificant things for almost an hour before Stephanie realized something was wrong.

"We aren't headed for the Plateau," she said suddenly. "Edema, where are we going?" she asked.

"To see Parno, dear," Edema said calmly.

"What?!" Stephanie demanded. "I told you I'm not. . .women aren't allowed-"

"I'm not 'allowed' or 'not allowed' to do anything," Edema snorted. "This has to get straightened out, one way or the other, before it becomes a problem. We're going to see him. You have two, perhaps three days to figure out what you wish to say to him," she said as she pulled a book from her travel bag. "I'd use that time wisely."

THE END

To be continued in the forthcoming book,
PARNO'S PERIL

A MESSAGE FROM AUTHOR
N.C. REED

I hope you've enjoyed Parno's Gambit. It was a challenge to write but it was also fun. It's always exciting to see something you've spent so long working on come to fruition

I wanted to say "Thank You" to the readers of the Black Sheep series, and express to you my appreciation for your patronage and your support, and most certainly for your kind words about my work. There has been many a late night when that encouragement was what kept me writing when I was ready to throw in the towel and give up.

If you enjoyed Parno's Gambit or any of my other works, please let me know with a review on Amazon, or Goodreads, or you can visit my blog at badkarma00.wordpress.com. There are links there to my Facebook page as well.

You'll find a lot of odd and end stuff there that I work on to piddle when I can't get anything else done. Feel free to leave a comment. I know that it doesn't get updated often enough but I do try to post important notices there, and ANY books released by me will always be posted there and on my Facebook page.

Again, thank you.

N.C. Reed

THANK YOU
FOR READING!

If you enjoyed this book, we would appreciate your customer review on your book seller's website or on Goodreads.

Also, we would like for you to know that you can find more great books like this one at www.CreativeTexts.com

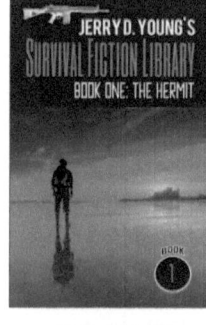

www.ingramcontent.com/pod-product-compliance
Lightning Source LLC
Chambersburg PA
CBHW022033120726
47899CB00001BB/158